Vexed with the Viscount

by

Jess Russell

Cover Art by *The Wild Rose Press, Inc.*

The Wild Rose Press, Inc.
PO Box 708
Adams Basin, NY 14410-0708
Visit us at www.thewildrosepress.com

Publishing History
First Edition, 2026
Trade Paperback Print ISBN 978-1-5092-6423-0
Digital ISBN 978-1-5092-6424-7

Published in the United States of America

Dedication

To Bliss, Gail, and Wendy with my deepest gratitude.

To my fellow writers—Collette Cameron, Fiona Davis, Hope C. Tarr, Bliss Bennett, Gail Eastwood, Wendy LaCapra, and Cynthia Capley—thank you for your encouragement, insight, and camaraderie.

To The Wild Rose Press for keeping my feet to the fire!

Special thanks to Anne Wonder, who has been a steadfast rock—from beta reads to spotting those elusive typos.

Heartfelt gratitude to Carol Cork, Barb Batlan, and Diane K Peterson for championing my books at every turn.

And finally, to my readers—thank you for reading, reviewing, and sharing. You're the reason these stories live beyond the page.

Chapter One

The Scottish Highlands, near Abernathy
Late March 1868

Dad burn nag!

Brendan Cavanaugh slipped from the horse and carefully checked its back left hock.

Yep, lame.

He knew he'd been flirting with disaster by hiring ol' Verlan. But he hadn't had much choice. The gelding was the only hack on offer in the tiny village of Abernathy. Should have stayed on, had a few more pints and convinced the barmaid, Jean, to spend the night with him. Not that much convincing would've been needed, not if that welcoming look in the gal's eye was anything to go on. By jingo, he would've been right home now, nuzzled into her ripe bosom, hands cradled around her lush bum, tasting her plump lips. But his itch to move on had been greater than his *other* itch.

Dang.

Verlan nipped at Bren's shoulder as if to say, "What about me?"

Having a lame horse wasn't the end of the world. Not unless a body felt like he *was* at the end of the world. Below him nothing but fields of heather. Beautiful enough, but beneath that beauty lay possible death, treacherous bogs that could swallow man and horse quicker than you could say *Jack Rabbit*. He'd been steadily ascending a rutted trail for a while now. The path getting steeper and wilder as the light faded.

Godforsaken Scotland. Why the hell had he decided to hie off to this wilderness?

He knew the answer. Fool that he was.

The sun was slipping fast. This far north you could count on light until nigh on nine. But once night came, it came quick as cream on a chill day. And as if the bogs weren't enough, fog could roll in so's a body couldn't see a hand square in front of its face.

The Black Hills had nothing on these Scottish mountains.

Only an hour or so ago, Orin Fraser, innkeeper at The Black Swan, had squinted through his pipe smoke, sipping the whisky Bren had stood him while he spun tales of ghosts and mysterious fairies who lured unsuspecting souls into life-sucking fens.

If he'd had the sense God gave a goat, he would've listened to the man. But he'd been eyeing bonny Jean, 'a course, and the tapster's advice had gone in one ear and out the other.

One of these days he might actually learn a thing or two.

"Eeeooow!"

The wail like a disembodied spirit, rose out of the fog.

Verlan shied, nearly jerking Bren off his feet.

"Whoa, there ol' boy," he whispered, his pistol now heavy in his hand.

Fog churned and danced through the trees. Their branches thrust upwards, caught in silver shrouds of finely spun webs. He had heard tell of these raft spiders doing their eerie work. The moon, just rising, striped the overgrown trail in shadow. Now he'd only to spy fairy folk or hobgoblins dancing under the stars at their nightly revels.

Hell, he should've seen the place by now.

Bren had no wish to be caught on this mountain after nightfall. Should he try and get back to the pub?

He gathered up Verlan's reins tighter and glanced back down the steep, rocky path. Traipsing up a mountain with a lame horse might be bad, but trying to retrace his steps would be suicide.

"Eeeooow!"

"Sh-i-i-t!" He leveled his pistol at the sound.

Something streaked by his feet. Verlan swung his huge head this time, knocking Bren sideways.

Then he saw it. A light.

A ghost? A wicked fairy?

Or salvation?

****

Callista Ainsworth raised her lantern as she stood in the doorway of her Highland cottage. The dratted cat always snuck out just as darkness was falling. But Gulliver could not resist the feral felines that hid in these woods. Well, he would return home when he grew hungry, scratching at the door, making a fuss.

After all, he was male.

It would serve him right to miss dinner.

Callie pulled her shawl tight around her shoulders and stepped back into the cottage, closing the door behind her. She poked up the fire and then returned to the letter she'd been reading—or rather re-reading—for the fifth time. She didn't receive many letters here in her highland exile. And when she did, she either wanted to revisit them over and over, or heave them into the fire. Not much middle ground. This missive, however, had her feeling a mix of the two.

Her little sister Helena, who, after her initial greetings, reported that the till-now-elusive Viscount Clifford, rumored to finally be in the country and ready to take up residence as the Ainsworth's neighbor, would be ripe for the picking. Next year might be too late to snare him. So, her father and stepmother had decided to launch Helena this season:

Please, you must come back to England! I cannot face entering society without you by my side to give me your steady guidance. I will make a hash of things! You know I will. And besides, I am already in love, with my dear Martin!

Martin? Callie shook her head. Her last letter extolled the young curate, Mr. Henry Dobbins, as being the most handsome man, she'd ever beheld!

Callie's hand drifted to her neckline, her fingers tracing the gold oval-shaped locket, feeling the familiar coolness and the nearly-worn-away chasing etched into the gold. *Only True Love.* Her mother's talisman.

Oh, but how could one ever be sure?

Certainly, Callie was no authority, given her past. But she'd been lucky enough to escape a loveless marriage.

She'd be damned if her sister would now have to pay for Callie's abdication.

A second letter—this one from her step-mother— lay on the table, likely conveying the same news as Helena's, but surely directing Callie to stay put in Scotland.

Damn, Hermione! It's too soon! Helena's only just

4

seventeen…

Callie pushed the letter aside. She'd open it when she needed kindling for the fire.

"Eeeooow!"

She smiled at the eerie, but familiar screech. Gully, now ready for his dinner, no doubt.

A scratch at the door confirmed her suspicion.

She pushed back from the table, rose, and crossed to the door. "Ready for your dinner now that you've done with your whoring? I should banish you to the barn for your appetites." Callie opened the door ready to give the shadow tabby a playful swat. But instead, her gaze encountered two muddy boots. Before she could raise her eyes, Gulliver snaked between the footwear then turned, letting out another loud yowl, this one less of hunger and more of protest.

Her gaze tracked upwards to buff-colored trousers spattered with more mud, then to a coat oddly trimmed in leather fringe and beads. Not the coat of an Englishman or a Scot.

Her gaze jumped to the stranger's face. A low-crowned hat shaded his eyes but didn't hide his thoroughly scruffy beard, which covered the lower half of his face.

Panic hit her belly, and Gully let out a hiss.

Why hadn't she taken a moment to grab her pistol?

Easy. Breathe.

The stranger smiled, exposing very white teeth—or perhaps they only appeared so white because of his dark beard?

He raised his hand and she leaped back, found the pistol which she kept primed and ready on the small table by the door, then leveled it at his breast.

"Whoa, gal, I was only going to remove my hat."
American.

"Who are you?" No one came to her door in the broad daylight, much less after dark.

"No one you need to shoot, ma'am. I can assure you of that."

Good God, his eyes were so *green*. And, hat now removed, hair of wheat and gold.

"The name's Brendan Cavanaugh. Bren to my good friends."

She ignored his flirtatious grin, one that no doubt worked on most females. But she wasn't most females.

"I'm staying near here—I think—but with this infernal fog I must have got turned around."

"Did you stop at The Black Swan?" She needn't have asked; she could smell whisky on his breath, and the Swan was the only pub in the village.

"Why yes, ma'am, I set there a spell."

"Orin Fraser gave you directions?"

"He did."

A rather unladylike snort escaped. "Mr. Fraser is a scamp who is fond of a good joke. I expect you are looking for the Belcher Farm?" Kinduggan Keep was the only other option, but by the disreputable looks of Mr. Cavanaugh, he seemed unlikely be a guest there. Besides, it was said the family had not visited the house in decades.

"Belcher?" He seemed unsure for a moment but then nodded. "That's it. Thought I'd do some fishing and the like."

"Well, you are about four miles away. If the weather were fair."

"Ah."

"Should have gone left at Pebble Rock instead of straight. That will take you around the keep."

"Pebble Rock?"

"The Scots will have their little jokes. Pebble Rock is the massive boulder perched at the crook in the road. The one that looks as if it could tumble down upon you if you happen to sneeze."

The huge head of an enormous horse abruptly appeared over the man's shoulder.

"Oh, sorry ol' boy, I'm forgetting my manners. Ma'am, this handsome brute is Verlan. He's a mite tired after having the gall to go lame on me."

Again, that smile.

The horse blinked his milky eyes and blew, his lips quivering as if he were apologizing for causing an inconvenience.

Callie could never resist an animal in need. But by Jove, she *would* resist that damned smile. Even with its dratted dimple.

Gulliver chose that moment to turn turncoat and rub up against the stranger's leg. The man, heedless of the gun she still held trained on him, bent to ruffle the cat's ears.

Gully never took to strangers.

The man took his time in standing. She felt his gaze, almost like hands tracking over her body as he rose.

Oh, hell. She must look a sight. Freshly washed hair hanging loose down her back, only her chemise covering her upper body, and a pair of old breeches she had fashioned nearly two years ago instead of a proper skirt.

She snagged her drab coat from a peg and shrugged into it, then lifted the lantern from the hook by the door. She gestured for the man—Mr. Cavanaugh—to step back and allow her to pass.

The gloom of dusk had snuffed itself to dark, and a chill hung in the air. She shivered.

Verlan was at least seventeen hands. She rubbed his velvet muzzle, gray with white whiskers. The horse blew his thanks and pushed harder into her hand, his warm tongue seeking salt.

Sweet old thing.

Mr. Cavanaugh loomed large as he laid his huge hand on the horse's neck.

She stepped back, lifting the lantern to examine the poor beast. Blackish scars checkered his swayed back and nut-brown hide. She cut a glance at the hulking man. Did he mistreat this animal?

But from Mr. Cavanaugh's gentle touch on the beast's nose, she doubted he could be cruel. "Left rear," he offered.

Callie handed him the lantern and then shoved her pistol into the waistband of her breeches. She ran her hand down the affected leg. Verlan poked his nose around to see what she was about. "Easy, boy."

Hot to the touch and swollen. Poor lad.

"I hate to be a bother…"

She stood and pulled her jacket more tightly over her body.

What to do?

He stood there, hands open in supplication, his grin shifting into a tight smile. Could she send him packing? Not really an option with Verlan hobbled so.

"There's a small barn out back," she finally offered.

He released a huff of relief. "Much obliged." He tipped his hat. If eyes could smile, she would swear his were doing just that.

His large frame still blocked most of the doorway. She stepped back and away from the horse to allow him to pass and lead Verlan off. As he moved forward, she realized too late she had not allowed enough room for him and his arm brushed hers. She jerked away from the touch and Verlan threw his head.

"Easy there," Cavanaugh said, though Callie was unclear if he was addressing her or his horse.

A shiver radiated up her arm, one caused not by the cold. Such a small thing—a voice, a touch—to affect her so. Still, she'd been alone for so long…

Hastily she pulled a blanket from her bed and then lit another lantern and handed both to him, taking care not to touch his hand. *Silly.*

"Thank you again, ma'am." He swept his hat back on his head.

"Mind the goats! Tansy can be rather territorial."

He grinned again as he set two fingers to the brim of his hat in a kind of insouciant salute.

He spoke softly as he led the horse away, a comforting croon no doubt filled with promises of ease. He couldn't be all that bad, not if he treated his animal with such kindness. Still, she would keep the pistol close, just in case. Shining white teeth, flashing green eyes, and enough charm to coax honey from a bee did not signal harmlessness. Past experience had certainly imprinted the lesson in her brain—and on her heart.

Chapter Two

Mr. Cavanaugh did not come back to the cottage that evening. She'd half expected him to return, attempting to charm his way into a meal, or at least a glass of whisky. But he never knocked upon her door. She finally pulled off the freshly washed and ironed gown that she'd donned in expectation of his return and took herself to bed, her pistol on her left and Gulliver tucked into the crook of her right arm.

Sleep, though, did not come.

After long hours tossing and turning, she finally lit a candle and reached for her book.

An American, she thought as she riffled its pages. What had his life been like? She'd read Alexis de Tocqueville's *Democracy in America*, and the eloquent impassioned speeches of Fredrick Douglas, but those books hadn't answered the many questions she had about life in the United States. Had he been in their Civil War? Seen Indians? Helped to free slaves?

But he had not come back to the cottage, and she would not—nay, *could* not—go out and disturb him, not just to satisfy her curiosity about his homeland.

Her book fell open to a favorite passage:

"I find it wholesome to be alone the greater part of the time. To be in company, even with the best, is soon wearisome and dissipating. I love to be alone."

She slapped the book down.

Mr. Thoreau's musings not as comforting as she usually found them. Not with the arrival of a handsome stranger who had her imagination racing to fill in his story.

Did he need another blanket? Perhaps a book?

She heard the splash of water, then a soft nicker.

She slipped into her wrapper, picked up the candle, and then made her way to the window.

Gilded in moonlight, the shadows of man and beast etched themselves against the pewter-colored water as he coaxed the huge gelding into the loch. Its icy cold waters would ease the swelling.

The white of his shirt caught the light. He picked at some sedge grass and held it out to his horse. Verlan nibbled delicately before dipping his head to drink.

The man turned back toward her cottage, and she stepped back like a thief. He would have seen the light from her candle. Fool!

"Eewow!" Gulliver gave her a knowing look from his perch atop the coverlet.

"All right, I'll come back to bed, you wretched cat."

Would the man's careful tending lead to Verlan's recovery on the morrow? Would he then continue on his way?

It had been twenty-four days since she'd entertained anyone other than her cat, goats, and chickens. Young Angus brought her supplies each month. So shy and deferential, he would only enter her cottage to haul in coal or a particularly heavy basket. On occasion he would accept a bit of bread and cheese and a pint on the bench but would never come inside. He always rushed to finish, then blurted "Need to get back down the mountain." Did he scuttle off so fast because he could sense how starved she was for company? Or because his mother had warned him of being taken in by the odd spinster who lived up the mountain?

Angus was due to return in another four or five days, depending on the weather.

Surely Mr. Cavanaugh would be gone by then. Gossip would not touch her. Much. But still, it would be better for all if man and horse moved on.

She got back in bed, moving the pistol from the coverlet to the side table. Ridiculous, to think that just because a man smiled at her, he intended her harm.

Gulliver nudged her and she finally lay down, his tail flipping across her nose as he settled.

****

She arose at five. The sun would be up soon. Nearly twelve and a half hours of daylight in the Highlands this time of year. Ample time to complete her tasks for the day and then some. But she didn't want to do any of them. The stranger in her barn called to her.

She dressed in the gown she'd put on last evening and tied on a fresh apron. Her hair, she scraped into a bun. She hesitated at the door, looking back at her bedside table, not for the pistol, but perhaps to spare a moment to look into the small, chipped mirror tucked away in the drawer?

"Ridiculous!" she said to Gully and pushed out of the cottage before she could change her mind.

Careful to silently slip past the broken barn door, she made her way inside. Pale arrows of light, catching dust from the hay, streamed from the knot holes and gaps in the walls and ceiling.

He lay on a pallet of straw, her quilt covering him up to his ears. A ray of sun baptized his head, gilding his hair to a burnished gold. She crept closer.

Quite utterly beautiful in sleep. This huge man, oddly vulnerable with his fist tucked under his chin, his lashes a smudge of dark against his cheeks. Another reason his eyes seemed such a remarkable shade of green, those striking dark lashes and brows.

The peace could not hold. Tansy, poking her head through the slats of her pen, bleated good morning, shattering Callie's secret observation. Once Tansy started, Floppsy and Myrtle had to chime in.

She turned to hush them but suddenly could not breathe.

An iron band of arm clamped her neck, while the other snaked around her waist, pressing her back against a wall of hard muscle.

Panic flared deep in her belly. She yanked her arm forward, ready to jab her elbow into his side. But no heavy cologne and beeswax filled her nose, only the smell of sweet crushed hay and leather. And no flickering shadows cast by gaslight over silk-papered walls, only morning sunlight dappling white-washed rough wooden walls. And, finally, no black superfine cloth of an elegant suit of evening clothes, but the plain, dun-colored wool of a working man.

Good Lord, how could he move so fast?

Before she could scream in protest, she found herself free. She stumbled, her own ragged gasp in concert with his jerky breath, hard and fast behind her. She resisted the urge to rub her neck and instead turned to face him.

He looked so contrite, she nearly laughed instead of rebuking him.

She did neither. "How is Verlan?" she finally said,

not knowing quite what to say.

"Verlan?" He waved his hands in the air, dust motes swirling with the gesture. "I nearly snapped your neck in two and you're worried about my dang horse?"

"I am worried you will be here another day."

His face broke into that wicked grin. "Couldn't sleep either, could you?"

Was she so rumpled? Her eyes bloodshot? Without a doubt her hair was a rat's nest. Perhaps she should have looked in the mirror… "I am unused to interlopers," she said raising her chin instead of smoothing her hair.

"So, you live up here all on your own, then?" His gaze slid around the tiny barn and narrow hayloft above.

"I do." Why did she have to sound so confrontational? She supposed she presented quite an odd picture to a stranger. She waited for the next question.

He only nodded once. "Seems like an ideal spot to me," he said almost wistfully.

No interest in why a woman—a gentlewoman— would live next to nowhere in the woods with a few cantankerous goats?

He cleared his throat. "I reckon I'll just tidy myself up now."

"Oh, yes, of course. I will leave you to your— ablutions then." She nearly tripped over Gulliver in her haste to flee the barn and that wicked, knowing smile.

Chapter Three

Who was this bewitching witch of the woods?

His dreams had only bred more questions. She spoke like a lady but dressed like a drudge. And lived alone, half-way to nowhere. She must be nearing—thirty? A woman, capable, strong—he had felt her tight bum and trim back against his chest and thighs when he'd nearly killed her here in her own barn.

Dang savage! Not even fit to sleep with the animals...

Still, she hadn't gone all vaporish on him. Oh, he'd felt her tense right up, but she'd got control of herself quick as beans on toast. Now dressed in a proper shirtwaist and skirt, smoothing her hands over her freshly pressed apron. Hands used to hard work. But despite her age and oddly solitary life, there was something fresh about her. Something untouched.

He shook the straw out of the blanket. Still smelled of her. Of sweet woman. He stuck his nose in it once more before draping it over the half-wall of the stall. Ah, silly fool, pining over a spinster who'd said she was ready to see the back of him.

Verlan's hock was a touch better, but couldn't carry a grown man, that was for sure. Best to give him another day or so.

No one was expecting him—well, that wasn't exactly true. His family had been expecting him for nigh on a year now. But the idea of spending a few days here in this oasis, with this woman—he didn't even know her name—gave him a sense of peace he hadn't felt since—well, in a coon's age.

His stomach growled. Right. Best to earn his keep.

He settled Verlan with some hay and wrapped the horse's hock in a plaster of cool mud while he munched. "Hold down the fort, ol' boy. And don't get too friendly with those goats."

He filled his water canteen and hoisted his Remington over his shoulder.

Several trails ran off from the cabin site. He took the one leading farther up the mountain.

Never failed, this balm of the woods, easing his often-tangled mind. Pine and earth filled his nose and lungs. So alive and vibrant, with its perfumed layers of wintergreen and bell-flower. His hearing adjusted to catch even the most subtle rustlings and calls within this glorious orchestra of the forest—a long-eared owl's hoot in concert with an irate chatter of a red squirrel.

Farther up the mountain he found snares. Expertly rigged, but empty. Did this woman have a man? Naw, she would have said so the moment he showed up at her door.

She could have lied about not being alone easily enough. But he had a feeling the thought never occurred to her.

His gaze snagged on a curious tower of rocks. A cairn.

He had made many a cairn in many a stretch of woods, but never anything like this. A nearly complete wheel of wedge-shaped slate, with a stunner of a mica-speckled Schist with a—by God, yes! A Trilobite fossil at its very top.

As he made his way toward the mountain's summit, he found more cairns dotting the woods, the topmost rock a clue as to which direction the next lay.

A fantastical treasure hunt.

He had no way of knowing, only his instinct. But he was sure she must have fashioned these. In society, his instincts weren't worth a tinker's damn. But in the woods, they were usually dead on.

A huge cairn made up of layers of thin, flat slate zigzagged up higher than his arm stretched straight over his head, each rock cleverly held in place, weighted down by the slab above it. He reached out to touch it but stopped as he caught sight of the topmost stone. A thin blade of rock that seemed to hang in the air.

He shook his head. How had she created such a monolith? One false move and the thing would have toppled and crushed her!

He discovered other sculptures, too, much smaller and made mostly of round rocks, set in minuscule divots where the next rock would nestle. Each creation astounding in its complexity. They must have taken a bucketful of patience to make, endless tries and topplings and then starting over once more. Just the selection of the rocks—coordinating colors and shapes— must have taken hours. He imagined her trolling the mountainside, searching for the perfect stone, testing the weight and feel in her hand then smiling.

Only he had to imagine her smile. Because he'd yet to see it.

He had that kind of patience when he was fishing, or whittling. Been a long while since he had done either.

Nearly at the summit, a trail along the ridgeline

opened to a rock outcropping with a doozy of a view of the valley below. The sun played cat and mouse with the shifting clouds, dappling the land. He could make out the spire of the church etched in front of the Abernathy Round Tower which rose above it. Then down Main Street to the roofline of the Black Swan where he'd spent much of yesterday afternoon. Always could spot something before anyone else. Smell too. Another thing he was good at: hunting—spying.

Up on a huge, flat boulder, sheltered in a stand of trees, stood a bower made of arm-thick deadfall lashed together and then covered with sheets of birch bark and pine boughs.

He hesitated. Surely her private spot. But he was Brendan Cavanaugh, and Brendan Cavanaugh didn't let rules and boundaries box him in.

A grand throne-like chair made out of slabs of rock dominated the space. A table, also made of rock, sat beside it. The back and seat of the chair were covered in thick moss.

He sat. A bit snug, but comfortable enough.

He imagined this woman—why the heck hadn't he asked her name?—sitting in this spot, surveying her kingdom far below. The cares of the world mere trifles.

Tucked in a crevice in the table was something wrapped in oilskin.

A book?

He unwrapped it. A journal.

He should put it back.

He flipped to the first page.

Perfect penmanship in neat and steady rows. He squinted his eyes, a trick that usually sorted out most words, but not these. Foreign.

French?

His ma had tried to teach Farren and Sara the language. She knew better than to tax his weak brain with such nonsense.

He flipped several pages, hoping to find something he could actually read. Nothing. Served him right for his prying.

Still, he continued as if by doing so he might learn something of this woodland witch.

A detailed drawing of a mushroom. Pretty good, but he was no judge of such things.

Other drawings. A goat—the ornery one, Tansy. Plants. And then a portrait. A young girl, maybe thirteen or so? Quite a beauty, or would be in a few years.

Yes, a young beauty…

Another face took shape in his mind. His Rosie…

He squeezed his eyes shut, as if the action might dispel his daughter's image. But instead, she appeared even clearer. Shy smile, same green eyes and dark brows as him, beautiful golden hair…

Damn, he was a coward. Running for nearly a year now. And from what? A young girl?

No, Rose would be nearly a woman now…

Would she even need him as a father? She had a proper family now with Farren.

Farren.

Land sakes, he missed his brother.

Hell, did he need to be struck dumb and blind to start figuring life out? Wasn't nearly being killed enough fodder to make a man step up to the plate? What a joke to have survived the whole damn Civil War with nary a mark upon him and then to be nearly felled by that psychopath, Rodger Milton. The man who had stolen his

Rosie, calling himself her father.

Standing over his grandfather's raw grave, Bren had vowed he'd be a real father to Rose, a better man than his own father'd been.

But what had he done? Gone an hightailed it outta there as soon as humanly possible. Oh, he'd had excuses—had to go back to the states to clear his name. Then a year of mourning to get through. Brendan Cavanaugh could always come up with some justification to put off his God-given responsibilities.

When would the tally of his actions be in his favor?

The answer seemed as indecipherable as the words in this journal.

He turned the page as if the book might miraculously provide a sign. Found another portrait of the young girl, her clear eyes looking out at him without any judgment. Her smile, a sweet secret. Tentatively, he traced the curve of her cheek. Would he ever dare to touch his own daughter with such tenderness? Would he ever deserve Rose's devotion and love?

****

Callie surveyed him from the shelter of the huge Scotch pine that stood lowering over the cottage. Such a swagger! So cocksure as he hefted a beam that must weigh thirty-five stone.

She stepped forward to offer help, a word of caution on her lips. But neither was necessary. He slid the wood into a newly chinked slot and then raised and slotted the other side in to form the new lintel on which the old barn door would slide. A few taps with a mallet and she could barely discern any seams in the joining. Nearly a year and a half since she had vowed to have it replaced, and now, in only a few short hours, it was done.

Again, his muscles bulged as his arms spanned the five-foot-wide door. Easy as hanging a painting, he fitted the fist-sized wheels onto the bar and then tested the ease with which the heavy door slid open and closed. He ran his hand over the ancient boards with a loving touch, then he stepped back.

Earlier, when she had gone to feed the goats, she had seen the deer hanging and dressed. A luxury, venison, for it was too difficult for her to process by herself. She restricted herself to snaring smaller prey—rabbits, grouse, and fish.

Three years and seven days now since she'd come to the Highlands. Books and animals her only companions. They had been enough, then.

But now…

He strode toward the loch, his gate an easy lope as if he had all the time in the world. Hips cocked forward, his gaze toward the clouds overhead, confident and ready for what life delt out.

She reminded herself she didn't like men with a swagger. Just a trick, to make themselves seem bigger, more consequential. Like a peacock flaunting its plumage. Pesky birds, peacocks, with not the most pleasant of dispositions. She preferred a good partridge any day.

He stripped off his shirt and plunged into the middle of the loch. He flipped and swam back to where he could stand. Taking handfuls of sand, he scrubbed his arms, chest, and belly. Muscles bulged and rippled. Skin shone glossy silver in the fading light.

She stepped closer. If he were not shy about showing his body, why should she play coy?

He turned, slinging water. Verlan also looked up.

"Oh, pardon, ma'am. I didn't see you there." He grinned but made no move to cover his naked torso.

She didn't know much about Mr. Cavanaugh, but the idea that he'd been caught unawares just didn't ring true. She remembered that band of iron arm around her neck, ready to snap it like a twig.

"Really?" she said, shoving her hands into her apron, "Then all this show is for—the birds?"

In answer, he grinned wider, confirmation of his shameless display. "And any other of God's good creatures who care to have a gander."

Callie shielded her eyes against the sun. "I suppose you should know my name if you'll be joining me for dinner."

His wicked smile growing even wider, he sloshed his way out of the water and picked up his shirt, using it to mop water from his chest. The weight of the water pulled his trousers low over his hips, revealing the jut of hipbones, arrogant, taunting…

"I was hoping you'd ask, Miss…?"

"Ainsworth," she answered rather breathlessly.

"Miss Ainsworth, pleased ta make your acquaintance."

"Callista Ainsworth," said with more assurance. "I'll expect you in an hour."

She turned before she gave in to the urge to find out what his wet naked skin might feel like under the press of her hot palm.

****

His presence—his man-ness—brought something alien into the tiny cabin. As if the room, which before his arrival had seemed spacious enough, was now filled with an "otherness." Wet man, leather, and saddle soap. And a musk that made her tongue press against her teeth.

Even the sound of his voice within the four walls changed the place.

Very well. He was handsome, without a doubt. But she had known other handsome men. In fact, several, even more handsome than Mr. Brendan Cavanaugh.

But not in a long while. And those men did not have that smile, that dimple, those laughing eyes...

Stop it! This man was simply a stranger who was lost and had a lame horse. That was all. She would play the Good Samaritan, give him shelter and a meal until he could be on his way.

Still, that green gaze seemed poised to devour...

"Dinner is served."

He ate with relish, using his bread to soak up every bit of venison stew. He did not speak much, intent on his food. After a second helping, he pushed back from the table.

"Now, that was the best stew I've had in a month of Sundays, Miss Ainsworth. I thank you. If you have a basket, I'll load up these plates and do the washing up before I mosey."

She didn't want him to leave, not yet. "I've a fine local whisky if you've a mind for a taste."

He stopped and stroked his now trimmed beard. "Whisky? Well now, that would be right nice."

When she turned back with the mugs of whisky, she saw he'd set a second chair next to the fire. The new furniture placement startled her. It seemed to change the entire interior of her cottage, yet again, making it smaller, and more intimate.

"You going to pass that whisky over, or are you having second thoughts?"

"Oh, yes. Here you are." She handed him the drink. "Orin Fraser will tell you his brew is the best, but Brian Belcher's is smoother, to my view. But perhaps you have already partaken, since you were headed to Mr. Belchers?"

He frowned but then smiled. "Naw, only Fraser's." He raised his mug. "I thank you."

They sat before the fire, whisky in hand. Gulliver, who had been napping next to the hearth, got up and laid himself over Mr. Cavanaugh's left boot.

Callie shook her head at the fickle animal then took a sip and watched the dance of flames.

He inhaled deeply from his mug and then eased back to look at her, his dark eyebrows raised. "You have a good nose for Scotch whisky, Miss Ainsworth."

Callie had a million questions. But, so unused to company, she felt oddly shy and out of her depth. So they sipped in silence. A silence not strained, but certainly poignant, as if both were poised to spill over. But with what? She had no inkling.

"Maryland, you said?" Unable to keep her curiosity at bay, she picked up on a thread of their dinner conversation. "I believe it is in the middle of the eastern seaboard, is it not?" Her gaze strayed to the large atlas tucked alongside Mr. Huntington's book, *Geography of the Heavens*. She longed to jump up and retrieve it but kept her seat.

"Smack dab, yes ma'am. The Mason Dixon line." He laughed, but it was harsh and grating in the quiet room.

"Ah. And, your family, what do they do? Do you live in town? Or perhaps on a farm?"

"We *had* a small spread—a farm."

She gripped her mug of whiskey. The question must be asked. "And did your family own slaves?"

"Naw, my ma wouldn't have it. Pa couldn't have cared less, but Ma stood firm. I reckon owning a person was something she just could not stomach."

"And what about you? Where did you stand?" Again, she hated that his answer could end their conversation then and there, but it was best to know these things outright.

"Oh, I expect I mostly stood where it was easiest." He nodded to the whisky bottle, his mug empty. "But, no, in that instance, like my ma, I could never cotton— pun intended—to owning a body."

Relieved, she passed him the bottle. He took his time pouring and then gestured to refill her mug as well.

"My ma never stood up to Pa, but God forbid one of us kids ever crossed her. A definite pecking order in the Cavanaugh family."

"And where did you fall in that order?"

"Lord, woman, you and your questions!"

"Yes, I am being unconscionably rude." She looked into the flames, feeling the heat on her cheeks. "The truth is, I am unused to company and I am a curious person. I had almost forgotten that. Perhaps you might indulge me as payment for the whisky, a meal, and a bed—or, rather, a place to lay your head," she amended when an unwanted flush flooded her neck and swept up her cheeks yet again at the thought of him in bed.

He only looked at her over his mug, his mouth hidden, then took another long sip of his whisky. "The thing you have to know about me is if there's an easy way out, that's the way I'm goin'. So, I escaped the pecking order, mostly. My brother, Farren, he

25

desperately wanted my folks' admiration, if not their love. But for me, it only took a few slaps, or being ignored, and I got the lay of the land right enough. Too much effort to try and worm my way into their hearts. If perfect Farren couldn't do it, sure as pullin' weeds in a drought, I didn't have a chance in hell."

"There was just you and your brother?"

He looked into the fire, his finger idly tracing the rim of his mug. "Sara. My sister, Saraphina Jayne."

The sadness in his eyes kept her silent. She waited instead.

Mr. Cavanaugh shifted his weight in his chair and tossed off the rest of his whiskey. "Sara, well, she escaped nearly all the Cavanaugh drama."

She shouldn't ask, but— "How do you mean?"

"How I mean is, she died." He winced and then abruptly stood. "And that bit of overly-bald truth-tellin' is my cue to take myself off to Verlan and those ornery goats." He smiled then. "Thank you much for your company, and the fine meal and whisky. I don't recall ever having a finer. I bid you good night, Miss Ainsworth." He made an elaborate bow, his hat sweeping the floor before setting it on his head, and then left the cottage.

Certainly, her prying had made him depart. Callie exhaled into the hush he left behind. He hadn't asked her a single question, and yet—somehow—his presence had stirred something in her that felt new and untouched.

Chapter Four

Three days later

After a day of foraging in the woods together, they had gone their separate ways.

How wonderful it had been to see her woods through his eyes. To show him her treasures. Clearly, he had spent many-a-day and night in the wilderness, knew far more than she about its secrets and wonders. "Hush, woman!" he'd exclaimed after she'd asked yet another question, exasperation and affection clear in his voice.

Tonight's dinner was grilled rabbit with greens and wild mushrooms. She found herself excited about cooking for him again. Wanting to impress him. Wanting him to stay…

After clearing their dinner plates, Callie cut a slice of bilberrie pie and brought it to the table.

He strolled around her cottage, restless, curious, examining her things, his long finger trailing down the spines of her beloved books, lingering over the little treasures nestled within the shelves, each a memory of a walk or adventure. The pieces of her life.

How huge he looked within these walls. His shadow long, reaching high onto the thatched ceiling.

What must he think of her, such an odd spinster-lady tucked into the Scottish hills? She found herself almost defensive as he examined the fragile wren's nest next to the curled knot of pine tree that she'd saved because it had put her in mind of a dragon's breath.

Had living alone made her secretive, territorial, without even knowing? Good gracious, she felt suddenly *shy*. She'd never been particularly shy before. Her father always frowning at the endless flow of questions spilling from her mouth without cease. *Why did this happen? What was that for? How did this work?* And when answers had not been forthcoming, she'd turned to books.

But she would not find this man's secrets between any pasteboard covers.

He picked up a bowl she had fashioned from a burl, turning it over, his long, elegant fingers tracing the whorls and grain in the wood, utterly absorbed. He had not stopped to pull down a single book, let alone open one, yet he seemed fascinated by a rather crude carving.

She would have been infinitely curious had she stumbled on such a person as herself. So she steeled herself for his questions, poised to defend her way of life. But he only looked, uttering not even a single query.

"Might I ask how an American comes to find himself in the Highlands of Scotland?"

He put the bowl carefully back on its shelf right next to the beautifully bound volume of poetry by John Keats. One that would unerringly fall open to *Bright Star*. She was glad he quickly passed it by.

"You sure do ask a lot of questions. Is that why you have all these books?" He gestured to the walls.

"Well…" It may have been a rhetorical question, but he had certainly hit on the truth. "Yes, I suppose so. I never got many responses from my father, or my teachers, for that matter. Once I learned to read, books became my world. And of course, out here there is little opportunity for scintillating conversation. Though Gulliver deigns to listen to me on occasion." The black tabby stretched, yawned and then settled back on his cushion, patiently waiting for a chance to lay across Brendan Cavanaugh's boot again.

His gaze raked over the walls of her cottage and then back to her, as if he were fitting the pieces of her life into a jigsaw puzzle. She sat up straighter.

"I guess you'd say I am on the run."

A criminal? Dear heavens! She shot a nervous glance to where her pistol lay on the small table next to the front door.

"Now, don't get into a twist. I'm not running from the law or anything like that. At least not anymore." He grinned, then took a sip of his whisky.

She eased back in her chair. She shouldn't press him, for he clearly did not want to elaborate.

But after long moments of silence, her curiosity would not be squelched. Besides, he would be gone soon. "On the run? From what, if not from the law?"

"If only it were as simple as a run-in with the law. But it's a sight more touchy than that."

"I see." But she didn't see at all. "Is it your family? I only ask because families can be tricky. I know mine is. My father, I hardly know. My stepmother, I would rather not know. And my dear little sister, I miss with all my heart." *Had she really rattled on like that?*

Then a thought occurred to her. A terrible thought. "Oh, is it a wife? Is that who you are running from?"

He looked at her startled, as if she had lighted on some hidden secret.

Dear God, was he not going to answer her?

Oh, hell and damnation. He *was* married and fleeing from his wife. But why were tears threatening? Why should it matter to her whether he had a wife or no?

She needed to tell him to leave. Now.

"Mr. Cavan—"

"Naw. Not married."

Dizzy relief swamped her breast. *Not married.* But Callie could not help but think wedged within those three words, there seemed a whole complicated history that remained unspoken.

"Are you?"

"What?"

"Are *you* married?"

"No," she replied, perhaps too hastily. But then a bubble of delight rose within her. He'd looked slightly panicked, too, when he quizzed her back. Perhaps her answer actually mattered to him. Perhaps he was even attracted to her as she was to him? Yes, that was the terrible truth of it. She *was* wildly attracted to this Yank.

He returned to his chair, adjusting his shoulders as if somehow his jacket had suddenly become too small. "I reckon I'm running from life. Lordy be, sounds lame when you say it out loud."

There was something so tender and wounded in his demeanor as he stared down at his untouched pie. Oh, he covered it up well, from the wicked grin that often didn't quite reach his eyes to the confident way he held his body. But as he pushed his pie aside, his finger thoughtfully tracing the burn mark on the table—made when she had been too impatient and set a boiling kettle down on the bare wood—belied his bravado. Perhaps he had confessed only because he would never see her again. But she felt as if he had given her a gift by disclosing a deeply held secret.

Running from life.

Her gaze strayed to the small table where Helena's letter lay. With Mr. Cavanaugh's arrival she had not yet written her response. "I mentioned I have a sister. I have not seen her in over three years. She has been wanting me to come for a visit. I have been resisting. But now it seems I do not have a choice. And so, I must give up my life here, at least for a while."

He sat forward. "Must be dire, the mess she's in, for you to shuck all this."

Was he being facetious? No. No he was serious. He understood this cottage and woods were a haven for her. Not many people would.

"Yes. Yes, her situation is quite dire."

He nodded slowly, his expression growing uncharacteristically serious. "Then you are right to go. I reckon there comes a time when life catches up to you and you have to turn around and face it." He spoke as if his words were meant for him as well as for herself.

Yes, she must face life again. Go back into the polite world, which in her experience was anything but polite.

Would she ever return to this cottage? Or would she be swept up in being the dutiful older daughter firmly on the shelf? Perhaps the doting aunt? Once entangled, a second escape might not be possible.

Life. Turning around to face it head on. And still so much she had not yet tasted…

Before her was a man bursting with life. Teeming with such, such—the word escaped her. She dreamed of experiencing physical love. But no one had ever dropped upon her doorstep to tempt her. Could divine providence have sent Brendan Cavanaugh her way?

Dire. Yes, that was a good word.

She set her mug on the table. And then as if she were plunging off a cliff, her hand drifted toward his, toward that burn mark in the table. She traced her half of the circle as he continued to trace his. They did not look at each other, just concentrated on fingers caressing wood.

The arcs became smaller, her finger venturing into his territory, his venturing into hers.

She could stop this. She could take her hand away, finish her drink and rise, signaling that it was time for him to go.

Or she could dare just a bit. She could lift her eyes to find his…

As her mind danced through tempting scenarios, she felt the touch of his finger. Such a small gesture but it hit her down deep. A thrill that rolled up into her belly and tickled her heart.

His gaze found hers, all bravado gone. Those eyes, vivid green pools, so endlessly deep. So vulnerable. Like a shy deer, uncertain whether she was friend or foe.

She eased her hand away and then stood. His body tensed, but he did not move. With trembling fingers, she found the top button of her blouse and flicked it open. His hand flexed once over the burn mark. She flicked the next and the next. By the fourth button, he straightened, tense, a hunter at the ready. She liked the look. She liked that she seemed to have all of his attention, instinctively knowing deep down he was excited and liked what he saw. It made her bold. Well, bolder.

She stepped from behind the table toward him.

At the sixth button he stood, the chair scraping loudly against the floor, the sound incongruous in the quiet room.

She did not have to undo the seventh button. His fingers found the small nub of colored cloth and easily released it, then the next two, until her bodice gaped. Living in the remote Scottish Highlands with only Gulliver and the birds to look on, she rarely bothered with a corset. She hadn't today.

The sight of her plain cotton chemise, one she must have mended at least a dozen times, seemed to excite him further.

He took a moment to shuck off his coat and then yank at his already loosened cravat. He swallowed, his Adam's apple bobbed in the thick column of his strong neck. She tentatively touched it, and it bobbed again, sliding from beneath her fingers and then rising to fill them.

Amazing.

"Wait. I'll be but a minute." He was backing out of the room. "I have an English Overcoat in my pack."

English Over—? Oh, a preventive. He was being careful. But she did not want to be careful. If he took more than two steps away from her, sense would worm its way into her besotted brain. She came after him and reached down to cup his genitals and gently squeezed.

"Ahhh!" Then he hissed. A good hiss, she thought, not one of pain. "Are you sure?"

She nodded.

"I will pull out."

She heard the words, not really knowing what they meant, only needing to feel him.

"Trust me, Callista." Her name in that deep, slightly Southern accent. Then he scooped her up right under her bottom and held her tight up against his hardness.

He carried her toward the bed, pulling her closer, his

hot mouth over hers. The soft rasp of his beard, a momentary shock, breath of heady whisky, then the press of his lips, his tongue, seeking, probing deeper as she opened, welcoming him. Wanting more.

She felt him shift. She clung to him, not wanting to give him the opportunity to stop. Not now.

But he was only trying to toe off his boots. Not so easy with her in his arms. He tossed her onto the bed.

She would have laughed if she were not so starved to have him back next to her. She slipped off the bed and pushed him down on it. The old rope groaned in protest at his weight. She took one boot—just like cowboys wore, she imagined—and pulled, then made short work of the other. She knelt between his legs. She had read about that—a woman taking a man's cock in her mouth. The idea intrigued her, but she ached below. She wanted him there.

He yanked his shirt over his head and then pulled her up to kiss her mouth again. He rolled back and to the side and she now lay partially beneath him. His hot mouth trailed over her jaw line, his soft beard tickling her, now skating down her neck, his teeth taking little nips of her tender flesh. Now over her collar bone and down to her—

"Ahh!" Oh yes! She had touched herself there, even pinched, but the sensation of his mouth on her nipple, his tongue teasing and laving and then sucking—hard!

Her hands skated over his body. Hard, bunched muscle, coarse hair, silky hair, the long length of him. An entire world to discover.

His hand moved from her breast down to her waist, then lower, bunching up her skirt and then dipping between her legs.

She pushed up against his seeking fingers.

"Ah, so wet," he crooned in her ear. "Are you ready for me?"

"Yes!" she cried.

Not really knowing what "ready" meant, only knowing she needed him, she grasped his tight buttocks and urged him on.

"Ahh!" Searing pain and burning. She'd read it would hurt.

"What the——" he began to pull away from her.

"No, don't stop! Please don't." Taking advantage of his surprise, she flipped him over, straddling his hips.

As his mouth opened in protest, she covered it with her own. All objections fled as she pressed her tongue deep inside. He groaned and then enveloped it. Teasing him, she pulled away only to fill the emptiness with her breast. Such sweet torture, but she wanted to be filled down there, where it was throbbing and wet.

She arched up, pulling him with her. As he laved her breasts, she found his bobbing penis and rose, her wetness guiding her, and then seated herself down onto him.

"Ahhh." he moaned, falling back onto the mattress while arching into her.

Capturing his hands, she rose and fell, seeking to find an elusive rhythm. Now, looking in his eyes, any doubt within him was glossed over by a haze of desire. Using her hands against his broad, muscled chest, she found her stride, sinking onto him only to push up, and then sink down again.

He seemed to like her taking charge. His hands now on her hips, he matched her rhythm, urging her tighter and faster, his green eyes never leaving hers.

The pain was gone, just an incredible fullness, a building within her body.

"Yes-s-s." The word came out in a hiss of breath, as he drove harder into her heat.

An incredible humming took over her body. The quaking seemed to be seated within her very core. It shocked her but she only wanted to ride its surging wave. She rocked above him as he pushed into her, throwing her head back, wanting only to be engulfed.

"Ahhh!" The sound rose from deep within her as her body exploded.

****

What the hell just happened?

The world still spun, and his body still hummed but he made himself rise on shaky arms to look at his still hard cock.

She lay next to him, eyes closed, a soft smile on her face. Her pert breasts rising and falling with her breath, the hollow of her belly echoing the motion, her rich, red snatch glistening with his seed.

A telltale streak of blood on her white thigh.

His dang johnson bobbed against his belly, ready for another go.

He heaved himself out of the bed. "Good God, woman, why the hell didn't you say something?"

She lazily opened her eyes. "I'm sorry, was I required to speak during the act? I understood it to be generally a silent activity."

"You know what I mean. Ignorant you are not."

"Well, I am certainly more educated than I was a few minutes ago." She turned on her side, her gaze raking over his body. "I must thank you for that, sir. It was truly—enlightening."

He looked for something to cover himself with. Dang it all, where was his shirt?

Wait. Sir?

He wheeled on her. "Generally, after a poke like that, I don't get called sir." *Shit, where the hell was his shirt?* He spun toward her again. "And it was a sight more than a few minutes!"

But that was the hitch. It hadn't been more than five at most. She seemed so hungry, so ready. *So experienced.* And, hell, he'd been downright starved.

"Jesus, woman. What the hell? You acted as if you knew what you were doing." He had managed to get his shirt over his head, but his cock was a stiff tent pole.

"Well then, my books have served me well." She toyed with a locket that hung between her breasts...

He spun away from the bedeviling sight. "Man alive, your books? What in tarnation have you been reading?"

"If a woman is industrious, she can find all manner of information."

"Jesus." He shoved his hands through his damp hair.

"I happen to be very industrious."

"If what just happened is any test, I reckon you could teach a dad-burned class on it. "

"I trust that to be a compliment? At any rate I shall take it as such." She sat up in the bed, her hair a riot of red over her white body.

A virgin. Shit. He'd never had a virgin before. Was there something he should be doing for her? She certainly seemed right as rain. And still tempting as the devil.

But what should a fella do?

He scanned the room as if it might give him an

answer. A silver frame winked in the light. A fine paisley shawl lay draped over a peg by the door. Hundreds of books lined the walls, mocking his thick brain.

Her posh way of speaking—Hell, even the dainty way she ate her dinner—

A lady! She was a blasted lady!

Idiot! How had he missed it?

Too concerned with himself he was, just like always.

He took a much-needed breath. "Listen, ma'am, I mean Miss Ainsworth. Damn, I mean, Callista. I—I'm sorry about all this. I reckon we—got carried away. And I—Well, I suppose, if you think we should... We, that is—I would like to offer—"

She jerked upright, straighter than a poker. "Mr. Cavanaugh. Please do not concern yourself." She held out a staying hand. "You took no advantage, and have no responsibility for me. I wanted this to happen. *I* made the choice. And have no regrets. I hope you have none, either. It was a mutually chosen joining, that is all."

"But you are—were—a maiden." Hell, she'd knocked him to a cocked hat.

"Mr. Cavanaugh—"

"Dang it, woman! Can't you at least call me Bren? Or Brendan, if you like?"

"Very well—Brendan. I am eight and twenty. My birthday is in five days when I will be nine and twenty. I am a confirmed spinster. Reading about sexual congress is one thing, but to experience it—" She shook her head. "Well, to experience it is quite another. Thank you for expanding my knowledge. That is all I require of you."

Require of him? He paced to the door and then back, nearly trampling the lady's cat. *Lady?* What the hell was a posh gal like her doing out here in the wilds of Scotland?

More like a witch!

And he'd nearly offered for her! Damn, he was impulsive, but to get hitched to a stranger on a whim? Or worse, because he thought he *should*? What the hell was this woodland witch doing to him?

It was a poke. One poke. And a quick one at that. But he was the one having vapors, not her. Callista Ainsworth was cooler than a Philadelphia lawyer.

"But you got on top," he gawped shoving his hands through his hair, trying to fit her actions to those of an untried virgin.

"Yes, I did."

"But no maid gets on top like that!"

"No?"

"No!" He spun around in frustration. "It just don't happen."

"You know this imperially? You've lain with a number of virgins?"

"Imper—? What? No! Never, but—well, you acted like you knew what you were doing."

"Again, I shall take that as a compliment." A satisfied smile stamped her too red lips. "My reading indicates that when the female is positioned on top, more of her pubis is engaged, and thus takes more satisfaction from the act," she said, as even-toned as if speaking of the weather. "I thought I should take advantage of the opportunity, since I doubt I will have another such chance to test the claim."

"Advantage? Well, I reckon for a quick po— encounter—you got your money's worth." Why did he feel like the one who'd been taken advantage of?

Still, his hands itched to find her waist and to pull her back against his cock. To bury his nose in her soft hair. And to find the sensitive spot where her neck met her shoulder.

"What are you doing?" she said idly stroking her cat who had jumped up to join her and seemed just as satisfied as his lady.

Lady. He shook his head. "Getting dressed."

"Oh." She bit her lip and pulled the sheet, soiled with her blood and his juice, to cover her body.

"Mr. Cavanaugh—I mean, Brendan…"

He stopped and turned to her. "Yes?"

"Well, as you mentioned, the act *was* rather quick," she said smoothing her hand over a wrinkle in the blanket.

"What?" He froze in the middle of pulling up his trousers.

"I was agreeing that our bed sport was—brief. Eye-opening and quite marvelous, but over before—well before I could savor it properly. I believe one should never squander an opportunity for further education." When he did not respond she added, "Perhaps we could have another—go? Try another position?"

"Position?" The boot he'd been struggling to put on dropped with a thud.

She smiled then, this woman-virgin—well, no longer a virgin now—with her open face and intelligent eyes. "Well, yes. There are an infinite number, I understand—"

Was this virgin trying to school him? "I know every position and then some, ma'am."

"Excellent. I do have one I've been particularly curious about…"

Dang, but this gal made a fella unsteady all around! How could she take the fire out of him and yet stoke it up all in one fell swoop?

"Of course you do. And which one would that be?"

"Number sixty-nine. It is where the man lays one way and the woman—"

"Yep, I'm familiar with it." Great God, heat swept up him to flood his cheeks and burn his ears.

"Ah, I am glad to hear it. Would you be willing to try that one with me?"

Well, dad blast.

****

Cold.

Callie fumbled for the blanket somewhere down near her knees.

Wait—

The spot next to her was empty.

He must have slipped out of her bed sometime in the early morning hours. Why hadn't she heard him? Because she'd been so utterly spent.

She pulled the blanket up over her body, wanting to be warm again. Wanting him to cover her again.

She'd had no idea. Oh, she'd presented herself as worldly, levelheaded, rattling off hard facts from a variety of books. But inside she'd been reeling.

The act had been a revelation. A wave of sensation that had swamped her entire body. A wave so very different from the solitary release achieved with her own hands.

She wanted that feeling again.

And had this man been at the point of offering marriage? Good heavens. She believed he had been about to do just that. What if she hadn't stopped him? In her love-stupored state, who knows what she might have said in reply!

Brendan Cavanaugh's misplaced chivalry was certainly at odds with the overweening American bravado with which he presented himself. As if he were so ashamed of his kindnesses, he had to qualify his actions, so that one didn't think too well of him. He seemed to need to play the rogue. A defense, no doubt. But against what?

The dim light of dawn filtered through the shuttered window. Gulliver stretched and then butted her shoulder with his head. Hungry and wanting to go out.

Callie rose and hastily dressed in the gown she picked up off the floor. A hot blush rose to cover her neck and cheeks. What they had done last night...

What her body had done...

She filled the kettle. Not just with the two cups she allotted herself every morning, but up to the brim. She set it on the hob then added a few lumps of peat to the stove.

She would make bread today. Did he like crowdie cheese?

She touched the burn mark in the table. She would never look upon it the same. And her chair. He had claimed it so thoroughly. She had been relegated to the guest chair, with its pristine cushion upon which Gully did not even dare splay himself—and he laid everywhere. She touched its twin cushion, cross-stitched last winter as she'd huddled next to the fire. Its colors still bright with poppies and butterflies fluttering amid green tendrils of grass, reminding her that spring would eventually come again. Those long, dark days...

Days filled with reading and things she loved to do, she reminded herself. But somehow the thought of another winter here made her want to cry.

Helena's letter still lay unanswered on her writing table. She *would* reply today.

She pushed open the door and took in a lung-full of air. Spring seemed to have suddenly descended upon her mountain. The tree trunks, dark arabesques amid a riot of new-green foliage blotted out the browns and grays. A whinchat chased its mate, zigzagging through branches where squirrels chattered in their comical and frenzied manner.

His arrival almost seemed to bring the season on with full force, as if he had magic within him. A silly thought, but on such a glorious morn, she wanted to believe in miracles.

She found herself grinning. There was such an easy, almost childish joy about him, something free and wild and untamed. That mercurial effervescence called out to something long-hidden within her. She laughed outright when she realized she'd been trying on his particular swagger as she crossed the side yard toward the barn.

With a shaking hand she eased the newly-fixed door open—so silent—her eyes adjusting to the dim light, her heart pounding with anticipation of touching him again.

But only two steps inside, and she knew.

He was gone.

Tansy bleated, wanting her food.

Life went on in her little barn. The everyday rhythm of her daily chores—ones that had shaped her day, giving her purpose and satisfaction, but now seemed just a long list of obligations, filling an empty space where none had been before.

She mindlessly fed the goats and even ruffled their heads. She gave a handful of grain to the chickens and filled the water trough.

A cold breeze whipped through the open doorway, and she shivered. Not spring quite yet.

She checked the carcass of the deer he had killed. Meat that would serve her for months to come…

Gully butted her legs. She looked down at his upturned face.

Oh, she'd forgotten to feed him, so eager to see— touch this man again. Her negligence tipped her into a sob that she'd not known lay just beneath her resignation.

Callie found herself collapsed on the dirt and straw-strewn floor, her quilt—the one she had lent to him, wrapped around her shivering body, the soft cotton soaking up her tears.

Such shocking grief over the loss of this man who she'd known only a few short days.

No—that was not entirely true. Her pain wasn't so much heartache over Brendan Cavanaugh—but more for her sheltered life, the one that had cocooned and healed her. But looking around her snug little barn, it struck her that perhaps this sanctuary was no longer what she needed. A new longing, pulling like a silken web, moored to a place deep in her soul, a tugging of which she had never even been cognizant until now.

She picked up Gulliver, burying her tear-stained face into the ruff of his neck. Bless him, the cat allowed her this indulgence, even going so far as to lick her ear.

Hefting his weight, she turned back to the cottage. After setting out a dish for him, she sat and pulled out a piece of paper.

My dearest Helena,
Yes, I wiil come....

Chapter Five

Barton Grange, Wiltshire, England
Three weeks later

"Three pitiful minutes. One-hundred and eighty seconds, and it's me yoked to this dad burn title and not you. Viscount Clifford, who the hell is he?" Bren frowned at his twin brother and then pulled at the choking cravat that felt more like a noose than a bit of fancy Irish linen. "Ma always got things ass-backward. Just had to set still long enough so we could organize ourselves properly down there and then everything would have turned out just fine and dandy."

"Hell, Bren, don't blame Ma. You elbowed me out of the way. Always had to be first," Farren stated as he waved away an insistent fly.

Bren snagged another glass of champagne from a passing footman and drank deep.

"Might want to slow down a bit. It'll be a long afternoon."

He'd just gotten home—only Ryeland Park, sprawled among the rolling hills of Wiltshire, wasn't his home. He didn't rightly know where home was anymore. Hadn't for a good number of years now—not since he'd left Hayland, the family farm on the Chesapeake. And even then...probably wouldn't have the sense to recognize home if it landed right in his dang lap. Now he was being trotted out to something called a Venetian Breakfast—which turns out weren't no breakfast at all, just a very fancy picnic with nary an Italian in sight—at the estate that bordered his grandfather's.

"Why do you think I'm drinking?"

"I reckon you'll do just fine with this lot once you get your feet under you."

Brendan looked over the array of English gals in their pastel gowns, chip bonnets, and fluttering fans, all trying to catch his eye. "I'd like to get something under me and it ain't my feet."

"Whoa, Bren. This isn't a dang husking bee. You can't just haul off and pull a girl onto your lap for a quick kiss. And these aren't girls at all, they're *ladies*. You may look but you don't get to touch. Because if you touch one, she's yours. These English hothouse flowers are carefully cultivated to entice the biggest bee. And you, my dear brother, given those three precious minutes, are the biggest bee in this garden."

"We'll see about that, little brother." He had a plan, but no need to inform Farren of it yet. Just play the nicely tamed pussy cat for now, at least until he got the lay of the land and could dodge all these dang rules.

"There's no shuffling off this title, Bren. It's yours, whether you want it or not."

Farren could still read his mind with hellish regularity.

"And I must tell you, Viscount Clifford, I'm mighty glad of those three minutes. Happy to have lost that particular race." Farr finished by raising his glass.

"God is a fella with a wicked sense of humor." Bren tossed off the rest of the sweetish champagne. It tasted cloying in his mouth. And these borrowed English duds felt more like a lunatic's strait-waistcoat than fashion. Oh, to shuck off these gloves, and in particular the blasted necktie.

"I don't suppose they have anything real to drink at these trumped-up gigs?" Would it ruffle these folks' feathers too much if he availed himself of the flask presently tucked in his breast pocket?

Naw. Best not.

"This being your first introduction to society, these folks are here to look you over. You need to keep your wits about you, Brendan." Farren jerked his chin toward two approaching ladies. "Here is our hostess and her daughter, come to meet the dashing new viscount."

Sure enough, a very attractive blonde in a huge crinoline was towing a gal, her daughter by the looks of her, in the brothers' direction.

"Ah, good afternoon, Colonel Cavanaugh. I am so glad you could attend our little picnic."

Little? Looked as if every table, chair, and piece of silver had been hauled from the house and out onto the lawn. Waiters in fancy livery were so thick on the ground a body could hardly turn without one of them shoving a tray under your nose.

Farren bowed and, after a subtle poke to his ribs, Brendan followed suit.

"Mr. Ainsworth and I are delighted your family has put your mourning aside and will, once again, be free to enjoy the delights of the season!"

Put mourning aside? As if grieving was only some peevish child to be set in a corner.

Damn Uncle Geoff for just up and dying right after Bren'd come back to England. If he didn't know better, Bren might have believed the cocked-eyed notion his uncle had hung on only until his ne'er-do-well nephew finally turned up. Daft thought.

Geoff had been Pa's older brother, the heir to the Clifford viscountcy. In the prime of his youth, while trying to save his brother's honor, Uncle Geoff had been thrown from his horse and trampled, leaving his legs useless and his brain addled. And all because Farren and Brendan's pa had a hankering for the wrong gal. If Duncan Cavanaugh were still alive, Bren would've wrung his neck. Not for his own sake—he deserved nothing better than an unloving father—but his ma and siblings hadn't.

"Miz Ainsworth, may I introduce you to my brother, Viscount Clifford? Clifford, our hostess, Miz. Ainsworth."

Wait, Ainsworth? Naw, God couldn't be that much of a trickster. Besides, these ladies looked not one stitch like his Woodland Witch.

Everyone did the do-si-do bow/curtsy thing again. God, what he wouldn't do for a swig of whisky and a plate of oysters.

"At long last! We hear you were recently recognized as a hero by your United States," the lady gushed.

"That is the rumor, ma'am. But you know what they say about rumors."

Desertion was punishable by hanging, so he'd hightailed it out of England to go square up his reputation with the Union Army. When all was said and done, he'd come out a dang hero. Seems spying for the winning side got you a medal instead of a noose.

"Handsome and modest! How delightful," Miz Ainsworth tittered.

"I am sorry Mrs. Cavanaugh was not able to attend

your party," Farren said before Bren could laugh at the overblown compliment. "She is currently in Town, assisting her niece, Lady Charlotte Sealing, to prepare for her first ball."

"Oh, well, I must excuse her then. I know what a deal of preparation goes into such an endeavor. Indeed, we will be hosting our own ball to celebrate my daughter's come-out." The woman gestured to a girl standing slightly behind her. "Helena, come."

The young gal stepped forward. "Colonel, you remember my daughter, Helena?"

"Of course. Miss Ainsworth." Farren greeted the chit with an elegant bow.

"Colonel Cavanaugh." The gal smiled at Farr, but then darted her eyes toward him, before settling back on his brother.

"Viscount Clifford, may I present my daughter, Miss Helena Ainsworth?"

A beauty. Blonde curls, a bow of a mouth, and quite a bosom beneath the tablecloth of lace that made up the collar of her dress.

"Pleased to meet you, Miss Helena." He took her hand and did a fairly dead on imitation of his brother's high-fallouttin' bow.

"Viscount Clifford," she murmured, dipping into a curtsy.

Blue eyes met his, then lashes fanned her blushing cheeks, before her gaze met his again.

The angel of silence descended on the group. A polite fella would have jumped in, made some inane comment. But no one ever accused Bren Cavanaugh of good manners.

The bothersome fly had found their little party and

now buzzed around Miz Ainsworth's décolletage. Her smile tightened as she oh-so-subtly nudged her daughter.

The girl's gaze now seemed fixed on his mouth instead of his eyes. And then the minx had the audacity to lick her lips.

But the deep frown stamped across her forehead put to bed any notion that she was flirting with him. Hell, he'd bet she wasn't more than seventeen, if a day. Not much older than Rosie—

He stroked his beard and gave her his wicked smile, the one that would make her think twice about travelin' down flirtation road with the likes of him.

Her frown released as her eyes widened.

"I reckon this will be an exciting time for you, Miss Helena. Are you looking forward to all the parties and hoopla?" He spun a silvery net of charm, a performance he'd perfected. After all, he was a good hunter. He had an instinctual understanding of his prey and could read all the signs—when to stalk and when to lay back. He would have a bit of harmless fun with her, and please Farren to boot.

"Oh, I suppose so. Mother has been planning now for weeks." She looked over at her ma who was showing Farr some rose bush that seemed to need his full attention. "It must have been very exciting, living in America. I understand you traveled all the way to California?"

He nodded seriously. "Got there with nearly all my parts intact, too."

She swallowed. He thought she wasn't going to take the bait but then her curiosity kicked in. "Nearly?"

"Well, a few Crow had in mind to relieve me of my hair. A course they had the right to it. I was poaching their kill. Still, a man has his vanity, Miss Helena."

"Of course. Why, any lady would be envious of such thick, fine locks as yours," she offered cautiously.

"And the color? I've been told it's as purty as a guinea flashin' in the sun." He turned profile and raked his hand through his hair.

The gal had not one iota if he was teasing or not.

He smiled and she followed suit. Albeit, a tentative version.

"But why would crows want to attack your hair? Are they different from our English ones?"

"Ha!" He winked at her. "Darn near as big as a Thanksgivin' turkey, they are."

She shook her head, her curls bouncing about her round cheeks. *Sweet young thing.*

"Well, Brendan," Farren said, returning to his side. "I reckon we should let our hostess and Miss Ainsworth get back to their company"

"Oh," Mrs. Ainsworth said, as if she just realized there were other guests in the garden. "Yes, we should let you meet the rest of the neighbors. It has been delightful, hasn't it Helena?"

"Yes, delightful," her daughter echoed, her head cocked slightly as if she could not quite figure him out.

"We leave for London at weeks' end, but we shall surely see you there, Lord Clifford. You must promise you will attend Helena's come-out ball."

"I shall, ma'am. And in the meantime, I'll be wary of low-flying English crows!" His laugh a boom amid the ladies' tepid smiles. Everyone did the bow thing again and he and Farr peeled off.

"She seemed taken with you," Farr said cautiously.

Bren grunted. His flask burned in his breast pocket.

He licked his lips, dry as three-month-old hardtack.

"Did you mean to be so charming?"

"Isn't that what I'm supposed to be?"

"If you really like her. Just be wary of laying it on too thick. Folks here take this marriage business very seriously," Farren said, batting at the determined fly who had followed them.

One snap of his wrist and Bren snatched the fly from the air and crushed it in his palm. When he opened his hand, the cream of his pristine kid glove was now streaked with black. The mark gave him a certain satisfaction, as did besting his brother.

Farren sniffed and shook his head. "Just letting you know the lay of the land, big brother. That's how it works here."

"You of all people know I'm not particularly good at working."

"Well, you could do worse." Farren gestured to Helena Ainsworth who looked as if she was getting a talkin' to from her mama.

"Naw, she ain't for me."

"Since when? Hell, she's just your type. Ripe curves and curly blonde hair. And seems to have some sense. Her pa has loads—"

"I reckon my tastes have changed." His mind strayed where it had gone so many times over the last three weeks, to the Scottish Highlands, and to a certain warm bed…

He shook his head, as if he might shake the picture from his brain.

"Bren, we've been over this before. It's your duty to marry."

"I don't do duty. You of all people should know that.

I see duty and I turn tail and run as fast as I can. God was cruel to both Uncle Geoff and me. Both of us no more viscount material than a pot of dirt. And worse, for the Almighty to take her great-uncle from my Rosie so soon after she found him."

Rosie had been laid flat by Geoff's death. Since she'd been rescued from that evil man, she'd stuck close to her uncle's side, seemed to understand him as no one else could. And he her.

Now Bren had to face Rosie and try to be a better father than his own had been. Not a tall order for a half-decent man, but not any job Bren was cut out for.

"Rose will survive. She has you now," his brother said, clapping him on the back.

"Oh, well shucks, that sets my heart right at ease." Poor gal. He'd courage enough to square up against a grizzly guarding her young and lived to tell the tale, but his beautiful, bastard daughter? She frightened the tar out of him. He'd barely strung two words together for her since he got back to England. And before that? They'd only been in the same room a half-dozen times—though she had been a devoted visitor while he was unconscious and mostly dead. But he figured that sort of loyalty was easier to come by when a body didn't actually have to talk back.

"Tell you what, little brother, you keep on raising my young-un. And while you're at it, you might as well do my courting for me too. Heck, they might never know it's you and not me. Just swear and drink a lot more." He took one last look at Miss Helena Ainsworth, who gave him a tentative smile—a smile that did not reach her eyes.

He dumped his glass on a tray. "I need some air."

Farren looked as if he might object but wisely thought better of it and just nodded.

Bren headed beyond the manicured gardens and tinkling fountains, beyond the giggling girls and stuffy matrons. His hand found the cool flask in his breast pocket as he slipped into the shade of the darkened woods.

Blessed cool hit his cheeks and the musk of earth filled his lungs. He took a long pull from the mouth of his flask.

The whisky burned the back of his throat, familiar and soothing, washing away the sickly-sweet taste of wine. The side trip he'd made to Brian Belcher's farm had been worth it. Ol' Verlan had not complained about the extra weight and the clink of the bottles in Bren's saddle bags. Nor had the horse complained when Bren stopped and nearly turned to head him back up the mountain, back to the cottage of the wild woodland witch. But sense kicked in. Besides, she might have gone already. She said she was going to see her sister.

Why the hell hadn't he asked where that might be?

He took another long pull on the flask.

An opening in the trees revealed a path. Someone had walked this trail recently. A woman or large child, he'd guess by the dampness of the earth and the impression of the boot. Must be downwind of him as he smelled no scent. Water off to the right. Maybe twenty yards or so. Stacked on a flat boulder nearly fifty yards away was something man-made. A cairn—

He heard a splash.

His senses kicked up a notch, ready for danger, or a thrill.

He ran toward the sound.

A largish pond.

No one.

Land sakes. The whisky on his tongue, the cairn in the woods had his mind filling with her.

Still, had to be a hell of a fish to have made that splash.

The bank was wreathed with cattail reeds, perfect for a fat bass to hide. Or a good striper. Maybe a rainbow?

Another splash, but this time subtler, from the far end of the pond. He crept fast along the bank.

What? In the distance he saw a figure. A woman, crouching behind the cattails gathering her clothes and then slipping into the woods. Tall, a flash of a white oval face, wild hair—red?

He stepped forward, ready to call out.

A twig snapped directly behind him.

Shit! He must be drunker than he thought. No one could sneak up on him. Hell, his instincts were dulled from lack of danger. He was getting soft.

He turned and was knocked sideways. A small person seemed to have launched themselves at him.

A woman.

Soft lushness against his body, the smell of roses and lavender hitting his nose. Her hands grasped the lapels of his coat. Her mouth found his chin and then skated up—

"What the tarna—"

Her hands now found his cheeks as she tried to fasten her lips to his.

"Come quickly!" A shrill voice from somewhere behind.

His foot met slick grass, and down they went.

Crack! His teeth met and his head rang as it hit what must be the hardest damned thing on God's green earth.

"Ooofffh!" The gal landed on top of him.

"What is going on, Hermione? Why have you dragged me down here?" A male voice, that one.

"There, Gerald! Look there! Sir! Unhand our daughter this instant!"

He would love to, but his hands were tangled in something. He yanked them free and heard a rip.

What the crap?

He closed his eyes and shook his head. Not good. His stomach heaved as his head pounded. The lady squirmed on top of him. Her knee finding—

"Oh, sh-i-i-it!" He curled up as she rolled away.

"I am sorry. That is—I—Oh, I—"

He should sit up. He should help her up. He should explain that this wasn't what it seemed...

"Bren, for pity's sake!"

Farren's voice. Thank God! An ally in this mess.

"I demand satisfaction, sir! You will make this right!" Yet another voice.

Bren squinted through the haze of pain. Blurred figures moved along the bank of the pond.

"Helena, are you well? Are you hurt?"

Jiminy Cricket, they were surrounding him. Now someone had come from behind. The woman from the woods?

"Can you sit up?" she asked.

"What the—?" Ignoring the pain, he turned toward the voice.

"Hush now," the woman said to the girl, but addled though he was, he would swear the words were meant for him.

His woodland witch? He couldn't make his eyes focus.

"Can you sit up?" the woman repeated.

"I think so," the girl said tremulously, levering herself up. She pushed the hair from her face.

Miss Helena?

"What the hell is happening—?" He blinked, trying to focus.

"Hush," the woman said, more firmly, and this time directly to him.

He squeezed his eyes shut and then opened them slowly. By God, his eyes and ears had not been playing tricks on him. He knew that face. He knew that *body*. His woodland witch in the flesh. Callista Ainsworth.

Ainsworth.

"What the...? What are *you* doing here?" None of this would make a lick of sense, even if his mind wasn't addled.

Miss Helena took the woman's hand. "This is my sister, Callista," she said with perfect manners, as if they were back at the garden party sipping tea instead of splayed out in the middle of the woods with half the damned guests looking on.

And her bodice—

Hell, that must have been the ripping sound he'd heard.

Callista Ainsworth hastily pulled her sister's shredded dress together.

"This is—your sister?" He looked between the two, trying to connect his Scottish witch with this English Cupid.

"Yes," they both said at the same time and then hastily looked at each other. Normally he'd relish such a comical moment, but his aching head wasn't allowing for much levity at present.

"You are hurt," his witch said, her attention back on him. Long fingers probed his hair, searching his scalp.

"Ahh!"

"A contusion. Look into my eyes."

Oh, yes, he knew the almond shape and deep blue color. A thick fringe of blonde/red lashes.

"No concussion. You will be fine. The head bleeds quite a lot."

"*He* will be fine?" The shrill voice again, closer now. "What of your sister? What of her reputation? It is Helena who has been compromised." The shadowy figures seemed to jerk like puppets on strings as they hovered on the periphery of his eyesight.

He turned back to Callista. "What the hell are you doing here?"

"Explain yourself, sir! What have you done?" He figured out the shrill voice belonged to Mrs. Ainsworth, the vanguard of the brigade.

"Done? Nothing. I only came into the woods to get away. Then suddenly this little gal—well, she surprised me, and I must have slipped."

"You expect us to believe that tripe? Our daughter is gently reared and not even half your weight!"

But he couldn't focus on the mother, not when his woodland witch was next to him. "You are this gal's sister?"

"Do not regard Callista." The mother gestured impatiently behind her. "Mr. Ainsworth, I beg you, take charge. Your daughter has been ruined!"

Where the hell was his flask?

There, right on the ground next to him. He reached

for it, but his witch already had it in her hands. She shook it and then dumped the last few precious drops onto his—

"Ahh!" He flinched as the spirits burned his scalp. "That's good whisky!"

"Hush." She deftly unwound the linen around his neck and began tying it around his head.

Her frowning lips so close to his. A few inches and his would meet them. Brendan laughed. He shouldn't have. His head hurt like the devil.

"Sir, I assure you this is no laughing matter!" Mrs. Ainsworth pushed an older man forward. "Mr. Ainsworth, say something!"

A tall man with a huge set of side whiskers stepped forward. Brendan tried to rise.

His witch stayed him with a hand to his shoulder. "Remain where you are for now. We shouldn't risk you toppling over again."

"Yes, ma'am."

She pressed a handkerchief against Helena's flushed and tear-stained cheeks.

"I have been dragged down here to witness—I know not what. Callista, are you behind this debacle? Explain yourself. Now!" the older man demanded.

"It was an accident," she said as she stood, dusting off her skirts. "Just an unfortunate accident," she repeated to the small crowd.

"What?" Mrs. Ainsworth jerked forward.

"I said, it was an accident," Callista said, somber as a parson at a funeral. "I saw the whole encounter and it was just as Mr. Cavanaugh claims, merely a misstep which resulted in a mishap."

"Callista, you will stay out of this. This has naught to do with you," the mother said, waving a dismissive hand.

"Well, actually it does," his witch said, matter-of-factly.

"How, Callista?" Mr. Ainsworth asked wearily.

"I advised Helena she should make sure she and any prospective husband are physically compatible before thinking of becoming seriously attached."

"You what?" Mrs. Ainsworth jerked forward again and then abruptly halted as if she might sully herself if she got too close.

"I believe a couple should *suit* each other—in every way. I think it is best to find that out as soon as may be if one wants to be truly happy in marriage."

Well, dang and blast. That was his woodland wench, all right.

"Happy in marriage?" Mrs. Ainsworth said as if the mere idea was utter flapdoodle. "You *think*? You *believe?* Who are you to have any opinion? You are an old maid. A spinster firmly on the shelf. You know nothing of love. And will know nothing of love."

"Mother, I—"

"Helena, do not speak. You have done quite enough." She pointed to Callista. "I knew it was a mistake to bring you out of *rustication*. But Helena insisted. You have been nothing but trouble since you refused to marry all those years ago. Three reasonable offers and one great match, all squandered! And coming back now, planting such disgusting ideas into a tender and impressionable girl!"

"But Mother, you told me to follow—" Helena looked miserable as her mother shook her head vehemently at her younger daughter. "You also told me to try to—"

"That is enough, Helena. You are overwrought and muddled. It is understandable given the circumstances."

Callista Ainsworth seemed to grow three or more inches, her face shifting from concern to understanding. "No, I will not stand by and do nothing. You will not practice your machinations on my sister as you tried to do with me."

"How dare you speak to me in this way! How dare you interfere in matters that do not concern you!"

"Oh, I don't know, Miz Ainsworth." Brendan used his silkiest tone, while itching to shake the living tar out of the evil shrew "But I suspect—" He grasped a nearby sapling and hoisted himself to his feet. The world swam and spots appeared before his eyes, yet he waved off any support— "I suspect Miss Callie here might know a thing or two about love."

"Pardon me?" The blonde biddy looked ready to burst like an occupied outhouse on chili night.

"Well, now." He was feeling a mite better. "You talk of Miss Helena being compromised. I reckon one fumbled kiss is small potatoes when compared to—"

"If you will excuse me—I—" Callista Ainsworth looked green as a new recruit.

She swallowed and swiped at her forehead. And then his woodland nymph ran hell-bent back into the woods.

Chapter Six

Moments later

Callie bent over double, her fists pressed against her belly.

Breathe. And swallow. Slowly.

She heard the crunching of footfalls. Not Helena. Heavier. A man. That man. *The* man. No denying his particular smell, that smile, those eyes...

Her stomach heaved again. Nerves. She had simply not been prepared to encounter him again. Ever. And certainly not at a garden party on her father's estate in the middle of Wiltshire with her little sister sprawled atop him. Such a situation would put anyone's stomach—and heart—in turmoil.

"Callista?"

One must admit to oneself when one was anxious. Half the battle of mastering nervousness was acknowledging it, breathing, then getting past it.

There. She was ready to meet his eyes.

"Good afternoon, Mr. Cavanaugh." She pasted on a smile. "Never fear, you're safe, at least from me. As my step mamma informed you, I am an old spinster and therefore of no account. But beware, she has her sights set on you."

"Your sister, Helena?"

"Ha! Helena is an innocent. No, Hermione. She is

the puppet master. Thus far I have managed to escape her scheming, but I am giving you fair warning she is a force to be reckoned with when she gets the bit between her teeth."

Surely the sight of him could not have caused her stomach to flip in such a manner as to make her cast up her accounts. Surely it had been from sampling that slightly suspicious bolete mushroom just before taking her dip in the pond.

But here he was! The man who was in part responsible for her joining society again. The man who had inadvertently caused her to hope for real happiness. That perhaps she could have everything in life. Real love. Perhaps even children...

Such fanciful thoughts. Her stomach flipped again.

He handed her his handkerchief. "Could you be in the family way?"

His question slammed into her, making her stomach heave yet again. Gentlemen did not speak of such things, but her reaction was not solely due to his faux pas. "Of course not. You pulled out."

"It doesn't quite work that way. Did you happen to skip that particular chapter?"

"Chapter?" Well, he was right. Not ever thinking to be with child she had indeed skipped to the more interesting passages. "No, I can't be."

"Have you missed your monthly?"

"That is none of your business, sir."

"Oh, I don't know, it just might rightly be my business."

"I don't have a regular menses."

"And I don't drink before eleven o'clock, most days, but that don't make me a parson." He looked so forlorn, as if the possibility of a child was the end of the world.

"If you must know, I did bleed just last week, so you may rest easy, sir." It was almost comical to see how he visibly relaxed.

"My upset is likely from a bad mushroom," she continued. "I am distracted of late and am not as familiar with English fungi."

Raised voices brought the present debacle to the fore. "We must get back."

"Must we?" His attempt at an English accent failed. As did his humor. "Can't we just hightail it out of here?"

"I wouldn't do that, big brother." A man who looked remarkably like Brendan Cavanaugh stepped through the trees. A twin. Identical, almost, if Brendan Cavanaugh had been clean shaven.

Dear lord, how much had he heard?

"Miss Callista, I am Colonel Farren Cavanaugh. My family and I have been living at Ryeland Park for the last few years. I understand you have been residing in Scotland?"

"Yes, I only arrived here two days ago."

"Ah. Welcome home."

Home? No, this estate had never been her home.

"We are also happy to have my brother, Viscount Clifford, back with us as well."

"Viscount?" *This American backwoods scamp, a bloody viscount?*

"Yes, he inherited the title from our Uncle Geoff, who died a year ago."

Viscount Clifford? The *viscount?*

Of course, it all made sense now. This man, *her* man, was Hermione's viscount, the one Helena had written about. The one who had brought Callie out of hiding so that she might save her little sister from a loveless marriage.

Anger rose to fill her throat. Damn, Hermione!

"Ah, hell Farren, you didn't have to bring that up, did you?"

"Oh, I reckon I did, as your ownership of the title still hasn't seemed to sink into that thick sap-skull brain of yours yet." He turned to her. "Pardon me for my plain speaking, Miss Callista. Now let's get on back and face the music."

****

With the help of Farren and Callista Ainsworth, Bren retraced his steps back to the pond and the firing squad.

"Callista, enough of your theatrics!" Mr. Side Whiskers huffed and puffed, waving his cane in their general direction. "Your behavior is unseemly. But why should I ever expect you to behave as you ought."

His gaze turned to Brendan. "Now, Clifford, how will you make restitution for this unfortunate imbroglio?"

"Imbro—? If you think you can catch this weasel asleep then you have another think coming. And I reckon since I'm the biggest toad in this pond, I'll insist you speak with more respect to Miss Callista here." He took out his flask and tipped it to his lips. Empty. Hell, he'd forgotten. She'd dumped the last of it on his thick skull.

"I am unclear as to your exact meaning, sir, but one thing is abundantly clear, my daughter has suffered some grave impropriety and must have her honor restored."

"I don't cotton to ultimatums, Mister A, especially when I'm innocent—least I am of this particular offense." He turned away from the sputtering

Englishman to address his brother. "Farren, if it's all the same to you, my head's clangin' like the dang Liberty bell. And I could surely use another drink."

A young man stepped forward. "I will have satisfaction!"

"Aw, shit." Bren tipped his head back, closing his eyes, wishing to God he would pass out.

"You have besmirched the honor of an innocent lady!"

Bren opened his eyes to see the man yanking his glove.

"Martin, please stay out of—"

"Helena, I will not stand by—" The glove stuck like a hog in the mud. Boy must have sweaty hands. Finally, he had to resort to using his teeth.

He stepped forward and swung. The sting felt like nothing next to the throbbing of his head. "Name your seconds, sir."

"Really? You want to do this?"

"Swords or pistols," the pup insisted.

Farren stepped forward but Bren stopped him, taking his arm. The poor young man looked ready to wet his britches.

The girl's father slid his cane between him and the young pup. "Henshaw, you are complicating matters. Desist." He pushed the man back with the stick as if he was herding a wayward sheep, then turned to face Brendan. "Clifford, what possible objection should you have to wedding Helena? You may not realize, new as you are to our society, but her portion will be *very* substantial. And she is only seventeen and very biddable."

"Beddable, you say?"

Mouths dropped open.

"Easy, Bren," Farren hissed in his ear.

"I assure you this is no game, Clifford. I don't know how it's done in the colonies, but we here in England take a woman's honor and subsequent marriage very seriously."

Despite the anger seething within him, Bren only gave a nonchalant shrug. "Might as well hang up your fiddle, man, 'cause I can seriously assure you, I ain't gonna dance to that tune."

God, his head felt like the very devil. He was being insufferably rude, but dang it, he would *not* be put in a corner. "Now, if the other's available, I might be willing to take her on." *Damn.* Words seemed to come out of his mouth with no connection to his brain.

And had he truly said them aloud? Mouths dropped open. Again. *Yep, looks like he'd said 'em aloud...*

"No need to *take me on*, sir." Lordy, his witch could sear the hair off a boar with that look.

He tipped his head in acknowledgement of her pluck. "Then I think we're done here."

The mother juddered, like an irate brood hen. "Do you think this is some joke, sir? No—no *gentleman*— would ever choose Callista over Helena."

Man, did he want to pitch the shrew into the pond. "All I mean is, if you're wanting to sell one of your daughters, shouldn't I have my choice as buyer?"

"I demand retribution! Swords or pistols!" Young Martin rose to his toes, waving his glove in the air.

"Mr. Cav—that is, *Viscount* Clifford, is obviously intoxicated." The freezing look his witch shot him nearly had him grinning. "No doubt being knocked on the head is only making him more addled."

"I agree. This discussion should wait until tomorrow." Farren grabbed Bren's arm. "Tempers are hot and passions—ah—that is to say—Mr. and Mrs. Ainsworth, your guests will be missing you, and I should take my brother on home. His head needs a good tending."

"What I need is a good whisky!" Bren shouted.

And then everything went black.

Chapter Seven

"Oh, Callie, I've made such a mess!"

Water sloshed as Callie sat up in the bath. The roll of toweling soothing her aching forehead fell with a wet smack.

Her little sister had burst into the bedchamber and unceremoniously thrown herself onto Callie's bed.

Poor Sharon, the girl hired by Hermione to accompany Callie from Abernathy to Barton Grange, stood back against the door, gawping.

"Sharon said you were not to be disturbed," Helena explained. "But she does not know our sisterly love."

Callie reached over and pulled a towel from the stack on the bench next to the slipper tub. Bathing in so much hot water was certainly a luxury she had sorely missed in Scotland. But Helena came first.

"Sharon, it is all right. Sisters have special dispensation. You may go and have your tea. And thank you."

The girl bobbed a curtsey and then quietly closed the door. Having come from the small village of Abernathy, and never having been in service before, Sharon was still in awe of the whole workings of an English estate. Rejecting Hermione's candidate for lady's maid, who, no doubt, would be in her stepmother's pocket, Callie had asked that Sharon stay on. The girl took her job very seriously and was quite devoted despite the fact that

Callie hardly needed a maidservant. After all, she had seen to her own needs for three years. Still, the girl was proving helpful. Callie had forgotten how difficult it was to don all the underpinnings and do up all the hooks and buttons required of a fashionable lady in society.

"Here, allow me to play lady's maid, since I have frightened off yours." Helena rose and handed Callie another towel before turning to cross to the window.

Who was this beautiful young woman with the sleek coiffure and fine silk gown? Where was the rather chubby adolescent, hair in pigtails, dressed in pinafores, she'd left behind three years earlier?

When Helena had run down the steps of Barton Grange two days ago to fling herself into her sister's arms, Callie had been shocked to feel her womanly figure. No matter how faithfully they wrote, letters could never convey the realities of physical change.

But when they pulled away to look upon each other, Callie could still see vestiges of the child within. She'd brushed the tears from those perfect cream cheeks only to have Helena hug her again all the more fiercely.

"Oh, thank goodness you are here! You are finally here!" her sister had cried.

Tears had filled her own eyes and spilled down her cheeks. "I am here for as long as you need me."

Now Callie stepped from the bath and hastily wrapped herself in the towels. But she needn't have been concerned with such modesty, thoroughly absorbed in her own anguish, Helena now clung to a drapery panel by the window.

"What must Martin think of me?" Helena turned from the casement and began pacing anew. "He was so very gallant, was he not? I don't believe he has ever ever fired a pistol or swung a sword before in his life!"

The sick headache, which had waned whilst soaking in the warm bath, returned with a vengeance. Now pressing at her temples and pounding the back of her head.

"I'm quite certain Viscount Clifford could kill my Martin with one bare hand." Her sister demonstrated by squeezing the bedpost and then abruptly released it with a dramatic shudder.

Yes, Callie was sure he could. Remembering how fast he'd pinned her against his body, his arm a vice around her neck. His strength, smell, his utter power...

Gulliver rubbed against her bare legs. He could always tell when she was unsettled. Callie bent and rubbed him with the end of the towel.

"And while Martin is no match for the viscount, I fear Mother is."

Callie let the towel drop and slipped into her wrapper.

Only a little over three weeks since he had left her. Twenty-one days if one were counting.

She remembered a knock at the cottage door only hours after he had left, rushing to answer, fumbling with the latch, an eager, *You came back!* on her lips. Wrenching the door open only to find Angus with her next month's supplies.

How her cheeks had burned as a confused Angus asked if everything was all right.

Then over the next weeks, putting her books in crates to be stored, laying her bedding in the cedar chest, which still smelled of rosemary and lavender from the past summer. Last walks in her woods. Retrieving her journal.

Would her cairns still stand when she returned? Would she ever *come* back?

Taking a final look around her cottage, which seemed just a bit shabby, a bit too empty, since *him*.

She thought she was blazing a new trail being independent, thumbing her nose at the rules that applied to the poor sots who needed them, who were enslaved by them. But what had he said? *There comes a time when life catches up to you and you have to turn around and face it.*

Being older, and no longer considered prime marriage material, could she now set her own course? Suddenly she had a thirst for a new adventure. She touched the locket at her neck. Perhaps she might still have a chance at true love?

Locking the door. Smiling determinedly at Angus as he helped her into the cart. Gully *eeowing* his outrage at being confined to a hamper. Nattering on with endless instructions about taking care of the goats and such, as she and Angus wended their way down the mountain to Abernathy. "Aye, Miss," he'd assured her over and over again.

Gulliver skittered out of Helena's path and jumped up on the bed next to Callie, butting her arm with his head.

What a tangle we are in, Gully. He is right next door. A fantastical miracle. The absurdity of it would surely make you laugh if cats could do such a thing.

"Mother has talked of nothing but Viscount Clifford ever since we moved to the Grange," Helena said without waiting for Callie to comment. "He was abroad in the United States when we first arrived, and then when he came back to England, she was all set to make introductions when the previous viscount died. It was all very sad. Apparently, his lordship was never right in the head after falling from his horse when he was a very young man. Anyway, Mother was thwarted once again. But now, well, you see she has him within her sights, and I fear she will win in the end."

It was a very good thing that her little sister could hold up her end of the conversation and then some.

Gulliver looked up at Callie and blinked once.

Yes, I know you liked him.

Callie blinked back. *I liked him too.*

"And now Martin thinks I am a wanton!" Her sister, now back at the window, pressed her forehead against the pane. "I'm sure he must." Her hands fisted in the curtains as she rolled her head back and forth over the glass. "He is kind and generous but how can he forgive me after I threw myself at a stranger?"

During Callie's first night at the Grange, Helena had expounded on her burgeoning love for one Mr. Martin Henshaw. And Callie, having come from such an eye-opening, soul opening, experience of making love with a man, had urged her little sister to at least kiss the young man first before committing solely to him.

Oh, why had Callie stuck her oar in? After all, her father was right. She knew nothing of romantic love. Nothing. One night of sexual congress with a stranger was not love. Simply a brief tutorial for the poor spinster who should never experience such things—tempting fate and flouting convention to seize one last chance.

Yet, the encounter had changed her. Had awakened something long buried within her. Hope for a full life. Hope of finding a mate whom she might admire, and who respected and admired her in turn. The prospect of a life so different from that of her own parents. So different from the sad and terrible fate of her mother.

Her beautiful, sad mamma. Only shadowy images remained. A forced smile, weary eyes, a tender but distracted touch as she stroked Callie's hair or traced the line of her brow.

After she had left—run off with a cavalry officer, some said, while others insisted it had been a groom from a neighboring estate, or even a gypsy, God forbid! Callie often lay in her bed and imagined what her mamma's dreams might be. She imagined her capturing whatever joy she chased. But Callie was sure she'd never found true happiness. Her poor mamma couldn't. For she'd been bound. First by an older man who broke her, and then by a child whom she'd never again be allowed to call her own.

Callie.

Why couldn't her mother just have forgotten her? She would've been so much better off. But she loved her child and that love had surely ruined her.

Because only three months after Antonia Ainsworth had run away, she'd miraculously returned.

Callie had been outside in the back garden of their old townhome in London hiding from her new nurse when she'd spied her mother through the large bow window. She'd immediately called out to her, then run up to the window.

Too high! Thorns from the rose bushes tore her hands and dress as she tried to reach the slightly opened casement.

I love her!

Her mother's voice. Heedless of her bleeding hands, she had stood there, now just listening.

You will never understand. I tried, God knows I tried. But I cannot—will not live without her! I love her! I must be with my heart, my love!

She remembered running into the house, her hands and face still bleeding. *I am here, Mamma! I love you too!*

She'd almost made it to the door of her father's study when the nurse called out to a footman to grab her. *No-o-o!*

As he carried her up the stairs, screaming, the study door opened and her father appeared, pulling her mother out by the arm. He stood there, his face rigid, one hand gripping her mother, the other clenched something that glinted in the fading light—her mamma's locket swinging from his fist.

Mamma!

Her mother flinched, as if her daughter's cry had been an actual slap. She took a step toward Callie, her arm outstretched, but then suddenly she shook her head, then, without a word, she turned away, disappearing back into the study.

Ma-a-a-mm-a-a-a!

She never saw her mother again.

Callie vowed never to be tethered to something—or someone—that would kill her spirit, her independence, take her freedom and shackle her to a life not of her choosing. She touched the engraving on the locket—*Only True Love*. She would honor her mother by living the life she'd never been able to have.

And by God, she would not see her beloved sister consigned to such a fate, a loveless marriage that would leave her open to the false flattery of illicit lovers.

"Come, Helena, you are making my head ache with

all that pacing. Sit next to me and we will sort this out."

Helena bounded over to Callie and then plopped down with a sigh, making Gully jump, his tail swishing in indignation. Helena immediately perked up. "One thing this unfortunate event has made clear is that I love Martin more than ever! I don't need to kiss anyone else. But will he have me now?" She slumped, picking at a loose thread on the coverlet.

When Callie made no answer, Helena set off on a different tangent. "How odd, that Viscount Clifford seemed not at all interested in me. Oh, he was charming enough while we conversed on the lawn, but he seemed much more taken with you. For he ran after you when you fled into the woods, even with such a nasty bump on his head. Why do you suppose he did that? I do not mean to sound ungenerous, but he had only just met you, hadn't he?"

A knock at the door saved Callie from replying. "Miss Callie, Mrs. Ainsworth would speak—"

"Stand away, girl. I will enter and leave any room in my home whenever I like."

Helena jumped up from the bed as her mother entered the room.

"When I did not find you in your bedchamber, Helena, I knew you would be here. Good heavens, Callista is not even dressed! Do not monopolize your sister." It was unclear to whom Hermione addressed this last comment.

But Helena dutifully answered, "Yes, Mother."

"Come now. You know your father does not like his dinner delayed." Gulliver jumped down from the bed to sniff Hermione's skirts. "I thought we decided that animal would live in the stables."

"Gulliver is quite fastidious and is never late for his dinner, Hermione. I assure you *he* will cause no trouble."

"*Humph*. Come, Helena, leave Callista to dress. Which reminds me, we must find something more becoming for you to wear on the morrow when the viscount comes. Possibly we can sacrifice Helena's green chintz." Hermione raked Callie's form with narrowed eyes. "Pity you got your father's height...and mother's hair... You will not shame this family. We must get the modiste in as soon as may be. In the meantime, come along, Helena. As soon as dinner is over, I must speak to Carstairs posthaste about a suitable option."

Helena ducked her head and followed her mother out of the chamber.

Yes, tomorrow. The viscount—Brendan—would come tomorrow.

****

Soothing hot water covered Bren's aching body, easing tense muscles. The back of his head still hurt like hell and had a knot the size of Texas, but at least his body was relatively clean. And no man could be too riled when his hand held a full glass of whisky.

"I won't ask how you're feeling. Frankly, you don't deserve to feel better."

He'd been expecting his brother to show up to play inquisitor, judge, and jury ever since they'd returned from the party. But did he have to interrupt a nice quiet soak? "Dang it all, Farren, I told you the whole mess was an accident. Am I to blame if I have the charm of a preacher at a church social?"

"*Humph*," was all the reply he got.

"Still, even if I were as charming as that Antony

fellow was to Cleopatra, no shy gal should be heaving herself at me like that."

"I agree."

Bren snorted and drank deep.

"I reckon her ma had something to do with her going off leash like that. What did her pa say? 'She's usually so biddable'?"

Hell, had he really responded by saying *beddable*?

"God knows nobody can make you do anything you don't want to, Bren. Remember when Ma tried to force you to eat liver?"

Bren grinned. "Never took one bite. Sat there until the stars came out and ended up asleep, my face planted in the vile stuff."

"Ma, she nearly beaned you with her best cast iron skillet. Damn near split the table in two instead."

"Never had to eat it again though, did I?"

"No, by God, you didn't."

Of course, neither mentioned that Farren had sat there next to him for hours urging him to *just take one little bite* so they could go and catch frogs.

"I did warn you about these English folk, big brother, yet trouble seems to follow you despite my setting out the rules." Farren helped himself to the Belcher whisky. "But, if it's any consolation, I expect Miss Helena was being *biddable* even whilst kissing you."

"Dang right. Only we didn't even really kiss. She got my chin." He rubbed the somewhat bruised area. "Did you hear how that woman spoke to Miss Callista? I'd like to snatch that harpy bald."

Farren gave Bren *that look*. The look that said, *I'm on to you so don't think of trying to pull one over on me.*

79

Bren took a pull from his whisky and waited.

"Just how did Miss Callista Ainsworth come to refer to you as Mr. Cavanaugh? From what I understand, you two had never laid eyes on each other before today. Am I correct in my thinking?" Farren paced before the tub, just like a dang lawyer.

Bren laid back in his bath and adjusted the toweling behind his aching head. "I reckon she put two and two together. You're not nearly as pretty as me, but she must know your surname is Cavanaugh and so just assumed mine was as well."

"Humm. Seems like there's a sight more to this tale than you're letting on." Farren topped his whisky. Bren held out his glass but his brother ignored the request.

Farren took a long pull and then held his glass up to the light. "This whisky is better than backfin crab on a biscuit. Where'd you say you got it?"

"I didn't. And go easy on that, I only have a few bottles left."

Farren scooped up the bottle and tucked it under his arm. Of course.

Bren shook his head. Should've just kept his mouth shut.

"Well, I'll go on over there to the grange tomorrow and sort things out," Farren said. "Good thing only Miss Helena's family and that Mr. Henshaw were privy to these shenanigans. I'm right sure Mr. Henshaw has no wish to sully the lady's name."

Bren closed his eyes and eased further under the water. What was his woodland witch doing now? Perhaps she was in the bath as well? Lordy, would he have loved to have come on her just a few moments earlier when she was in the middle of that pond...

Something slapped the water, making him jerk upright. "Hell, Farr! You made me dump my dang drink."

A wet piece of toweling floated in front of him. He balled it up and heaved it back at his brother. Farren deftly ducked, the rag slapping the tiled wall and sliding to the floor.

"Then pay attention! I said don't drown yourself in your bath, Viscount Clifford."

Bren sank under the water to avoid the sound of the inevitable slamming door.

Water filled his ears and pressed against his eyelids. He made himself relax and began counting in his head. How long had it been since he'd tried this trick? His best, six minutes and thirty seconds, give or take a second or two.

Maybe six minutes would have been long enough to have saved Sar—

His hands fisted as he curled into a tight ball, drawing his legs up against his body.

Danger! A flash of yellow,

I can't lose my other half—

What number was he on? He'd lost count.

He held himself beneath the water until his lungs burned and his head thumped with blood. Only when he feared he might pass out did he finally burst out of the water.

His chest swelled, gulping cool air. The towel behind his head had slipped and was now floating around his knees. The water felt tepid and the glass he'd set by the side of the tub was empty.

What the hell was he doing here?

He was supposed to be a father, a brother-in-law, an

uncle, and now a dang viscount. He didn't know the first thing about any of it.

And then this newest business with that young gal, Helena, having a go at him. And meeting his witch again. As if God was saying, *No, lad, you're not quite done with this lady.*

Bren heaved himself out of the water and then stepped out of the huge tub. Water ran down his body, pooling on the floor. He watched as it found the slope and ran across to hide under a glass-fronted cabinet.

Another mess.

Farren would go and smooth things over tomorrow and all would be well. Farren was the diplomat of the two. Bren stirred things up, then Farr came in and calmed them down. Dang it all if Farr didn't have a boatload of charm as well as smarts.

But Bren had learned a thing or two about weaseling out of things, especially while spying in the war. Yup, he had his own way of smoothing. When he couldn't run, he'd been forced to learn to talk his way out of just about anything. And, talk his way into just about anything, too.

Why should he let Farren smooth this road? And what could be so bad about courting Callista Ainsworth for a few months during this London Season? In the end, she'd see sense and throw him back for a better fish. It didn't need to come to anything.

After all, she wasn't with child. Dodged a bullet there. Hell, his witch was likely as relieved as he. A raw deal to be shackled to him.

Still, he could play the game. He was good at games. He usually won, even if he had to cheat just a bit.

And time would peel away the gloss of his charm. She would eventually see the man he truly was, and they would go their separate ways. No harm no foul. And Farren would be happy his big brother was taking things seriously, for once. Winners all around!

Bren crossed the room and reached for the wet towel he'd heaved at Farren. He wrung it out over the tub, then dropped it down against the wet floor. dang satisfying, the sound of that slap. He used his toe to pull the wet linen across the tiles, sopping up more of the spilled water. Yes, satisfying. He picked it up, gave it a good hard wring, and then got down on his knees and began to scrub in earnest.

He stood, surveyed his work. *Damn fine job.*

Now what duds did a fella wear to go a courtin'?

****

The dreaded knock came all too soon.

"Miss Callista, you are summoned to the gold drawing room."

"Thank you, Rutledge. I will be down directly." The footman bowed and left.

"This blue poplin suits you so well, Miss," Sharon said, adjusting the fall of the skirt. "So much better than the green." Turns out Sharon was a deft hand with a needle. The bust had been adjusted and a panel of darker blue chintz had been added to the sleeves and hem. Callie's hair had been somewhat tamed.

"I know the fashion used to be for smooth perfection, but I've read styles are changing. I believe we should celebrate your curls."

"I don't know much about what is currently in vogue, Sharon, but I do appreciate your being so diplomatic. I suspect this mane cannot be brought to heel, had you five hours and as many flat irons."

But looking in the mirror, Callie could not help but

gain a bit of confidence for this upcoming meeting. She touched her locket for good luck.

Helena was already in the drawing room when Callie entered. Poor girl looked thoroughly miserable. Likely she had not slept much, either. Their father stood by the window, looking out at the sunshine as if it was a personal affront. Hermione hovered over her daughter, barring any possible escape.

Helena was certainly under her mother's thumb. Unlike Callie, her little sister sought to please her parents, to capture the elusive title Callie had tossed aside. Old Rupert Henshaw's son, Helena's Martin, was one of the wealthiest men in the county, but had the unfortunate distinction of being in trade and that simply would not do for the likes of the Ainsworths. Too close to their own social standing.

What a pickle. And all Callie's fault.

"Colonel Cavanaugh," the footman announced, and then stood aside.

"Good morning, Mr. and Mrs. Ainsworth. Miss Ainsworth, and Miss Helena." The colonel bowed.

Her family waited, everyone primed toward the doorway.

It remained empty.

Hermione was the first to step forward. "We are very pleased to see you, Colonel Cavanaugh. Has Lord Clifford been delayed?"

"Oh, I reckon we can sort this all out without my brother."

"I'm sure I don't understand. How can this be *sorted* without the viscount?"

"I reckon I can sort for myself, little brother." Brendan Cavanaugh's large body filled the doorway. "I am sorry to be tardy, but I had to find some proper courtin' duds. Farren, I told that valet man of yours you wouldn't mind if I snagged a few of your things."

Callie's heart bumped up against her throat at the sight of him. He was wearing an outrageously tied cravat and what looked to be highly polished cowboy boots. His tanned face was still rather pale above his newly trimmed beard, but his ubiquitous grin was firmly in place.

And aimed squarely at Callie.

"Lovely day we're having. I feel fit as a fiddle. I can see that Miss Callie and Miss Helena are in good form as well. No worse for wear from our little mishap." The large drawing room seemed to have shrunk in size with his presence.

"Well, yes, I expect you have the power to make things right, dear Clifford," Hermione said a tight smile pasted on her face.

Dear Clifford?

"As I said yesterday, Miz Ainsworth, I won't be trapped into marriage. Pardon to Miss Helena, but I reckon she doesn't have much interest in marrying me, either. And Mr. Ainsworth, I am sure you are keen to see your daughter happy?"

Her father seemed surprised to be addressed. "Well, of course we wish her to rub along well with her chosen husband, but—"

"Good. And I am sure you believe Miss Callista when she says what you saw was hogwash. I was distracted, and I'll own just a bit foxed, when I slipped and took Miss Helena down with me. I apologize."

"As friendly neighbors, I think we can agree nothing untoward took place. A simple accident, word of which need not go beyond this room," Colonel Cavanaugh echoed his brother's argument.

Hermione started to speak and then looked to her husband. "Mr. Ainsworth, what have you to say? I cannot imagine you would allow such a breach of decorum to go unchecked?"

Callie's father drew out his pocket watch, opened it, frowned, and then snapped it shut. No doubt his strict routine of morning papers and coffee had been scuttled by this hasty meeting. "The gentlemen have explained the situation to my satisfac—"

"What of your other offer?" Hermione cut her husband off and moved from behind Helena, easing her way toward Brendan Cavanaugh like a spider to a fly.

Callie's skin prickled.

"You expressed an interest in our Callista." Hermione licked her lips. "Indeed, I believe you seemed quite taken with her."

All eyes now focused on the viscount.

"I am."

Dear God. He said the two words so casually, yet his green eyes bore into hers.

Hermione nearly stumbled and caught the edge of a nearby table.

"You would marry *Callista*?" Her father fumbled, nearly dropping his watch. He hastily slid it into his pocket.

Brendan Cavanaugh spread his hands wide. "Well, let's not put the cart before the horse. But I reckon we could give courtin' a go."

"Why?" Helena asked the question that was surely on everyone's mind. "You don't even know my sister. Do you?"

Good heavens, she did not want to open the

Pandora's box of their time at the cottage. "I am right here, Helena." She made herself turn to the viscount and meet his remarkable green gaze. "Lord Clifford, I thank you for your—interest—but it will come to nothing. I won't marry you."

"Callista, do not be so hasty." Her stepmother held out her hand, a treacly smile on her face. "As your sister says, you do not yet know the viscount. None of us do. Perhaps we should all take the season to become better acquainted? It would not do to dismiss the generosity of a kindly neighbor." She turned to Brendan. "And once you've come to know our girls better, my lord, I am quite sure you will choose—well, you may change your mind."

A possible peerage once again in their parent's sights, Helena would bend to their wishes, if he could eventually be convinced to take her. And, honestly, why wouldn't he?

But Helena was clearly in love with Martin Henshaw. At least her little sister thought she was. Callie would never allow her sister to sacrifice her happiness simply to satisfy her social-climbing stepmother.

"Aw, no need to look so forlorn, Miss Callie." Brendan Cavanaugh shot her that wicked grin. "What's the harm? Come on and give me a shot."

Why was he doing this? He could have skated around these machinations. Her parents could blow hard but in truth they had nothing to hold him to any promise. If they rolled the dice, crying their young daughter's ruination, only Helena would be hurt in the end. Oh, a few old dowagers might cut the viscount for being a scamp, but when all was said and done, a title was a title, and that fact superseded any alleged impropriety.

The beginnings of a plan formed. If she drew the viscount's attention from Helena, her sister would be free to pursue her Martin. Callie had the entire season to dissuade Brendan Cavanaugh. No doubt once he got a look at all the young and eager beauties on offer, she would pale and then fade away. Why did the plan not fill her with relief? No time to examine her feelings. They were waiting for her answer.

"Very well, Lord Clifford. I will see you in London."

Chapter Eight

Two weeks later
Curzon Street, London

"I will not have this family shamed, Callista. You must make an effort to be in your very best looks, even if Clifford does in the end decide that Helena is more to his liking. And of course, it goes without saying that we expect you to be more than civil to him, as well as to the rest of the *ton*. Agreeable. Charming, even, if that is at all possible for a girl as recalcitrant as yourself."

Since the family's arrival at their townhome in London, Hermione had shifted her unrelenting attention from Helena to Callie.

The modiste had been summoned and Madame Yvette brought a hive of seamstresses that now buzzed about, holding swaths of luscious fabric up to her face to be approved (or mostly rejected) by Hermione.

Callie remained a silent pincushion. Better to let her stepmama rail on to her nodding and tsking audience.

"And I will not have the *ton*—especially that Lady Wilton, who thinks herself better than everyone else simply because she happened to catch an earl—wagging their tongues, claiming we keep you in rags—No, a darker blue." Hermione waved her hand dismissively at Madame's offering of a pale egg-shell blue voile. "No sense in even attempting to pull the wool over anyone's eyes by putting her in the colors of a young girl."

The draper hung her head and backed away as yet another lacky stepped up with an alternative offering.

"So." Hermione tapped one finger against each of the fingers on her other hand. "The green silk, the amethyst in duchess satin, then the darker blue that matches her eyes—yes, that one. We must play up her best features."

"And I believe we chose the striped taffeta as well, Ma'am," Madame said, consulting her notebook.

"Oh, yes." Hermione squinted at Callie, her mouth pursed. "Is there anything to be done with her hair? It is so very—wild."

Madame *tsked* and proceeded to dig her fingers into Callie's tresses. "It is unfortunate the hair is so very curly. I have had some success with ironing, but there is always a risk of burning. Perhaps a pomade?" The woman pulled a strand from Callie's chignon and then released it.

Both she and Hermione sighed as the strand sprung and then bounced against Callie's neck.

"Hopeless!" Hermione cried.

"But she does have excellent skin, Madame," the modiste rushed to reassure. "And we can certainly play up the color of her eyes—quite a lovely shade. Rather unusual, that deep blue."

Hermione sniffed. "You must come back for the day dresses. And I suppose she must have a riding habit. I'm sure the viscount rides."

Madame's eyes gleamed in anticipation at such a large order.

"But it will be all for naught if you act a fool, expecting some grand declaration of *love*." Her stepmother said the word as if it were a disease one must avoid at all costs. "I expect Clifford will see sense in the end and offer for Helena. But if he remains fixed on you and you do not accept him, then I wash my hands of you. You may go back from whence you came. Your father has been too lax with you, and far too generous. That will stop."

Ah, Callie had been afraid of this. Hermione was vindictive, and her father craven. Since Hermione had not given him a son, having suffered several miscarriages, and one heartbreaking still birth, which had delayed Callie's come out, her father had largely gone along with whatever his wife dictated. Callie's meager allowance would be cut to shreds if she did not tow the line.

"I said I would participate in the season, Hermione. And I will, but know that I cannot—will not, force any gentleman's hand."

****

The much-anticipated night of Helena's ball finally arrived.

With the head of the household a mere mister, the Ainsworths did not typically draw the *creme de la creme* of society. But *somehow* word had got out that the newly found Viscount Clifford was to attend, and so acceptances had rolled in.

Callie stood with her father, Hermione, and Helena as the guests were announced.

"Lady Hazelton, how kind of you to come! May I present my daughter Miss Helena Ainsworth?"

Helena dipped into a curtsy. "Your ladyship."

Her ladyship's quizzing glass went to her eye, as she stepped back in order to assess Helena. "Pretty. Seems quite young."

"She is seventeen, Lady Hazelton." Hermione beamed.

"And who is this?" Her ladyship had moved on to Callie.

"Oh, this is my stepdaughter, Miss Callista Ainsworth."

"Weren't you out *several* seasons ago?" the matron asked, as if Callie might have been lately raised from the dead.

"Yes, your ladyship." Callie offered a fixed smile. "I came out in eighteen-sixty."

The lady raised an eyebrow, then nodded once, decisively, and moved on.

Most of the guests that followed Lady Hazelton greeted Callie, too, as if they were not entirely certain she was not a figment of their small imaginations.

Just over four years since she had last stepped foot inside this ballroom on Curzon Street. Memories flooded, making her insides lurch—not with a child, thank God—yet her stomach still did not seem to have received the message.

Being trussed up in this infernal corset did nothing to help her nausea. She smoothed the skirts of her new frock, a deep midnight blue she secretly loved.

But now the gown seemed tight despite having been fitted only a little over a week ago. It felt more like a sausage casing than an elegant gown, especially as it pressed against her breasts which had been uncharacteristically sensitive of late. Her curling hair had been miraculously tamed under Sharon's deft hands into an elegant chignon, a few stray curls allowed to escape around her face and down her back. She wore her mother's locket which she had insisted on wearing, despite Hermione thrusting various garish gems at her.

Callie longed to touch it now—run her fingers over the engraving, feel its familiar warmth. But her hands, encased in kid gloves, were occupied adjusting her skirts to curtsey to guests, and to hold an intricately carved ivory fan, depicting Zeus pursuing Leda.

Ah, if only she could escape. Escape the confines of this dress and the cage of steel that made it bell and sway. Shuck off the tight slippers, and the pins digging into her throbbing head. To feel free…to disappear…

Had she made a mistake coming back?

The ballroom swelled with simpering smiles, breathless giggles, and the coy flutterings of eager young hopefuls, with their grand gowns and shiny faces, all snares for catching a husband. Such elegant desperation.

Poor wretches.

She had been one of them, as Lady Hazelton had reminded her. Coming out at the ripe old age of one and twenty. Terrified to fail, yet even more terrified to succeed. Despite being labeled a bluestocking and the daughter of a lowly Mister, her huge dowry had several of the season's most illustrious gentlemen circling her.

But none had been interested in her as a person. Oh, some had fooled her for a while—one in particular.

Lord Percy Blanchard.

A hot flush flooded her neck and cheeks. She glanced at Hermione who had admonished Callie that, while blushes could be quite fetching on most young ladies, given her very white skin and red hair, she should avoid them at all costs.

Percy, as he had asked her to call him after only a few meetings, had been so very attractive. He could have had any girl that season—or so it seemed to Callie, for she'd been so smitten she assumed every other girl must have been as well. But he did not want every other girl. He seemed to want only her. And she saw only him.

One evening, after an intimate dinner party held in his family's honor, he drew her into the picture gallery of this very house. The walls were mostly bare, save for a scattering of portraits—Hermione glittering in her jewels, Helena as a solemn young girl, their father caught mid-frown behind his desk. Nothing of her. The rest were starchy, bewigged ladies and gentlemen, purchased by her stepmother to lend the illusion of heritage.

Callie had been about to point out the portraits—nervous to be alone with him, but so very excited.

Then Percy grabbed her from behind, shoving her hard against the pilaster, his hand painfully squeezing her breast. She froze, unsure what to do. He turned her roughly, his mouth colliding with hers, sticky with drink, reeking of spirits.

Shocked and confused, she'd tried to kiss him back.

But then his mouth opened, and his tongue forced its way inside. Shocked, she pushed at his chest, but he only pressed harder, his teeth bruising her lips, his hands capturing hers.

He turned her around toward the wall, her face scraping against the flocked wallpaper, his arm crushing her chest, the other yanking up her skirts.

She tried to speak, to tell him to stop—but no words would come.

"Lord Percy? Callista? What is this?" It was her father.

Percy had stepped away from her. She turned, thankful for the intrusion, feeling shaken and confused.

Hermione stood there with her father.

Still in shock, Callie reached for Percy's hand, wanting to present a united front. But he had not even looked at her, simply fishing out his handkerchief to wipe his mouth.

"You said five thousand?" his only reply.

Why wasn't he smiling and tenderly asking, *Callista, will you consent to be my wife?* Callie shook her head, as if by doing so she could make sense of this terrible scene.

Hermione did not hesitate in answering. "Five thousand a year, along with fifteen hundred acres near Portsmouth. And we'll make good on your gambling debts."

Callie would never forget him turning to her, his gaze raking over her as if he were assessing if he could tolerate her person even for such a handsome price. "I'll take her." Then he turned away to once again address Hermione. "No banns. We'll do a special license. I need the blunt as soon as possible. Send the contracts to my man on the morrow." He dropped his handkerchief on a nearby table and stopped in front of Hermione. "My vowels," he said extending his gloved hand.

Hermione smiled. "As discussed, you shall have them when the deed is done, my lord."

Lord Blanchard sniffed. And then, without even a backward glance at Callie, left the room.

The next morning, Callie told her father she would not marry him. Hermione had been furious and Percy Blanchard, livid. But, to give her father credit, he only seemed sad—if such a thing could be believed. Certainly, he'd been furious with his wife. And so, after a few months of refusing to participate in the rest of the season, Callie had made her bargain with him, conceiving her plan to go to Scotland.

Yet now terrible hope warmed her. The yearning, banked like embers low in her gut, had now reignited. A hope that might just engulf her.

All because of that damn Yankee.

But where was he? The family had waited in the receiving line for the arrival of the viscount and his brother, but finally, after many hissed whispers, Hermione signaled the orchestra to begin.

As if the music had summoned him, Brendan Cavanaugh appeared at the top of the stairway.

Only this man was not Brendan Cavanaugh. This man looked every inch a viscount.

"Viscount Clifford and Colonel Farren Cavanaugh," the majordomo intoned, his voice carrying over the orchestra. Though he could have whispered the introductions, for the entire ballroom had hushed the moment the two men appeared in the doorway.

The matchmaking mamas subtly edged their daughters forward.

Callie steeled herself, expecting his gaze to fix on one of those bright young hopefuls. Waiting to slip into the shadows to nurse her anguish rather than watch him captivate some delighted beauty. But instead, he scoured the room like a hunter until his eyes caught on—her? Only then did he smile.

She nearly turned around, so sure there must be some worthy beauty just behind her. Indeed, the rest of the company stood in some amazement as well, as he and his brother descended the stairway and crossed the crowded ballroom, his gaze never wavering from hers.

His smile, just for her.

"You shaved your beard." Good heavens, why begin with such a statement? Why could she not perform a simple curtsy and greeting?

"Well, don't that beat all, Farren. The gal can tell us apart even all slicked up and looking like dang bookends." He slapped his hand against his thigh.

"I may be old, but I'm not shortsighted." She missed the beard. Because without it, he was even more handsome.

"Your Lordship." She dipped into a curtsy, then turned to his brother. "Colonel, thank you for accepting our invitation."

"Oh, I don't think we could have avoided it." Farren Cavanaugh smiled, looking remarkably like his brother. "I regret Mrs. Cavanaugh could not make the journey to town with us. After her niece's ball—well, she was a might tired, and so I took her on back to Ryeland Park for some rest."

"I am not surprised to hear she is in need of some quiet, Colonel. I was only on the periphery of the preparations for this ball and would give much to be able to join Mrs. Cavanaugh in the country."

"Oh, she'll be right as rain in a few weeks. She was very disappointed not to meet you, though, but hopes to do so in the very near future." He winked. "Well, I reckon I'll say hello to our hostess. If you will excuse me, Miss Ainsworth?" The colonel bowed and then began to edge his way around the room toward her parents.

"So, how did you know it was me?" her Yank asked, stroking his freshly shaven cheeks.

She snorted. "You are clearly you and he is clearly him."

"But how can you tell?" It seemed important to him that she give an answer.

"What do you mean, how can I tell? Yes, you have shaved, and tonight you are even dressed alike, but you are not alike." He waited for her to continue. "The corners of your eyes crinkle whereas your brother's do not, at least not in the same way."

Lord Clifford shook his head. "Most folk see us as two peas in a pod. We used to have a lot of sport tricking folks. Our schoolmaster in particular."

She spent a moment imagining him as a boy. And then pitying the poor teacher.

"How else do we differ?" he asked, clearly enjoying pushing her.

"You have a tiny scar just by your left eyebrow. And your mouth—really, there are a million differences. Not to mention your scent—why, it's entirely different from that of the colonel."

He sniffed his shoulder, a frown on his face. "I don't expect I smell anything like myself at present. Farren's man dumped a boatload of French cologne on me. I don't think it'll come off in a month of Sundays."

She shrugged. "Well, I've been told I have a strong olfactory sense."

"I reckon you do at that if you can still smell me under all this fancy juice."

"I can't help it. I am—observant. I pay attention to details."

"Heck, woman, I could've used you in the Black Hills. You'd have made a right fine tracker, I reckon." He smiled and his eyes crinkled. He took a moment to look about the room. Hermione smiled and waved her fan at them and her father even managed an approximation of a smile. "Speaking of tracking, your folks are like hounds around a cornered fox."

"Pardon?"

"This big fancy do I reckon is what we used to call shooting fish in a barrel. All slicked up and fattened we are, ready for the taking. My question is, who's the prey and who's the hunter?" He looked again at Hermione.

Certainly, he had a point. Her stepmother would never be satisfied until either she or Helena secured a peer of the realm.

"I either marry you or your sister has to pony up. And we know darn well she wants no part of me. I reckon that young whippersnapper, Mr. Henwitt—"

"I believe you are referring to Mr. Hen*shaw*."

"Right. Mr. Trigger Happy, the fella looking at me like I'm a fox in his henhouse. He'd have something to say about me poaching his territory. Can't say as I blame him."

Callie turned from Brendan Cavanaugh's wicked smile to Mr. Henshaw's narrowed eyes, clenched hands, and lethal stare pinned squarely at Viscount Clifford. If a timid gentleman's looks could kill, Brendan Cavanaugh would be lying dead at her feet.

"How about we dance?" He nodded to the center of the room where couples were gathering in preparation for a waltz. Martin Henshaw caught Helena's hand before the older gentleman Hermione was towing toward her could engage her.

"You dance?"

He shrugged. "I know a jig or two. I reckon you'll direct me well enough."

"This is a waltz. *You* must lead."

"Humm. I recollect I liked it right fine when *you*

led." He waggled his eyebrows.

A hot blush rose. Good heavens! No doubt he was thinking of her straddling him in the firelight, their eyes locked on each other, her fingers laced in his as she held on, rising and falling, pushing up against him, trying to get even closer…

"Now, don't go getting all hot and bothered and distracting me, else I won't be able to manage this waltz. At least in a waltz, I get to hold on to you instead of prancing around all on my own like a chicken at a bar-be-que."

Yes, anything but stand here with the eyes of the *ton* on her. "Lead on, sir," she said with more bravado than she felt.

He guided her to the very center of the floor.

"Look how happy your mamma looks." He nodded toward a beaming Hermione, now surrounded by the most influential ladies in attendance this evening.

"She is not my mother."

"Well, she's certainly filling a mamma's shoes. Like it or not, circumstances are conspiring against us. Even I recognize this. Me, who is as contrary as they come."

"It's only because she knows you were just playing a joke on us all, offering to court me. And she knows you'll turn your attention away once you discover what a sharp-tongued shrew I am, allowing her to manipulate you into making an offer for Helena."

"Playing a joke?"

"Yes, a joke! You didn't mean a word of that ridiculous proposal. You only did it to shock and upset my father and stepmother. You do not want me as a wife." The words came out more strident than she'd meant. She felt exposed and oddly vulnerable.

His smile dimmed just a bit. "Are you so sure of that?" his voice deep and soft in comparison.

"Yes, I am." *Damn, still defensive.*

She drew a breath and managed a brittle smile. "Why would you? I'm twenty-nine, hardly a beauty. Look around, Your Lordship."

She paused, waiting as he dutifully glanced about the room. Nearly every gaze was fixed on them—some furtive, some openly bored, others tinged with shock or thinly veiled contempt. Hermione's face stood out, smug with triumph. Of them all, perhaps only Helena and the colonel looked on with anything resembling support

"As you can see," she went on, quietly, "the *ton* doesn't much care for me monopolizing such a prize as the new Viscount Clifford. All the young beauties will be setting their caps for you."

He turned back to her, expression unreadable. "Ouch. She 'your lordships' me. After everything we've been to each other, could you at least spare me the honorific?"

Heavens, he was such an American. And in that moment, she adored him for it.

****

Land a mercy, did she clean up well. He would have offered up a compliment, but she'd have just shot him one of those cutting looks, like he didn't have any more sense than a toad.

He hated crowds. A man needed elbow room. Out of habit when he first arrived, he'd scoped out the room for the nearest exit. Behind him, some French doors that led out most likely to the terrace. Good. Two more doors at opposite ends of the ballroom, one in each corner. Likely for the servants' use. Either would do as well.

Boy, did he wish he could waltz her right out one of 'em and into the cool evening air.

Instead, he played nice, setting one hand at her waist and clasping the other about hers. Even wearing these dang gloves, he could feel her heat. Her fingers seemed to meld into his. He rubbed his thumb along the small of her back and she arched, just the tiniest bit. His cock twitched in response. He'd never been so happy to hear the fiddles commence—

But only after a few steps and a fancy turn, he knew he'd miscalculated. The movement of their bodies, so perfectly matched, only intensified his want.

It didn't help that her dress pushed everything up till he had a devil of a time keeping his eyes where they should be. Or his feet, for that matter. Dang dance was trickier than he'd remembered, but he reckoned that was because of the gown and her bosom and well, Callie.

"You must've had one of these do's." He nodded generally to the company and the opulent room.

"Yes."

"That's all I get? Callie-of-one-million-questions-but-not-any-answers?"

Her gaze left his and fixed somewhere over his left shoulder. "I didn't take."

"Didn't take? Not the story your stepmama tells. You had a passel of proposals by season's end. Why didn't you accept any?"

He would swear his footing was perfect this time, but still she stumbled. Not visible to any of the folks standing on the perimeter of the crowded room, just noticeable to him because he happened to have his arms wrapped around her.

When she remained silent, he reckoned he'd let his

question slide on by. He didn't like anyone prying into his past; why shouldn't he give her the same consideration? He held her just a tad closer and took her into a rather dramatic turn.

"The answer is very simple," she finally said after he'd twirled her from one end of the room to the other. "I did not fall in love."

Suddenly the other dancers seemed too close, the room too stuffy, this fancy cologne too overpowering. Then there was the dang problem of how to swallow the lump in his throat and make some sort of rejoinder.

"Well, I am new to this game, but I thought you *ton* folk didn't set much store in the notion of love. At least not within marriage." He laughed, but even to his ears it sounded hollow.

"You are correct. Love is not deemed important in choosing a marriage partner. It is not even looked for in some cases."

"I'm used to a girl sitting in my lap because she thinks I'm pretty, not because I'm some peer of the realm with buckets of money. But ever since I landed this title, I've suddenly got all manner of gals round me like flies on a steaming pile of shi— Well, you get the gist of it."

That got a small smile out of her.

"Now Farren, he's a lot smarter 'n me. He got the brains. I got the good looks." He gave her his best roguish smile, but she only offered an unladylike snort that made him want to rear back and howl with laughter. Not a gal to be taken in by easy charm, Callista Ainsworth. "But where Farren isn't so clever is, he jumps right in with his heart. He does dang cartwheels trying to get people to love 'im."

She made no reply.

"But I reckon his circus tricks paid off, in the end. He got his Nora, after all."

The music was winding down. She was looking everywhere but at him.

They had a mighty attraction for each other. But love? He shook his head.

The only thing that would've pushed her into marrying an ignorant rube like him was a child growing inside her. But there was no child.

Thank the good Lord.

There was no child…

This gal was no shallow doll to toy with. He should leave her be.

Still…

She had been waiting for love.

Was still waiting for love.

Gosh darn it.

Chapter Nine

The Crystal Palace, just outside London
A week later

Over the next week, he and Miss Callie Ainsworth played cat and mouse. Every time he set his sights on her, some well-meaning lady or gent dragged another eligible miss into his path for inspection. He was many things, but downright rude—at least not without provocation—wasn't one of them. By the time he disentangled himself from the matchmaking mothers, fathers, aunts, and grandparents, Callie was either already dancing… or vanished. These damned ballrooms were packed tight enough to suffocate a man. And worse, she hadn't even shown her face at half the outings.

He'd finally bribed the Ainsworth's coachman to give up the sisters' schedule.

The Crystal Palace, this coming Thursday. At least there he might be able to breathe.

Thursday evening came but Bren hadn't caught sight of either of them, even though he'd been over the entire building twice. No small feat, as the thing was near the size of his entire farm back in Maryland. Had they changed their plans? Over a week since he'd danced with her at her sister's ball…

The fireworks would be starting soon. He hated them but couldn't make himself give up on her yet. He moved outside, walked along one of the many paths winding around the glass palace. Along the perimeter, he spied a tall woman walking alone up ahead of him. A long coltish stride, a stray wisp of red hair curling from beneath her bonnet. His pace lengthened and his heart knocked in his breast.

"Miss Callie. You're harder to pin down than a rogue steer." Lord, it was so good to see her.

"Your Lordship." Her gaze did not meet his, even after they'd finished the bobbing and bowing that came before any conversation.

Shadows hid her face. He moved to expose her to the lamplight, but she ducked her head.

Callie Ainsworth, shy? Not the gal he knew. Had he made such a blunder that she couldn't even look at him?

"Step out with me for a while? I'm just a mite afraid of these dark corners and could use a brave soul by my side."

She looked behind her, down the pathway, her profile catching the light. Now that he got a good look at her, she didn't seem all that well. Her eyes had shadows etched below them and she looked even paler than usual.

"What, nothing to say? Come on, at least give me hell for my lame courting."

She turned back to him. "I—that is—I don't think—"

"Callie!" Helena Ainsworth hurried down the path to her sister's side. "Oh, good evening, Lord Clifford." She curtsied. "Isn't it a grand evening? The fireworks are starting soon, Callie, and you promised to sit with me and Mr. Henshaw."

"Oh, yes. Yes, I did. If you will excuse us, your lordship?"

"Would you like to join us, Lord Clifford?" Miss Helena turned her pretty smile his way.

But there was no matching smile on her sister's lips.

He wanted to rile her, to tip her backwards over his arm and plant a kiss on those frowning lips.

She was waiting for love.

"Naw, I 'spect I'll mosey on." He made sure to bow before he turned to walk—no, by gum, saunter—down the dimly lit path to nowhere.

Dang, this attraction made no sense. She was old, tall, had wild red hair and next to no bosom—well, seems like from the other night at the ball, she had a handful more than he recalled. None of the things he usually sought in a lover. But what fixed his flint was how danged smart she was. Oh, he might have her fooled for a spell, ducking and dodging, but soon enough she'd discover he was just an ignorant horse's ass. She loved to read, while he hated books. He'd much rather muck about outside, especially atop a horse.

But she loved to ride, too—though maybe not horses...

Hell, she was one of those complicated females, the ones that took a lot of work.

He flinched at the sound of a firework hissing in the night sky. Dang war had ruined the spectacle for him. He should just turn around right now and mosey on back to Clifford House, forget all about her...

"Lord Clifford."

He turned around.

She was back without her sister. But didn't seem happy about it, her mouth pulled tight, hands firmly clasped in front of her, clutching her reticule as if it held her reason for living.

He couldn't bear to listen if she was gonna let him down easy.

"I know," he said before she could speak. "It was a harebrained idea, this courtin' business. No need to explain. We'll just keep avoiding each other these next few weeks."

"I am increasing."

"What?" The boom overhead had drowned out most of her words. But he could swear she'd said she was having a baby.

"I said, I am—pregnant."

No boom this time. At least not in the sky. His heart was another matter.

"As it turns out, I am going to have a child," she repeated again, this time slowly, as if he were a sapskull. "Your child."

The sky exploded. He spun away from the noise, nearly dropping and rolling.

"Oohs" and "ahh's" had him jerking upright. No battlefield, just the delight of the crowd at the gosh-blamed finale.

She looked at him as if he was an almighty fool. Or worse, with pity.

Stupid idiot!

The applause from the crowd seemed to echo his assessment.

"Are you well? she asked, a frown on her face.

Another boom sent a shudder through him. "After-effects of war. I'm fine." He tried to smile.

She looked uncertain. "Yes. Well." Seeing him so shaken seemed to have thrown her off her tact. She cleared her throat. "To be frank, I *had* bled when you found me getting sick in the woods. I *did* think it was a bad mushroom. So, I didn't think I could be. I didn't want to be. But it seems a little blood is often normal in the early stages. Since then, I have read a great deal about the signs… I would not have bothered you with it until I was certain. And, well now—it is certain. I suppose if one believes in retribution for breaking the rules, then perhaps I am being punished now."

He had no words. No way to comfort her. To comfort himself. It was all too new. Too sudden, as if the bottom had dropped out of his world and he found himself suspended in air with no foothold.

He reached for the flask in his pocket. *Shit.* Much as he needed to dull his ricocheting mind, *she* likely needed him to be reasoned and responsible.

Responsible. Hell. All his dang fault. He'd had to have this beautiful thing she'd seemed so eager to give. Could not deny himself. Selfish clodpoll.

She stood frozen in place. He reckoned if he dared touch her, she might just shatter into a million pieces.

Smart and sassy and so beautiful standing there in the half shadows.

But she'd wanted love. She wanted a fella who was worthy of her. Dang, she'd taken herself off to the God-forsaken Highlands rather than be trapped in a loveless marriage.

She didn't give a fig for the only thing he had, his fancy title.

"I am right sorry."

Her head jerked up, her gaze meeting his for a long moment, then slowly sliding away. "Well, I had a say in the matter." Her lips drew together tight as a miser's purse.

Yes, she had at that. Flipping him over on his back

that night in her cabin and riding him until they'd both exploded. He'd been so catawampused he hadn't been able to pull out all the way. Damn.

"Why didn't you tell me sooner?" A stupid thing to say. He knew it the minute the question left his lips.

"Because I didn't know." Her hand wound around the strings of her purse tighter and tighter. "Never having been pregnant before. As I said, I bled over six weeks ago. I thought 'that is that.' It was finally over. But it wasn't." She froze up solid again.

Laughter ran along the edges of the gardens. People were beginning to drift along the paths.

"Callie. Callie, girl. I am right sorry," he stupidly repeated and tried to take her hand.

She shook her head vehemently.

Damn, he couldn't get anything right.

"I should have resisted you there at the cabin. This is my fault, Callie."

That riled her even more.

He didn't know the right words.

And yet he did know.

There was only one thing to say.

Words he'd vowed never to say to any woman, so's he could right the mistake of inheriting this dang title. Not marrying, not siring a boy child, meant Farren, or Farren's children, would inherit after he was gone.

But now his brilliant plan was colder 'n a wagon tire.

"I reckon we should get married, then." The words came out clear and matter of fact, spoken like a man in charge. A responsible man. A stranger…

She cracked then, seemed to shudder so that her entire body shook.

He pulled her into the deeper shadows, not wanting

to expose her to the stares of passersby.

"Oh, lordy, gal, what have I done to you?" He pulled her against him, his hands stroking her beautiful, soft hair.

They stood there for a long while. Finally, she pulled away and sniffed. She tried to open her purse, but her hands were still tangled in its strings.

"Here, let me." He picked at the fine ribbons until the mouth of the purse loosened and then opened. He pulled a dainty scrap of linen from within and dabbed her eyes and then her nose.

She seemed happy enough to submit to his fussing.

"Now, we best get you back to your sister. Miss Helena and her Mr. Henwitt are likely near ready to call out the guard, you've been gone so long."

She nodded and sniffed again, then took the handkerchief from him and wiped her face. At last, she gave a good strong blow of her nose.

For some strange reason, the fact that she didn't care a hill of beans for dainty niceties made his dang heart squeeze up tight against his throat.

"Now, we can sort all this out tomorrow. Let's find your sister before I get challenged to another duel."

She nodded and sniffed again, then lifted her head and strode out of the shadows and into the lamplight.

Chapter Ten

Her note came by footman with the dawn.

He didn't need to read much of it to decipher her intent.

...too hasty...not myself these days...raise the child on my own...perhaps back to my cottage? Or, maybe the Continent.

He crumpled the letter into a ball, then saddled up a horse.

After knocking three separate times on the front door of the house on Curzon Street, a rumpled-looking footman finally answered. He looked like he'd been asleep.

What the devil time was it?

The answer, it didn't matter. This needed to be sorted as soon as possible.

Bren didn't wait to be admitted, he just strode into the hall. "I'm here to speak with Mr. Ainsworth."

"Lord Clifford, pardon, my lord. I don't believe the master is receiving at present," the footman stammered.

"Well, I reckon he will be when you tell 'im I've come to ask for his daughter's hand in marriage. If not him, then I'm dang sure that Miz Ainsworth will be right pleased to receive me."

The footman bowed, then gestured toward a set of open doors. "Would you please wait in the drawing room, your lordship, while I see if—"

"What are you doing here?" Callie called from the top of the stairs. She looked like a young girl, her hair in a long braid hanging over her shoulder, her face newly scrubbed and pale, her cheeks bright in the dawn's light.

"What do you think I'm doing?"

Callie waited until the footman disappeared. "Did you not receive my letter?"

"I got it." He didn't realize just how angry he was. "You seem to be forgetting it's my child, too."

She came down the stairs. Mad as he was, he still had such an urge to take her in his arms, just like last night, when she'd been so forlorn.

She said nothing as she passed by him and entered a drawing room. He followed her and then shut the doors behind him.

"I am perfectly capable of raising the child on my own. My parents will make a fuss at first, but then they will see reason. I will simply go away again—"

"I don't' reckon you heard me. As you said last night, it takes two to make a babe, and I will not shirk my part in it."

"But we—we are not in love. Our marriage would be a lie."

"Well, I agree, the circumstances are not perfect, but lie or no, we must marry."

Suddenly the doors were flung open and a dressing-begowned Mrs. Ainsworth, hair under a cap, rushed into the room. Mr. Ainsworth followed close on her heels.

"Lord Clifford, what a surprise!" the lady cried.

"Good day, Miz Ainsworth, Mr. Ainsworth." Bren remembered to bow like a formal suitor would. "I am sorry for the earliness of my visit, but what I have to say can't wait. I've come to ask for your daughter's hand in marriage."

Callie *snorted.*

Hermione Ainsworth hesitated just long enough to show her hand, then summoned a brilliant smile, quick as a cardsharp flipping an ace. "Oh, how wonderful! I assume you are asking for—Callista's hand?"

"She's the one, ma'am." He turned to Callie, who frowned like he was the very devil.

"This is astonishing—yet utterly delightful! Oh, my dear Callista! We will have such a jolly time planning the wedding. We must have St. Paul's, of course. Surely, either that or Saint George's! We may have to wait until next year until one is free, but no matter. T'will be the most spectacular wedding of the season!" The lady clapped her hands like Bren had just performed a hat trick. "Gerald, the ballroom here will have to be redone post haste! We shall need to accommodate no less than two hundred guests for the wedding breakfast. Or perhaps a new house entirely!"

"Hermione, desist." Gerald Ainsworth crossed to a chair and sat. Then he waited, hands folded over his chest.

"But the tradesmen must be engaged as soon as may be, if we are to have a hope—"

"Woman, no more!"

"Don't you understand, this is our chance to rise in society! I will finally be able to put that odious Lady Trunket—"

"Hermione, you will leave us." Mr. Ainsworth sat up poker straight, never taking his eyes off his daughter.

"But, Ger—"

"Now," Callie's father said with a definitiveness that rivaled the Almighty.

"Well, of course, she is your daughter, you must deal with her as you will," she said, her tone far more doubting than her words. But when he made her no answer, the woman finally wheeled, her chin high, her robe snapping like sails in a squall.

She hadn't gone far, Bren reckoned. Likely huddled by the keyhole, desperate to hear any shred of the impending conversation...

A cue if ever there was one for him to state his case. "Mr. Ainsworth—"

"I am with child." Callie cut in, her tone matter-of-fact.

Mr. Ainsworth received the news as he might a change in the weather.

Bren rocked forward on his toes and then back. "Well, I wouldn't have led with that, but yep, that is the case, sir. I reckon we put the cart before the horse, so to speak."

Callie stepped forward. "I have told his lordship that I am very able to raise the child on my own—"

"Sir—"

"Do you love him?" Her father's words, as well as his gaze, were fiercely intense.

Her answer came in a mere moment. "No."

Bren felt the monosyllable hit his chest like a shot. He should not have been surprised, but somehow he had hoped she might soften her response, give him even a smidge of hope...

Her father's hands flexed against his chest, but otherwise his face registered nothing. He turned to Bren then. "I see. And Clifford, do you love her?"

Hell, he admired the heck out of Callista Ainsworth. But love?

"No," he said, but quickly added, "We don't know each other all that well, yet, sir, but I do hold your daughter in great esteem. And one thing I know for certain: I will never abandon my child."

Bren waited for her father to speak, but the man seemed lost in thought, no longer staring at his daughter's face, as if he couldn't bear to look at her.

"Callista," he finally said, his tone pained and weary. "Would you leave this child without a name? No. As Lord Clifford has put it so succinctly, you have made your bed and now you must lie in it. A child should be supported by both its parents."

Callie jerked fully upright as if she had been suddenly pulled by some unseen puppeteer. "Both parents, you say? By God, you of all people dare to say such a thing to me! I have lived with your disdain, but I will not live with such hypocrisy. At least spare me that," she cried out, with a razor-like sharpness Bren had never heard from her.

Gerald Ainsworth seemed to shrink within himself. His hands collapsed into his lap and he stared at them as if he were not sure what to do with them. What had happened between father and daughter that she would turn so?

Bren was just about to speak when Ainsworth stood.

"My opinion, nor your stepmother's opinion, is of no account to you, it would seem. But I would ask you to please consider your sister, and the love I know you bear her. Helena is truly an innocent. Her chances of a good marriage, and ultimately, happiness, will certainly be damaged if you—disappear yet again."

At the mention of Helena's name, Callie's shoulders slumped, and her head dropped. She fiddled with the gold pendant she always wore.

Both men watched as she walked to the window and looked out. The rising sun gilded her profile and hair. Almost like an angel, she looked.

Not like him to be so fanciful. But the idea was so striking, he was sure he'd remember her just so for a long, long time.

She turned her back to the lighted window to face him. "Very well. I will marry you. For the child's sake, and Helena's."

Well, that hit like a hammer. Not for him, no sir.

Still, damned if he didn't want to halloo to the rafters. Didn't make a bean of sense. His entire plan to hand the peerage to Farren? Shot to Hell.

He'd be marrying a woman he barely knew, and having yet another child who would only become disappointed in him. Yet the feeling of intense relief stuck.

"And we will keep the child a—secret—for now," she finished and then quietly turned and left the room.

"Right." Mr. Ainsworth broke the silence. "I'm going to get a brandy and then we'll get to the settlements. Would you care to join me, Clifford?"

Should he run after her? Try to at least take her hand? Naw, best to let her stew a while. Women seemed a sight more tetchy when they were with child.

"Yes, sir, I reckon I could do with a nip, thank you."

Chapter Eleven

Barton Grange, Wiltshire

"Dear Mr. and Mrs. Ainsworth, I am overjoyed Brendan and Callista have decided to return to the country for the wedding! I am slightly prejudiced, but I believe there is nothing as splendid as Wiltshire in early summer.

"Wiltshire!" Hermione sniffed in derision, holding the note from which she'd been reading at arms' length, as if it were some foul rodent instead of a note of welcome. But quickly began reading again.

"Will you please join us for an informal family dinner this Thursday at seven in the evening. I am longing to meet Miss Ainsworth before she becomes my sister-in-law! Nora Cavanaugh."

Hermione threw the invitation down next to her uneaten breakfast. "Wiltshire, indeed!" she repeated.

Hermione fussed and fumed, but she was getting her peer. Of course, the wrong daughter had secured him, but one could not have everything in life. "And all this rush! We should have had a grand wedding at St. Georges and a wedding breakfast for at least two hundred. Not even held at our own estate but shunted off to Ryeland Park's tiny chapel. Mr. Ainsworth," she said, pointing her fork at his paper. "I knew we should have built a chapel instead of that ridiculous folly."

Callie took a sip of tea. Now cold.

"Still, I suppose it is best to get the deed done as soon as may be. We certainly don't want another Percy Blanchard scandal." Hermione shuddered dramatically. "Did you know he married the Earl of Sutton's eldest girl, Lady Beatrice? Nothing to look at, but a title and a fortune nearly as large as we were offering for Callista."

Callie had not heard of his marriage. Poor Lady Bea.

Gerald Ainsworth continued to read his London Times without comment.

"But this wedding is all so higgly piggly! No time to even make a proper bridal gown in white. That reminds me, Callista, you must try on the yellow silk again. That village woman got the flounces all wrong. I suppose we shall have to rely on that Scottish chit. But praise heavens the new gardener has sorted out the hothouse. He has assured me the tuberoses and gardenias will be at their peak."

Just the thought of the heavy scented flowers made Callie's stomach roil.

A maid entered with a piece of paper. "Madam, beg pardon, but Cook wanted me to give you the newest menu as soon as possible." The poor girl extended the paper as if she were a suppliant before her sovereign.

Hermione snatched the paper and then began reading. "No, no! This is all wrong!" She glared at her husband, who paid her not one jot of attention, and then at Callie. "Well, there is nothing for it. I will speak directly with the woman after breakfast." She waved the maid away.

Her stepmother's voice faded into the background as Callie pushed her food around her plate.

I'm right sorry.

Those three words a refrain in her brain, a thrum over her heart.

I'm right sorry.

He didn't want this marriage, not truly. Oh, he'd agreed to a fake courtship, but only to stir up the *ton*, and specifically her stepmother. But marriage? No.

The existence of a tiny babe clinging to her womb had changed everything. The merry chase had lost its thrill and he'd been caught.

I'm right sorry.

Oh, if only she could bottle the look on Brendan Cavanaugh's face when she had told him of the child and shake it out whenever she needed a good laugh. Or a good cry.

Only there was nothing to laugh at now.

Her life as she had known it, the quiet days spent at her cottage counting birds, marking nests, building cairns, seemed like years ago. How had it gotten away from her? How had she allowed her life to be usurped so?

She hoped this marriage wouldn't change him. Wouldn't kill the reckless, irreverent man she love—

Only she didn't love him. She didn't even know him.

Once Hermione had finally accepted that the wedding was fixed for the very next Friday at Ryeland Park, she'd whisked the family out of London and back to the Grange to begin preparations. And to avoid any gossip about such a hasty marriage. Time enough to bask in her coup after the deed was done, and the viscount truly bagged.

Callie had no idea if her father had confided in his wife about the babe, but knowing her father, she suspected not. However, Hermione Ainsworth was no dullard. Two and two always made four, whether one liked it or not.

It had been just over a week since she had last seen him. Endless days longing for the sight of him and eight days dreading the same.

Tonight. Her last evening as Callie Ainsworth.

Only the day before, she had crept through the woods and fields of the Grange and into those of Ryeland Park. She'd passed a charming cottage that reminded her a bit of her Scottish retreat. This one was larger, two stories instead of one and appeared uninhabited. Someone must visit often, though, for a neatly tended garden thrived just on its side next to a well pump. Who took the time to nurture this tiny plot?

Beyond the woods, a graveyard lay on a slight rise nestled within a copse of beech trees. *Geoffrey Colin Clifford, Viscount Clifford, beloved son of Martha and Colin*, read the newest grave. The late viscount's parents lay beside him.

"Callista!" Hermione exclaimed as she rose from the table. "No running off into the woods today. You have a fitting and then that girl will attempt to do something with your hair. Why you rejected Carstairs in favor of that Scot I will never know."

Hermione's voice faded as Callie sipped her cold tea.

Would she be buried there, too? Resting for eternity next to her husband?

Husband.

****

Bedecked in a beautiful leaf-green gown with cream-lace insets and an embroidered sash of pink and purple violets, her hair somewhat smoothed, tendrils pulled down to frame her face, Callie supposed she was as ready as ever to face the evening.

As the carriage drew up to Ryeland Park, Helena took her hand in hers and squeezed. "Isn't it lovely, Cal?"

She squeezed back in reply as she couldn't trust her voice not to break.

A beautifully sculpted, multi-tiered fountain stood before the house. Within its splashing water, charming mermaids and aquatic creatures frolicked, granting it a sense of whimsy. They rounded the fountain and stopped in front of a large portico. The manse's light-colored stone façade gleamed opalescent in the deepening dusk. It seemed every window was lit and thrust open to admit a breeze. How utterly welcoming. Quite the opposite of Barton Grange whose wings jutted out at all angles, each competing with the next, as if to say, *look at me, aren't I impressive!*

Yes, Callie thought. *It is lovely.*

The butler, a Mr. Pratt, welcomed them into a front hall very nearly the size of her father's, but again, there the comparison ended. Instead of marble statues and enormous urns holding nothing, warm tapestries hung from the walls and a profusion of wildflowers mixed with flowering branches filled several gayly-painted vases. The room spoke of family and contentment.

"They are here!"

A gaggle of children raced across the checked marble floor to surround the Ainsworths.

"This is her!" A little girl about the age of six or so claimed Callie's hand and held it up as if it were some sort of trophy.

"If you will please follow me?" Mr. Pratt seemed unflappable as he culled Helena and her parents from the group to usher them across the hall.

A ginger-haired boy took Callie's other hand as she and the children trailed behind Mr. Pratt and her family. "Uncle Bren says you can spot a bird nearly as good as him, is that true or is he telling us a tall tale?"

"Uncle Bren would never tell a tall tale!" another boy objected.

Uncle Bren seemed to be a favorite.

"Is that your real hair?" The little girl tugged on Callie's hand, an incredulous look on her face more suited to a woman of forty.

"May I?" Another girl found Callie's arm, her fingers skating up over the kid skin of her glove, to her bare arm and then to her shoulder where she gently touched a curl. Her entire body canted toward Callie. "Yes, it is real, and washed with rosemary and verbena."

Good heavens! The child was correct.

"No need to show off, Aggie." The forty-year-old child stepped in front of her friend. "Aggie is blind so she can see more than the rest of us."

Indeed, now she looked more closely, Aggie's gaze seemed unfocused. "Ah, yes, I expect she does. And who are you?"

"Mum named me Marigold. Mari for short. And that is Rose!" Mari pointed toward a beautiful blonde girl about Helena's age who stood by the door where Callie's family had disappeared. A soft smile lit her face.

"Uncle Bren calls her his Shy Bird." Mari tugged her hand and Callie bent toward the little girl's upturned mouth. "Rose is from the charity home, but not like Phillip and Ernest. She was—special."

Charity home? And what exactly did *special* mean?

Rose had crossed to the group. Mari immediately took the older girl's hand and pulled her toward Callie. "Miss Callie, this is Rose," the little girl said as if she were a diplomat introducing heads of state.

Rose dipped into a curtsy. "Pleased to meet you, Miss Ainsworth. I look forward to us being—good friends." Her startling green eyes darted to Callie's and then back to the floor.

"Thank you, Miss Rose. I am sure we shall."

"Mum has been wanting to meet you so very much," Mari declared, once again commandeering everyone's attention. "She has been sad-happy all at once. Sad, cuz Opal has gone, but happy that Uncle Bren is getting married," Mari continued.

"Oh, and who is Opal?" Callie asked, so curious about this wonderfully odd family.

"No one knows much about Opal," Mari said ominously. "But she was Mum's first. Then Aggie. But *I* am third *and* the youngest! Well, I am until Mum has the new—"

"Mari, I believe Miss Ainsworth is ready to join the adults now. Let us go in and make our curtsies," Rose said pulling the little girl ahead.

Certainly, this Opal was yet another mystery. Why was Nora Cavanaugh so distressed by the girl leaving? As for their Mum being happy for her brother-in-law, well, Callie hoped the countess's happiness would be prophetic.

"Miss Ainsworth," Pratt intoned as he stepped aside to allow Callie and the children to enter.

Then there was a flurry of introductions. Mari and Agnes and Billy, and Diana, and so on. What a contrast was this gay and rambunctious assortment of relations to her own staid family.

A woman appeared at her side, the children's beloved, *Mum*, and the famed, Countess of Havermere, now Nora Cavanaugh.

"Ah, I see they pounced on you the moment you crossed the threshold—and no doubt pummeled you with a hundred questions." She gazed at the children with sheer love. "Well, I suppose it was too much to hope for. They have been as eager to meet you, as I have." The smile remained, but when her gaze lifted to Callie, it was with the searching intensity of someone trying to see into her very soul. "I am Nora Cavanaugh. You must call me Nora, and I hope I may call you Callista?"

"Uncle Bren calls her Callie." Mari rose onto her toes and then nearly toppled into Agnes. "Will you be our Aunt Callie?"

"Hush, Mari of-a-million-questions." A boy, Phillip, if she remembered correctly, with a hair lip and perfectly sculpted hair elbowed Mari while gazing adoringly up at his Mum.

Callie smiled at them both. Indeed, Mari reminded Callie of herself when she was about that age. "I would very much like to be your Aunt Callie."

A cheer went up from the group that had the rest of the company turning their heads.

"I fear we shall have to work a bit more on our decorum for the next social event. Now, bid good evening to Aunt Callie, it is time for bed."

Farren Cavanaugh joined them. His hand came to rest protectively on his wife's waist—or where her waist would have been had she not been with child. "Nora, a pack of wild hooligans seem to have invaded Ryeland. I wonder what they have done with the children?"

"We are not hooligans, Uncle Farren! We're the cavalry, come to protect Aunt Callie!"

"I want to be a spy like Uncle Bren!"

"And I'll be Chief Spotted Elk of the Lakota Sioux tribe. Uncle Bren says he was the bravest!"

"And there, you have done it again, Colonel." Nora Cavanaugh laughed up at her husband. "You have managed to stir them up just when they should have been encouraged to calm themselves before bed."

He grinned at her.

"Best get some good sleep tonight. You all have a passel of work tomorrow. Coins to wrap up, rose petals to gather. And—" he leaned down to whisper. "—I found some old cowboy boots to tie onto the back of the carriage!"

The children burst into chatter, each competing for jobs, and then bargaining, and finally capitulation.

What would her own new family with Brendan Cavanaugh be like? She sought his eyes across the room. He had been watching her, even with Hermione chattering away in his ear.

Clearly Nora and Farren Cavanaugh were very much in love. Could she and Brendan one day share a similar joy?

"I'll be but a moment, Nor. Just want to corral this herd and tuck them in." Her husband raised her hand and tenderly kissed the inside of her wrist and then he crossed the room to follow the children.

How extraordinary. Her father would no more delay his dinner to tend to her or Helena—especially with guests—than he would dance about in his underclothes.

Brendan continued to pretend to listen to Hermione,

and now Callie's father, who had joined them. Her betrothed's eyes remained focused on her. They didn't crinkle with their usual mirth though. He seemed subdued and rather withdrawn, as he had been since he had proposed.

"Thank you for being so tolerant of the children. They so wanted to meet you, and as you can see, the Colonel and I are not the strictest of parents," Nora said.

"They are utterly charming."

"Yes, they are dears. I am sure Brendan told you how they came to be with us. Such a terrible situation. But one that gave our family many blessings."

Now was not the time to admit that in fact, no, Brendan had not told her much of anything. She changed the subject. "You will not remember, my lady, but I met you once before, very briefly. You and your former husband, Lord Havermere, attended my come-out ball. It was a great coup for our family."

"Oh, goodness. I am sorry not to have remembered. I must have been just married." A cloud crossed her lovely face. "I was…well, I was very unhappy then."

Indeed, Callie did remember how utterly beautiful the young countess had been, but also, how sad she'd looked. "I need not ask if you are happy now."

"Ah, yes. I never dreamed of such a blessed life. Farren is—well, he is simply the best man I have ever met. I sincerely hope you and Brendan will find the same kind of happiness."

Callie said nothing, her throat suddenly tight.

Nora Cavanaugh's prayer was for the future, Callie realized. Was it so evident that no love existed between them at present? Forcing a smile, she nodded.

Nora Cavanaugh leaned forward suddenly and gave

her hand a sympathetic squeeze.

Callie would likely have made a cake of herself, so strong was the urge to throw herself into the dear lady's arms, if Mr. Pratt had not just then appeared at their hostess's side.

"Thank you, Pratt." Nora Cavanaugh turned to the company. "Would you all come in to dinner?" she called out to the assembled guests.

Brendan came to take her arm, a smile fixed on his face. "I warned you we are a wild bunch. Want to back out?"

His hand felt warm and solid against her, and a looping buoyancy shot from her deepest place up into her belly, around her heart, and then back down again. As if the floor had collapsed for a moment, leaving her suspended, and just as suddenly been restored solid beneath her slippered feet.

Callie brushed her still-flat stomach, remembering how the Colonel had touched his wife's swollen belly with such reverence. Oh, if only she and Brendan had half such a love!

But they barely knew each other.

Only one thing was certain: there was no backing out now.

****

With dinner finished, the men rejoined the ladies for tea. Brendan made his way over to her side.

"I see you met my Rosie." His right hand twitched. A telltale sign of his nervousness, despite his smile.

"She is charming. If I had a pence for every time I heard *Uncle Bren*, I would be rich."

"Well, happens I am their only uncle, so I wouldn't set much store by it."

"Nora mentioned there was some terrible tale involving the children. She assumed I knew. I didn't tell her otherwise." She waited for him to reply. When he didn't, she continued. "I am told you call Rose your 'Shy-Bird'. And she is from the charity home, but somehow *special*? Has she been with the family long?"

"Oh, a while now." He shoved his hand in his pocket and rocked up on his toes.

Callie had an inkling there was much more to this tale. "You say, '*Your* Rosie'?"

"Rose Cavanaugh."

"Cavanaugh?"

"Yes, Rosie is my—natural daughter."

At least five emotions flooded her body, each vying for purchase. Outrage, shame, worry, fear, frustration, bitterness. Stupidity won out, quashing all those feelings. Why had she not seen it? The girl had the exact coloring of a Cavanaugh.

Callie managed to tamp down all feeling. "Oh, that might have been something to mention."

He had the good sense to at least look down at his boots. "Yep. I reckon so."

"Any other shocking secrets you've been keeping from me?" she asked.

He looked up under those stubby black lashes, a contrite grin quirking his lips. "A passel, I expect. Nothing dire as all that."

"No other children?"

He shifted his feet. "Well, Rose had a twin sister. Lily. She died."

Dear God in heaven. It got worse and worse. Anger flared, but his face, so stamped with grief, quickly snuffed it, replacing it with pity.

"Oh, I—I am sorry." *How did she die? And when? Were you close?* But one question she could not hold back. "And their mother?" Best to know this history here and now.

"Dead," he hastened to say, no doubt seeking to tamp her panic. His hands twitched again.

She would have insisted on hearing more, but the look on his face was one of such pain that she did not have the heart to pry. "I see," she said, though she really didn't see at all.

"Well, I'm glad we got that out of the way." He put his hands in his pockets and then pulled them back out again. "I think I'll get a drink. Can I fetch you something?"

Can you turn back time? Can you make my heart beat normally when I am around you? Can you save me from disaster?

She shook her head. "No, nothing."

He made a beeline for the sideboard which held an array of crystal decanters.

My God, he'd had an entire life before her. Of course, logic would deem it so, but what a naive fool to assume his must have been as staid as her own.

"So, soon-to-be-sister-in-law, welcome to the Cavanaugh family." Farren Cavanaugh had taken his brother's place by her side.

She should have accepted Brendan's offer of a drink. Or twelve. "Thank you. I think."

"Ha! I assured him you wouldn't take on about Rosie. I reckon you're about as levelheaded as they come. Am I right?"

"If you mean I prefer the truth to secrets and lies, then you are correct."

130

"Well, sharing his unvarnished truths may take a bit of time for my brother. He plays the chatty, affable fella, but he's pretty slow to talk about what really matters."

Callie only nodded.

"You and I don't know each other well, but I have a hunch you'll be good for him," Farren continued after taking a sip from his glass. "He's rough around the edges, and avoids conflict until it's unbearable. But once he's riled, well, there's no better champion than my brother."

Is that what happened when he first offered for her hand? He got *riled*?

"I know my brother down to his bones, and have never seen him so fixed on a woman as he is on you. He wouldn't tell me much of his travels up north, only that he met a woodland witch in the land of fairy folk and she set him straight."

Had Brendan spoken of her to his twin? Oh, how she wanted to believe his words, even just a bit.

"None of my requests, supplications, or even downright threats had any effect on his thick skull. But after only a few days with you, he returned a new man— well, not new, but a better man. At least, one willing to try. You must have some magic in you to have turned him back toward home and family."

Magic? Might he have wanted her even without the child? She looked for Brendan, hoping to see some sign that might be taken for an omen. But he'd disappeared.

Don't be a fool, Callista Ainsworth. The only alchemy between them was forged through the babe growing within her.

If Farren Cavanaugh thought his brother was marrying her because he *wanted* to, perhaps the Colonel did not know his twin as well as he imagined. Still, she did not disabuse him of the notion. Why didn't she tell Farren Cavanaugh the unvarnished truth, that any magic she possessed was because of the natural miracle of the child growing in her belly?

"He's had a passel of heartache, my brother. But I think you just might be a woman he can unburden himself to, a woman who can help him heal."

"I fear you give me too much credit." The recent revelation of his having a bastard daughter only served to highlight that they knew nothing of each other.

And the child had a mother, too. Who had she been to this man who would be her husband by this time tomorrow?

"Oh, I don't think so. After all, you are magical." He favored her with a lopsided grin. The one so very near to that of his brother, but, if one looked closely, not the same at all.

It would take work, not magic, to make this marriage last.

"Least ways, I'm hoping this time he'll find some peace."

This time? How many others had come before her? Certainly, Rose and Lily's mother had been one of Brendan Cavanaugh's paramours. Had he loved her?

The Colonel took another sip of his whisky.

Questions burned on her tongue. So much death. Rose's sister, Lily; Brendan's own sister; his parents; Rose's mother. Surely other women in his past, too. Then his childhood, his role as a spy in their Civil War, and Rose being one of the rescued children but somehow special. The list of questions went on and on, pelting her brain.

But now was not the time to probe. Because her husband should be the one to reveal his own history. If he did—if he could—their marriage might have more than a chance.

Callie remained silent.

"Just don't lose heart. Bren is tight as an oyster around its pearl when it comes to feelings. He'll run any physical gauntlet, but emotional pain, well, you'll likely just see the back of him when it comes to that."

She said nothing, though she felt like a starved child, in desperate need of any small scrap of knowledge.

"Hard on himself, my brother. And dang if most of the time he deserves it. But still, not nearly as much as he believes he does. Try to love him, Callie. He deserves a chance at love."

Farren excused himself to speak with an approaching servant. At the footman's words, Farren glanced quickly around the room, his eyes coming to rest on Callie.

"Is everything all right?" she asked.

"Oh, just—just one of the children. A nightmare. They get them from time to time—ghosts from the past. If you'll excuse me, I'll just go and see to her."

"Yes, yes, of course."

Heavens. Once again, she could no more imagine her father pulling himself away from guests to soothe a frightened child than the moon turning to cheese.

Would Brendan be like his brother? Or more like her father?

Where was her bridegroom?

She crossed to the French doors and then out into a small conservatory. Immediately she could see he was not within. She almost turned back but the idea of facing questioning looks and putting on a brave face made her linger. A drift of purple clematis wreathed a whimsical iron balustrade, as if a lady had casually left her colorful shawl draped over the railing. Thick mist rose from the damp ground, streaking the glass walls with rivulets of water. Callie stepped closer to the glass and swiped a small area clean with her gloved hand. Peering through it, she could just make out the front entry of the house. Now she remembered, when they were driving up to the manse, she spied the winking glass room, thinking it a charming addition. She could hear the splashing of the fountain beyond.

A carriage stood in the drive. A guest? She did not think anyone else had been invited. And why would anyone arrive after dinner?

The carriage door stood open and a woman appeared framed within it. She wore a bonnet with a veil, but her figure was still youthful and even lush.

As if she sensed her presence, the woman turned toward Callie. The lamplight caught the sparkle of a jeweled brooch. A butterfly?

She was talking with someone who Callie could not see. She swiped more of the window as her breath fogged the glass.

Her cheek nearly pressed to the pane, still she could not see. Then the person stepped forward. A cap of golden hair, wide shoulders, long legs.

The Colonel?

No, he was soothing the disturbed child.

If only she had a better view. The impatient huff of her breath fogged the glass. She swiped again.

The man must be Brendan.

He said something to the lady who laughed and then

disappeared inside the carriage. Brendan looked around before joining her.

A fine but steady rain began to fall, making her view hopelessly blurred. Still, she pressed against the cold, wet glass, heedless of her ruined gloves and now tear-stained cheeks. Who was this woman? What was she doing at Ryeland Park?

The only answer, a low rumble of thunder.

Jealousy sprung up from her belly making her heart race and her cheeks flush despite the cold glass.

What were they discussing? Was this woman a paramour who had been surprised by her lover's hasty marriage? After all, as demonstrated by this evening's events, Callie knew next to nothing about her future husband's past.

More clouds had moved in, and the already meager light was fading fast, she would be missed soon. But so would her bridegroom-to-be. Would the assembled company assume the couple was simply taking a private moment together?

Oh, what a joke this sham of a marriage was!

Brendan finally re-emerged from the carriage. He spoke again and then leaned into the carriage once more. Finally, he stepped back and firmly closed the door.

As the carriage trundled around the fountain and then down the long drive, Brendan never took his eyes from it, not even long after it disappeared.

Oh, what had she done?

****

"Whoa there, Rosie gal!" His daughter nearly barreled into him, her eyes looking behind her even as she raced down the stairway. "Where's the fire? Did you have a bad dream?"

Tarnation. What did a good father do when his child had a nightmare? Here she was, nearly sixteen, and in her night clothes. Could he give her a hug? Hell, his clothes were wet with mist. He shoved his hand through his damp hair.

Rose looked toward the balcony overlooking the front entryway. Her profile so like Sara's. True, his Little Sprout had been a few years younger when— But he imagined his little sister would have looked very much like his beautiful daughter if she'd made it to her sixteenth birthday...

He stepped in front of her and laid a hand on her shoulder. "Rose?"

"I—I—that is, I couldn't sleep. It is very exciting, with the wedding tomorrow. I had thought to go to the music room and practice my part of the duet. Oh, dear, that was supposed to be a surprise. Agnes and I have been working on a new etude for the occasion."

"Well, that sounds grand. Thank you. And have no fear, I'm a dab hand at keeping secrets."

Rose smiled tentatively and nodded, but couldn't seem to hold his gaze.

But why would she confide in him? Heck, she was closer to his brother and Nora than himself. Even this evening, she'd beamed up at Callie, far more at ease with her than him, even after having just met the gal.

"I reckon we're all a bit restless." He looked out the large window and into the night sky, thinking of the star he had wished upon a few moments ago. Heaven knows he would need all the luck he could get. "You sure you are all right?" The gal still seemed skittish. Hell, given recent events, he was darned skittish as well. "Rest assured, there ain't no ghosts at Ryeland Park. No dead folk, at least. Now there might be a few memories that haunt you now and again, and I am sorry for that, I truly am. But I aim to make dang sure no one ever harms you from here on out."

Again, why would she believe him? History damned him as a fraud. He hadn't taken care of Rose, hadn't even primed her for this meeting with Callie. Just as he hadn't alerted Callie he had a nearly grown daughter.

"You like Miss Callie, don't you?"

"Oh, yes! She was so kind to me. I only hope she liked me as well."

"Is that what's worrying you? Believe me, if Callie can stomach me, she'll certainly love you. Of that I'm dead certain."

"Oh, it's all so romantic!" Rose cried, ignoring his assertion. "Not so long ago, I used to imagine the perfect wedding would be a grand one at Saint Paul's in London. But now, I think if two people love each other so very much, why would they ever want to wait? You must love Miss Ainsworth—Callie—very much?"

It was a question. Rose's observations of the two of them was likely at odds with her notion of a couple so in love they wanted to marry by special license. She was too innocent to even think of other reasons.

"Well, Rosie, love is a funny thing. It can just sneak right up on you and catch you by the tail." Rose did not need to know he was speaking of his daughter and his love for her, rather than his soon-to-be bride.

"Yes, that is exactly how I want to fall in love! Being grabbed by the tail!"

Bren had to laugh at her utter innocence.

"Oh, I hope she will love me as she must love you. I do want us to be a family." Rose threw herself into his arms.

He wanted that as well. But he had so many failures in his past. Was it possible to put them all behind him? Well, God knows he'd try. He prayed his secrets could stay secrets. After all, wasn't it best for all that they did?

On the spur of the moment, he handed her the bunch of cornflowers he'd picked to give to Callie and then sent her off to bed.

How long had he been gone from the party? When he arrived back in the drawing room, the Ainsworths were anxious to leave. Callie was nowhere in sight. They seemed to assume she was with him. Some bridegroom he was. Even the little posey he'd gathered for her, he had given away to the first gal who he needed to please.

He found her in the small conservatory looking a mite lost among all the huge palm trees and exotic flowers. Good thing he'd given his wild offering to Rosie. Right paltry, next to all this glorious profusion.

He watched her for a moment, listening to the tat of rain against the conservatory's glass.

"Callie?" he finally called out, wanting her attention.

She looked up, startled, as if caught hiding.

"I wondered where you'd got to." He shoved his hands in his pockets. Hell, and why shouldn't she disappear when he'd abandoned her?

"Your folks are ready to leave." He held out his hand to her.

"Oh, yes. Thank you." She didn't take his hand, instead she tucked hers behind her back as she brushed by him. Well, he deserved her ire. But when he started to follow, she stopped and turned back to him. She said nothing for a long moment, seemingly fixated on the shoulder of his coat. Self-conscious, he brushed the beads of water from it.

"Did you love her?"

"What?"

Her eyes found his. "Rose and—Lily's mother. Did you love her?" She bit her lip as if the words had escaped.

"Oh, Callie-gal. Iris was—" he broke off, staring out at the rain. "Well, I was really just a boy."

"Yes, but did you love her? Iris?" Her voice was stronger now, more insistent.

He shifted his feet and thrust his hands in his pockets. What to say? *Had* he loved Iris Darvan? It had been so long ago. He'd been foolish and young and thoughtless, so utterly smitten—

But is that what Callie wanted to hear?

He shoved his hand through his damp hair. Taking a chance, he answered, "I—I reckon—I did?"

"Thank you." She nodded once. "Thank you for telling me."

He tried to take her hand again, and this time she let him. He squeezed her fingers. He wished he'd had his pitiful flowers to give her. To tell her he'd picked them because they matched her eyes. Anything to give her some assurance of his lov—

Heck, what he really wanted was to kiss her. To bring them back to their night of love. He hadn't kissed her since the cottage. And why shouldn't he? She was to be his wife!

He pulled her close, taking both her hands in his.

"Ahem." Farren stood just outside the French doors. "Time enough for canoodling this time tomorrow. Miss Callie, your stepmama is anxious for you to get on home."

"Oh, of course." She stepped away from him and he released her hands. Right, no kiss this night. The loss of her made his nose prick and he blinked.

As he solicitously handed her into the carriage, he couldn't help thinking of her question. *Did you love her?* Honestly, he didn't know. But could he love this woman?

More importantly, could she ever love him?

Chapter Twelve

Her wedding dress, the palest-yellow silk, hung like a ghost in the corner of her bedchamber. Its skirts fluttered as a stray breeze found its way into the room, as restless as the woman who would soon wear it.

What was Brendan doing now, on the eve of their nuptials? Was he regretting his rash offer? Was he saying goodbye once more to the veiled woman?

"I won't let you do it!"

Helena burst into the bed chamber without knocking. Again.

Callie had been avoiding her little sister.

"You moved away to Scotland rather than marry without love. I will not have you sacrificing yourself for me!" She flopped on the bed next to Callie. Gulliver, in resignation, simply moved farther down to the foot of the bed.

"Sacrifice? Heavens, Helena, you sound like Mr. Dickens's *Little Dorit*! Viscount Clifford is hardly a toad, dearest—"

"But Martin and I have it all worked out!" Helena's eyes sparkled as she took Callie's hands in hers. "We are going to elope. You will come with us. We have money enough. I was afraid before to cross Mother, but you have given me the strength. You have taught me I can have true love if I fight for it."

What a sight, her sweet sister radiant and full of

romantic fervor. Oh, the beautiful vigor of young love!

"I was such a foolish innocent!" Helena rose and began pacing the room. "This marriage of yours is entirely my fault. I got you into this mess trying to please Mother, hoping a handsome peer of the realm could make me feel as Martin does. It was silly. I should have known you meant I was to kiss Martin when you counseled me to explore further before truly committing. But I had to try with the viscount. He seemed so charming. I had to see if there could be any spark." She stopped her pacing and turned to Callie. "Say something, please. I could not bear to lose your love even while gaining Martin's."

Callie crossed the room and took Helena's hands. So beautiful and white. So untouched by work. "You have nothing to apologize for, sweet sister. You did not make this mess. I did."

"I'm sorry, but that is nonsense. Martin agrees. I threw myself at the viscount. I am the one who is ruined. You must not be the one to suffer for my idiocy. I simply will not let you marry where there is no love."

Callie smiled. "Helena, you will break my bones if you squeeze any harder."

Her little sister gasped and dropped Callie's hands as if they were on fire. "Oh, I am so very sorry!" Then she took them up again only to kiss them.

"Come, let us sit." Callie pulled her sister toward the bed.

"But we have not a moment to lose! Martin is ready and waiting for my signal."

Signal? Did they actually plan to bring her along to Gretna Greene? Oh, she almost hated to thwart the clandestine plots of such sweet innocents…

Helena seemed unlikely to give over her scheme, unless Callie yanked that innocence away. And she was tired, so tired, of lying, of keeping secrets.

"I cannot go with you, my dear. I am with child."

It really was rather comical, watching Helena's mouth drop open and her eyes blink wide.

"Come. Sit."

And so. her tale unraveled. The lame horse, the dinners, the laughter and the tenderness. The extreme want.

"I wondered why you called him Mr. Cavanaugh when you had not ever met him before."

"Ah, clever girl." She kissed her dear little sister's forehead. "Promise me to keep this child a secret? It is— still early. You know I do not like falsehoods, but I would not have you, or your mother, made a subject of gossip because of me. Promise, Helena, you won't tell a soul, even your dear Martin."

Helena, still in some shock, nodded her head. "Yes. Cal. I promise."

"So you must call off Mr. Henshaw without delay. And you will have your church wedding soon enough. And that is my promise to you."

****

Helena and Hermione had already departed for Ryeland. Her father stood waiting for her by the carriage, fiddling with his pocket watch.

"Callista—you look—well."

"Thank you." She looked him straight in the eye deeply aware she'd not been alone with her father in years.

"You are not wearing it—"

"Pardon?"

"The locket," her father said, his mouth pulling tight as if he'd just swallowed bitter gall.

If he'd said Gulliver could dance on the dining table, he couldn't have astonished her more. "No. Not today."

He opened his mouth and then closed it.

She waited. But after a suspended moment, he only shook his head and took out his watch again. "Well, we had best be on our way." He snapped the case closed and then extended his hand to assist her into the carriage.

Silly disappointment flared and then died, now just a hard lump in her throat. Still, how odd to feel his hand in hers if only out of dutiful courtesy.

Once settled, she reached for her locket, only to find the round smoothness of a string of pearls. Already she'd forgotten—It lay safely coiled in a small box on a table next to her bed.

As she stared out the carriage window, the clatter of the horse's hoofs on the pea stone lent a comforting cadence to the silence inside, like the tat-a-tat of rain on a roof...

She'd found the locket on her eleventh birthday when she'd been tucked up in the attics—her refuge on rainy London days. Which were many.

Her gift had been a handsome leather journal. Of course it had been selected by her newest governess, Miss Petticord and not her father, but Callie hadn't much cared, only eager to begin chronicling her life's journey.

An old, deep-seated, winged chair, a moth-eaten Aubusson rug, and a brass carriage lamp with a broken pane, cobbled together to create her little oasis. Right at home among all the castoffs. After all, wasn't she just another?

She'd needed a table to begin her writing. After

poking around, she discovered an exquisite ladies' writing desk hidden beneath a dusty Holland cover. Perfect.

Moving the piece had proved harder than expected. Her hand slipped and the drawer had slid open, nearly crashing to the floor.

Inside, she spied a few stray hair pins, a broken fan, and beneath them, a stack of writing paper.

Antonia Ainsworth—

Her mother! Callie ran a fingertip over the raised letters, and then held the paper to her lips, as if she might summon her beloved mamma. She breathed deep, but only smelled the musk of neglect. She laid the papers aside.

What other treasures might the desk contain? Digging into the very corner, her fingers found a hard, smooth oval.

Could it be?

Her breath caught as she pulled it out, its long chain sliding against the drawer's wooden bottom.

Yes!

Her mother's golden locket.

Callie remembered as a young child grabbing the shiny object as it swung over her mother's breast on its long, chain, and her mother gently prying it from her fingers.

Why would her mother have left such a treasure? Callie had never seen her mother without the trinket. The broken chain perhaps? No, now she remembered, the last time she had seen the locket it had been clenched in her father's hand.

Callie carried it to her lamp. A dull tarnish covered both the chain and oval case.

She used the edge of her sleeve to polish the metal, an engraving—

Only True Love.

With trembling hands, she sprung the lock, so eager to discover some new secret of her mother.

Nestled inside she'd found a braid of hair, one strand copper-red, the other two, white-blond.

The red must be her mother's—too deep a red to be Callie's. But the blond? Not her father's, his was coal black.

Would Gerald Ainsworth have given his wife such a gift? The heartfelt inscription seemed so unlike the father she knew.

If not her father, then who?

A handsome, young man who had taken her mother all over the world—to places where she could not bring a young daughter? Callie had clasped the token to her breast, imagining this beautiful couple stealing into the house to gaze longingly upon Callie sleeping, and then disappearing with the dawn's light.

Only True Love...

Yes, Mamma, she had whispered and then kissed a golden oval as a sort of benediction. *I will only have true love.*

Using one of the hair pins to secure the chain, she'd hung the locket around her neck.

"Miss," Edgar, the footman, stood at the now open doorway.

Callie had looked up surprised. No one ever bothered her up here. Not since Miss Petticord, after a few skirmishes, had finally understood if she stayed out of Callie's way, Callie would stay out of hers. A good bargain all around.

"Your father would see you in his study, now."

And her father never called her to his study.

When she entered, he was reviewing some papers. She waited for several minutes.

He seemed uncharacteristically lost in thought. When he finally looked up his eyes were glassy. He hastily covered the papers with another document and rubbed his eyes.

He stood, his hands flexing by his sides. His gaze dropped to the locket and then snapped back to her face. "Where did you find that?"

She raised her chin. "In the attic hidden away, with my mother's things. It was hers, wasn't it?"

He said nothing, but he didn't need to. His demeanor told it all.

"I want to wear it."

Her father looked as if he would forbid it. But to her surprise, he turned away without speaking. He laid a hand on the rain-streaked windowpane, rested his forehead on it and closed his eyes.

She started to leave the room thinking she was dismissed, but remembered she'd been summoned and her curiosity made her ask, "Why did you call me here, sir?"

He turned back to her as if he hadn't a clue as to what she was talking about. Then he seemed to mentally shake himself.

"I am going to remarry."

Callie had known this was coming. Indeed, she'd often wondered why it had taken so long for her father, who made no secret of desperately wanting a son, to choose a new bride. Gerald Ainsworth was still fit and, she supposed, rather handsome. Certainly, he had enough money to attract even the *crème de la crème*, if the lady were desperate enough.

Still, Callie had felt blindsided with the declaration. "Who?"

"No one you would know. A lady named Hermione Semple. We will marry in a week's time, next Tuesday."

Shocked at the timing, but not surprised that her father would never have thought to at least introduce his only daughter to his betrothed before planning to marry. Still the news stung. Callie started to leave the room once again but stopped and turned back. Clasping the locket she'd asked, "Why now?"

"What?" her father barked, his eyebrows rising at her forwardness.

Callie stepped up to his desk. Something was not right. She reached for the papers he'd laid there.

Her father lurched forward, but his desk was huge and she, determined. He stepped back, resigned.

Feeling oddly victorious, Callie scanned the top sheet of heavy velum—a special marriage license. She tossed it aside revealing—

A death certificate.

Antonia Dorthea Ainsworth. In the year of our Lord, September 15th, eighteen hundred—and fifty.

The words swam as she blinked her eyes, seeking to make sense of the date.

Only a fortnight ago?

She looked up at her father but when he remained implacable, wild, pent-up rage welled up within her.

She screamed, skirting around the desk to get at her father. Desperate to rake her nails into his stoney face. To make him feel!

He stood there utterly still as she pummeled his

body, tearing at his cravat and lapels.

"No-o-o-o! No-o-o-!"

She was pulled away. A footman—Edgar, she thought—but she was so blind with rage, it could have been anyone.

She'd raved against the bands of his arms, but he was tall and strong. Finally, her throat raw and body spent, she sagged in his arms.

"Let her go," her father's voice. "And leave us."

When the arms released her, she collapsed to the floor.

He waited until she sat up, wiping her eyes and nose with her sleeve, heedless of the expensive silk.

"My mother—she was alive all this while?"

Silence, for the longest time. Then finally—

"Yes."

That one syllable, a knife in her heart.

"But now she's dead?"

"Yes. Dead."

He stood there, ram-rod straight as if he were facing a firing squad.

"Why?" The one word croaked from her mouth. "Why? She repeated, stronger now.

At first, she thought he would not answer. Then he said, "I thought it best."

She shook her head in disbelief. "You thought it best to keep my mother from me?"

He closed his eyes. Again, she did not think he meant to answer. She was just about to repeat the question when he stood straighter and looked her in the eye. "Yes, I thought it best."

She pulled herself up from the floor, needing to see his face to comprehend such heartlessness. "You thought it best that she never return to be the mother I so wanted and needed? Or, that I might go to her?"

He flinched as if she had slapped him. His gaze dropped from her tear-stained face to her chest. Only then did she remember the locket around her neck. She touched it now, and her father closed his eyes, and then turned away once again looking out the window.

She had been dismissed. But the set of his shoulders and his raised chin spoke to her more than any further explanation could. The interview was over.

She'd looked at his still-handsome profile. It had never occurred to her that there had been a colossal impediment as to why her father hadn't remarried. Callie'd made up stories how he had loved her mother so much, he could not bear to replace her. But even with her vivid imagination, she could not make that fantasy ring true.

He couldn't because her mother had been alive. And, God knows, he would never suffer the shame of divorce.

She looked at the papers on his desk—the marriage license and the death certificate. An inkwell lay on its side, black ink soaking into the heavy velum. His pens, scattered, the blotter on the floor.

A mess. She had made a mess in her father's inner sanctum, just as he had made a mess of her childish fantasies…

"Here we are," her father's voice interrupted her memory.

The carriage turned into the gates of Ryeland Park. Callie looked over at her father as they made their way around the fountain toward the chapel. Nearly the same distinguished profile as that terrible day, just a few more lines and gray side whiskers.

She closed her eyes. Her wedding day...

She should be wearing her locket, with her mother by her side, marrying a man she loved—

Once again, the death of childish wishes...

****

Though the chapel's aisle could be no more than twenty feet long, it might as well have been five miles. The heavy scent of Hermione's prized gardenias and roses filled the stilted air. Callie swallowed, praying her stomach would settle. Her hand strayed to the neckline of her makeshift wedding gown. Panic rose and quickly died. Again, she'd forgotten.

Only True Love.

Would she ever wear the locket again?

The Chantilly veil provided a gauzy cocoon, making the world outside appear a hazy dream. Yet, here, unmistakably, at the end of forever, stood the viscount.

For on this June morning, he certainly appeared every inch, Viscount Clifford. Ramrod straight, his hands clasped behind his back, he stood as if reporting for some loathsome duty instead of his nuptials. Sun-kissed hair, now darkened with pomade, lay sleek against his head. The points of his snow-white collar crisp, a froth of fine lace at his neck, the wink of some gem nestled within its artfully layered folds a sparkling contrast to the dark midnight-blue of his super-fine morning coat. She could not tell if his eyes were fixed on her or somewhere just over her left shoulder.

The music wound down and stopped as she and her father approached the altar. Someone coughed in the ensuing silence. The sound seemed to jerk the viscount out of his stupor. He nodded once to her father, again as if in response to some silent order, and then turned to face the vicar.

I'm right sorry. His words when she had accepted his proposal.

Only he hadn't proposed, not really.

The vicar—Mr. Holland, if she remembered correctly—began to speak. "Dearly beloved...If any man has just cause...Brendan Christopher Cavanaugh, do you take...Love, cherish, obey...Till death."

"I will." His voice was strong, almost harsh in contrast to the soft cadence of Mr. Holland.

The vicar continued in his sing-song tones.

Twenty-four candles on the altar's left side. Now the right... Twenty-one, twenty-two. Number twenty-three shuttered with a puff of breeze, threatening to extinguish itself. She gripped her prayer book, willing it to remain lit—

The lulling voice had stopped. Utter silence. She glanced from the lit tapers to Mr. Holland. Apparently, she must respond.

"I will," she guessed. And then looked directly into her soon-to-be husband's oh-so-green eyes.

He stood straighter as if the two words she had spoken were a heavy yoke about his neck.

I will.

It was done. She had promised. Vowed before all assembled and God to love him—

Only True Love.

But there was no love between them, other than the physical kind.

Could there be? Could the attraction grow into something meaningful? Could a child forge a bond of love between its parents?

Loving the child would be easy. Ever since the pregnancy had been confirmed, a fierce love had been brewing within her. Her hand now strayed to her belly dozens of times a day. Not even a tiny bulge yet, but this unknown being had already inspired an overwhelming sense of protection in her.

She thought she understood her mother better now. The pull a child could have upon your soul. The price of having this miracle. Callie had resigned herself to being a spinster, but if she must marry, it would only be for love. Real love.

What a terrible irony, that she had unwittingly followed in her mother's footsteps—caught not by marital love, but the love of a mother for her child.

Yet, looking into her soon-to-be husband's eyes, her vow was not entirely a lie. Well, perhaps the obey part. But she did care for him, too.

How could she not? He had taken her in, just like all the others, with his effortless charm, with his lust for life. But what was worse, she thought she saw who he really was at his core, deep down beneath the layers of bravado and charm. Saw the child who had put on a brave face, thumbing his nose at a father who had never cared for him. And a mother who had spent all her love chasing after a man who was incapable of giving it and so had nothing left for her children.

"I pronounce you man and wife."

He lifted her veil. Her gauzy world suddenly focused into stark relief, his beautiful face only inches away. The pads of his gloved thumbs touched her cheeks, his fingers at her temples as he bent to kiss her mouth. The cool press of his lips against hers. So utterly tender. So entirely different from the last kiss they had shared, weeks ago in the dark of her cottage when his tongue had thrust hot and wet.

He pulled away, his green gaze seeking, hopeful.

He offered her his arm. Before taking it, she looked back to the altar. The candle still burned. It had not gone out.

Chapter Thirteen

Finally over, all the wedding folderol. Getting the special license. Signing the settlements saying who gets what and where it'd all end up after he passed. And parading down the aisle in church, her in all her finery, he in his best suit. Staring all the while at boots shined by a man whose sole job it was to take care of only his clothes. When the fella'd tried to fasten up his britches, Bren'd nearly flung him into the middle of next week.

Everyone had trooped back over to the Grange for the wedding breakfast. He'd never set foot in the place before today. Cold and formal. So English.

This was his new life now. This valet. This peerage. These estates.

And this woman. His wife.

Agnes and Rose valiantly played their surprise ditty, children running riot about them all the while. Mr. Ainsworth ready to snatch them up and tan their hides. Nora and Farren trying to shush and corral them. Quite a circus, one he would have thoroughly enjoyed if it weren't *his* circus. He nodded, smiled and drank deep.

Applause broke over the company, and Rosie and Agnes stood and bobbed their curtsies.

Callie hurried over, thanking them for such a lovely gift. He took his cue and followed.

"That was just the best jig I ever heard!" he offered. "Thank you, ladies!"

"We did a much better job when we practiced at home early this morning," Agnes said, judiciously.

"Well, you did have a fair amount of competition this afternoon," Callie said, as she took each of their hands. "I particularly enjoyed how light a touch you both have and how you listened so closely to each other. Most impressive."

Heck, she knew just the right thing to say. Not praising overmuch, but honest in her appreciation. So much better than his ham-fisted compliment.

"My ma used to play the fiddle right well," he heard himself say. "We kids loved to listen to her of an evening."

Rosie looked up at him with eager interest. "Did you ever play, Pop—pa?"

Poppa. Though she stumbled over the name— Poppa—now that was real music to his ears. Made him wish he could say yes.

"Naw. Your Uncle Farren tried. He was always wanting to make a good impression on our ma. But what was heaven in her hands turned t'a bunch of caterwaulin' noise in his."

Ah! He earned smiles.

He watched as Rosie shadowed Callie about the grand room. He wished he could join them, insert himself into this new friendship that Callie seemed to form with such ease. She took his daughter's hand without a thought as she laughed at something Rose said. Why couldn't he be that comfortable with his own child? Too dang full of guilt, most like.

He hung about the side of the room until the cake had been eaten, the champagne drunk, the toasts made, and finally the goodbyes said to the Ainsworths.

Miss Helena wept as she threw herself into her sister's arms. "Oh, Cal, you were so lovely today! I am sure you and Clifford will be happy—you must!"

Callie gently peeled herself away and smiled, touching her sister's cheeks. "That is my plan, my dearest. And you know how I like to accomplish what I have set out to do."

They'd piled into carriages headed back to Ryeland. Nora had admonished several of the children for wanting to ride with him and Callie, but Callie only laughed and said, the more the merrier. He was just as happy not to be alone even on the short journey back to the Park.

Nora and the children had all gone to bed. And Rosie had given them both kisses and taken herself off as well.

"Callie, why don't you go on up too. I'll just let you get—settled—and then I'll be along shortly."

His bride nodded once, looking rather weary. Maybe he'd be in luck for once and she'd be asleep by the time he joined her...

Hells bells, he was scared witless of this skinny woman with the capacity to lay him flat with her perfect blue eyes.

He turned back to Farren. "One more?" He headed for the whisky bottle, not waiting for an answer.

Farren raised an eyebrow.

"Aw, come on, one more. I can't go up until she performs—well, whatever ladies do."

Farren snorted and then nodded. "One. A short one." He held up two fingers, indicating an inch.

They settled back with their drinks, both staring silently into the waning coals of the fire. They had no need to talk; Bren knew his brother was wishing him well and hoping this marriage might make him happy, finally.

"Bren," Farren sat forward, his drink held lightly between his fingers. "Last evening, after the dinner—"

"I know. I shouldn't have ducked out of the party, but I just needed some time to myself. Telling Callie about Rosie, and—well, I want to make a go of this, Farr. She's remarkable. So dang smart." He looked up at the ceiling, as if imagining Callie up there waiting for him. "I just need a chance to get my feet under me. I need to start fresh."

Farren looked as if he wanted to say more and then stopped himself. He reached out and touched Bren's knee and squeezed.

His brother's gesture surprised him. They usually didn't touch each other except for teasing punches or slaps on the back.

"I will do anything in my power to help you find peace and fulfillment," Farren said when Bren gave him a questioning look. "I want you to have what I have."

And then he squeezed Bren's knee once more before setting his unfinished drink aside and rising. "And, that being said, I reckon I'll go on up and see if Nora's awake."

"Land sakes, Farr, she's about near ready to pop. That can't be safe?"

"Ah, big brother, you have much to learn," Farren said smiling down at him. "I bid you a good night."

"Goodnight, then."

Should he have one more? The whiskey glinted deep amber in its bottle. His old friend. His liquid courage.

Lands, she had been a sight in all her wedding finery, her veil hiding her eyes.

Yet when he had bent to kiss her at the end of the ceremony, her cheeks had been wet with tears.

She had wanted love.

The bottle was in his hand, the stopper out.

Naw, best not. Couldn't only think of his own needs, not anymore. He had a nearly grown daughter, another child on the way, a title. And now a wife.

A wife who was waiting for him upstairs.

The whisky stayed in the bottle and his feet found their way to the door of his bedchamber.

Nora had wanted to move out of the grand chambers reserved for the viscount and his viscountess, but Bren wouldn't have it. Why disturb everyone when they would be perfectly content in his room here in the west wing. Quiet there at the back of the house, and a pretty view of the gardens to boot.

But now he began to second guess his decision. Would Callie care who had what room?

Not that any chamber in Ryeland Park could be called inferior. Heck, his bed—a behemoth with fancy curtains and gilt curlicues—stood nearly as grand as the one in the master's chamber.

Guess it was more the notion that *any* bed would feel odd, sharing it with a wife. How much better to be back in Callie's cabin on the tiny bedstead with its faded quilt.

Still, he probably should have consulted her about the bedchambers. A husband asked his wife about household matters, didn't he?

Should he knock? He shoved his hands through his hair and then tried to flatten it back down. He wiped his hand on his trousers, shifted the candle and wiped the other one.

Shit. Just go on in!

He turned the knob and pushed open the door.

"Me-e-e-o-ow!"

Bren nearly dropped his candle.

Gulliver. He had forgotten Callie had brought her cat to Ryeland.

Gully butting Bren's legs eased his nerves. He bent and ruffled the cat's head. Gulliver immediately rolled to expose his belly, a glutton for attention—something Bren totally understood. He had yet to look at the bed. When he did it was empty.

She stood by the window, her flame hair a cascade of rippling waves down her back. She had left it loose, as it had been that first evening they'd met.

His cock bobbed its approval.

This wing of the house had not yet been fitted with gas jets. The firebox still held a few glowing embers, and candles shed halos of light on either side of the bed.

Gulliver stretched, yawned, and then settled himself on a footstool in front of the fire, already seeming right at home.

The little speech he had prepared—*I told myself I would never get myself into a marriage where there was no esteem. I swear to you here today I will try to honor and respect you. I will try to be a better man. To at least aspire to be the man you deserve. And our child deserves*—hung heavy on his tongue.

"I reckon you must be done in," he heard himself say instead.

She turned from the window to face him head on.

"Sweet Jesu." A fancy silken wrapper, tied loosely at her waist. And clear as a May sky, nothing beneath it.

"I know you had a full life before we met. You have traveled, lived through a war, experienced real tragedy. Had other women." This last part she tacked on like a hasty afterthought. He was so dang nervous, the hope she might be just a tad jealous stifled any grin. "You are much more—experienced—than I. But I am hoping we will be able to build trust. We may not have love, but I would ask you for honesty. And to give me a chance to be a wife, a mother, and—your lover. I would like you to give me that chance." She sniffed, a sort of period to her little speech.

"Give *you* a chance?" He shook his head. "You're the one getting the runt's share, Callie. I want to set my past aside as well. I want to try to begin again."

"Good, then we are in agreement." She nodded her head once and then cleared her throat. "I would like to proceed with the lover part." She ignored his gawp. "I've been waiting very patiently to do this again, and you will not put me off."

"Well, dang," was all he could manage.

What took his fancy valet at least forty-five minutes to accomplish this morning took Bren about forty-five seconds to undo this evening.

She only had to pull the slick belt of her robe and let it slide down her body. Blessedly, she waited until she had his full attention before doing so.

He could have stood there and ogled her beauty for—well, another forty-five or so seconds, if he weren't so darned hot for her. But he was across the floor and had her in his arms in less than one.

He hissed as his hot length met the cool, satin skin of her belly—

Her belly.

Damn it all! He jerked away from her. "Is this safe?"

"Every book I have read says that sexual congress while with child is permitted." She reached down for him, using both hands to grasp his cock. "And while you

161

are apparently on the larger side when it comes to the male appendage"—she spanned her hands and then flexed her fingers against him— "that should not be of concern, either."

"Well, don't that beat all? I never thought I'd be so glad to marry a dang blue stocking!"

"I thought we'd start with me on top and then move on from there."

Chapter Fourteen

Two weeks later

Bren stepped outside, dragging in a deep breath of fresh air. The scent of damp earth and clipped hedges grounded him, but it didn't loosen the knot in his chest.

Farren was right behind him, boots crunching on the gravel. "You'll get the hang of it, Bren. Kincade's just used to my way of doing things," he said, voice smooth, reassuring.

Bren let out a rough exhale. He'd sat through Farren's meeting with Ryeland's steward, drowning in figures and ledgers. Numbers flipped, letters tangled. It was like school all over again—frustrating, impossible.

"It's no use, Farr. I can't do it. Better you take the reins, and I take Callie back to Scotland."

Farren folded his arms. "Bren, Ryeland Park isn't mine. It's yours. And maybe your wife will have something to say about running off again so soon."

Running off...

Bren forced a grin. "Callie? Naw, she's my Woodland Witch. She'll be happier in Scotland. Misses her mushrooms and critters, I expect."

Only... would she? He hadn't asked. Hadn't dared.

Farren rocked back on his heels, staring at the gravel. "You're not running."

Bren huffed a laugh. "Naw. Just choosing a different

path." He clapped Farren on the shoulder. "Don't worry about me. Or Callie. We'll manage at Kinduggan. Maybe a few cobwebs to fend off, a ghost or two to keep us on our toes, but we'll manage."

"Ghosts?" Farren gave an uneasy chuckle.

No. Not ghosts. Not the kind that rattled chains and moaned in the night.

The kind that whispered *you don't belong here.*

Bren swallowed down the thought and smirked. "I'm only joshin'." He punched Farren's arm. "But if a haint's taken up residence, Callie'll make short work of it. She's magic." He said it lightly, but the words tasted bitter. His easy teasing just a mask over the inferiority gnawing at him.

"If you'd just give yourself a chance—"

"Farr, let me have this." More bite in his voice than he liked. He took another breath, slower this time. "Give me a chance to know my wife without having to play the damned viscount too."

Farren studied him for a long moment, then offered a faint, reluctant smile.

Bren turned away before he caught even a flicker of pity. He looked out over the estate—his estate. *Hell.*

Squaring his shoulders, he faced his brother again. "It's only for a few weeks. A couple of months at most. Then I'll be ready to face the *haute ton*. I promise."

Farren met his gaze, searching for something, then nodded.

They turned to look out over the land. Bren was sure Farr saw opportunity, and promise, while he saw only endless responsibility. Give him the woods any day.

"Bren, there's something I've been meaning to tell you. The evening before you got married—" He hesitated, uncharacteristically tongue-tied.

Bren arched a brow. "What is it, little brother? Don't tell me you're about to offer marital advice?"

Farren snorted. "Ha! Give *you* advice? I know better than that. You're as contrary as they come."

"Contrary as a Missouri mule."

"Naw, it's just—"

A footman appeared at the garden entrance. "Lord Clifford, pardon for the interruption, but you've a caller."

Farren stiffened, like he'd stepped a mite too close to a rattler.

Bren's grin widened, covering the flicker of unease in his gut. "Whoa there, little brother, no need to shy. Probably just another dog-and-pony show. Folks wanting to gawk at the American rube turned peer of the realm, and his unconventional, spinster bride." Yet another reason he needed to get out of England.

The footman hesitated. "Lady Clifford asks that you join her in the drawing room."

Bren clapped a hand on Farren's shoulder. "Come on in with me, Farr."

"Bren, I need to—"

"Come on, it can wait. Didn't you say a husband is supposed to support his bride?" A slow grin stretched across his face. "And I've got the sudden itch to put these posers in their place."

Farren hesitated, looking like a man who'd swallowed a bad oyster. Bren didn't give him the chance to argue, waving off the footman and heading to the drawing room.

The door stood part way opened. Bren held out a staying hand to his brother.

"Lady Clifford."

The voice alone was enough to conjure an image—haughty, severe, wrapped in lace and stiff-backed propriety. Bren peeked into the drawing room, just as Farren sagged against the doorframe.

"Where were you keeping yourself all these years past?" the old biddy demanded. "I am sure we are all eager to know." She waved a hand over the sparse gathering, as if an entire *salon* of rapt guests hung on her every word, rather than just two spindly women who had to be her daughters—identical in their sharp noses and even sharper eyes.

"I lived in a cottage in the Highlands, Lady Trunket," Callie answered easily, no hesitation.

"Indeed!" Lady Trunket's turkey neck disappeared into the ruffle at her throat.

"I had no plans to marry and so thought to indulge my own wishes—with my parents' blessing, of course."

"You are very... modern."

Bren bit back a grin, watching his Callie-girl run circles around the old bird. Almost made him forget, for a moment, what a fraud of a viscount he was.

Straightening, he stepped into the room, throwing on his easy confidence—too late realizing he hadn't changed his coat. The snug fit across his shoulders made him feel like a boy in borrowed clothes. And his cravat? Hell, he should've stopped at one of the fifty mirrors in this house to tidy it up.

"Lady Trunket, Miss Trunket, and Miss Mary Trunket," Callie introduced smoothly. "May I present Lord Clifford and Colonel Cavanaugh."

He and Farren bowed in unison.

Lady Trunket's gaze flitted between them,

assessing. It took her mere seconds to decide where her favor lay. Her eyes softened, chin lifting in satisfaction as she inclined her head toward Farren.

"Viscount Clifford," she pronounced, her voice rich with approval. "How delighted we are to finally meet you! What a relief it must be to leave the colonies behind and take your rightful place in England."

Farren's lips twitched, but before he could open his mouth, Bren shot him a look that said, *Let it play out.*

"At last, Ryeland Park will be in the hands of a viable viscount," Lady Trunket continued.

Her daughters nodded in eerie unison, their thin-lipped smiles barely qualifying as polite.

"After all, these lands require proper stewardship."

Bren flashed her a grin, all charm. "Do they now? And here I thought Ryeland required crops and sheep."

Lady Trunket blinked, her lips pressing tighter. Bren felt, rather than saw, Callie suppress a smile from her place by the hearth.

A hush settled over the gathering, all three ladies' gazes shifting to him, raking over every inch. Lady Trunket squinted, lifting her quizzing glass as if searching for something but coming up empty.

Bren nodded toward Farren. "You've got a good eye, Lady Trunket. Alike as we are, my brother here is the very picture of a gentleman."

She sniffed. "Quite so."

Farren turned to him. "Bren, you really ought to tell her."

"Oh, I'd hate to contradict a lady," Bren said, tilting his head toward Lady Trunket. "Especially one so certain."

The pinch at the edges of the old biddie's mouth

deepened. "What are you implying?"

"Only that my brother's done well, hasn't he?" Bren said lightly. "Holding things together while I was in the States, trying to keep myself from the firing squad."

Lady Trunket's brows knitted. "Firing squad?"

Farren exhaled, stepping forward. "My lady, I fear—"

She held up a gloved hand, cutting him off, her attention locking onto Bren. She studied him as one might an unruly hound that had wandered inside and was eyeing the finer furniture. "Ah, the famous younger brother, back from gallivanting around the continent. I suppose it is good that you have come home as well. I trust the viscount will be a stable influence on you."

Across the room, Callie sat with her tea, her gaze bright with amusement. The warmth he saw in her eyes steadied something deep in Bren's chest.

He inclined his head. "Aye, I'm learning. But then, I find expectations can be rather tedious, don't you?"

Lady Trunket looked as though she'd bitten into an Indian turnip.

"Lucky, ain't I, to have so much help?" he continued. "My younger brother's the real farmer of the two of us. And Lady Clifford—well, I reckon she's a true expert in all things genteel."

Callie set her teacup down with a smile. "Indeed. My husband is too modest. I believe he manages... awkward situations rather well."

Lady Trunket's mouth worked for a moment, her gaze bouncing between Callie, Farren, and Bren. "Your husband, Lady Clifford?"

"Yes. I fear, Lady Trunket, you've made a small *faux pas*."

Silence stretched between them, taut and brittle. Bren relished the discomfort a bit more than he probably should.

Lady Trunket's lips parted, her gaze darting to Bren, searching for confirmation of this absurdity.

Bren stepped forward and offered an exaggerated bow, his grin widening, though in truth, the joke was beginning to wear thin. "Brendan Cavanaugh, Viscount Clifford, at your service, ma'am."

A strangled sound escaped Lady Trunket. Across the room, Callie snorted.

"An easy mistake, your ladyship," Bren said, forcing a charm into his tone he was far from feeling, but it hid the unease creeping up his spine. "Heck, we used to bedevil our teachers all the time, didn't we, Farren, you pretending to be me, and me trying to imitate you."

The flicker of dismay was brief, but there it was— that moment where she struggled to reckon her world to this new and atrocious fact.

"I do hope you'll pardon me, your ladyship, for having a bit of a jest," Bren continued. "It's been a while since we've had the chance to play that particular trick. And I do like to make life a bit more exciting when I can. No use in being a pompous boor, is there?"

But even as he spoke, the truth pressed in—he might have won this round, but her ladyship's initial assessment was dead to rights.

Farren *would* make a far better viscount. Bren was just an imposter, struggling to squeeze into a title that fit him as ill as his too-tight coat.

****

Bren lay in bed, hands folded behind his head, watching as Callie brushed out her hair. He thought about offering to do it for her—he loved the silky weight of it in his hands—but decided watching was better. The rhythmic strokes of the brush soothed him in a way he couldn't quite explain.

"You handled Lady Trunket brilliantly today," she said at last as she glanced at him in the mirror, lips curving.

"Did I?" He felt a momentary glow at her praise, but truth snuffed it quick enough. "She thought Farr was the viscount."

"A reasonable mistake." Another long, deliberate stroke through her hair.

"A sight too reasonable."

"You are identical." She finally laid the brush down and rose to cross to the bed.

He didn't want to talk. He just wanted to bury himself inside her and forget. To hear the unique music of her little gasps and moans, and then out-and-out cries.

Lively and inventive, his wife. These first few days of marriage, when he pressed into her body, she never held back her exuberance, letting him know exactly what she liked. And gol darn, she liked a whole passel!

The sweet utter completeness he felt after the act— such a deep and abiding peace, and yet so dad gum frightening—was becoming even more important than the lovemaking itself. How the two feelings could exist within his breast, he could not fathom. But he knew it to be true. He couldn't imagine a day when he'd tire of loving her.

As if, for the first time in his life, he truly belonged somewhere.

Callie pulled the tie of her robe, and the silk shushed down her arms. She caught it just before it hit the floor, laying it neatly at the foot of the bed. He smirked. Why she bothered to put the darn thing on in the first place, he'd never know. It always ended up on the floor.

He reached for her, pulling her down onto the bed beside him and stroking a hand over her arm, her flank.

"I've been meaning to tell you, Helena knows about the baby," she murmured as she curled against his side.

His fingers stilled on her skin.

"I had to tell her," she said, propping herself on one elbow. "She'd hatched some romantic scheme to elope with Martin Henshaw and take me along. Wanted to save me from a loveless marriage."

Callie bit her lip, as if regretting that last part slipping out.

Bren exhaled slowly. Well. It was only the truth.

"Right," he said after a beat. He squeezed her hand. "I haven't told anyone. Not even Farren, though he usually knows my thoughts before I do." He hesitated. "Nora might suspect. She's perceptive that way."

Callie nodded. "I think, though, it's best we don't tell Rose. At least, not quite yet."

"I'll leave that to you," he said, tracing a slow path along her arm. "Still early days?"

"Yes. Early days."

His hand drifted lower, but she caught it. "Speaking of Rose…"

Bren stilled.

"I need to know what happened to her."

His body tensed as if bracing for a blow.

"Mari mentioned that Rose was one of the charity children," she continued, searching his face. "That she was… special. If I'm to be a mother to her, I need to understand."

Be her mother… How wonderful that sounded. Could they be a real family? Could he be the father Rose deserved?

He was the very last person to fill his wife in on his daughter's life. He inhaled deeply through his nose, as if air might wash his soul. "Nora would know. She's the one who finally tracked Rosie down, not me. Leave it to a woman, to sort out the truth."

"What can *you* tell me? I understand Nora found you and Rose at this charity home?"

Dang it. She wouldn't let this go.

He sighed. "It's a long story."

"I happen to have time," she offered quietly.

He shoved his fingers through his hair. Could he put her off? Naw, Callie and her questions, he could only dodge them for so long.

"I spent nearly a year trying to find her," he said at last. "I knew Lily was… gone." His throat tightened. He never spoke of Lily. "But Rodger Milton found me first. Locked me in the cellar of his 'charity home' for months. I had no idea my girl was just upstairs the whole time."

Callie paled. "Why was she special?"

Bren gave a humorless chuckle. "Milton had *chosen* her. Just like he'd chosen Nora to be his wife—his perfect little family." His jaw clenched. "Sick bastard."

Callie squeezed his hand. "I'm so sorry. For you. For Rose. And for Lily…"

He swallowed hard. Confession felt like taking a dose of castor oil—probably did some good, but tasted damn awful going down.

After a long silence, Callie shifted, snuggling into his side.

Ah, now he could lose himself in her. He started to

cover her body.

"So… when were you going to tell me you wanted to return to Scotland?"

He pulled away from her. "What?"

She laid her hand on his chest. "Nora mentioned it. Assumed I already knew."

Bren winced. Dang. He'd meant to tell her—*ask* her—right after the wedding. But he supposed he wasn't used to consulting a wife. Not to mention the fact that she'd probably put up a stink.

He gave her a sheepish look. "I was thinking we might go back, for a sort of honeymoon. Back to our roots." He watched her face carefully as she absently traced circles around his left nipple. "My grandfather still has that spread near the Belcher farm. You may recall, I was headed there when I met a certain woodland witch who stole my heart."

He caught her hand—so damn distracting—and pressed a kiss to her palm. "So, what do you say?"

She was going to say no. He'd abide by it. He had no right to drag her off again just because *he* wanted to disappear.

"I know it's a lot to ask," he added quickly. "You've only just reunited with Helena, and I'm asking you to leave her again. But it would only be for a month or so—"

"Yes," she said.

Bren blinked. "Yes?"

She pulled her hand from his and went back to touching him. "I think it's a *very* sound idea."

He had already opened his mouth, to give her another reason to go—but damn if his wife wasn't full of surprises.

Before he could say anything else, she straddled him, warm and soft and suddenly *everywhere*.

"Well," he murmured, voice rough, hands settling on her waist. "That's settled, then."

Her hands slid over his chest, teasing. "Now that we've finished talking…" She leaned in, her breath warm against his lips. "I want you."

God above, but he would never get tired of hearing that.

He flipped her onto her back with a growl, stealing her breath with a kiss.

And for this moment, at least, there was nothing but her.

****

Saying goodbye to Rosie was something he could not avoid. Best get it over and done with. He'd thought about asking her to come with them. But it wouldn't't've been fair. Utterly selfish to expect her to give up her home here at Ryeland with Farren and Nora and their kids. She'd begun to get past her grief over the loss of her Uncle Geoff. Why would she want to traipse up to the wilds of Scotland?

He found her in the corner of the garden devoted to Lily. She'd shown it to him with a touch of nervous pride days ago, but he'd already known it—had stood at its edge the night before his wedding, cornflowers in hand, unable to cross the threshold.

God, what he wouldn't give to turn back time.

"You've done something real lovely here. Lily'd be proud."

She smiled and ducked her head at his compliment. Her finger stroked a velvety petal. "I've added a new specimen. I think Lily would approve. White is—was—

her favorite color. It's rather showy—she preferred the delicacy of lily-of-the-valley, but it only blooms in the spring."

"Well, we'll remember come next April and plant a whole field of it."

She offered him another smile, this one more sure.

"Now then, I reckon you have heard Callie and I are going to Scotland for a bit. A few weeks. I expect you to hold down the fort here at Ryeland. Don't let Mari run roughshod. And make sure Agnes lets you have some time on the pianoforte. You play mighty pretty."

"But Poppa—"

Poppa. He'd miss hearing that. Miss her.

She flinched. "I am sorry." She shook her head. "I cannot call you Poppa."

He'd thought they were making some headway with getting closer, but he reckoned he still deserved his daughter's reticence. "That is all right, Rosie, I understand." he replied, a smile hiding his disappointment.

"No." She shook her head. "I don't think you do understand. "I called—him—Poppa." She swallowed. "I would like you to have a different name, something that is new."

Dear God, she associated Poppa with Milton. She wanted to put that evil in the past. She wanted a brand-new name for her real father. He tempered his burst of joy with what he hoped was a fatherly response. "Well, now, that sounds very reasonable, Shy Bird."

"How about Pa? You called your father by that name, I believe."

As much as he wanted to agree with anything she suggested, he had to shake his head. "Truth to tell, I don't have all that fond a memories of my pa, so if it's all the same to you, could we find another name?"

She looked up at him, not with judgement but with a shared sense of kinship. How did he deserve this miracle? He reached out to take her hand. "We'll set our brains to it and come up with just the perfect name."

She nodded.

"Now, Callie and I are expecting you to have this garden in tip top shape by the time we get back to Ryeland—'

"But I am not staying here at the Park."

His daughter looked up at him with something that bordered on mulish resolve. What could she be about?

"Now Rosie, I know Agnes has been hankering to go off to some fancy school, but I don't cotton to you leaving your family. You belong at home, with people who love you."

"Yes, I agree."

"Then what's this all about?"

"I don't reckon in Scotland they will set such store in my being born on the wrong side of the blanket."

Reckon? Set store? Then what she said hit him. Had someone been taunting her, shaming her for his mistake?

"I am coming with you and Callie. You are my father. I am your daughter. Am I wrong to assume you would want me?" She rushed on before he could form a single sentence. "I do understand you might not wish to acknowledge me publicly. But I thought—"

"Acknowledge you publicly? Oh, my Rosie gal, I reckon you should be the one worried about acknowledging me publicly!

He took her hands in his. They were so soft and white, her fingers long and elegant. "I am no one to admire." He could have left it at that, but he needed to be straight with her. She needed to know what she was signing on for.

"Here are some hard truths about your old dad. I didn't have such a grand childhood, but I brought most of my troubles on myself. It was my actions that ruined what little love we managed to have within our family. I bear the responsibility. If it weren't for your uncle, Farren—well, I don't rightly know what would have happened to me."

"But you are a hero. You have a medal given to you by the President of the United States, Mr. Grant himself."

Bile rose in Bren's throat. This beautiful young girl—a part of him—wanted to believe he was a good man. Believe he was somehow worthy.

He could tell her a tall tale, put some shine on the sordid truth. But he'd only let her down later when she saw through the gloss to the real man. He drew her down to sit on a stone bench near an arbor and sat next to her.

"The truth, darlin', is I joined the war a bit later than most. See, I was out west chasin' bank robbers with a man named Pinkerton. Plenty of excitement there, a lot of high drama, which I suppose I've always had a hankerin' for."

He'd been sitting in a bar in Deadwood when a news reader came in to read out the story of the bloody battle at Antietam. *It is estimated that nearly 23,000 men fell in the fighting, with thousands more left to suffer from their injuries.* While the man read, tears streamed down his cheeks and into his dusty beard. Even old Hugh MacIntosh, the orneriest trapper you ever saw, who never showed an ounce of emotion, wept, shaking his shaggy, white head.

"Anyway, Pinkerton left to join the North, and I decided it was high time I came on home to do my part. But I got in a terrible fight with my pa and so I told him I was going to join up with the Confederacy just to bedevil him."

Rosie sat in rapt attention, listening to his tale.

"I knew in my heart it was wrong. The notion of aiming a rifle at my other half—your Uncle Farren—well, I just couldn't do it, no matter how much I hated my Pa. I guess I wanted our nation to stay together as well. The nation, and the chance to end slavery. Those things seemed a sight more important than any war with Pa. So, I got back in touch with Pinkerton and started spying for the North."

"It must have been very dangerous," Rosie offered, her eyes wide.

"Well, you're right. Sometimes it was plumb hairy. But mostly my job was just counting."

His daughter looked at him rather dubiously.

"I know, it don't sound like much. See, I wasn't much of a soldier type fellow, but out west I was good at calculating heads of cattle. Sounds odd, but it's a gift I had. So Pinkerton put me to the task of estimating the size of Confederate troops. Most of the spies exaggerated their reports, puffing up the numbers. That made the northern generals too cautious, holding back when they should've been charging ahead. So if I could get the numbers straight, maybe we could stop all the bloodshed sooner."

Rosie nodded, her dear face so very serious.

"Sometimes, Shy Bird, the smallest things can make a big difference, even something as simple as counting heads."

He would not tell her of all the death, the rotting flesh covered in flies, on the dead as well as men still alive. The senseless waste of life. The brutality against his brothers, fellow Americans. It was enough to let his daughter know a bit about his life. The good and the bad.

"So, I'm no hero, Rosie. Your Uncle Farren is the hero in this family. He is my better half, a far better man than me. Trust me, you'll be better off with him and your Aunt Nora."

Rose turned and picked up a spent flower. She set it in her palm then closed her fingers around it. She turned back to face him, a determined look in her green eyes. "You never knew Lily. She was my better half as well. She thought she was the bad one, but she wasn't. She was the strong, good half. She took care of me. But then she was gone."

Oh, if only he could turn back time. How far would he have to go back to make things right? A very long time. Certainly, back to that summer day—a Sunday afternoon in July…

He squeezed his eyes shut, but the memories rushed in, stealing his breath.

Danger!

A flash of yellow

The smell of yeast

Sara's thin soprano voice, Shall we gather at the Ri-i-i-ver…

His Hare's Ear fly with its red silken thread and tiny gold bead

I can't lose my other half!

A small, warm hand tucked in his…

"Will you take me?"

Bren gasped for air and shook his head to clear away

the past. His Shy Bird, Rosie, had risen to stand next to him, a worried look on her sweet face. She'd taken his hand.

No matter how much Bren strove to be a better man—better father—he could never bring back the youth of his two innocent daughters, his Rosie and her Lily.

"Rosie, for sure you and Lily deserved better than you got as far as parents go." Poor words for such misery. "I left your mama with you and your sister in her belly. Now, truth to tell, I didn't know it at the time, but chances are if I had I still would've left. You see, that's what I do. I leave."

"But not anymore. You won't leave anymore."

He wanted to promise her he wouldn't. That he was committed to her, to this marriage and the new child she knew nothing about, and even this title and new way of life that was so foreign to him. He wanted to assure his Rosie he would always be by her side. But he knew himself too well. He didn't want to lie to her. He didn't want to lie to himself. Not anymore.

Another chance to be better. Another chance to make amends. How many more would God give him?

"Are you all packed, Rose?"

How long had Callie been standing there? Brendan looked between the two women—for suddenly his fifteen-year-old daughter had become a woman with a mind of her own.

He turned to his wife—his wife, the idea still new to him. "So, I reckon you knew about this all along?"

"I did. And if you had eyes in your head, you would've seen it as well."

Thank God he'd married a woman with some sense.

"I know!" Rosie rocked up to her toes her arms flapping at her sides. "I have the perfect name for you."

"Goodness, what name is this?" Callie asked looking from Rose to him.

"We have been trying to think of the perfect name for Rosie to call me." He turned to give his full attention to his daughter. "Well, don't keep us in suspense, what is it?"

"Da!"

"Da?"

"Yes. I believe that is what the Scot's call their fathers." Rosie looked as if she'd hung the moon.

And his wife, the stars.

Yep, just a slice of heaven here in his midst.

"Well, then, Da, it is!"

Chapter Fifteen

She heard the burble of a stream in the distance. The call of a mourning dove to its mate, its song low and plaintive. A slight wind ruffled the boughs of pine hanging just over her blanket. The limbs cast lacy shadows across the face of the man lying beside her. A large, blond, god-like man...

He smiled, and she smiled back, hoping his had been meant for her. Why couldn't she be sure? He was so close, yet somehow so very far away. If she reached out, could she touch him, make him real?

But she dare not.

Could she be content to only gaze at him, though? To never be held within his arms? Feel his kiss upon her lips?

No! She wanted all of him.

Her hand trembled, reaching toward his cheek—

A flurry of brightly painted wings, a fluttering murmuration, swirled about him, completely covering his body.

So beautiful!

So unsettling...

Gently she swept the butterflies aside, needing to see him again. To make him real.

The fluttering mass dispersed, revealing—

Nothing. No one. The beautiful golden man had disappeared.

Only butterflies remained. Thousands and thousands of blue and gold butterflies.

Her breath caught in her throat. Her heart fluttering too fast, faster and faster, trying but failing to keep pace with the beating of their wings.

Where had he gone?

She turned and saw him far below, now framed in an open doorway, an endless staircase spooling between them. She cried out as she rushed down the steps.

He stood silent, unmoving. But no matter how fast she ran, she could not reach him. The staircase grew longer, and longer...

Butterflies dove past her head, warping in the air, forming a fluttering curtain between them.

Impatient, she pushed them aside.

Once again, the golden man had gone.

In his place now stood a veiled woman. Butterflies swirled about her head then disappeared. All save one, which rested on the woman's breast, its jeweled wings beating like a heart.

The woman raised her head, then reached up to remove her veil—

"Mamma?" Callie whispered.

Her mother gazed straight into her daughter's eyes. But she did not hold out a hand, did not rush to embrace her.

Instead, she turned away, disappearing through the doorway—

Callie jerked upright. The rock of the train must have set her to dozing. How mortifying.

She swiped at her mouth, happy to discover her glove came away dry.

But he wasn't looking at her anyway, his gaze fixed

out the train window. She shifted her sore bum while tentatively rolling her neck.

This was not the first time she had dreamed of the veiled woman and her mamma. The image of that clandestine meeting between Bren and the unknown woman in the carriage lay heavy on her heart, manifesting in this recurring nightmare.

"Edinburgh!" The shriek of brakes punctuated the conductor's announcement.

"Callie." Brendan turned from the window. "What say we press on to Perth tonight? And then, depending on the time, we could go on up to the keep?"

What?

He read her horrified silence but continued. "Heck, it's only six. We could get to Perth by eight or so and still have three hours of daylight." He grinned. The idiot.

"There is no getting round the villagers meeting the new Viscount Clifford. Though, I suspect those who frequent The Black Swan have already had the honor."

He hung his head. She had hit on at least one of his reasons why he'd proposed hieing on to Kinduggan.

"And, besides, look at poor Rose," she continued. "The child is done in. And frankly, so am I."

His head jerked up. He looked so terribly contrite, as if he had made the worst of blunders. "Ah, heck, I never thought—"

"Please take yourself off the rack. I am as anxious to get to the keep as you, but I think it best we keep to the schedule as planned."

"Right, yes. The schedule." He nodded like a good school boy. There was something so sweet and vulnerable in his manner. Oh, did she want him right then and there.

Of course, there were only two rooms to be had at the Inn, and so Callie had suggested that she and Rose take one and Bren the other. Oh, the look of disappointment on his face. Yes, she knew the feeling, but Rose was paramount.

They got a bit of a later start than expected. Brendan, now fully immersed in his role as tour guide, had insisted they must see the famous castle before pushing on to Perth. And so they had.

"Now, folks, before we even step into the castle, you need to know about this spot we're standing on—this Castle Rock. It's not just any old hill. This is a volcanic rock, and it's been the site of a fortress for over a thousand years."

Oh, to watch his delight as he ushered his daughter around.

"And we can't forget about Mons Meg." He slapped his hand on the barrel of a huge cannon. "This thing was built in 1449, and they say it could shoot a cannonball the size of a man's head."

Rose stooped to look down the barrel. She was certainly in awe of both the castle and her Da.

When they arrived in Perth, Angus, dressed in his Sunday best, waited for them in an open carriage.

The boy jumped down from his perch. Hat in hand, hair slicked like obsidian, the boy nearly tripped as he made his bow to the ladies.

"Angus, you look well!"

He seemed to be incapable of uttering a reply. Clearly, the poor man could not reconcile Callie of the cottage with the Viscountess of the keep. And Rose looked expectant and nervous at the same time. Yes, they all seemed just a bit out of sorts.

"Aye, thank you, Miss—I mean ma'am—I mean your ladyship. Pardon. May I assist you?"

"Thank you, Angus, but I think I'd better hold on to Gulliver here. As you know, he can be cantankerous."

The boy nodded, then fell silent.

"And how are the goats? Is Floppsy still off her feed?" Angus had got his sister, Lizzy, who had some schooling, to write to her.

He nodded but then shook his head. "Nay, your ladyship. That is—" He shook his head again and squeezed his hat. "They are all in fine form. 'Cepting Tansy, who got into the garden once. But only the cabbages were lost."

Her little life… Could it have been only a few short weeks ago that she had been thoroughly immersed in her garden and snares and wandering the woods for mushrooms?

"Ah, well, I expect she regretted that a bit later."

Callie meant her reply as a little joke, but serious Angus nodded like an old sage. "Aye, she did, your ladyship, bleating and carrying on for all the world to hear."

Brendan, returning from seeing that the luggage had been loaded onto a cart, was introduced and poor Angus got flustered all over again.

Several hours later, as they approached Abernathy, Callie could see the villagers hung about in little knots in front of their cottages. Waiting. She suspected most of them had never encountered a personage as grand as a viscount.

The village was a relic of another time, its thatched cottages girdled with ivy, their windows adorned with flower boxes where house cats lounged, subtly watchful as they sunned themselves. Now and then, a tail flicked at a passing villager, as if to say, *Yes, I know I am beautiful. You may look all you like.* Indeed, they were the only creatures unimpressed by the arrival of the new Viscount Clifford and his family.

Gully stirred in his basket, whiskers twitching, but after a sleepy yawn, he settled back down. Clearly, the cost of curiosity, apparently, exceeded the reward.

On Main Street, the *Black Swan* and the medieval kirk at the lane's end were fine landmarks, but both were dwarfed by the Abernathy Round Tower. Its ancient stone loomed over the village, casting a long shadow down the street. So familiar, yet now strangely foreign as Callie gazed at it from her newly vaunted status as viscountess.

The vicar, Mr. Dougan, had made it his business to be on hand for their arrival, standing humbly by as they alighted.

Bren shoved his hands into his jacket—Callie had come to recognize it as a habit when he was nervous. But then, with the ease of a man who refused to be out of sorts for long, he flashed a roguish grin and stuck out a hand.

"Good afternoon, Mr. Dougan. I'm right pleased to meet you."

The man's head nearly collided with Bren's outreached hand as he bowed deeply. When he straightened, he looked at Bren's offering with some horror, as if he had not the least idea of how to navigate such a greeting. Sense won over and he duly pumped Bren's hand.

"Lord Clifford, we are so pleased your family has come back to the neighborhood. It has been so long since the keep has been occupied. Such a tragedy about the young master, Lord Geoffrey. And may I offer my sincere condolences on his passing this earthly realm. And of course, that of your grandsire as well. I never had the pleasure of meeting either of them, but there are a few still in the village who have very fond memories of them both."

"Thank you, Mr. Dougan. That is right kind of you. I reckon you must already be acquainted with my wife?"

Callie had encountered the vicar on a number of occasions while visiting the village. He'd always been polite, but it was clear he had not quite known what to make of her. Indeed, most of the village had treated her with varying degrees of discomfort. Some, like Angus, offering a tentative friendship, others only disdain.

"Lady Clifford, may I offer my felicitations." The vicar bowed again. Callie nodded and smiled. Mr. Dougan had tried mightily to find out her history when she had first arrived in the village years ago. Who could blame him? As shepherd of his flock, he needed to know if he should shun her or embrace her into the fold. She had toyed with styling herself as a spinster, but could not abide a lie. In the end she told him she was here to rest her nerves—not a lie at the time—and to write a book. Not a lie either, at the time.

Rose hung back, standing next to the carriage. "Ah, Rosie, come and meet Mr. Dougan!" Bren held out his hand to her and she came forward. "This is my daughter, Rose Cavanaugh."

"How do you do, Miss Cavanaugh?" If the vicar had any questions about how a girl of nearly sixteen fit into their little family, he did not give one hint. The vicar immediately rose in Callie's estimation.

Rose bobbed a curtsy. "I am well, thank you, sir."

A sibilant hiss of whispers rose from many of the bystanders. No doubt they were attempting to place a near grown woman into the Clifford family.

"I see you found your way in the end, your lordship."

A giant of a man with a shock of white hair stepped out from a group in front of the Black Swan. Orin Frasier, the publican. His grin as broad as his shoulders.

"Ha!" Bren slapped his thighs before hailing the barman. "I reckon I did. Much obliged to you for the directions, even though you sent me down a few sidetracks along the way. But, as you can see, it was worth it." He turned to Callie and took her hand as if she were the prize at the end of his meandering journey.

"Led by the fairies, you were, Lord Clifford," Fraiser said, his eyes twinkling.

The vicar snorted his disapproval, his expression one of long-suffering patience. Callie could almost hear the sermon forming in his mind about the dangers of drink, loose company, and idle hands.

Bren, unconcerned, turned back to the gathered villagers. "Next time I'm in the village, I'll stand you all a whiskey as my thanks!"

A cheer went up, and Callie bit the inside of her cheek. He was far too comfortable here, too easy among the rougher men of Abernathy.

"I will just duck into the livery stable to say a quick howdo to my ol' pal Verlan, who I must thank as well for his part in leading me to my future bride."

As Bren strode off to the stables, a little girl pulled away from her mamma and stood in front of Callie and Rose, a posey of flowers in her hand.

"Oh, thank you, my dear. These are just lovely, aren't they Rose?" Callie said, accepting the bouquet of Bell heather.

Rose gave a tentative smile and nodded.

A woman joined the little girl and sunk into a deep curtsy.

"Pardon, your ladyship for me comin' ta you without your askin', but I wanted to thank you again for taking on our Sharon. We are so very honored to have her in your service."

"Oh, Mrs. Barrett, I was hoping to see you! I have another letter for you from Sharon." Callie fished a letter from her reticule. "I expect she wrote that she is staying at Ryeland Park with my sister-in-law while we are at the keep. I will not have much need of a lady's maid while visiting Scotland, and the Countess has grown very fond of your Sharon. She is near her time, and I understand Sharon is very good with infants?"

"Aye, that she is, m'lady! She near reared this one"— she waved a hand at the little girl—"from the first hour she was on this earth."

Callie did not mention that Sharon also seemed quite smitten with the head groomsman at Ryeland Park. And suspected the attraction was at least part of the reason the girl was staying in England.

"Please accept this basket as a small thank you. You may get a bit peckish on the drive up to the keep."

"Thank you, Mrs. Barrett, you are very kind and thoughtful." She took the basket, laying the posey on top. Gully poked his head out of the hamper Rose was holding to sniff the contents. Finding nothing to his liking, he swished his tail and settled back down.

Mrs. Barrett and her youngest curtsied again and

then crossed the narrow street back to their cottage.

"And how is the venerable Mr. Verlan?" Callie asked as Bren returned to hand them back into the carriage.

"Bigger 'n ever. If I thought he'd make it up the mountain, I'd bring him along with us this trip."

"Ah, but instead you gave the ostler money to keep him like a king, did you not?"

"There! I always knew you were a witch! Come on, we need to get on the road."

"Leavin' afore I get a chance tae pay ma respects?"

A new voice—thick with drink.

From the shadows of the Black Swan, a figure stumbled forward. Brian Belcher.

Callie had met him once before when she had come down to the village. That is where she'd discovered his fine whisky.

His coat was two sizes too large and tattered at the cuffs, his boots scuffed and rundown. He wove through the crowd like a ship that had lost its rudder, one hand bracing against a post, the other flung outward in grand generosity. He reeked of ale, pipe smoke, and regret.

And yet—

Bren lit up.

Callie had seen him polite. She had seen him amused. She had certainly seen him charm people into forgetting why they'd been annoyed with him in the first place.

But this?

This was ease.

"I've been savin' that case o' ma brew for ye, yer lordship!" He made an awkward bow.

"Ah, Mr. Belcher! You are well met." Bren strode

forward, grinning like they were long-lost brothers. He clapped the man hard on the back, nearly sending him sprawling.

Belcher let out a half-laugh, half-cough. "Telt ye, did I no? There's nae finer whisky in a' Scotland."

"Scotland? I'd venture to say near the world over! Certainly rivals Kentucky Bourbon," Bren declared.

Callie caught the vicar's sharp inhale a moment before he cleared his throat—loudly.

Mr. Belcher gave a pleased, lopsided grin. "Aye, weel, I wasna sure I'd ever see ye again. Sure as the fairies dance, they've been busy—an American turned peer o' the bloody realm, eh?"

Callie bit back a smile. Of course. Bren had met Brian on the mountain—after stumbling into her cottage—when he'd gotten himself thoroughly turned around in the fog. And now here he was, greeting the man as if he were the most reliable fixture in the county.

"We would be honored," the vicar said, pointedly, "if you would stop and take tea at the vicarage now, Lord Clifford."

A heavy silence fell.

The crowd stilled, waiting. Callie swore she saw a few villagers exchange knowing looks.

Belcher hiccupped, peering between Bren and the vicar. "Tea? Och, tea's all well an' guid, but a man o' yer standin' deserves somethin' wi' a bit mair fire tae it." He wagged a knowing finger. "Aye, somethin' strong. Somethin' puts hair on a man's chest."

Orin Frasier let out a roaring laugh, slapping his knee. A few men joined in. Others simply watched.

Poor Mr. Dougan, however, looked as though he had just bitten into a particularly sour lemon.

Bren hesitated. His gaze flicked to hers—just a heartbeat, just long enough for her to feel the weight of a choice.

Then his reckless grin returned.

"Tea sounds lovely, Vicar," he said, "but I reckon we should get on up to Kinduggan while the light is good." He turned to Brian Belcher. "Can we give you a ride?"

****

"Is Kinduggan far?" Rose asked once they had all settled into the carriage, Gully's basket between her and Rose. Mr. Belcher had declined the ride, as he had his cart, and no doubt more drinking to do in the village.

"About six miles yet. Is that about right, lad?" Bren turned around to speak with Angus.

Poor boy, so astonished to be addressed, got the reins twisted as he tried to turn to face the viscount. "Aye, my lord. 'Tis a fair stretch. But the weather has been kind, so shouldna be many ruts in the roads. I expect we'll be there in two or so hours. Three at most, your lordship."

Callie's cottage lay somewhat near the keep, but she had never visited. Apparently, the old Viscount Clifford had not been in residence for nearly forty years. Not since his heir, Bren's Uncle Geoffrey, had been thrown and trampled by his horse. After that, the family had needed to be near civilization and doctors.

Callie found herself squeezing Rose's hand as they crossed a rather dubious stone bridge to make the final turn up the steep and, despite Angus's prophesy, deeply rutted drive.

Kinduggan sat nestled within the clove. Made of native granite, the manse seemed to rise right out of the land itself, not something made by the hand of man. She looked to her husband and met his gaze. "It is a fine house, is it not, Rose?"

"It is just as I imagined it to be, Da." The girl smiled.

Relief wreathed her husband's face, and he grinned.

But Callie felt the girl's hand tighten within hers. Callie's heart bobbed in her breast. Yes, they were both nervous.

She made herself turn away from her husband's brilliance and back toward the house.

Certainly, it was not nearly as grand as Ryeland Park. But that suited Callie perfectly well.

Ivy curtained much of the house, adding to the feeling that it had risen from the ground. A large field of heather and gorse spread like a quilt on its western side, and a small orchard lay to its east. Ben Crannoch rose steeply behind. Late afternoon sun still shone brightly on its southern face. Dark water lay some distance to the left of the parkland. A lake, or loch, as the natives called it.

A line of servants spilled out of the front door— someone must have been at the watch. They stood at attention just below the front steps.

"Welcome to Kinduggan, Lord and Lady Clifford!" The man who looked ancient enough to be in the grave— the butler?—rose from a very decorous bow.

Bren nearly stuck out his hand but instead slapped his thigh. Callie squelched her smile. What would the poor fellow do if offered a handshake from a viscount?

"Callie, Rosie, this is Mr. Billings. He and his missus have been in charge of this house since before the flood, I reckon."

"Mr. Billings." Callie nodded and turned to the lady who could only be his wife. "Mrs. Billings."

The lady curtsied. "Your ladyship. Welcome."

"Your lordship. I trust you have had an easy journey?" the butler asked.

"Easy enough. Once we say howdy to everyone, I reckon the ladies are a might tired. And I could do with a wash."

"Of course, your lordship." He gestured to his wife. "Mrs. Billings is housekeeper." Next was the cook, Mrs. Green, who had to be Mrs. Billings' relation. Yes, the relationship was confirmed when Callie inquired. Then there was a pot boy, Philip, and two maids of all work, Martha, and Harriet, also relations of the Billings'. The girls both looked to be about Rose's age.

Bren had said they would be here for a few months—a kind of honeymoon. Could Scotland be a place of magic for them? It certainly had had that effect on her back at her cabin when she had seduced him. Well, seduction might be perhaps too subtle to describe what she'd actually done, when she'd literally leapt on him. Could Kinduggan possess a bit of alchemy and transform them into a real family?

Chapter Sixteen

Their first night at the keep was as awkward as a three-legged table. The staff bowing and 'Your lordshipping' him, then sorting them into assigned rooms, a whole dang suite for the master and mistress. Seems in these places a body could not just sleep with his wife, you had to have a whole warren of rooms separating you.

Well, thank the good Lord his wife had a keen sense of direction. He had barely removed one boot—he had not brought Mr. Olivier, his valet, to Scotland—there stood Callie, in her dressing gown, tendrils of hair still dripping and cheeks flushed from a recent bath.

"I waited as long as I could for you to come to me. What with the packing and travel it has been five days. I will not wait another. No, not another minute."

His boot dropped with a thud. "Right then. Let's get to it."

He almost didn't hear the tentative knock on the door as he dropped his second boot to the floor. Callie clearly hadn't heard it as she launched herself at him, lips finding his, one leg snaking up his thigh.

Should he ignore the knock? He was Lord of the Manor now. It might be important—

Callie reached down to cradle him. Whoever it was surely would have the good sense to just go away.

But a second, more insistent knock must have

penetrated his wife's passion-sodden brain. Her leg tightened for a whisker before sliding back down to stand firmly on the floor.

"One moment," she called. As she stalked through the chamber connecting his room to hers, she efficiently scraped her riotous, still-damp hair back into a bun and cinched the sash of her robe. He followed in her wake.

She opened the door to Rose. A shaking and terrified Rose.

"I—I—am so sorry, Callie." Rose wrung her hands and shook her head, staring at her slippered feet.

"Come in, Rose, dear." Callie opened the door wider.

"Oh!" Rose took a step, then caught sight of him and drew to a stop. "Oh, dear, I didn't think—that is—of course, you are married now."

"Now, hold on now, Shy bird," he said, laying a hand on her arm before she could flee. "I was just coming in to say goodnight to the missus before turning in."

Callie gave him a look as if to say, *that is the lamest hogwash a body could utter.* Then she turned back to Rose. "Tell us, my dear, what has frightened you so?"

"I'm sorry. I couldn't sleep. It is so light out and there are so many strange shadows—" Rose pulled her wrapper more tightly around her. "I thought I heard—something moving overhead."

"Ah, most likely just some varmint up in the rafters," he offered, with a grin. "Probably a rat, or mayhap a coon."

Again, he got another look from Callie. *Coon? And that will steady her nerves?*

Yep. His daughter looked even more frightened now.

"It can be daunting, and sometimes even a bit frightening, adjusting to a new place. Especially one as old as The keep," Callie said, setting her arm about Rose. "I am sure your father will sort the—critters—out tomorrow, but for now, why don't you sleep here with me tonight?"

"Oh, I don't wish to—intrude." But she moved not an inch from Callie's side, clearly still afraid.

"Well, as your father has said, he was just saying goodnight. Isn't that right, Brendan?"

Dang it all. He looked at the bed he'd hoped to share with his bride, then back at his wife and daughter. "Right." He nodded, trying to convince himself that he was actually going to leave and go sleep in his cold, lonely bed tonight.

Callie tapped an impatient toe until he finally leaned in and kissed Rosie on the forehead, then gave him her cheek. He dutifully kissed it.

"Well, goodnight, ladies. Reckon I'll see you in the morning, then."

"Goodnight, Da." Rose ventured a smile, while Callie simply nodded her head once and then turned her attention to Rosie.

Back in his own bedchamber, he nearly tripped over his boots, which still lay on the carpet where he'd dropped them.

He snorted. Sleep would be impossible.

On the morrow he'd speak to Billings about the critters in the eaves. Heck, they'd always had a squirrel or two somewhere at the old farmhouse at Hayland. Even the tiniest chipmunk could sound like the calvary going full tilt when scurrying overhead in the dead of night.

Maybe he'd make some snares. A worthwhile use of

his time, and something he was actually good at. Get his daughter settled and back in her own bed. And himself in his wife's.

Should he go up in the attics now? Naw, he'd only scare his Rosie more with all the noise.

Better just sit tight here.

Dang, was his wife a sight in that robe, with her hair still dripping…

The front of his britches bulged, a stark reminder of his need. He pulled a heavy winged chair in front of the still-glowing coals in the firebox and then poured three fingers of whisky. He inhaled the peaty smell and then took a long sip. Not nearly as good as Belcher's …

His hand had drifted between his thighs. He slid farther down in the chair, his legs splayed. Four quick flicks had his falls open and his pecker free.

He closed his eyes.

The image of her filled his brain—flushed from her bath, spikes of still-dripping-hair soaking her silken robe at her shoulders and down to her breasts. As if she had impatiently jumped from the slipper tub and into her robe without stopping to do much drying. Her want so vivid in her parted lips, her sparkling eyes, her dancing fingers as they pulled him to her.

God, was she lovely…

And his…

He snorted. Just not tonight.

He took another swallow and then set the drink aside.

Now using both hands, one on his shaft, the other fondling his balls—gentle and then not-so-gentle tugs. Slick wet pearled at the tip of his cock. He squeezed and hissed as his thumb brushed over the sensitive head, the juice allowing his hand to glide smoothly up and down.

Her breasts were so beautiful—just a bit more than a mouthful... No, bigger now, the nipples just slightly darker than before, and larger, too.

Those pert breasts bouncing as she rode him, arching into him, crooning his name. Her long, pale neck exposed to his mouth, his teeth. Her buttocks firm and pulsing in his hands—filling them so perfectly.

He squeezed, the blood building, making the flesh impossibly tight and full. His hand now moving in a frantic rhythm that he knew so well, and yet, this fantasy of this woman—his wife—made it all completely new.

He jerked as his seed shot out, spilling hot on his thigh and down to the hearthstones below.

Sweet relief swamped him as he collapsed back into the chair, staring at the creamy wet running down his leg. For the first time he considered its power. The power to create a living being. A child. His child. And hers. Their child. A child made from—love? And why not? Why could they not find love?

Dawn was still hours away—so many hours of daylight in the Highlands. So much time to fill.

He poured another drink.

****

He awoke with a start.

His body cramped and neck aching from spending the night in a chair. The bottle next to him was empty. Likely the reason his head felt like a ten-pounder.

What time was it?

Full daylight outside. But the dang sun came up as early as five in the morning here at Kinduggan.

Were his ladies still abed? He dared not check, not with his young daughter possibly still asleep.

Sweet Rosie, so shy and scared of most everything. He hadn't seen that until looking in her face last night.

Well, he would teach her that critters were nothing to be frightened of—at least not a squirrel, or even bats if you didn't bother them. So much to teach his daughter.

He found them in the library. The door cracked open, allowing him to view a slice of Callie and Rosie

Heads together, they were looking at some large book that spanned both their laps. His Shy Bird pointed out something on the page and Callie bent her head closer. She said something Bren couldn't make out and they both laughed.

Sara and Farren had often been so, heads together over a book, sharing a joke. He'd ached to join them. But they seemed so cozy and happy. He'd only be a third wheel. Besides, likely he would not have understood the joke and feel like a sapskull.

Just like Sara and Farr, best to leave the two women to themselves. Rosie would learn a site more from Callie than she would by his side, that was for darned sure.

So dang smart, his Callie. And so self-sufficient. She didn't really need him, did she? Well, except at night—then she seemed to need quite a lot of him.

Was her body aching as much as his was this morning?

Well, today he would scour the attics for scat, set some snares, patch some holes. He wanted Rosie comfortable and happy here at the keep.

And he wanted his wife in bed next to him.

But dang it, he was a selfish cuss. Because he wanted more than her nighttime hours. He wanted all of her, all the time. Morning, noon and night. But not just her body, he wanted to be a part of her whole world. Just like all those years ago he had wanted to be a part of everything Farren and Sara were doing.

When Callie looked up from the book toward the door, Bren pulled back, out of sight. Had she seen him lurking? Why couldn't he just sashay on in and take over the room like he always did?

Scared. That's what he was. When a body wanted something too much, disappointment always followed. He'd learnt that lesson over and over again until…well, until he learned to not want. And if he did, he knew to be cooler than a three-day-old spud.

Dang fool. Running away to Scotland, thinking he and Callie could escape together, recapture the simplicity they'd shared at her cabin.

But Kinduggan Keep was not her cottage.

No, Kinduggan meant responsibility, just as surely as Ryeland Park did. Sure, he might no longer be under the critical eye of the *haute ton,* but he still had a daughter to parent, a passel of servants to command, a pile of paperwork and estates to manage.

And a wife, too, who would soon give him another child. Another twenty years of responsibilities and the burdens of fatherhood.

What had he been thinking? The problem was, he hadn't. He'd just known he *had* to get the heck out of London, of England, before the weight of responsibilities had him exploding, just like the mine General Burnside had sent sky high under the Confederates at Petersburg.

A tactic that hadn't helped the Union one damned bit.

He snorted. Running away like a danged coward again. Just like always…

He risked another peek into the room. Still poring

over their book, they didn't see him at all. Only Gulliver caught sight of him. And then, as if he knew just what Bren longed for, the danged cat swished his tail and settled himself smack dab between the ladies. Splaying himself right over their book, commanding their full attention.

"Oh, you are a very bad boy!" Callie crooned, shaking her head even as she ruffled the fur under the beast's chin.

Gully only rolled onto his belly. Bren watched, jealous as a green-eyed monster, as his wife snorted a laugh and moved her hand to accommodate the cat's needs. Lordy, he envied that feline. Able to just do nothing, be adored, and not have to do a darned thing to earn love.

Right. Better to take himself off into the attic. Then maybe explore the south side of the mountain? Maybe pay a call on Brian Belcher. He surely needed to replenish his whisky. Might even sample a dram or two...

But, boy howdy, did he envy that cat...

****

He grabbed his gun and headed into the woods.

The south side of Kinduggan would wait. As would bedding his wife. In the meantime, he'd slake another thirst.

Land aplenty attached to the estate, but most of it lay straight up. No farmland, thank the good Lord. And the only outbuildings—the stables, the dairy, and a spring house. Not much to keep up.

Suited him just fine.

He found himself heading up a track which forked into the old, rutted road he'd traveled weeks ago, after he'd fled from Callie's cottage. The one that had led him to Brian Belcher and his whisky.

Seemed like providence. And just like that earlier time, Bren found Belcher on his front stoop, rocking and smoking his pipe.

"Ah, yer lordship! I wis hopin' ye'd come by." Belcher rose, raised his cap, then made a deep bow.

Bren shifted his rifle from his shoulder to lean on it. "Ah, heck, enough with all that 'yer lordship' hogwash!"

""Whit, an' have the vicar breathin' doon ma neck for no' showin' proper respect tae ma betters?"

Bren chuckled. "You didn't stand on such ceremony with me when we first met."

"Weel, tha were afore I knew ye was the viscount of the keep. Kept that bit of information tae yourself when last we met."

Bren leaned on his rifle and shoved his hand in his pocket. "I've never been much for rules."

The man grinned. "Weel, if ye dinnae want me followin' the rules, then I expect we ought tae hae a few drams."

Bren checked the height of the sun. Still low in the eastern sky.

Belcher didn't miss his subtle hint on the earliness of the day. "Ah, come on, man. At least let us drink a toast ta yer bonny bride!" Belcher crowed, and before Bren could object, he'd ducked into his cottage and come out with two mugs and a bottle. "Tae the Viscount and his lady wife!"

"Well, I don't know about raising a glass to the viscount, but I sure as hell will salute his bride!"

Bren took a sip and smiled. The familiar burn in his nose and then the rich roll of flavor over his tongue, sliding down his throat to warm his belly, already easing his worries. Some kind of magic, to take grain and water and make it taste like heaven…

They settled very agreeably in two huge wooden-armed chairs that looked out over Belcher's fields. Well past time for planting. Looked as if they'd stood fallow for years. Only a few stubborn stalks of barley stood yellow and brittle shuddering in the ruffle of wind.

"Belcher, I've had many a whisky in my years, but this must be one of the finest. How'd you get the note of leather into this moonshine?"

"Leather, ye say?" Belcher sniffed the brew and then took a judicious sip, rolling it around in his mouth. "By God, yer right! Whaur did ye get such a fine nose?"

"I reckon I have to credit my pa for my handsome mug. My brother and I look just like him."

Belcher gave an amused snort. "Nae, I'm no' speakin' o' yer bloody beak, as you rightly know. I'm meanin' yer sense o' smell."

Bren swirled the whisky in his mug. "Always could smell things no one else could. But I learned a sight more about using *all* my senses when I lived with the Pawnee, one very lean winter back in fifty-eight. When your ribs are near poking out of your chest, missing a sign can mean the difference between life and death."

"Pawnee? Now that sounds like a tale worth another drop." Belcher leaned forward to top off Bren's cup.

"Perhaps…" Bren closed his eyes as if doing so might stave off bitter memories. All he said was, "Whisky proved no friend to my native brothers."

Belcher nodded slowly. "Aye, nor my da, either."

Both men eased back, the creak of wooden rockers a steady and comforting. A crow flew across the horizon, its caw measured and repetitive. A warning to others to stay away. Likely a snake down in the tall grasses.

Belcher sat forward, his rocker groaning. "Whit else d'ye smell?"

Bren took another sip, then closed his eyes and held it for a few moments in his mouth. Finally, he swallowed, then stared down into his mug. "Oak, peat, smoke, a hint of apple—no, apricot, as well as the leather."

Belcher slapped his thigh. "By God, it's uncanny."

Bren drew deep through his nose, inhaling the rich perfume. "Could do with a bit less fruit. And maybe a note of pine instead as a finish? But it's a damn fine brew, Mr. Belcher. Damn fine."

Belcher sipped, closed his eyes, and held the liquor in his mouth just as Bren had. "Pine? Bless Stingy Jack, ye may hae somethin' there!"

But Belcher's enthusiasm proved short-lived, his grin gradually fading as he sank back in his chair. He stared into his mug, "Weel, this 'Water o' Life' will dry up soon enough."

"Why?"

"Only have a few wee casks left." Belcher shook his head. "Grand Da wis the whisky maker. Ma da an' me? I reckon we were just the whisky drinkers." He took another long pull then raised his mug, a kind of benediction to his confession.

"Surely you must've learned some of the art from your grandpa 'fore he passed. Did you never brew a batch yourself?"

"I watched him plenty as a wee lad. Even lent a hand roasting the peat, working the auld hand mill. But the older I got, the wilder, and by the time I learnt a scrap of sense, my Grand Da was in the ground."

"That sounds right familiar." Bren raised his mug to his friend for a toast, but the gesture was half-hearted. Two tricks from the same deck.

Bren gulped down the rest of the brew, not even savoring its richness. "Well, I best get on."

Belcher looked up as if he just realized Bren was still there. "Right. Back tae the missus."

Bren nodded, then set his cup on a nearby table.

Belcher rose, using the arm of his chair to steady himself. "Weel. I thank ye for the visit. No' many come by these days. I dinnae get doon tae the village as often tae sell or trade, as there's no' much anymore tae sell."

Bren looked once more over the fallow fields. No, harvest of barley this season to make more of his grandad's brew.

"Used to be thick with it." Beside him, Belcher gave a grunt as he jerked his head toward the field. "Shoulder-high come Lammas. Birds used to fight over the stooks."

"Do you still have your set-up?" Bren asked.

The man's gaze narrowed, his blue, red-rimmed eyes locking onto Bren's as if seeking to gauge his interest and perhaps even worthiness. "Aye."

"Show me?"

Bren was just about to retract his request when Belcher muttered, "I'll fetch the key."

Bren released the air he'd not been aware he held, and taking his cue from his host, remained silent as Belcher led him up a ragged neglected path. Almost reverent, the man seemed, as if they were on some holy pilgrimage. The only sounds, the old crow and the rush of clear mountain water running over peat, pine roots, and limestone.

At the top of a rise a barn rose from a stand of pine. Belcher fit a key into a lock big as Bren's fist, then pulled the door wide.

Windows on the south side let in some filtered light, but it took a moment for Bren's eyes to adjust to the dim interior. The first thing he saw was a copper still. It stood, in pride of place, at the very center of the room. Bren gestured, asking permission to inspect it more closely. Belcher gave him a small nod.

"This is whaur Granda made his Water o' Life," Belcher finally declared. As unnecessary as the statement was, it said everything about his immense pride.

"My family ran this still for five generations. Through excisemen, famine, an' worse." Belcher reverently ran his hand over the bell curve of the tarnished copper as if it were a beloved child. Then, as if he'd been burned, he pulled it away, making a tight fist. "Jist took a couple ne'er-do-weel drunks tae shut it all doon."

He turned away and gestured Bren to follow him up a ladder to the loft of the building. Even dimmer up here, but Bren could make out several casks stacked against the wall.

"Been in the family since ma great, great, great, great grandpa hauled them up from the continent," Belcher explained in response to Bren's raised eyebrow. "His prize for fightin' for the British."

Bren reached out and brushed a finger against the well-worn patina. His eyes adjusting to the dark, he made out a fine, close grain, dark with age. "French oak?"

"That's right. Originally held sherry."

"Where I come from, they burn the inside of the

barrels before they put the whisky in 'em. Adds more caramel and vanilla. Deepens the color, too." Bren leaned in to sniff the wood. "Yep. These here look and smell like they have a char on them, but in Tennessee the insides look like a dang alligator's hide."

"Alligator? Weel, I'll be." Belcher rocked back on his heels, thumbs stuck in his pockets.

"I spent a few months working at a still in a little town called Lynchburg," Bren said. "A man there— name of Nearest Green—could read mash like dang tea leaves."

He'd forgotten how much he'd loved that time. Hunkered down beside the still, listening to Uncle Nearest go on about wort, and wash, and charcoal... And Bren had been good at it. He'd forgotten that too.

Belcher let out a low breath, gaze drifting toward the casks. "Could surely use a man wi' talents like that." He scratched his chin, voice turning thoughtful. "No' much oak left tae be had in Scotland or Ireland these days. Took near all of it tae build the British navy."

Belcher nodded toward a stack of aging barrels piled by the far wall. "Those have seen better days. I always meant tae fix them, but I'm no' a cooper. An' besides..." His voice trailed off. "Who am I leavin' it all tae, anyway?"

"You never married?"

"Nae. Marriage wis no' for me."

He did not say more, and Bren did not press, suddenly so grateful for his little family back at Kinduggan.

Belcher crossed the loft to the pile of broken casks. More old French oak, the maker's mark still visible on the top. Their iron bands had slipped, and the staves had separated. The wood needed to stay wet in order to swell to the proper size to support the bands.

"My Grand-da gave me this little book." Belcher pulled out a thin handmade book about the size of a folded handkerchief. "Has all the measurements for each cask's dimensions, and how many gallons per cask. And a few other secrets." Belcher laughed. "He told me if I ever showed it to anyone, I'd have to kill them"

Bren snorted and shook his head.

Belcher gave a wry chuckle and reverently tucked the little book back into his coat. "No' tha it much matters now," he said, voice lighter than the weight in his eyes.

Bren studied him for a beat, the scent of peat smoke and aging spirits thick in the still air between them. There was something here—a history, a skill, a legacy—left untended, much like the man himself.

And for the first time, Bren felt something unsettling stir in his gut. *There but for the grace of God go I.*

He shoved the thought away.

Belcher stretched, yawning. "Weel now, reckon ye've better places tae be than listenin' tae the bletherin' o' an auld sot. The missus'll be waitin', nae doubt."

Would she? Not likely—until time for bed. Then she needed him sure enough.

"Aye," he said easily, clapping the man on the shoulder. "But I am right honored that you showed me this place. Right honored," he repeated, and he stuck out his hand. "Damn fine whisky, Belcher. And damn fine company."

Belcher snorted. "Pah! Yer either daft or drunk already." But there was something close to gratitude in his farewell nod.

As Bren stepped from the barn back into the crisp mountain air, he told himself he wouldn't come back up here. Wouldn't let himself sink into another man's regrets, wouldn't let the shadows of what could have been whisper to him in the stillness.

But he knew better.

He turned to see Belcher framed in the doorway. "See you around." He held up a hand.

Belcher only stared back in reply, already sinking into the barn's dim light, where old casks and old ghosts waited, undisturbed.

Chapter Seventeen

A week later

Callie pulled yet another beautifully bound book from the crate and inhaled deeply. Leather and the musk of its straw packing. She ran her fingers lovingly over the title, *The Moonstone*. No time to cut the pages, alas. Not with so many new books to catalogue and shelve.

What a surprise to find three large crates in the middle of the library floor. A note—in Brendan's hand, difficult to read—

From your cabin. And a few more to fill all these walls.

A childish-looking hand. Had he much formal schooling?

She sighed. So much she still didn't know about her new husband.

She tucked the folded slip of paper, already slightly worn at the creases from her fingers running over it, inside her bodice. She'd place it with her other keepsakes later, in the small wooden box she kept on her dressing table.

She had not seen much of her husband over this last week. Where he went, she did not know. But when he returned, he usually had the smell of whiskey about him. She might have suspected he spent all the time drinking away at Brian Belcher's farm if not for the fresh game that appeared every evening in the kitchens. Rabbits, grouse, even a deer one night. Mrs. Green had begun to complain to Callie of not having the mouths to eat all this bounty.

True to his word, Brendan had made short work of the vermin in the attics. Billings had nearly been apoplectic when his lordship had declared he would make war on the "critters" himself, and insisted he at least take a potboy along. Young Phillip certainly had a far greater appreciation for his master after witnessing his skill in setting traps and patching holes firsthand.

After a few false starts, Rose had begun sleeping in her own room. Gully had been a huge help in that regard. After being inadvertently kicked off Callie's bed during a quite vigorous session of lovemaking, he had wisely decided that snuggling with Rose was far better for his sleep and disposition. Apparently two males in one bed was one too many.

Each night Brendan came to her bed ardent and ready. Their lovemaking, hurried and almost desperate, as if they thought they had only a finite amount of time together and they must use it or forfeit it.

Afterward, when they both lay sated, he would usually make some randy comment. Some inane sophomoric quip. Had he been any other man, she would have scoffed, telling him how ridiculous he sounded. But Brendan appeared so utterly delighted with himself, and with her, almost childlike in his joy and satisfaction. Funny, to regard not only his jokes, but the coital rush, as innocent rather than indecent. But both made her feel as if she'd been swept up right off her feet and spun around, like a child on a merry-go-round, her heart pounding in cadence with her laughter.

He liked it best when she rode him. He would grin up at her, sometimes with his huge hands behind his head. Then, when he couldn't take it any longer, grasping her hips and buttocks and taking charge, driving into her even as she bore down on him.

But beyond learning his preferences in bed, she still did not know very much about him. About who he was deep inside. She had her instincts, yes, her suspicions and hopes, too. But as yet he had not told her much of his history. And patience had never been her strong suit.

****

Bren smiled. Turns out this viscount title was good for something. Only took a note and some blunt, and mountains moved. Or rather a few crates of books. Hell, he would buy the dang Taj Mahal to see the look of wonder on his gals' faces. Chances are his ladies would spend weeks sorting and pouring over their treasure trove.

So dang industrious.

Right. Industrious.

He looked at his desk littered with wood shavings, his whittling—silly little figures, for Rosie, for the baby—a slingshot, and a bit of wire he'd twisted into a newfangled snare, which had captured not a rabbit, but an old boot.

Beneath the mess lay the estate papers Farren had handed to him just as they were leaving for the keep. Predictions on crop rotation, ditch drainage, sheep management. Beneath those, drawings and specifications for gas lighting to be installed at the keep, and a new bridge to replace the one that got washed out every year.

All reports he couldn't make head nor tail of.

And then, on the very corner of the desk, a pile of rocks he'd collected from his hikes. At present, a record stack of five rested, one on top of the other. The last one a doozy, nearly the size of a robin's egg, poised perfectly in the dimple of a pristine white kidney-shaped stone. His very own cairn.

He'd started with one stone and each day, after careful consideration, had added another. Could he add one more? Somehow, he had the crackbrained notion that if he could keep this little tower standing, his new world would remain stable as well.

He selected a nice flat stone, hefting its weight, his thumb searching for any groove or rough patch. Could he dare?

"Da?" Rose stood in the doorway.

He squeezed the stone, feeling like a boy caught slacking at his chores. He hadn't heard her coming.

"Rosie, I thought you were in the library at your lessons?"

"Oh, yes, I will be—that is, we have been sorting all our lovely books." She seemed to want to say more, but instead shook her head. "Angus came with the post and so I wanted to give you this." She took several steps into the room and held out a letter.

Letters always bothered him. Usually bad news. Even if they weren't, a body was still obliged to write back. Not something he'd ever been much good at and mostly avoided.

"Well, I thank you for the prompt delivery."

"Is it from Uncle Farren?" Rosie asked with a timid smile.

He glanced down at the writing. Words swam before his eyes, but he could make out Farr's distinctively bold penmanship. "Yes, indeedy, Shy Bird."

"I wonder if Aunt Nora has had the baby?" Rose clasped her hands together, nodding to the letter.

Dear Christ, she wanted him to open it and see? Wanted him to read the letter to her?

"Well, now, Rosie-gal, I expect that news will have to be a surprise," he said, winking at his daughter. "You know how I like to give surprises." He gave her his biggest shit-eating grin.

God bless her, she smiled just as big right back at him. Hell, he'd have to teach her how to recognize a scamp when she saw one.

"You'd best get on back to your sorting. If Callie thinks I've been a distraction, she'll have my hide."

"Oh, yes, of course." She turned to leave then stopped. "But you will be sure to tell us any big news, whatever it turns out to be?"

"Assuredly!"

She smiled again and then left the room.

Oh, wouldn't it have been grand to have been able to share the letter with his daughter.

Now, with something bordering on eagerness, he cracked the seal, already planning how to reveal if the child were a boy or a girl.

Bren took a breath. Even though Farr always was careful to print, words shifted and got turned around. If he looked at them just the right way, they sort of got in line enough for him to make some sense of them.

Bren,

Hope this finds you well. No news yet on the babe, but I reckon it won't be long now. Maybe by the time you get this, Nora and I will have a new little Cavanaugh to add to our tribe.

Aw, shoot. No surprise for his ladies. Bren focused again.

I tried to tell you the night of your wedding, and then again when you were leaving for Scotland, but I just didn't want to saddle you with an extra worry. I hope I did right.

Iris Darvan has resurfaced.

Bren squinted and read the line again, sure he'd got it wrong. But no—he traced a finger over each letter, I-R-I-S—surely those were the letters that spelled the name of his old lover.

A dang cavalry of memories stampeded through his mind, making his heart pound. Some wild, some painful, some even full of real joy. All complicated, though, and near overwhelming.

He'd honestly thought her dead. The Iris he remembered lived at the very top of her lungs and that kind of living got a body killed with great regularity. Hell, he should have been dead ten times over.

But, dang it all! Why hadn't Farren told him?

She arrived in a hired carriage the day before your wedding, just after dinner. She asked for the master of the house, and the servants, used to that being me, I was called to see to her. Hell, I thought she was dead. Your old pal Gillingham said as much.

With the wedding and all, I panicked. Gave her a bunch of money. Told her to go back where she'd come from.

I thought that'd be that—

Hell and damnation! Bren could have told his brother Iris would never let them off so easy. After he'd recovered from being shot by that lunatic Milton, he'd decided to look for her, just on the chance Gillingham had lied. With Rose found, it seemed only right to try once more to find her mother. If he was being honest, the search had given him yet another excuse to dodge the role of father. He'd taken a boat to Callais and then on to Paris, and poked around some, but he hadn't looked all that hard or long before deciding he needed to go back to the States to clear his name. Yet another delay to fatherhood.

But she came back for more. I didn't oblige her. Told her the well was dry, and to skedaddle. Hell, I probably shouldn't have paid her off in the first place—

Damn right! Bren nearly crushed the paper.

—but I got rattled, what with the Ainsworths all under our roof and the wedding the next day.

Why had Farr not allowed him to settle his own affairs?

Hell, who was he foolin'? In the end he probably would have done the same thing, given her money and hope that was the end of it.

This time, I used your title as Viscount to put the fear of God in her. At any rate, she has no idea where you are, so you're safe up there at Kinduggan. I want you to be prepared, though; when you come back to England, you might have a thorn in your side.

Your Brother,
Farren

P.S.- She never once asked about Rosie. I didn't know quite what to do or say, but I didn't get a good feeling about her, and so I didn't say anything about Rose, just let it lie. I didn't want Rose to be a pawn in the mix.

Oh, dear God, Rose... This time Bren's fist closed around his brother's words.

Be sure and tell us of any big surprises... she'd just asked of him, and he'd just promised.

Rosie never talked about her mother, so he never mentioned her, either. And, true to form, he wasn't one for opening a can of worms unless he was going fishing.

Some father he was.

Surely Rosie believed her ma was dead. How else could she square Iris never coming back for her girls— her girl.

Would Iris try to wheedle her way back into her daughter's life? And did she have the right? Certainly, she could make trouble. The Iris he knew would not hesitate to use every trick in her book to squeeze as much money out of him as possible.

A memory rose hot and fierce. They'd lost at the tables—well, Iris had. Any money he'd had was gone. And so, high time to visit his grandpa.

He'd never forget seeing the joy on his grandpa's face when he'd arrived, and then the terrible disappointment when Bren had cavalierly demanded his share of the Clifford money. The old man had been furious. And why not? His grandpa had known nothing of the tall tale his pa had told about his family in England. Turns out it had been all hogwash. The reason Duncan Cavanaugh had never come home to England was not because his father had been cruel, but rather because he couldn't face his own demons, the part he'd played in his brother's terrible accident.

Bren had come back to Iris empty-handed, sure Iris'd simply laugh and draw him into another wild romp. But she'd lit into him, calling him a useless Yank. Shades of his pa, who had known just how to level his son. When he'd tried to calm her, she'd thrown her silver-backed brush at him. He'd railed back at her and then high tailed it to the nearest bar. When he returned the next morning, sure she'd be cooled off by then, he'd found the room cleared out, nothing left but a worn deck of cards and an empty bottle of gin. He never saw her again. But then, he hadn't made much effort.

Dang it all!

Lordy! He'd have to tell Rose.

And Callie…

Bren ripped the crumpled paper in half, then again, and again, and again, until it lay in tiny bits on the desk. Just as he had with his schoolwork, frustrated he couldn't form his letters or make the words make sense.

Lazy, good-for-nothing halfwit!

Bren could still hear his pa shouting, still feel the belt stinging the backs of his hands, his open palms. His ma, silently looking on, or worse, turning away and going on with her breadmaking or darning.

Bloody hell, you'll never amount to anything! His pa's very posh accent would always come out in full force when he was raging. Or drunk.

Yep, good-for-nothing. Hell, even his own brother knew he couldn't handle his responsibilities—

Too much, all too much. He'd chosen this tower room for its location, at the very top of the castle, with its view of the valley below. King of his castle—what a joke. Now the walls seemed to mock him.

One swipe sent the tenuous tower careening across the desk, crashing into all the rest of the mess.

One tiny wooden horse, one he'd intended for the new babe, lay smashed to bits.

"Damn, Iris!"

****

"I'm sorry I'm late!" Rose called out as she hurried into the library.

At the sound of her voice, Gulliver lifted his head, yawned, and burrowed deeper into the folds of Callie's skirts.

Over this past week, Rose had become Callie's shadow—always near, seeking reassurance and approval. She needed far more of Callie than Helena ever had. But then, Helena had always had a mother, even if Hermione Ainsworth's presence had been more ceremonial than truly maternal. Her father's obsession with producing a son often left Hermione indisposed— whether from grief, disappointment, or her own relentless ambition. During those absences, Callie had stepped in gladly.

Now, she had another chance to nurture. Brendan's daughter had begun filling both her days and her heart.

Callie'd discovered Rose's education had been spotty at best. She'd been raised as an ornament, taught to perform, to charm when summoned. But that would change. Callie would see to it. The girl deserved the chance to learn anything she set her mind to.

And beyond Callie's role as teacher, and dare she say, mother, there was the house to manage, the staff to coordinate, and—perhaps most enticing—an entire library of books to catalogue. She shouldn't have time to miss her husband. Yet she did.

"Angus arrived with the post. Da had a letter from Uncle Farren. I brought it to his office," Rose announced.

"Was he there?" Callie tried not to sound too eager.

"Yes, but he didn't open it. He said if there were news of the baby, we'd just have to wait."

"Of course he did. You know your Da—he'll turn even a scrap of news into a grand production."

"And I received a letter from Agnes!" She waved the paper in the air. "Agnes is learning Braille! Look—run your fingers along the bottom of the page." The girl nearly danced over to where Callie was sitting.

Callie took the letter and then dutifully brushed her fingertips over the paper. "It tickles."

"Close your eyes—you can feel it better that way." Rose had plopped herself down next to Callie.

She did. "Ah. Yes. I feel the patterns now. But what do they mean?"

"I didn't know either. Agnes calls it Braille, an alphabet for the blind. I wonder if Da might purchase a book about it, so I can learn to write to her properly."

"Oh, he'll be delighted to. You must ask him."

Rose hesitated. "But he's already been so generous. We have so many books…"

Callie heard the same note she so often did—too cheerful, too careful.

Trying too hard to be good.

To be perfect.

When Callie had asked Rose to play something on Kinduggan's ancient pianoforte Rose had flinched at the slightest wrong note. Nora had hinted at the horrors of Milton's "charity" home, but even that word felt grotesquely misapplied. Children sterilized. Others, experimented on. Rose had been the favored one. Groomed to be the perfect daughter.

"I think he'd be thrilled to buy you just about anything your heart desired. Certainly, another book," Callie said gently. "We both want you to have every opportunity."

Rose ran her fingers again over the page. "Agnes wrote this part says, 'Friends forever.'"

"Do you miss Agnes and your other friends from the Park?"

Rose took a moment to consider her answer. "Yes, and no. Before coming to Ryeland, I didn't have any real friends. I was sometimes allowed to play with a few of the children from the west wing, but only once in a great while. I was used to being on my own." She smiled then. "I must confess sometimes I found the noise at Ryeland a little overwhelming."

"I can well imagine! Mari alone, with her endless questions, would try anyone's nerves." Callie did not add that she had been very like Mari at that age.

Rose smiled and carefully folded the letter, smoothing the paper. "I miss my Uncle Geoff most."

"I think it is time to take a break from our chores and have our tea."

"Oh, but I have done nothing as yet to help this morning." Rose hastily tucked the letter into her pocket and stood.

Callie took her hand and pulled her back to sit beside her. "Well, you may earn your keep by pouring out."

Rose smiled and began to lay out the teacups, turning each handle to align precisely with the largest cabbage rose on the saucer. Her exacting placement a glimpse into how she survived her prison-like existence.

"I never had the pleasure of knowing your uncle. Will you tell me about him?"

A genuine smile bloomed on the girl's face. "Some people shied away from him, finding him grotesque, too damaged. But they did not know him as I did. I suppose I gravitated to him because I am damaged as well." Rose's tone, so matter of fact.

Callie quelled the urge to reach over and squeeze her hand.

She had cobbled together only the bare skeleton of Rose's terrible history—indeed, she was not sure she could stomach the details—but poor Rose had known this world, albeit only from the periphery, but day in and day out she had been groomed by this madman. Perhaps she would air some of her memories? Callie waited to see if Rose would continue.

"Uncle Geoff and I just seemed to understand each other, even without words. Much like Agnes can, in some ways, see so much more than the rest of us. I think if one has a deficit, other parts take over and become stronger." She shook her head. "Well, somehow Uncle Geoff and I could talk without talking, if that makes sense."

"Yes. I believe your Da feels that way with your Uncle Farren." Callie took the cup from Rose.

"Exactly! Lily and I could do that, too, even though she was so much smarter than I. She took care of us."

"And your mother?"

Rose's cup rattled in its saucer and tea sloshed as the girl looked up sharply.

Callie hated that she was so curious about the woman who had come before her in Bren's life. The woman with whom he had created two souls. "You do not have to speak of anything you don't wish to, Rose. You know that, don't you?"

Rose carefully tipped the tea from the saucer back into her cup and wiped the side with a napkin. She did not drink. "Mama, she was very beautiful. She always had admirers. Sometimes Lily and I were helpful, and sometimes—well, sometimes we were not. Then Mother Lockhart would take care of us, often for a few days, occasionally for several weeks. Then months…"

Callie knew that longing feeling. "You must have missed her very much."

Rose looked up at Callie as if she were surprised at the question, then she nodded slowly. "Yes," she whispered, almost as if to herself. "Mama, she always came back…" She adjusted the angle of her teacup handle once more to the correct position.

Callie swallowed. "I'm sorry, Rose. You've lost so much."

At nearly sixteen years old, Rose could appear oddly young and girlish at times, and yet at others, so wise, so melancholy. The poor child had seen too much in her tender years, but not enough in the later ones.

Rose placed her teacup on the table and then smoothed her skirt. "I expect you will look forward to being a mother," she said with almost a stoic resignation.

Callie took Rose's hand. She longed to place it over the barely-there swell of her belly—to share her joy. But she and Brendan would tell her about the baby in due time. "Yes. Yes, I will."

When she looked up from their joined hands, Rose's expression had changed. Was it fear? Or something harder to name? Did she think a babe, one born in wedlock, would render Rose "unhelpful", as with her mother?

Rose jumped up. "Oh, stupid me! I have been so absorbed in my own tale, I forgot, you have a letter from Helena." Rose fished in her pocket and then handed Callie an envelope.

Callie smiled at the familiar scrawl. "Ah! I was wondering when I'd get a letter. Let us see what Helena has to say." Gully flicked his tail and Rose nodded vigorously and sat, her smile once again fixed and bright.

"Would you care to wager if my dear little sister is still in love?" The cat merely yawned.

"Oh, but Mr. Henshaw and Helena seem so very devoted to each other!"

Callie nearly laughed at Rose's concern. She would not disabuse the girl of her naive assessment that love endured, instead she popped open the seal, eager for news.

"'My dearest Callie, Oh, life is such a tangle!" Callie read aloud, and continued, "'I thought Mother would begin to accept Martin now that you have married Brendan. But it seems she is more determined than ever that I should look even higher! When will she realize I will not give him up? Oh, how I miss you and your wise advice!'"

Apparently, Helena did not remember that Callie's "wise advice" had led to all sorts of trouble.

"Ah, you see, they are still in love," Rose said with a satisfied sigh.

Callie read on. "'Which leads me to my plan!'" Callie shook her head. "Oh dear, not another plan!"

Callie resumed. "'Well, it was not entirely all my idea. You see, while I was in the park reading your letter and feeling very sorry for myself, I met a very nice lady who lent me her handkerchief—for as you know I never seem to have one about me. I confessed how I longed to see you again before—'"

The baby came. Callie skipped over that part, hastily adding, '"too long"' to finish the sentence.

"'She said I should not delay. That life was too precious to squander. It was as if the dear lady were speaking the words of my own heart! I declared to her then and there that I would go to Kinduggan. And so, I shall!—I will certainly send a prayer up to my angel—for that is what I have dubbed my dear Mrs. Gillingham—who insisted I keep her handkerchief, (embroidered with angel's wings!) and this grand idea.'"

"Mrs. Gillingham?" Rose looked up.

Callie skimmed the page. "Yes, that is the name of her 'angel'." Callie shook her head, smiling at her sister's melodrama.

"…an angel?" Rose frowned. "Is that all she says?"

Callie picked up the thread. "'I will write again when I have everything in order! Please give my love to Rosie and Brendan tell them I shall see them soon! Your loving sister, Helena.'" Callie smiled. "No doubt she was eager to get this in the post as soon as may be, else her letter might have arrived after her!"

Rose was oddly silent.

"Rose? Are you not pleased? You must not worry that Helena will be punished for leaving England. For all their bluster, Hermione and my father will bow down in the end. As a viscountess I do have a bit of power, and I will use it if need be."

Rose picked up a piece of shortbread but only crumbled it between her fingers, then wiped her hands on a napkin. "It will be lovely to see Helena." She stood abruptly. "But I must get to work." She set her cup down. "I've done nothing this morning."

Callie set aside the letter and absently took up the next book to be cataloged. She watched Rose for a moment. Should she press her to confide more of her feelings?

No, give her time. Cavanaugh's seemed to require time to reveal their secrets.

She glanced down at the title, and then snorted. "Gulliver's Travels! Now I am in a quandary." Callie rose and crossed the room. "Should it go on our travel shelf, or in the novel section? Or perhaps under cats? What do you say, Gully?"

Suddenly she was enfolded in a fierce embrace from behind. Rose's arms wound tightly around Callie's waist, her cheek pressed against her back.

Callie stood very still.

"Oh, if only we could stay here safe at Kinduggan forever and ever!" Rose cried.

Heavens! The mercurial emotions of youth. But Rose's outburst felt more than that. A tip of something vast and dark, submerged just beneath the surface.

Would Rose—or her father—ever trust Callie with their pain?

Chapter Eighteen

That evening Bren stumbled back from Belcher's with a raging headache, climbed the ninety-seven winding stairs, and made himself confront, once more, the mess of his desk.

He swiped it all aside then found a stack of pristine paper. How long he sat in front of one blank page, he couldn't rightly say. It included mending his pen—three times; Mrs. Billings trudging up those ninety-seven steps to call him into dinner; him telling her he wasn't hungry; and using the chamber pot at least twice before finally managing to write Farren's name.

Did he admonish his brother for not telling him immediately about Iris? Or did he tell the truth and own that he was glad Farren had dealt with her? He squeezed his hand and yet another page was rendered useless.

He finally raised his head and discovered the room had grown cold and dark. His belly rumbled. Time for bed, praise the Lord. He'd deal with all this in the morning.

"We missed you this evening," he heard as he pushed the door open to his wife's bedchamber.

Ah, hell. No just slipping into bed now. Callie and her dang questions. Hidden snares to trip you up. The most innocent ones could catch you in something you didn't want to be caught in.

In theory, *We missed you this evening* wasn't even a

question, but he'd have to be a fool not to realize the host of implications behind her seemingly innocent statement.

He grunted. What was there to say? He'd been rude. He'd just have to make it up to her.

He reached for her, but she deftly eluded his grasp.

Ah, dang. Worse than he thought.

"Rose was very quiet at dinner tonight. I hope we have done the right thing bringing her to Kinduggan. She was a little weepy this afternoon. I wonder if it is her menses?"

Jumpin' Jupiter! Menses?

"Do you think she is missing Ryeland and all her friends there? Has she spoken to you about her feelings?"

Feelings?

Apparently, wives and husbands discussed feelings. This was new territory. He and Farren'd just sort of known what each other were thinking, without any of this poking and prodding. Sara used to talk about feelings, but she'd been gone so long, he'd buried the memory of her so deep that any influence she'd had on him was long gone.

"What did Farren have to say?"

Ah, an honest-to-goodness question. But one he did not want to answer.

"I assume there is no news of the child, else you would have shouted it from the rafters."

He could only imagine casually saying, *No, just news of a long-dead ghost, one who may up-end our little family.*

"No, no babe, as yet."

Silence.

He *would* tell Callie about Iris. But not tonight. Not

when they were just getting to like each other. He reached for her again.

"She needs you," Callie said, her tone matter-of-fact. "Rose," she clarified.

Did she? Did either of them need him, truly? What the heck was he good for? A poke and a joke, but beyond that? He couldn't see.

"Well, give Mr. Belcher my regards next time you see him."

Dang it. How did she know? Witch.

"My nose might not be as good as yours, but I certainly recognize his brew."

Rivaling Farren, she seemed to be able to answer him even when he said nothing. Was her tone just a bit accusatory?

"Yep, its whiskey, and I've been drinking a fair amount of it."

She looked as if she might have one or ten other questions brewing. He steeled himself for the barrage.

Then she gave him her school-Marm look along with a little *humph*. "Well, next time don't come back empty-handed."

With a frown, she turned. Not toward him, like she had every other night, but away.

"I bid you goodnight."

He stared at the back of her head.

Hell.

Her soft snore came so fast he rose up on his elbow to make sure she was really asleep.

Yup, sleep of the innocent.

He flopped back on the bed. Still, she didn't stir.

He sucked in air, then held his breath and began counting.

Chapter Nineteen

He woke with a start. She was no longer beside him. The imprint from her head still there but cool to the touch. Gone a while now. Full daylight streamed through the window. How long had he slept?

He wasn't all that savvy on how a woman's mind worked——but he was pretty darned sure wives tended to scold husbands who drank too much...

He had a sight to learn about his woodland witch. And he'd better start learning quick.

He frowned. Probably in the library, or maybe out foraging? So far, when he'd quizzed Mrs. Billings on his ladies' movements, she told him her ladyship and Rose tended to stay inside or within the keep's gardens. He suspected Rosie was not keen on venturing too far from civilization. A'course he didn't know for sure, but given her life before Nora found her, he could understand how the gal seemed skittish about most things. He'd like to change that. He'd like to show her the wonders of the forest. Teach her about something he knew about. But feelings? And her menses?

"Hello, ladies!" Bren took the plunge and entered the library instead of lurking behind the door.

"Da!" Rosie stood up leaving her book on the settee.

His daughter didn't seem any worse for wear.

"Are you coming to join my lesson?" She bent to retrieve her book and then held it up to him. "See, we are studying your United States and its constitution."

His daughter crossed the room, holding the book out to him. "We are just reading about its new fourteenth amendment. Would you like to take over?"

He stepped away from the book like it was a rattler. "Would love to, Rosie gal, but I can't stay. I have to—have to help out Mr. Belcher with some—business this morning."

Callie just *humphed* and went back to her sorting, while Rosie fixed him with a too-bright smile.

"Shall we see you at dinner, then?" she asked, tucking the book behind her back.

But she hadn't fooled him. After all, he'd seen that look too many times on too many people not be able to spot disappointment under a heap of goodwill.

"You surely will!" he said with more gusto than he felt, capping it with a theatrical salute. Rose giggled and Callie snorted as he turned and escaped.

Trouble was, Rosie's disappointment stuck to him, like he'd been tarred and feathered with it. What would his sweet daughter say if she really knew her Da?

He started up the familiar track to Brian Belcher's but stopped. Sure, Brian would likely be expecting Bren to share a bottle or two along with a few companionable stories, but the notion of getting foxed just didn't appeal to Bren today. Maybe snare a couple of grouse for dinner? Or some of those yellow chanterelle mushrooms Callie was so fond of? Hell, what with traipsing up to Belchers every day, he'd not even explored the east side of the mountain.

He found a somewhat over-grown path not ten or so minutes into his hike. Dense forest on either side, but definitely used by humans as well as animals.

The skyline opened after another half-hour or so, then, after making a turn, a clearing appeared ahead. He could smell the remnants of a fire—some pine and apple wood, but mostly peat.

The thatch roof of a cabin appeared through the trees, its daub and wattle walls pocked with native stone. Tiny, round windows of colored glass winked in the dappled sunlight. Only needed a wizened elf to come strolling through the doorway to complete the picture.

And, by gum, there he was. A squat old man with a long gray beard and an ancient hat crowned with a hodgepodge of what looked to be capercaillie and gold pheasant feathers.

"You're lordship."

Ah, heck. Hadn't even uttered a word and the old man already had him pegged. So much for thinking he could pass for a native.

"You set a good snare, Lord Clifford."

Traces of human presence here and there had alerted Bren he didn't have the woods all to himself.

"I'm Tam Cree. I used tae be gamekeeper for yer grandsire."

A grin split his face. Someone connected to the past, who knew his family. "Mr. Cree. Brendan Cavanaugh. Pleased to meet you."

The old man squinted, raised his chin and then cocked his head. "Heard tell yer faither went off tae America. Good tae hae ye back hame. Ye are hame now, aye?"

"It seems I am. Got a fancy title and wife to keep me tethered."

Again, the squint and now a pursed mouth. Tam Cree looked him over a good long while. "Will ye tak a wee cup o' tea, m'laird?"

"I am right parched, Mr. Cree. Thank you." He had nipped at the whisky in the flask he carried in his rucksack, but a cup of tea would be very welcome.

He set his sack and rifle by the door before ducking to enter the tiny cabin. The place looked a bit like the one Callie had called home.

Mr. Cree moved to the fireplace where a kettle hung over embers. He added a lump of peat to the fire and then lifted the lid of the pot, adding a pack of dried leaves.

More herbs hung from the rafters, and mushrooms in shallow wooden bowls sat in the sunniest windows. The cabin was tidy as a pin. The place spoke of a man who had lived there for some time and who had honed his way of life to just the essentials, seasoned with a smidge of what gave him pleasure.

A glass-faced cabinet took pride of place opposite the fireplace. Bren stepped closer. Bugs! The case was full of carefully preserved bugs. Big, small, glossy, hairy, all varieties. All clearly labeled on velum cards. He squinted. Too fine a hand for him to decipher.

Mr. Cree's collection put him in mind of his grandpa who had one very much like this one. Bren'd spied the bugs when he'd come to Ryeland and stupidly dismissed him as an old toff who wouldn't spare him the money he'd come asking for. Bren had only scoffed at him when the old man asked him why he needed the blunt. Hell, he'd almost demanded the money, believing it only his due. Or maybe, afraid of telling the viscount his eldest grandson had been cattywampused by a doxy named Iris Darvan and who required a lot of money. What a contumacious coward he had been.

"My Grandpa liked bugs."

"Aye, that he did. Fair obsessed, ye might say."

He looked at the man with real interest. "You must have known him some?"

"Had that honour, I did. Ye favour him."

"Yes, well, us Cavanaughs, we all look alike."

"That ye do, but I wasnae talkin' about yer looks."

The man's gaze met his—quiet, unwavering. Like he was taking Bren's measure and not expecting him to come up short.

"You should meet my brother Farren. My twin. Spitting image of me, but he's all hero—certainly more like my Granddad than me. I guess I'm more of the black sheep, like my pa."

Mr. Cree made no reply. Instead, he dipped his head once, like he heard more in Bren's words than what had been said aloud. Then he looked up and gave a smile—not amused, not pitying. Just—knowing.

"Did you know my Pa, too?" Mayhap the younger version of his father hadn't been so black and angry.

"Aye, I did. Used tae take baith the young masters fishin'."

"You did?" Hard to imagine his pa and his Uncle Geoff as boys. Geoff young and strong, standing on the edge of the water, casting his line. His pa, four years younger, mimicking his older brother. Much like he and Farren had done...

"Master Duncan didnae hae the patience for it. He'd get bored and jump in the pond, splashin' aboot like a banshee."

"That sounds like Pa."

"Do ye like tae fish?"

"Love it."

The old man nodded as if he could see right into

Bren's soul.

The kettle shrieked. Mr. Cree shuffled over to the hearth to pour their tea.

Bren turned back to the case of bugs. The carcasses didn't interest him so much, but the cabinet did. It was made of what looked to be yew and featured some of the best joining he'd seen. But what struck him most was the utter simplicity of it. Heavy furniture with an Egyptian or Rococo flair was all the rage today, but this cabinet paid no mind to fashion. Sleek, like some of the furniture he'd admired so much when he'd visited San Francisco's Chinatown. Bren would bet the farm Tam Cree had not been anywhere south of Perth, let alone traveled the world.

"You know something of wood?" The old man offered him an earthen mug of brew.

Bren inhaled deeply and then nodded. "Oh, I whittle some. Used to make little odds and ends, years ago." One Christmas he'd given Sara a three-inch-tall carving of a hero of hers, Susan B. Anthony. She'd launched herself at him, nearly knocking him to the floor. *She's so perfect! So utterly perfect!* Sara'd cried. But when she died, the miniature carving had disappeared along with just about everything that reminded them of their sweet Sprout.

He took a sip. Earthy tasting, maybe the mushroom chaga with hints of honeysuckle and rosemary. He set the cup down, then nodded to the cabinet. "Where'd you get this beauty?"

"I didnae get it."

"Surely it didn't come with the place." It stood out like an exotic gazelle amid the cottage's everyday barn critters.

"Nae, and it wasnae brought by the fairies, either." The old man laughed, showing several gaps in his teeth. "I fashioned that piece nigh on seven winters past."

"You? You made this?"

"That I did. A man's got tae find summat tae keep his hands busy while waitin' on his maker."

Bren took a second look at the room's other contents. Sure enough, more gems revealed themselves. An elegant chair in the corner, sturdy and deeply seated yet looking for all as if it were light as air. An arched stand for a lantern, made of wood, but cunningly fashioned to look like a single blade of wheat.

"You've been up to Brian Belcher's place," the old man said, seemingly out of the blue.

Ah, heck, he didn't think he'd spilled any whisky on his duds. And he'd chewed some birch bark along the trail. He breathed into his hand just to make sure. "What gave me away?"

"Didnae take much guessin'. A wee nip on the road. And a glint in the eye o' someone who's tasted somethin' rare."

Uncanny.

"His da—" the old man shook his head. "Weel, 'tis a shame the brew will end with young Brian." Mr. Cree's blue eyes bore into Bren's.

Now Bren shifted from foot to foot, like he was back in the schoolroom under Miss Nettie Gordon's sharp gaze, clueless and cornered.

When Bren didn't respond, Mr. Cree continued. "Weel, I suppose the apple dosna' fall far from the tree. Though I don think the boy is lazy. Just—beaten doon by life."

Bren knew something of that, but never allowed

himself to wallow in his pain for long. Never did a lick of good—

Then a thought sprung up fast as a dandelion. "Mr. Cree, do you know anything about cooperage?"

Maybe it was the tea he was drinking, or perhaps Tam Cree was in fact a fairy, but the old man's huge smile did not disabuse Bren of the notion that there was something otherworldly at play.

Why the heck hadn't Belcher just asked for Bren's help?

Bren snorted. That danged title—Viscount Clifford of Kinduggan Keep. By God, Bren wouldn't let it dictate what he lent his hand—or nose to!

"I've got a harebrained notion to help Mr. Belcher get his still up and running. Fill those casks once more." The second the words left his mouth, doubts swarmed— fast and filthy, like flies on a heap of dung.

"Cooperin's no' for the hasty. Takes a fair bit o' patience, an' a steady hand." Tam Cree brushed a speck o' dust from the top of the cabinet, then looked up at Bren.

"But I reckon if a man's got the will—and the knack—he'll come by it soon enough."

By God, it seemed this old man knew Bren's path before even he did.

Heck, he'd just been drinking the days away until he could crawl back into his wife's bed each night. But what if he could do more? What if they could actually revive Belcher's brew?

"Belcher's Brew is a fine enough name. But I'm thinkin' Kinduggan speaks far more tae its smooth elegance," Tam Cree offered.

Bren's mouth dropped open, now not all sure this

wizened old man was not of the faie world. He smelled his tea.

"Ha! Ye should ken wi' yer nose—just plain chaga, rosemary and honey. Nae potion."

Bren found himself grinning. And then out and out laughing.

"I've a bit o' a woodworkin' shop oot in the barn yonder. Mayhap bring doon one o' them barrels, and we'll take a look-see? I'd be glad o' the company."

"Sounds like a right fine plan, Mr. Cree." Bren took a long swig of his tea, then ran his hand along the satin-smooth "bug" cabinet. "And I would surely love to learn how to make something as fine as this. I've never seen the like."

Tam nodded slowly.

Bren stood up straighter as if he'd managed to pass some unknown test.

"I could also show ye some fishin' spots, if ye're of a mind tae catch some Brownies."

"I'd like that very much, Mr. Cree."

"If we'll be workin' together, ye might just call me Tam."

"Only if you leave off 'my lording' me."

Tam nodded again and then crossed the room to sit by the fire.

Quelling his urge to run right up to Belcher's to lay out his grand plan, Bren instead demonstrated the patience Tam Cree believed he had, pulling up a small rustic stool to sit opposite the old Scot.

Together, they sat and sipped and contemplated the glowing embers.

The last time he'd felt this kind of peace, he'd been in Callie's cottage, sipping Belcher's brew. Now, with

Tam Cree—well, the man just seemed to settle his soul.

He wanted to express his thanks, the deepness of his—feeling, but one look in Tam Cree's eyes told him he didn't need to say a thing. Just being was enough.

Why could he not feel this ease with the women in his life? Were they so fragile they couldn't bear the weight of his flaws?

Callie was strong as they came—thumbing her nose at society, carving out a life in the mountains. And Rosie... well, his daughter seemed to dote on him, even after he'd given her a taste of the man behind the smile.

Heck, the truth of it was, he was the fragile one.

Tam, who had been watching the glowing embers, stroked a gnarled finger over the fine curve of his chair, his eyes glinting with something deeper than firelight. "Aye. A man needs summat tae shape, tae mend, tae pour his soul into. Elsewise, the cracks start showin' in ways ye cannae patch."

Bren blinked. He hadn't said a word about his buried fears, but damned if the old man hadn't sniffed them out anyway. And despite the revelation, Tam Cree seemed to accept him all the same.

Chapter Twenty

"What are you doing up at Brian Belcher's all day?" Callie pulled the coverlet aside, the welcoming gesture at odds with her suspicious tone. "And don't tell me you're just raising a glass with the man. You've got that look—like Gully after a dish of cream. There's more to it."

He came in from his bath warm and damp, eager for their nightly romp. But her folded arms—breasts swelling above like temptation itself—stopped him short. She cleared her throat sharply, dragging his gaze back up. Sure enough, her mouth wasn't ready for his kiss, but held tight in a flat line. Her brows lifted, braced for whatever foolish thing she suspected he'd done.

Should he tell her about the whisky? Would she disapprove? After all, he was pretty dang sure aristocrats didn't usually dabble in low trades like distilling. Could he lie?

"Brendan, I don't like surprises," she said, almost as if she could read him easy as one of her books. "I need to know what lies before me, and where I stand."

A dang witch, she was. Why did he think he could ever pull one over on her?

Her hands had fisted in the sheets, as if she were about to face a dose of castor oil. "I do not know much about sustaining a marriage, but honesty seems the least one should expect from a spouse. And I, for one, have had enough of deceit."

Deceit.

God above. Had she found out about Iris somehow? Even though he'd ripped up Farren's letter and hadn't written back? Could she have heard from Nora?

He swallowed hard.

"Brendan, what is it you're not telling me?" Her voice above a whisper now. "Are you using Belcher as an excuse to go somewhere else? To… see someone?"

"See someone?"

Hell, she thought he was sneaking off to meet a mistress?

Relief washed over him. She clearly didn't know about Iris Darvan.

But the tightness in his chest remained. His own wife—his brand-new wife—thought he needed someone else? That she wasn't enough? That she suspected he could be so low-down and double-dealing?

Time to come clean.

"I'm helping Belcher make whisky," he said.

Her eyes narrowed. "Whisky?"

He crossed his arms, trying for confidence. "His brew's near gone—some my fault—so now I'm helping him make more."

She stared at him.

Then burst out laughing.

"What's so damn funny?" He propped himself up on his elbows.

"Turns out my beak is good for something besides looking pretty," he muttered. "Belcher says I've got real talent. And I'm not giving it up."

She wiped tears from her cheeks, then leaned forward, bracketing his face with her hands, and kissed him square on the nose.

"Oh, I'm a puddle-headed idiot," she said, then kissed him again, softer this time.

He blinked. This truth-telling business might actually be worth a damn.

"You're not mad?"

"Mad?" She shook her head. "You've found a passion. That's a good thing."

"Passion, huh? If passion makes you this giddy, maybe I could rustle up some more."

He rolled over her, smug and half-hard already. She met him with eager limbs, wrapping herself around him like a burr on a shoat.

****

Not another woman. Just *whisky!*

She laughed again as he burrowed his face into the side of her neck and growled. Not to be outdone, she rolled on top of him preparing to pin his arms. But he had other ideas. They ended up on the floor.

"Oof—are you hurt?" His voice laced with panic, his hand reached for her belly as if his touch might calm the babe inside. "Callie, dang it all, are you hurt?"

She smiled up at him and shook her head.

"Are you sure?"

"Oh, yes, quite sure." *Whisky.* He was making bloody whisky. She laughed again at his frown.

"Let me help you up. Easy now." He lifted her gently and set her on the bed as if she were made of spun glass.

"Oh!" She pressed a hand against her throat, searching...

"What? What is it?" he said, scanning her body with his eyes and hands.

"My locket. It must have broken." The familiar weight no longer around her neck.

He took the bedside candle and dropped to the carpet. She raised up to her elbow to look as well from the side of the bed.

"Here it is." He held up the trinket. "The clasp must have broken when we rolled off. I'm right sorry, Callie. I can mend it, I'm sure."

She took it from him. Her mother's locket. *Only True Love.* Could love find its way into this forced marriage? She looked up into her husband's eyes, so forlorn, becoming so dear. Oh, she hoped so. She dearly hoped so.

She laid the locket on the small table next to the bed. A little pool of winking gold. "Now, where were we, sir?" She reached out to him and pulled him down to her, wrapping her legs around his tight bum and pushing up into his hardening penis.

"Whoa, Callie-girl! While I'm happy to tick off every possible position, it's not a race. We have the rest of our lives, no?"

Would they? Could the bliss they miraculously achieved together in bed be sustained? Or would he tire of her some day?

Without realizing, the nagging fear lent a frantic energy to her lovemaking—she must embrace as much of this experience before the embers cooled and then died.

"Just you lie back now, and let me show you how slow can be just as good. Better, even, upon occasion."

He stroked his thumb over her brow. Had she been frowning?

"Relax. Nothing for you to do," he crooned.

"Nothing at all. Just lie still and let me…do for you."

His thumb stroked again.

She bit her lip. "Do nothing?"

"Not a dang thing."

"I'm not sure this will work. I like to be—involved."

"That's just it, there's no work involved, just relax and feel."

Was he dissatisfied with their congress? After all, he was so much more experienced than she. Oh, she was a keen learner, but books were one thing, years of experience quite another.

"Very well, I will try," she said. Heavens, her voice made her sound as if she were girding her loins for battle, not pleasure…

He smiled at her, his dimple showing.

"That is, I will not—try. I will just…be," she amended.

"There's my good student."

He started at her…feet?

There was a newness in his touch. A discovery of languid lingering.

Oh, the things he did to her. So hard to lay still under his sweet torture. Yet so worth the exquisite pain.

"Not yet, my Woodland Witch. Hold on a while longer," The deep rumble of his words, warm and round against her ear.

Sounds squeezed between her lips she did not recognize as her own. Or even human. And yet he took them in stride. Indeed, they seemed to spur him on, to do even more miraculous things to her body.

"I can't—I need—now!"

And, bless him, he did as he was told. He filled her in one swift move right up to his hilt.

She gasped as she seemed to come apart. Then utter peace as she lay spent in his arms.

When she could think again, she decided she liked the idea of doing the same thing to him—slow torture. no movement, and total control. Might she even use her stockings to keep him contained? She smiled at the thought. Yes, definitely stockings. The pretty ones with the embroidered violets…

He hovered over her, grinning at her as if he'd hung the moon. And, by God, he had. He seemed fascinated with her breasts and belly, trailing his fingers over them.

"Hello, little sprout," he whispered to the slight bulge in her abdomen, a bulge that had appeared almost overnight earlier this week. "You took your first tumble today. I promise to be there to pick you up. Always." He dipped to nibble around her navel, his lashes tickling her sensitized skin.

She set a hand on the crown of his thick, golden hair. Would he be there, always? Would this family be enough for him?

"You are so beautiful," he whispered, almost as if testing how the compliment felt and how it would resonate with her.

Beautiful? She wanted it to be true, but the word felt—extravagant.

"No need to flatter. I know my looks are quite common."

"Really? Common, you say?" He gave another wicked smile, the one he knew curled her toes. He flopped down, his hip and side snug up against her, one arm threaded behind her head. She could feel the thump of his heart.

"Sara would tell you different."

Sara... His sister? Callie dared not breathe.

He was quiet for so long she thought perhaps he had gone to sleep.

"My little sister would often impart her wisdom on her two older, clod-headed brothers," he finally said, his voice a soft whisper. "Once, I remember, we were walking through the woods together, checking snares. Farren got saddled with mucking out the barn, so it was just the two of us. I was grousing about how unfairly Pa was treating me, feeling right sorry for myself. She told me to hush and to look down. She asked me what I saw. 'A bunch of leaves,' I told her, sure she was setting me up for some joke, or worse, some test of book learning. Sarafina Jayne was smart as you."

Callie remained silent as he traced the edge of her ear with the tip of a finger. "Anyhow, she bent down and picked one up. A leaf, a red one. 'In September, the first red leaf is a treasure,' she told me. 'But then come autumn, they seem as common as grain in a chicken yard. But you only have to pick one up, turn it in your hand, to remember each one is one-of-a-kind. A miracle.'"

He turned and touched her hair. "You are my red leaf, Callie-girl. One-of-a-kind. My miracle."

Such a gift, his beautiful flattery. But more precious, that he'd shared something of his beloved sister.

Should she ask for more?

No, not yet.

For now, she'd treasure her very own red leaf.

A beginning.

Chapter Twenty-One

A few days later

Bren shifted from foot to foot after he'd spread out the plaid blanket and settled the hamper.

What to do now? Dang, he should have brought his fishing gear! Would Rose like to learn to fish? Did he have time to go back to the keep for it?

The picnic had been Callie's idea. She'd pretty much demanded he join them. Hell, he'd been all too happy to take a day away from his work with Belcher. The man had taken to this new beginning like he'd found Jesus.

"We'll revive a wee dram of the old soul!" Belcher had crowed.

Today, the grain they'd unearthed was soaking, and Belcher would be busy changing the water for the next day or so.

Callie had shucked off her boots and stockings. Ones that reminded him of just the other night...

He shoved his hand through his hair. Boy, would he like to make good use of this fair day, that plaid blanket, and those stockings...

"Ah, it feels good to be outside and have my toes in the grass."

Rose, mimicking Callie, removed her boots and stockings, too.

"Da, come and sit." Rosie patted a spot beside her on the blanket.

Would now be a time to bring up Iris? Would Rosie be upset knowing he'd kept her mother from her? Or did she just want to let sleeping dogs lie? If only he knew—

"Brendan, do you intend to give us crimps in our necks? Sit."

He looked at his smiling ladies. No, now was not the time to blow up their first outing as a family by bringing up the past. He sat.

"What's to eat?" He rubbed his hands together and gave them what he hoped was a wolfish grin. A grin that made Rosie giggle, much to his satisfaction.

"We just broke our fast not an hour ago," Callie snorted. "Do not tell me you are already hungry again."

"Woman, I am always hungry." He wagged his eyebrows at Callie over Rosie's head. "After all, I had the laborious job of toting that hamper all the way from the keep. Mrs. Green must have packed a side of beef in there."

"I believe she has outdone herself," Callie exclaimed as she and Rose began to unpack the huge hamper.

Indeed, it seemed to contain enough food for an entire regiment and then some.

"And here is the *pièce de résistance*!" Rosie pulled out not a side of beef but—books.

Instead of hunger pangs, panic hit his belly.

Could he simply lie back like some pasha and demand his ladies read to him? He'd sidled out of reading hundreds of times in his life. He'd been dang inventive to avoid the shame. Once, while on a raid, he'd received a note—this one not in braille. He'd thrust it at the young infantry boy by his side only to have the lad admit, with a red face and a stammer, "Sir, I'm sorry, sir. I got no reading." Bren had pretended to read the dispatch. Hell, he'd nearly lost their way and gone into enemy territory.

"Da, I brought this one just for you." Rose held out a book at least two inches thick with a title that looked like gibberish.

His teeth met and ground, even as he smiled.

"But perhaps you have read it already?" she said when he didn't immediately take it. "I know it was very popular in your Civil War."

Civil War? Bren squinted to look once again at the title. French. Dang if it wasn't, *Les Misérables*. He reached out for it. "We called it, Lee's Miserables." He flipped open the book, daring fate. Tiny writing, all running together. What the hell had he been thinking? Not thinking. Wanting to impress his daughter and wife.

He tossed the book away. "Let's go for a swim!" He leapt up from their blanket and slapped his thighs in anticipation "Who's coming with me?"

"Swimming?" Rosie's mouth gawped like a beached fish. "But it looks so cold!"

"Cold? Naw. What's a little chill next to a good swim!" He shucked off his jacket and then checked the height of the sun in the cloudless sky. If he kept his shirt and britches on, they'd likely dry out soon enough. Had to remember to preserve a bit of modesty around his young daughter.

"But we've nothing to wear."

Of course! Girls couldn't get into the water in those rigs—huge skirts and petticoats…

Danger!

A flash of yellow, a sweet sing-song voice...

He shook his head, wanting to rid himself of the dark memory.

"Besides, how are we to admire you if we are busy flailing around in the water?" Callie asked. "Much better to have a grand audience of two ready to applaud you when you return."

Rosie still had a smile on her face, but it looked mighty forced, and her hands fisted in her skirts, as if she needed a tooth pulled.

Oh, heck. He hadn't seen it. Hadn't been paying close enough attention. Now he did. Rose was afraid of the water. One look at Callie confirmed what had just smacked him upside the head.

"Show-off? You think me a show-off, do you?"

"The biggest in all of England, and Scotland, too, I'll wager. Not to mention your United States," Callie stated.

Rose giggled

"And you, Miss Rose Cavanaugh? What say you?"

Rose bit her lip and then nodded.

"Well, I reckon I must oblige you ladies and give you something to gawp over."

Eleven strides to the edge of the water. The last two over freezing round stones and through sandy mud.

The cold hit him like a lariat's lash as he sloshed through the water—sharp, sudden, but nothing compared to the sting of shame. He resisted the urge to look back, drew a deep breath, and dove.

****

Oh, this wonderful man and his fearfully defiant bravado...

But she'd seen the flash of panic in Brendan's eyes

when Rose had brought out Victor Hugo's *Les Misérables*. In the next moment he'd jumped up, slapped his thighs with a relish Callie knew he didn't feel, distracting them with the declaration of his intention to swim.

Callie suddenly recalled his note—the one he'd tucked inside the gift of books. Careful, yet very simple penmanship.

She'd never seen him reading a book, or even a newspaper. Not at her cottage, not at Ryeland Park, not even here at the keep, despite the books he's so generously sent.

Could he not read?

Had he given her the books not for show, not as a token, but simply because he wanted her to have the world she loved, even if he couldn't enter it himself.

Rose suddenly stood.

"What?" Callie stiffened, jerked out of her musings.

"Da. He hasn't come up."

The surface of the lake was glass. Not a ripple. "He must have done. You likely just missed it."

"No." Rose shook her head vehemently. "I *have* been watching. It has been too long." She ran to the edge of the water, her shawl dropping on the stones.

Callie stood, shielding her eyes from the sun and scanning the water. *Where is he?*

Rose waded into the water, heedless of her skirts. The green wool of her dress floated up around her waist, her hands fisting tight against her breast.

Callie debated shucking her skirt, but feared taking her eyes from Rose and the surface of the lake.

She hissed as icy water engulfed her feet. Pain rushed to her head as the cold took hold.

How long *had* he been under?

Rose teetered, nearly up to her neck now, her frantic gaze jerking back and forth from shore to shore.

Had he hit a rock?

No blood.

No sign.

Not one ripple.

Slick, algae covered, stones nearly had her pitching below the water's surface. Instinctively, her hands found her belly.

Too long. Dear God, too long.

"Brendan! Brendan!" she called out, knowing he couldn't hear her, but needing to do something.

"Da!" Rose joined her. "D-a-a-a—!"

Had Rose seen him? Callie turned back toward the girl. But Rose had sunk below the water line. Callie could only see her arms, flapping, flailing…

No! Damn these heavy skirts! Arms searching, she found the fabric of Rose's dress and yanked it. The girl's head broke the surface, her mouth open, gasping.

And then, a powerful surge burst from the water directly in front of them, a glistening body heaving upwards.

Bren!

Callie did not know at this point who was holding who up, Rose or herself. They both clung to each other, attention utterly fixed on this Poseidon, whipping his head, slinging water, gasping in triumph, a grin spreading over his face!

Grinning? She stared in disbelief. His daughter had nearly drowned!

And then, even worse, he laughed. "I thought you ladies weren't going to join me."

Rose, who had managed to gain her footing, tried to answer his smile.

"Where the hell were you?" Callie practically screamed. "Rose nearly drowned trying to find you!"

"Drowned?" His smile dimmed as he took a step toward his daughter.

"I—I am fine. I slipped. I—it was silly." With shaking fingers, she swiped at the wet mat of hair that covered one eye and tried to smile through chattering teeth.

"Where were you? Did you have a reed in your pocket? Were you trying to scare us?"

"No!" He turned away and hit the water with his fist. Then turned back to them. "No," he repeated, now softer. "I was only holding my breath. It's just something I do. A challenge. I've done it since—since I was a boy."

He turned away and then back to them. "You have to believe me, I never meant to scare you. I never meant—" He broke off, then, gasping as if it were he who were truly drowning.

What was happening? She had never seen him so vulnerable—well, once before. Sitting at her old, scarred table at the cottage. Just before he had made love to her. Yes, there was some of that same look then.

Did Rose see it as well? Or was she too shaken to see the desperate pain in her father?

He raised his hands as if he wanted to reach out to them. She would have gone to him then, but she was holding Rose up and did not dare let go.

"Come, Rose, I think we must let your Da off the rack," she said, trying to make her voice light. "If only so we might get out of this cold water before we freeze."

He remained mute.

She took Rose by the shoulders and guided her back onto the beach, their heavy, sodden skirts dragging through the sand and stones. Rose shivered even though the sun was strong and warm. Callie settled the girl on the blanket and gave her a shawl, pulled it tight around her.

When she finally turned back toward the loch, Bren still stood with water up to his chest, staring sightlessly down at his hands floating like pale fish on the surface.

A razor-thin blade of alarm sliced through her, shocking in its sting. Surely, he would not. God in Heaven, he could not—

Pain lanced through her feet as she pounded over the rocks and sand, armfuls of wet skirt slowing her.

"Da?" Rose's plaintive call echoed Callie's own fear.

He paid no attention, still staring at his hands, sinking lower, lower...

She plunged back into the lake, not knowing what drove her but knowing she must.

He had turned from the shore back toward the center of the lake.

Surely, he must hear her splashing, her heavy breathing. Surely, he could not ignore Rose, crying out in fear.

Dear God, if he disappeared again—if he—if he left her—

She had not been prepared for such a feeling, such a terrible sense of danger, such an appalling loss of control—

When she reached him, she froze, now just behind him but uncertain how to approach. Should she lay a hand on him? He could disappear in a flash.

"Brendan," she said with more confidence than she felt. "Bren."

His body jerked at the sound of her voice.

"Bren, she is well. We are both well." She touched his shoulder, found his hand in the water with her other. She threaded her fingers into his. "Come, Rose is worried."

He looked at her then, the pain in his eyes so palpable it shocked her. She gritted her teeth and raised her eyebrows giving him the school-marmish look he seemed to love. "And now I am suddenly famished."

He blinked and looked toward the shore and his daughter, then swallowed, his eyes, mouth, and the hand gripping hers tightening, squeezing, as if he might shatter her bones.

Something broke open in him. Tears, not lake water, but tears streamed down his face.

"I didn't mean it—I would never— I'm so dang sorry, Callie."

"I know, my love. I know." Tears came hot over her cheeks, recognizing his for the precious gift they were. "It is over, in the past. You are forgiven. It is over."

Oh, she would swear this huge, hulking man had suddenly become a vulnerable little boy. She smiled into his glistening eyes.

"Come now, my love. Mrs. Green has packed all your favorites. And, it was meant to be a surprise, but she has made her famous clootie dumpling. We will be so busy feasting, that books will have to wait."

He stared at her for a long moment, then, without warning, scooped her up into his arms. Miraculously, his body was all heat. He murmured something into her hair she could not hear as he carried her out of the water and set her on the blanket.

Rose, who had followed Callie to the water's edge, trailed quietly behind them, somehow knowing how fragile her Da was.

Callie busied herself with removing the sodden shawl from around Rose, fishing a tartan out of the basket, and wrapping up the shivering Rose. Then she pulled another blanket and held it out to him. He took it and wrapped it not about himself, but around her. He worked a long time adjusting its folds, making sure each one was tucked in tight. Then he took a step away.

She had the sense that she must step away as well. She returned to the blanket on the ground and sat.

A heavy silence hung between them, thick with uncertainty.

She would not let this outing, which began with such joy, end in sorrow. "What a trick, Lord Clifford! I can't imagine holding my breath for a fraction of that time."

He shook his head, as if shaking loose a painful memory.

"I was holding my breath just now as if I were under water," Rose offered, teeth chattering through her smile. "And I couldn't last long at all."

He looked so forlorn. Big, dripping man, huge hands dangling uselessly by his sides. Gorgeous and so unhappy. "Stupid, silly trick."

"Well, I don't know about silly, and I am not sure I would like to see it performed again without warning. But amazing all the same, Lord Clifford."

"Oh, yes! Quite amazing, Da!" Rose shifted to sit on her knees. "I am afraid it is all my fault. I panicked. If I had only waited a bit longer! But you were under so very long…"

"Rosie, you don't swim do you?" Bren finally asked.

Rose looked between the two of them and then sat back on her heels, pulling the blanket up around her coloring cheeks. She shook her head.

Bren's eyes squeezed shut, his hands fisting against his thighs.

"Da?" Rose shifted to her knees again. "Da, would you—"

He must have heard the tentativeness of her tone, for he opened his eyes, giving her his full attention.

"Would you teach me? Would you teach me to swim?"

He glanced toward Callie, as if she should be the one to provide an answer. But Callie only smiled.

"And would you teach me your trick?" Rose asked. "How to hold my breath like that?"

Oh, how Callie longed to gather her in her arms—so kind and generous even in the face of her fear. So wanting acceptance and love, but daring to grant it first, before it had been granted to her.

Brendan smiled then. "Heck, Rosie, there's no shame in admitting to not knowing something. Course, I'm not the best person to give out advice when it comes to learning. But there's always time to be taught a thing or two, even for a fellow of my advanced years. Isn't that right, my love?"

My love. He had heard her, was acknowledging their new closeness. One that went far beyond the bedroom where they lay cocooned in the dark of night.

"Oh, yes. One is never too old to try something new." And indeed, she did feel new, remade.

He clapped his hands and then rubbed them

together. "Right! But first things first. Nothing like a full belly to warm us up and then you get right back on the horse!"

What a mercurial man! A word from his daughter could transform him from utter shame to buoyant happiness...

He sat down to the plate Callie handed him. Her cold fingers touched his warm ones and they shared a look. Then he sat back, propped on his elbow, a big lounging cat, and dug into the food as if he hadn't eaten in three weeks. His grin was huge, the sun shining on his cap of golden hair, dimple winking.

"Now then, Rosie, the trick is to think of the water as your friend..."

Oh, but how marvelous he was!

Yes, somehow, being baptized in that freezing lake they had all come out renewed, ready to become a real family here in the brilliant light of this glorious day.

Chapter Twenty-Two

"That was quite a trick you played on us today."

He just grunted. After an energetic poke like that, he'd been certain she would've just drifted off to sleep.

"You mentioned it was something you did as a boy?" She turned to him, her arm propped under her head, her gaze fully fixed on him. "How did you start? Was it a dare with Farren?"

More questions.

"*You* never talk about *your* past," he dodged. Might've been childish, but he still hadn't told her about Iris Darvan being alive, asking for money. Hadn't mentioned her to Rosie either.

But he had made himself a promise—if either of them asked him straight, he wouldn't lie.

Still hadn't written to Farren either.

"Perhaps because you've never asked," she said, calm as you please.

Well, that landed like a punch to the gut.

Before Callie, he hadn't cared to know women too deep. Most seemed to like him just fine without all that talk. Never figured any woman could take Farren's place anyhow. Women were there to feed his hunger, sing a sweet tune, maybe get set up on a pedestal now and then. But they were messy with feelings, and how could he hope to sort out theirs when he'd never known what the hell to do with his own.

Farren got him. Always had. No need to explain.

Women were too damn much work.

Only—he'd been wrong. Some were worth it.

Like Nora. Farren said they'd found something real. And dense as he was, even Bren could see it.

But Farren wasn't him. Sure, they looked alike, maybe even talked alike—but that's where it stopped. His brother was decent, honest, steady. The kind who deserved someone good.

Bren? What did he have to offer a woman like Callie?

Hell, he hadn't even known he was starving for love. Not till she found the hollow inside him—buried under years of not giving a damn. She'd gone and poked at it.

He hated her for that.

And damn it, he loved her more than anything for it. For digging up that soft spot only Farren had ever seen. For wanting to fill it.

"Yes, I would like to know you." Her mind, not just her body.

And maybe, just maybe, his curiosity wasn't a way to dodge. Maybe he really did want to know what made her *her*. Turned out, all he had to do was ask. Simple as that.

"Very well," she said. "What would you like to know?"

Suddenly his head was full of questions, tripping over each other.

"I'm imagining you as a kid, nose in a book."

"You are correct." She smiled.

Stupid how good it felt to get that right.

"Your ma teach you to read?"

A shadow crossed her face. Damn. First question

and he'd already made her clam up.

He was about to cut in with a joke, maybe touch her knee—but she beat him to it.

"She never had the chance. I never really knew her."

Hermione was Callie's step mamma, but he'd not known that her ma had died so young.

"I remember she loved to trace my brows. 'Beautiful wings to see the world,' she'd whisper, like it was our secret. After she left, I used to imagine the kind of dreams she might have had. I pictured her out there, chasing down happiness, though I doubt she ever caught it."

Left? Hell, he'd thought she'd died.

"I'm sorry, Callie-girl. Didn't mean to bring all that back up."

"Oh, no. I don't mind speaking of her. It is good to bring her into the light now and then."

"She left?" he asked, frowning.

Callie nodded. "She was caught far too young— only seventeen, Helena's age. Bound to a man she loathed."

His spine went stiff. Trapped—was that how she felt?

But her hand found his. He gave it a squeeze, trying to reassure her. Or maybe himself.

"And then she was caught by me... ensnared more deeply. Because she loved me. She came crawling back. Begging to return. All because of me."

"What happened?" he asked. He had to know. Had to see how this story carved out the woman beside him.

"He sent her away. And no one spoke of her again, as if she'd died. I was four—no one'd ever explained what death meant. I asked for her so many times that finally my nursemaid sat me down and told me. That was how I learned the word 'dead.'"

She fingered the locket at her breast.

He'd taken it to Tam's, and together they'd fixed it. *Only True Love*—Tam had read the nearly worn-away words out loud. Inside was a coil of braided hair—red and blonde. Maybe hers and Helena's? He remembered it swinging from her neck that night at the cabin, catching firelight as she rode him. She'd smiled when he gave it back to her, whole again.

He tried to picture her at four—a mop of red curls, big serious eyes, reaching for her mother's hand to show her some tiny treasure.

Callie's grip tightened in his. She took a steady breath. "When she came back to beg for me... that was the last time I saw her."

Jesus. He knew that kind of loss. The kind that cleaves a person in half. But there was one brutal difference. Like her father, he was the one breaking apart a family.

"Is that why you got all fired up when your pa said a child should be raised by both its parents?"

"Yes. He threw her out. Couldn't forgive the betrayal. But he wouldn't free her, either. So I grew up motherless."

"Do you hate him, your pa?" Waiting for her answer felt like digging his own grave—slow, steady, and damned inevitable.

"I did. Once. But not anymore. Hate is too strong a feeling to waste on my father. I neither hate him nor love him. I was merely a pawn in his campaign to dominate her. A bargaining chip. Had I been a boy, it might have been different. But I was what she wanted—so I was the one thing he'd never give."

"But you forgave him?"

She shifted her hand inside his. He realized he'd been squeezing too hard.

"They should never have married. That's the truth of it. So yes, I forgave him. He could never grasp her brightness, much less match it."

Ah, hell. Was history already repeating itself? A child the only thing tethering them together?

And then there was Iris Darvan. Would Callie side with her? With a mother who'd been separated from her children—one lost to death, the other to an evil man?

Now Iris was back. Did she know Rosie was alive?

Was he doing the very thing her father had done— keeping a child from her mother?

He turned from Callie, stuck in a tangle of terrible thoughts. Already off in the weeds of what he'd done.

She touched his shoulder.

Not more questions. Not now.

Her finger traced one of the scars across his back. The one his father had given him.

"Thank you for listening."

He grunted, still too deep in the mess of what he should do—and what he knew he wouldn't do unless forced.

"I wonder what happened to you, that you prefer letting people think the worst of you rather than setting them straight?"

He pulled away, sat up, swung his legs over the edge of the bed.

"Nothing to set straight. Don't go painting me a hero, Callie. You'll only end up whitewashing in the end."

He grabbed his robe and left, barefoot and aimless, the door clicking shut behind him like a quiet curse.

Chapter Twenty-Three

She had believed, after the incident at the loch—his ill-considered trick that had gone so terribly awry—they had made some measure of progress toward building a real trust. It had frightened them both, pulled at buried wounds, and she had hoped the vulnerability it unearthed might draw them closer. But now he had withdrawn again, retreating into himself with that quiet, impenetrable stillness that unsettled her far more than anger ever could.

She would not forgo the delights of their lovemaking—pleasures that had grown more tender, more reverent—but still, she longed for something deeper. If only they might learn to share not only their bodies, but their thoughts—the innermost landscapes of their hearts and minds.

As content as she'd imagined herself over the more than three years she'd spent at her cottage, she now knew how severely lacking they had been. Oh, part of her had loved the solitude, the rigor of living on her own. Being responsible for only herself and her animals. How hard it had been, and yet, in retrospect, how very easy.

This—this attempt at building a family—was the far more arduous endeavor. To carry new life within her, to offer her love to a man marked by sorrow, and to open her heart to his nearly grown child, whom she was only beginning to understand and already loved with an aching, maternal fierceness—this was hard. And yet, how she wanted them. With a desperation so fierce, it frightened her.

Meanwhile, the babe within her grew. Her abdomen, once flat, had taken on a gentle, unmistakable curve. Her breasts had grown fuller, tender to the touch. She would be a mother—soon enough. And she wanted a father for this child. Not merely a name or a figure, but a true presence. She wanted Bren to stand beside her—not as a shadow of himself, but as a man willing to claim them both.

And still, the image of the veiled woman haunted her dreams.

Who was she?

She should have asked him—openly, plainly. She, who demanded truth of herself and of everyone around her, had hesitated on the very eve of their wedding. She had turned away from confrontation, allowing the question to fester. And now, this woman had become a burr in her thoughts, irritating her dreams, and worse— embedding herself in the quiet spaces of Callie's heart.

Was their love so fragile that it could not withstand honesty?

The rainy weather had kept her indoors for nearly a week. But today bloomed fresh and clear. A few fickle clouds intermittently blotted the sun, casting dappled shadows on the fields far below. Such order in the valley with its neatly tended squares, mapping where one parcel started and stopped. Tidy civility.

She turned back to gaze at the keep. Home. Her home for her family. The stone walls seemed softer now, laced with climbing wisteria. The mullioned windows winked as they caught the light. How amazing what sunlight could do to a vista—what it did to one's well-being.

It felt good to be out of the house. She had been holed up for too long, being teacher and friend, and dare she say, even mother to Rose. At least, she hoped they were on that path. But, just like her Da, Rosie held heavy secrets as well.

Rose was ensconced in the library reading about her new passion, the United States. Callie had asked if she wanted to go for a walk in the woods, but Rose shook her head declaring she wanted to finish these next chapters on, "The Way West".

Callie was just as happy to go out on her own. The fresh air might clear her tangled mind. Stop her from confiding her worries to Rose or probing too deeply into the girl's past.

A path took her into the east side of Ben Crannoch. The recent rain brought out the tang of pine mixed with earthy loam.

The trail had been used with some regularity. Had he come this way? Likely. Perhaps there was another loch this direction. He liked to fish.

Occupied with thoughts of her husband, she didn't spy the cottage until she was nearly upon it.

A setting for a children's story book. Gem-like windows in green, red and blue were set deep into the walls. Its thatched roof looking like a cockeyed hat, lacking only a feathered plume of smoke as its finishing touch. The front door stood slightly open.

"Good day?"

She pushed it wider and blinking, her eyes adjusted to the gloom. Tidy. Only dull embers in the grate. No one about.

She would have liked to have explored further, but clearly someone lived here, and she would not trespass.

She closed the door just as it had been and then continued down the path. Not far she discovered yet another building. A barn. It reminded her at once of the one at her cottage. Indeed, the door looked to be exactly like the sliding one Bren had fixed for her not so long ago.

That door stood wide open. She ventured inside.

A wood shop of sorts. A large table dominated the room. On top of it lay several slabs of roughly cut wood in various lengths and widths. The light from a window fell on one piece.

In this fantastical place, she almost felt as if it was calling to her. She reached out and touched the plank. Dark whorls of deep red and brown marked its surface, and two-thirds of the way down a huge burl, roughly twice the size of her head, bulged. If one possessed a vivid imagination, one could imagine it as a face trapped within the wood.

"A beauty."

Callie turned at the sound of the voice.

An old man stood in the doorway. He nodded, a soft smile on his face. He seemed not at all surprised to see her standing in his little barn.

"Ye've a good eye." He stepped closer. "A fine piece o'wood, that."

"My apologies. The door was open."

"Aye, it stays open often as not." He nodded his head toward the knotted wood. "Most folks would pass this piece by, seein' as it's flawed." He crossed to her and pointed his gnarled finger at the burl, then passed his hand lovingly over the knot's face. "But I'm thinkin' it's what spoke to ye. The burl forms from some hurt in the tree's life. We cannae say what, most times. It's a mystery. But the tree answers back wi' a fortress. A shield o' sorts. Protectin' itself."

Callie had an odd notion that the old man was no longer talking about wood.

"Often the most beautiful and interesting piece is passed over because it's no' perfect."

This wizened old man seemed to be able to see right into the very heart of her. "I am sorry to intrude. You have caught me prying."

"No matter. You are curious. That is a good thing, yer ladyship."

"Ah, so you know who I am."

"Who else?"

"Right. Of course."

"He's no' here."

"Oh! Am I that transparent?"

He shrugged. "I've lived a few years longer than ye, and I fancy masel' a keen observer of nature—human an' otherwise." He touched the wood again. "Ye'll need tae dig deep tae reveal this one's beauty, but mark me, if ye spend the time, ye'll no' be disappointed."

Again, it seemed the old man was no longer talking about wood.

"It's raw yet. Needs care tae reveal its secrets. Its beauty's just beginnin' tae show—aye, but there's more, if ye're gentle, and patient. Give him time."

Callie jerked her gaze up to meet his bright blue one. *Him?* Had he said, give *him* time?

He continued to stroke the wood lovingly.

No, she must have heard wrong. But still, she could not help but liken this multifaceted specimen with her husband.

"Ah, Mr.—?"

"Cree. I'm Tam Cree, ma'am."

"Well, Mr. Cree, I thank you for the—lesson."

He pulled at his beard and nodded, a knowing smile on his lips. "Aye, grown folk like tae pin things down and name them 'fore they've had a chance tae breathe. A child's got the right of it—he sees a mountain o' possibilities in the simplest o' things."

Chapter Twenty-Four

"Has Rose asked you for a book on Braille?"

"What?" No poke. Now it was her turn to ask the questions. He'd been dodging her ever since finding out her pa had kept her from her ma—afraid what she'd say if she knew he was doing the same to Rose and Iris.

"Agnes is learning to read Braille, and Rose wants to be able to read her letters."

"Well, I happen to know Braille." It seemed a safe enough subject.

"You do?" She sat up now, all attention.

"Come to think on it, it's probably not the same as what Agnes is learning. I'll get Rosie the book."

His wife shook her head. "I am sure she would be very interested in your version of Braille. I know I am."

"Aw, it's not so interesting. Us spies used it in the war. Needed to read messages, even when there was no light, so we used Braille." Dang talk of war, when all he wanted was love.

"Truly? How interesting."

What would she say if he told her that he was better at reading Braille than words on a page?

"When I'm interested in a subject, I like to explore it thoroughly," she said as her fingers parted his robe and then trailed down over his chest toward his stomach. He grunted, but she seemed oblivious to the blissful torture she was inflicting. "Now, we've already ascertained, that

I am an open book. Turn any of my pages and I will tell you my story. But you are not quite so easy. Let's see…if you were a book, I'd have initially chosen you for your glorious cover.

"Then I'd have hefted your weight and felt you to be substantial." Her tone was so utterly matter-of-fact as her hand drifted even lower. "I usually like to read from the beginning, but I sense that is not how I will learn you best."

"I'm not sure there is all that much to learn." He swallowed. He wouldn't remind her that she didn't even get to choose this particular book.

"Oh, but I disagree. I expect there are chapters where you have yet to cut the pages."

"Well, I do have one very secret chapter—best read in Braille." He guided her hand to his cock.

Her fingers danced away. "No. I am more interested in your innermost thoughts." Her hand settled over his heart.

"My thoughts? Heck, my brother usually did most of the thinking between the two of us. I was more the brawn of the pair." He wriggled his bum to remind her of a certain bit of him.

"Oh, I imagine you have plenty of your own thoughts and opinions, completely unrelated to Farren's."

How could the gal be touching him in that way and yet sound like she was reciting from a dang recipe book?

What the heck just happened to his possible poke? Gone, he suspected when his wife shifted back to get a better look in his eyes, thereby leaving his nether region like a bobber without hope of a fish.

"I understand books are not a favorite of yours, but

I plan to study you, sir. Inside and out." She gathered the loose ends of his robe and pulled him toward the bed.

Now this was more like it. He followed her like an eager pup. When she pushed him onto the bed, he made sure his robe fell entirely open. "Well, you may *study* me, ma'am, to your heart's content." He shifted upwards on the bed, hoping to make her aware of his need.

"Very good. Now, let us start with the cover."

"I like the sound of that."

"Well, the cover is exquisite. In fact, it is so tantalizing that one might just gaze at it for hours and not even bother to open to its story. But I am greedy, and I want to devour the whole thing. I want to be able to reread favorite chapters that make me laugh."

She slipped the silk fabric off his shoulders and pulled his arms from the sleeves.

Better and better.

She ran her hands over his limbs almost as if she were a dang sawbones. He smiled.

"And I want to cry over the sad parts." She abandoned his nether region to touch his jawline. "How did you get this scar?"

Dang.

"What, that little thing?" he asked as she traced its slender ridge. "Most folks never even notice it."

"Why? It's plain as the nose on your face?"

"Why? It's plain as the nose on your face."

He shook his head. "You'd have made a right fine spy, I reckon."

She seemed to consider his words carefully before answering. "Yes, I believe I would have been, at that." She lifted a leg over him and settled her cooter right on his belly. "We are going to go over every inch of your body, and find every scar, from the tiniest little scratch to the biggest doozy, as you would call it. And you will tell me the story behind each one." She touched his jawline again.

"I have a much more impressive one right down here you could get acquainted with." He pulled her hand down to his upper thigh right next to his bobbing—

"No, I will not be distracted." She slipped her hand from his and tapped the scar on his jawline. "I am in charge. and I want to know about this one."

"That little ding's nothing. Farren has one from that particular escapade, but his is a real doozy." Her arms, now folded under her breasts, pushed them up and together, while curling tendrils of hair provided a curtain for the show. "Woman, if you want this tale, you are going to have to cover up."

"Oh, very well. I've no wish to be a distraction." She found the ties of her robe and cinched it tightly about her still-slim waist. "There, is that better?"

"Better? Naw. Better would be no talking at all."

She gave him that schoolmarm look.

"Right. We were eleven. Farren and I were supposed to be riding the fences, looking for places that needed mending. Only we weren't. We were playing Texas Rangers. That time I was the horse thief, and I just took off without any ready, set, go."

Callie, thoroughly immersed, rocked ever so slightly as if actually on a horse. He raised his knees, giving her a sort of backrest, and conveniently snugging his cock between the two.

"I tore across the south field." The smell of newly cut alfalfa had been as thick in the air as midsummer mosquitoes. "Farren was gaining on me. I swerved and headed for the trees. A dang fool move. But, well, hindsight is twenty-twenty."

Tree limbs had reached out as he whizzed by. He'd felt invincible, dodging them like a knight in a jousting tourney. "I *halooed,* throwing my head back. Farren did the same, only longer and louder, trying to outdo me." He shook his head. "Didn't see the branch. My little brother lay on the ground cold as a wagon tire. Three days before the dang fool decided to wake up. And three days I slept nary a wink curled on the floor by his side."

"That was good of you."

"Naw, just wanted to make sure I was there front and center so he could cuss my sorry hide and then we could get to the business of getting our stories straight. 'Course, I got tanned right good no matter the tale we hatched."

He grinned, tugged the tie of her robe. "Speaking of tail, I've a hankering to know a sight more about yours."

She batted his hands away as if he were an annoying bee.

"I'm not quite finished here." Callie touched the puckered scar on his chest. "Now, this could certainly be categorized as a doozy. Did you get this one in the war?"

"Would've been heroic, to take a bullet in battle, but I can't claim that distinction. Lots of heroes in that war, and no heroes at all. Plenty of honor and plenty of outright cowardice. Naw, I got this on this side of the pond, courtesy of Rodger Milton. They say, 'Only the good die young'. Apparently, the Almighty has a lot more in store for this sinner," he finished, hoping his quip would lighten the mood.

She bent to kiss the scar. "What about this one?" she asked, her fingertip tracing the thick, shiny welt just over his left flank.

Take care of your sister!

Her gaze found his, questioning. He must have stiffened at her touch, at the memory of his mother's words—

Could he lie, or distract her? It would be easy enough. She'd learned not to press him when he grew evasive.

He could. But he was so tired of it all. Tired of lying, tired of playing the fool...

"I got that one just after Sara died."

He hoped that brief answer would be enough for her, that she would move on to another spot. Perhaps the burn he'd gotten when battling a fire at Fort Randall when the Sioux had had just about enough of the white man ruining their land.

"How? How did it happen?" she asked with infinite care, as if prying open a fragile shell.

Nope, she wasn't going to let this one go, was she?

Memories flooded in. Burning hot pain in his head, uncontrollable shaking that left him too exhausted to raise a finger, let alone rise up to take a sip of water his stone-faced ma forced between his cracked lips. Farren hovering in the corner of the room, rocking back and forth, his eyes glazed.

"My Pa took a horsewhip to me."

"What!"

"Oh, he had a right to be mad. Farren is my other half, but Sara, well, she was our family's heart. I broke our heart."

She waited, a tiny frown on her face, her mouth set as if there were hundreds of words pressing against her lips desperate to be released.

The pain—too strong—he peeled away from it, exposing a happier memory.

"I remember so clearly the day she was born. Pa, a glass of whiskey in his hand, still full, sloshing onto the carpet as he paced the room below my folks' bedroom, muttering under his breath. It seemed to go on for hours and hours, the waiting, but, Ma, she never cried out. Not once. Then finally we heard a little mewl of a cry. Pa slammed his whiskey down and charged up the stairs. His *haloo* of triumph told it all. A girl. 'Course, Farrer and I wanted another brother. But Ma got it right this time and produced the most beautiful little gal you ever wanted to see."

Callie touched the swell of her belly.

"Pa insisted she be called Sarafina—I know why, now. The name of the gal he'd tried to run off with here in England, the one that got her neck broke by his thoughtless actions. Jayne was added as a concession to my mother. But we never called her Sarafina. Instead, we had a million nicknames for our beloved girl. Sage, Seraph, Sasha, Finni, Sprout. Mostly Sprout."

The great pressure built behind his eyes, his body hot with shame, his heart squeezing within his chest. So easy to tip into tears, into the abyss of sadness and grief. He squeezed his hands into fists, his fingernails biting into the callused flesh.

The joyous memory evaporated, leaving only heartache and pain. He shut his eyes against the onslaught. That terrible day when he'd brought Sara home.

He'd made himself look toward his ma. If she had made one gesture of kindness, one twitch of compassion, he would've succumbed to the terrible grief and broken right there at her feet. But when he looked in her eyes, there was nothing. The sight of his mother turning away from him to clear the table, moving her three loaves of rising bread in preparation to lay out her dead daughter's body ended his boyhood then and there. No more crying. No more feeling. He had to be so vigilant against the pain that would sneak up on him and gut him, sure as a badger.

But his Pa? Oh, he'd been very real. Once he'd taken Sprout's body and gently laid her on the table, he came for his son. Bren had welcomed the blows. Farren tried to intervene but was too weak. Bren had ended up crawling into the barn to sleep for the night. His eyes nearly swollen shut, his lips torn and bloody from his teeth, each breath a torture against his bruised and broken ribs.

When he'd recovered enough—nearly two days— he'd headed straight back to see her—But they'd gone and buried her without him. No time to waste in the heat of July. Had to set her in the ground as soon as possible.

He'd dragged himself to her graveside, a fistful of Queen Anne's lace, buttercup, and blue devils in his shaking hand. No gravestone yet, just a beautifully carved cross. Before he could lay his pitiful offering on her grave, he'd been knocked sideways, his head ringing with terrible pain.

Don't you bloody dare! his pa had raged, his speech clipped and posh. The true Brit always came out when he got riled. *You dare come here, you who killed her? Your very breath sullies the ground in which she lies. If I ever catch you in this graveyard again, I will whip you so hard, you will never be able sit on that worthless arse again!*

He'd been nearly as tall as his pa, then. Yet his father outweighed him by fifty pounds. All bones and gangly arms and legs, he'd been. All snot and unshed tears. All show and callous bravado.

All a sham. Just a dang sham.

The man he'd become had truly been forged then and there over Sprout's grave. A man who could not really be touched. Who laughed at danger or punched his way out of it. Who loved women but only on the surface, only making love to their bodies, never allowing them to touch his heart.

Still, pain and doubt wormed its way in. At the oddest moments, when a body wouldn't expect it. At the sight of a flower—the white flesh of his wife's breast—the swell of her belly...

As the years passed, he'd got better at seeing it coming. Managing it. Till the pain receded and it was a little itch now and again.

But lately that itch had begun to grow. He'd begun to feel more. More joy. More pain. More expectation. More love.

Love? Could he truly love anymore?

He glanced again at Callie. She was looking back at him much like she had the day of their picnic, when they were standing in that freezing loch, and she'd held out her hand to him. Again, waiting patiently while he retraced his steps over this terrible road of memories. Waiting for him to come back.

She had called him 'my love' that day, and he'd echoed her words. Filled with awe, and so frightened, so very frightened...

"When she died, every bit of joy in our family died with her. I killed the only thing my father ever loved.

Farren forgave me, but my ma—" He shook his head. "And Pa, well, now he had a real whipping boy. His anger had always been there—a seed. But losing Sara was a storm of grief that soaked him to the roots. After that, his rage grew wild.

"He caught me by the grave and hauled me up till my feet left the ground. Told me to never go there again. Well, a course, I couldn't stay away. Sure thing you tell me no, I'm gonna do it anyway. So, true to his word, the next time he found me there, he gave me a beating I'll never forget."

Bren laughed. "Poor old man. Those beatings never did stop me from going to see Sara. But when I stood up from her graveside, finally bigger and stronger than him, he backed away. I think by then he'd had his fill of raging at me. After that, it turned inward, and he just seemed to give up on life. I reckon his anger was all he had left and when that went, he had no more reason to go on living."

Callie said nothing. She untied her robe and lay herself fully over him, as though determined to shield him from all that had ever wounded him. Somehow, she seemed to find each hollowed space in him and fill it— with warmth, with a fierce tenderness, with love beyond any words.

His arms came around her to bind her body even more closely to his. Only the wetness in the crook of his shoulder betrayed her grief.

And then, his own tears, sliding down his cheeks, melding with hers.

Chapter Twenty-Five

He lay spent and loose limbed next to her. How could he think this would ever get old? She felled him each time they made love. Like a great pine, toppled by a whisper.

He held her closer, her head tucked under his chin, her finger making looping circles over the fine hair on his chest. Would she be up for another poke?

He began looking forward to the night, not just for their lovemaking but to ask her questions. He was finding he loved discovering her secrets.

They had continued exploring his scars, at least the ones on the outside. The tales he wove about them weren't exactly tall, but aimed to entertain, not just inform.

Still, the resurrection of Iris Darvan lay like a piece of shrapnel left to fester over his heart.

He'd finally written to Farren. And he would tell his ladies about her—soon. Very soon. But he was loth to make war when there was the option of love.

It was his turn to ask a question. She was patiently waiting.

It wasn't hard to come up with one—or twenty, for that matter. This one had been tickling him for a while. "How did you end up at your cottage?"

Her fingers stopped circling and found the locket that lay between them. He felt the brush of her lashes against his chest.

"I made an agreement with my father and Hermione that I would go away if they would not force me into a loveless marriage."

Well, he'd asked for it.

"Hermione and I never got on. She wanted me married and out of her house. She also wanted to break the bond between Helena and myself. And for once, I obliged her—wholeheartedly. I fancied myself in love with him."

Jealousy flared, hot and bitter.

"Everyone was so pleased. Even my father seemed proud of me. Not proud that I was smart or learned, but that I might finally marry—and a peer of the realm, no less." She shook her head. "When I found out Hermione had bought his considerable debts to force him to the point... I rebelled." She fiddled with her locket again. "His lordship threatened to make a scene. In the end, my father swallowed his pride and paid him off. He had another daughter to launch, so he cut his losses. By then, I was five-and-twenty. Thoroughly on the shelf, and 'used goods.' So, I took the opportunity and escaped to Scotland."

Bren's hands curled into fists. God, he wanted to throttle the bastard.

But the man didn't matter. What did matter was her courage. The trust it took to share this. The raw, unguarded truth of it. With nary a shred of shame.

He drew a breath—and let it go with a rush.

"I can't read," he said.

There. It was out.

He waited, every muscle taut, as her hand stilled.

And then—blessedly—her fingers moved again,

tracing slow circles against his skin.

"Well," he went on, grateful she hadn't thrown him out of the bed, "I can read a little. And write. But it's damn hard wrangling the words into order. They jump around—kind of like fleas on a griddle."

She said nothing.

He nearly tried to fill the silence with a joke—but then she spoke.

"I wondered why you didn't help Rose with her history lessons."

He braced, waiting for her to fix it. Offer to teach him. Tell him it could be overcome. But—nothing.

"Is that it?" he asked. "Is that all you have to say?"

She sat up, eyes bright in the dim light. "No, of course that's not all I have to say. I have much to say. But what I really want you to hear is this: I am so very proud of you. And I think that is quite enough for the present."

She kissed the patch of skin just above his pounding heart.

"Now," she murmured, "no more talking. No more reading. Not for the rest of the night."

She pulled him down to her.

"Cover me," she breathed into his ear, threading her arms around him.

"Cover me with your beautiful body… and come into me."

Chapter Twenty-Six

"Are you afraid, Rosie?

They stood at the edge of the loch. The lap of icy water nibbling their toes.

"A bit, Da."

"Good. Good to admit when you're scared. Only then can you thumb your nose at your fears."

"But Da, you're not afraid of anything, are you?"

"Afraid? Me? Let me tell you a story. When I was out west, I was by my lonesome a fair bit, often camping out when the cold would near freeze the hair off your head."

Rosie gawped appreciatively at his exaggerated tale.

He crouched down and she mimicked him. So attentive.

"Lots of sounds in the night. Critters come out then. Small uns. Big uns, too," he whispered. "Sound bigger when you can't see 'em in the dark."

"Just like the critters in the attic," she whispered back.

"Just like." He nodded as he imagined Tam would.

"But they're not so frightening if you know what's making the noise," she said, ever the good student.

"Exactly! You get to know the particular sounds of where you're at—the birds calling to one another, or the grizzlies grubbing for food. Mice scrabbling in the eaves. But knowing the music of the woods—or a house—

makes you less fearful. Remember that gal. The more you know about a thing, the more you understand it, and finally, you might even begin to love it."

Hell, when had he become so philosophical? Sara would be right proud of her big brother.

"I love you, Da."

Her words hit his heart like a fifty pounder and nearly felled him. No one, save Sara and Farren, had ever said those words to him—except a lady or two caught up in the throes of passion, and that didn't count.

This little gal was so dang brave. Far braver than he ever was—unafraid to risk her heart.

"By golly, I love you too, my sweet Rosie. I surely do."

"Thank you for teaching me."

"Oh, I reckon I got a lesson myself this afternoon. You are a very good teacher."

"Me?" Rose smiled even as she shook her head.

"Oh, yes. And one of the bravest people I know."

He blinked away threatening tears. How much she looked like his sweet Sara. His Sprout.

"And now, since you're so darned brave, I figure I might as well be too."

"But you are braver than anyone I know, Da."

"There's brave, and then there's *brave*. I'm mostly brave on the outside, but not so much on the inside." He touched the place over his heart.

She nodded, her face serious.

"So I'm gonna tell you a secret, a secret I've been afraid to tell you for some time. Afraid you'd be ashamed of me." He took a steadying breath. "I can't read." Only three simple words behind a boatload of shame.

"Oh!" Rose exclaimed before covering her mouth

with her hand. Was she ashamed?

"I know it's an odd thing, a grown man who can't read," he hastened to explain. "Did you ever study another language, Rosie?"

"Oh, yes! I had to study French with—before, when I lived—with him. My accent was lacking."

"Ah, my Ma tried to teach me too, but she gave it up right quick when she saw how poorly I took to it. Anyway, when I look at words on a page, they sort of look like French to me. The letters get so mixed around, I can't even tell a d from a b."

"That must be mighty frustrating."

"Mighty. And that was why I was such a dang fool at our picnic, holding my breath for so long. Showin' off. Wantin' to prove I was good at something."

No. Not shame. Acceptance. Those kind and accepting eyes never wavered from his.

Tears gathered in his eyes as she reached out and took his shaking hands in hers.

"Da! I have a wonderful plan. Since you are teaching me to swim, I will help you with your reading. Is that a fair trade?"

"Well, I don't know if it's fair. Seems to me you'll be working a sight harder teaching me my letters than me teaching you to dog paddle."

"Well, would you also teach me how to hold my breath for so long? That'll make it fair, won't it?"

This sweet gal, with her open, kind eyes. So like his beloved Sprout. Such a gift.

That's when the idea came to him. A surprise, just for his new family...

Chapter Twenty-Seven

The next day

Bren hung by the half-opened door, eavesdropping on his two ladies.

"What do you suppose the surprise could be, Callie?" Rose stood by one of the walls of bookshelves, absently taking out a book, only to return it without even looking at it.

Callie seemed distracted as well, stroking Gulliver with one hand while the other held an unopened letter.

"I wonder if the surprise is riding lessons?" Rose took down another book and ran her hand over the cover.

He couldn't see his daughter's face, but he could read her body well enough. Scared as a rabbit in fox territory. She'd made good progress with her swimming, stubbornly tenacious despite her deep fear. Making her get up on a horse—well, he reckoned *that* lesson could be put off for a while yet.

"Heaven knows what your father has up his sleeve. But you may be assured the revealing will come with no little fanfare," Callie said, ruffling Gully's neck.

If that wasn't a cue, then a fox never raided a hen house. He pushed open the door.

"Hello ladies!"

Rose wheeled, a smile on her face. "Good morning, Da!"

Callie set her letter aside and folded her hands in her lap.

"Well, now, what're you all up to today? Seems as if you've finally wrestled all these books into some order."

"Nearly." Rose almost danced over to a shelf nearest the bowed window and pointed to a row of books. "I have made a new section just for you, Da. Some adventure stories with wonderful illustrations."

Callie sat there looking like a cat in cream. Her smile full of warmth for him. He lapped it up. Heck, confession seemed to bring their little family together instead of breaking them apart.

Maybe he could even risk telling them about Iris? Yes, he'd tell them. Not today, though. Not just yet. Just a few more days…

"Angus arrived with the mail, Da. Nothing from Uncle Farren, but I have another letter from Agnes. Can we read it together, since you already know Braille? And Callie received a letter from her Da." Rose stopped to take a much-needed breath. "Oh, and don't forget, we have our swimming lesson this afternoon, remember?"

"Ah, right. Hummm…might have to put that off for today, Rosie gal. I, myself, have suddenly got a rather full plate. So full, I best be off!" He made a show of slapping his thighs and then rubbing his hands together and finally heading back toward the door.

"But what about the surprise you promised, Da?"

"Surprise?" He turned back and nearly laughed at Rose's crestfallen face. She had yet to understand her ol' pop's humor. Callie, though, only shook her head, smiling.

"You said you had a surprise for us. Didn't he,

Callie?"

"I certainly hope he does. I hate to be led down the garden path."

"Oh, I did say something about a surprise, didn't I?" He made a show of patting down his trousers and then his jacket. "Now where in the tarnation—Ah! Here it is!"

He whipped out the card from his sleeve. "Voila!"

"How did you—? Rose gawped.

He would have to thank ol' Grady Pembroke, a master at sleight of hand, for the look of downright awe on his daughter's face.

Rose eagerly took the card from his hand and then opened it. She frowned, but soon her face broke into a huge grin. Her fingers skated over the paper. "It's ... an invitation!"

Callie drew closer to take the card from Rose. "How do you know? There is nothing written here."

"Ah, but there is! You just have to look with different eyes," Rose proclaimed, mysteriously.

Callie shook her head, playing along. "I've never needed glasses to read a note before! No, there's nothing written there, I'm sure of it."

"But there is!" Rose cried in triumph. "Don't you remember, it's in Braille! Da's using Braille to send us his message."

"Well, then you will have to decipher it, Rose. I can't make heads or tails of it." She handed the card back to Rosie.

"Viscountess Clifford and Miss Rose Cavanaugh are cordially invited to..." Rose frowned, her fingers sliding over the paper again. "I must have it wrong. Christmas? Christmas in July?"

"Christmas in July? Are you quite sure?"

A frown of doubt crossed the girl's face, but then she nodded, certain now. She laid the paper flat then grasped Callie's fingers, moving them across the page. "This says Christmas, and this says July."

Bren clapped his hands together. "Right as rain, my Shy Bird. Christmas in July!"

"Seems there must be a story behind this malarkey," Callie said raising an eyebrow and trying not to smile. "Tell us about this holiday."

"I think it is self-explanatory, my dear viscountess."

"Yes, I can deduce that much, Clifford," she said teasing him with his title. "But is this a Cavanaugh tradition, or something you have just invented?"

"Lordy, why must women dissect everything? Can't you just take it as a lark and let it go at that?"

But both his ladies remained mute and darn near mulish, their arms crossed.

"No, I can see that you can't. Very well, Christmas was my little sister Sara's favorite holiday. Smack in the middle of the hottest part of the summer, she'd already start badgering everyone to get ready. Make our gifts and decorations, dig out old family recipes, practice all our favorite carols. And every year she wrote a puppet show she put on single handedly"

Memories rushed him. Sara's tongue poking out as she concentrated on painting the face of St. Nick. Ma getting her fiddle down from the high shelf where she stored it, her long fingers brushing the dust from its curved belly. Pa hauling in a huge block of ice as a surprise for his beloved little girl. Farren singing, *God, Rest ye Merry Gentlemen,* like some puffed-up opera star. And him, wrestling the biggest yule log he could find out of the woods. His pa had lit into him for his folly.

Who would light such a thing with the temperature still nigh on eighty, long after sundown?

Bren tensed, anticipating the fierce slice of pain the memories always brought.

But today, gazing at his daughter's eager, up-turned face, he only felt the swell of his heart.

No, he'd not been wrong to open this long-sealed memory. He was stronger now. His new bride and nearly-grown daughter had made him stronger.

"One year Sara just couldn't wait. She announced that we'd have Christmas early this year, at the very end of July. Of course, Ma said that'd be sacrilegious. But Pa, well, he couldn't deny his daughter anything. And thus, Christmas in July became a Cavanaugh tradition."

Rose clapped her hands. "Oh, what a wonderful surprise! Da, I wish I could have known Sara. I know I would have loved her."

Familiar guilt rose from his chest to fill his throat. He swallowed it down. "Oh, not a doubt in my mind, Rosie gal. And she you."

"Now, I must get busy!" he exclaimed, careful to keep his eyes from meeting Callie's. We only have a week to prepare!"

"I will make puppets and write a play for the occasion!"

"Well, then I fear I must put my father's letter aside and inform the staff of this grand event!"

Callie crossed to the desk where she took out pen and paper. "Mrs. Green has been longing to try out her great grandmother's special recipe for Tipsy Laird. And we will have the pheasant you killed just yesterday. I saw some girolle mushrooms on my latest walk I can gather to use in the stuffing."

"I wonder if Harriet and Martha will help me with the puppet show? Would you mind if I took them away from their work for a few hours each day? I already have an idea!" Rose joined Callie at the desk.

"Of course, the more the merrier!" Callie said.

"One more thing to add to your list," Bren said. "On the night before, on Christmas eve, you must wear your nighty inside out!"

Both Rose and Callie paused in their writing. "Inside out?" Rose asked. "Why?"

"Guaranteed to bring snow!" he declared before heading out the door.

Seeing his two ladies, shaking their heads with laughter, then as they bent over the desk, making a list, was all the gift Brendan Cavanaugh needed. Now, he had to get busy if his own offerings were going to be finished before Christmas.

Chapter Twenty-Eight

"Christmas was never so merry!" Rose exclaimed midway up a ladder, hanging more tinsel on the huge blue spruce whose gold-flocked star nearly grazed the room's fifteen-foot ceiling. "

Callie could not help but smile, remembering Bren and Phillip, squeezing the behemoth though the doorway and then hoisting it up while Callie, Rose, Martha, Harriet, and even Mrs. Billings, stood around the parameter offering advice on where to set it to make sure it stood straight. Old Mr. Billings directed the entire process from the safety of the doorway, while Gully merely lounged from his favorite perch, an ottoman near the fireplace, no doubt plotting how best to scale the tree.

They had managed to transform the dark and cavernous room, made even darker by the dimming light of an approaching summer storm, into a winter fairyland. Paper cut-out snowflakes hung from the chandeliers, spinning in a stray breeze. Hundreds of tiny candles had been laboriously fixed to the tree's branches. A crude puppet theatre, fashioned from a cast-off table, a wine crate, and a moth-eaten brocade curtain stood next to the tree. Rosie, Harriet and Martha had been working on their production day and night.

"You may see our theatre," Rosie had declared, "but the puppets will be a surprise!"

"Despite the imminent threat of a—what would your

Da call it?—ah, yes, a toad strangler, I believe Sara Cavanaugh must be looking down on our preparations and giving her blessing," Callie said, surveying the room.

"I hope we shall always have Christmas in July!" Rose turned from her labors to give Callie a huge smile.

"Yes! Folk may shake their heads and think us strange, but we will simply laugh and carry on as if decking the halls in the heat of summer were normal as butter on toast."

"Our very own private holiday. One just for our family," Rose whispered, almost like a prayer.

The child stirred within her belly as if to concur.

"I don't know if I will be able to wait to give Da his gift!" Rose looked out at the darkening sky. "I have been working so hard on it all week."

"Another? Besides your puppets?"

Rose nodded, a mysterious smile lighting her face.

"Well, I know better than to try and divine any Cavanaugh secrets. I will just have to bide my time."

Callie had agonized over what she might give to her husband. In the end, she decided the babe in her belly was gift enough.

"I guess I must have not worn my nightgown properly last night," Rose said after a rumble of thunder split the air. "Da said I should wear it inside out, but maybe I put in on backwards instead? Saint Nick brought rain instead of snow!"

"Never mind," Callie reassured. "We are snug inside, and Mrs. Green has prepared enough food to last us till All Hallows Eve, at the least!"

"Your ladyship, Miss Rose, you have a visitor." Mrs. Billings stood in the doorway, wiping her hands on her apron.

"A visitor?" Callie frowned. They weren't expecting anyone. "Who is it, Mrs. Billings?"

"A lady ma'am. She would not give her name."

Could it be Helena, come to surprise them? It would be just like Bren to come up with such a lovely and unexpected surprise. Callie glanced toward Rose, searching for any hint of collaboration. But the girl looked just as surprised as Callie.

"Well, whoever she may be, we can hardly send her away in this weather, can we? Please show her in, Mrs. Billings."

The bit of greenery she had been trying to hang on the mantle fell. So clumsy these days. She bent to pick it up. Not quite so easy with her growing belly.

"Mama?" The word, said tentatively, as if Rose were testing it on her lips. "Mama?"

Callie's heart pounded. Rose had never called her mama. She gained her feet, only to see Rose's gaze not fixed on her, but turned toward the doorway. And no shy smile on the girl's face, only shock.

Callie followed her gaze.

Not Helena.

A stunning woman stood in the doorway. She turned from Rose to Callie, her brooch winking in the candlelight.

A butterfly.

****

"That's enough o' yer polishin', lad. Nae such thing as perfection. Just get them wrapped up wi' a nice tidy bow an' be on yer way afore ye get doused in this wet." Old Tam held out his hand for the shammy cloth Bren had been using. "It's a bonnie thing ye've made. Yer lady an' wee Miss Rose'll be fair gobsmacked, I'll warrant."

Bren gazed about the neat-as-a-pin woodshop, every tool in its place. His office now nearly as tidy as Tam's shop. Certainly a far cry from the mess of his past.

"Never would have managed it if I didn't have you to bedevil me. I thank you, old friend. I never was much for giving thanks, but I do now. I feel so darned lucky to be in my shoes I almost can't stand myself!"

The old man looked at him a long time. So long, Bren nearly ducked his head in embarrassment. Finally, Tam nodded, carefully tucking the shammy in his coat pocket. "Weel now… that puts a smile in ma auld heart, lad. It surely does."

Bren wrapped a square of muslin around each of his two gifts, tying up the ends with bright satin ribbons. Yes, they were finished. And he was right proud.

Dang, but he couldn't wait to see their faces when they discovered what lay inside!

He took one last look at the old man standing in the middle of the shop, his gnarled hands hanging by his sides, his blue eyes steady and kind.

Nearby branches lashed the windows as wind whipped around the shed. Tam was right. A summer storm was churning over the mountain.

"Wait one minute. I have something for you." Bren ducked out of the cottage. The sky roiled above the twitching tree limbs. He hefted a small cask from the cart he'd brought and then dashed back inside.

"We couldn't have Christmas in July without a little something for you." He set the cask on the table and stood back. "This is the first of the new Belcher Brew. We took your advice and are calling it, *Kinduggan*." Belcher had burned the name into the bell of the barrel, right above the stopper. "Course it won't be any good for another three or so years, but I expect us to crack this open then and have a dram or two when its ready. So don't be goin' anywhere, Tam Cree."

The old man smiled and ran his hand reverently over the re-made cask. "Ye did a fine job here too, lad."

Somehow Bren knew Tam was meaning more than just the art of coopering.

"Should've brought summat for you an' the lasses as well," the old man said, lines of regret marring his forehead.

Bren touched his heart. "You have. You do," was all Bren could manage through the sudden thickness in his throat.

Tam looked at him and slowly nodded. "Best be off wi' ye, then. This storm'll wait for nae man nor beast."

He loaded the gifts into the cart, tucking them against the padding he'd remembered to bring, then secured them with a length of rope. One yank as a test. All secure and safe. And lastly, he covered them with a tarp. He turned and waved farewell to Tam who stood in the doorway, then started down the track.

"*God rest ye merry gentlemen let nothing you dismay. Remember Christ our savior was born on Christmas Day. To save us all from Satan's power when we were gone astray…*"

Hell, he couldn't carry a tune in a bucket. He sang even louder as he made his way through the ever-darkening woods toward the house. No, toward home. And family.

"*Oh, oh, tidings of com-om-fort and joy, comfort and joy. Oh, oh, ti-i-dings of com-om-fort and joy!*"

****

The woman who had haunted Callie's dreams stood in the doorway.

The same woman Bren had met that evening at Ryeland Park, day before they'd married.

Rose's mother?

The angel of silence had descended on them, as if they were actors on stage who had forgotten their lines.

"Mama, we—Lily and me—we thought you were dead."

"Really?" The woman set a hand on her breast, making the jeweled butterfly shimmer in the light.

Rose nodded. "We waited and waited, but you never came back."

She took a step toward her daughter, but Rose remained poised on the ladder, a bit of tinsel still clutched in her hand.

"But didn't I tell you I would always come back, my sweet Rose? And when I did, you and your sister had vanished!"

Rose flinched at Iris's raised voice—just a flicker—but Callie saw it. Not everything forgotten. Not everything forgiven.

"You'd run away, old lady Lockhart told me. I believed you had left *me*. I thought *you* were—dead." But then she shook her head as if to dispel those terrible memories. "But now I have found you! At last!"

She turned to Callie. "Lady Clifford, forgive me. My arrival must be rather a shock to you. To both of you." She nodded to Rose. "But I simply could not wait another day, not once I found out my beautiful flower was still alive and well!"

Callie knew she should speak. Hospitality, kindness—the roles she was meant to play. But her instinct screamed for distance. She wanted this woman gone, tucked back into the hazy realm of nightmares.

Yet there she stood, luminous and surreal. Older than Callie by some years, age had not dulled her brilliance; it had refined it. Her thick, coifed hair gleamed pale gold, just a few shades darker than Rose's. Her lips were full, almost too ripe. Her eyes, shockingly blue, were framed by lashes so dark they looked painted on.

Until now, Callie had thought Rose looked purely a Cavanaugh. But here was the other half—undeniable, vivid.

What must this woman have endured, believing her daughters gone?

Had her life resembled Callie's own mother's—a slow slide into dependence on strangers' kindness, her wits, her beauty?

Images rose unbidden: her own mother, too thin, copper hair slipping free, that sudden, irrepressible smile that transformed her from merely pretty to radiant.

But what of Rose? What was she feeling, faced so abruptly with the mother she'd long thought lost?

Callie was getting better at reading the girl's quiet moods, but now, she couldn't read her at all. Rose clung to the ladder and her tinsel as if tethered to both.

How old had Rose been when her mother disappeared? It hardly mattered now. She must welcome this woman. Politeness insisted on it. She should call for tea, offer a seat.

But she did nothing. Said nothing.

"Oh, Rose, I have missed you so!"

The woman crossed the hall, arms half-raised, as if afraid the girl might vanish if touched.

Something in the woman's smile—too rehearsed?—set Callie's nerves to bristle. But then again, how could anyone be expected to act naturally at a time like this?

Rose leaned back into the tree as though she might disappear among the branches.

"Oh, my goodness, my flower, you are nearly the image of me when I was your age," the woman whispered. Then she sighed and turned back to Callie.

"Mr. Jasper, the painter—he once saw me in the park and begged my mother to let me sit for him. But she was terribly strict and forbade it."

She shook her head with a laugh. "But you—you must be painted just so. Hair down, that darling pinafore. In fact, we ought to be painted together."

She reached to touch the hem of Rose's apron, smiling up at her daughter.

"Oh dear, I'm rambling. Forgive me. I'm just a bit flustered." She touched the hem of Rose's apron and smiled up at her daughter.

"Oh, dear, I own I am just a bit nervous and rattling on." The beauty stepped back and dropped her hand.

Callie was about to ask the lady to have a seat when Rose spoke.

"Mama…"

A breath. A blink. A step down the ladder.

"Yes, my love?"

"Lily—she is dead. She died."

"Oh, poppet," the woman cried out as she reached her arms up to her daughter. "Yes, I know. Come, let me hold you."

Rose looked to Callie, wide-eyed, as if she needed permission.

What Callie would give for such a moment. For her

own mother to return—to embrace her again. A flare of jealousy rose and died just as swiftly.

She gave Rose a small, steady nod.

Obedient as ever, Rose turned back and descended the ladder. Her mother gathered her in a sweeping embrace.

"Oh, I've dreamed of this moment! But now that it's here, I can scarcely believe it. Are you actually real, my flower?" She pulled back to look more closely at her child. "But my, how you've grown! Nearly a woman now! How could you run away like that? My heart nearly broke. But I suppose Lily must have led the charge—she always had to have her way in things, didn't she? Just like your father."

The woman looked up through her lashes at Callie.

Your father.

Bren, her husband.

Suddenly Callie felt herself the interloper.

"I'm so very sorry," Iris said, her voice hushed. "I should have been there to keep you safe. I should never have trusted myself to that—" She broke off. "But we needn't speak of such sadness now."

"But you were gone for so very long." Rose stood straighter, her voice more determined. "We were so afraid. Why did you not send us word?"

"Oh, but of course I did! I wrote faithfully. Did you not get any of my letters?"

Rose only shook her head.

"Well, let us not linger in the past. Not when we have so much to be thankful for now that I've found you again." She glanced about the room, as if seeing it for the first time. "I see you're celebrating."

"Please forgive me. I have been rude. Won't you sit

down, Mrs...." Callie's voice faltered. She did not even know the woman's name.

"Darvan, Lady Clifford. Iris Darvan." She crossed to the settee with effortless grace. "I confess, I'd be glad to sit. It has been a very long journey to find my blossom."

The name meant nothing to Callie. "Please, make yourself comfortable, Mrs. Darvan. I'll ring for tea."

"Tea would be divine, my lady!" She settled her voluminous skirts with practiced ease. "Has no one ever spoken of me?"

Callie looked to Rose, but the girl only stared at the bit of tinsel she still held, absently pulling it through her fingers.

"Well, I shall not take offense, I suppose." She patted the seat next to her for Rose to join her. "I am here now and eager to become fast friends."

A sudden gust of wind swept through the hall. Paper stars spun on their threads. The flames on the tree's candles danced.

"Ho, ho, ho! Merry Christmas! I ran into Saint Nick, and he gave me these parcels to pass along. Said you had to open them right away!"

Callie didn't turn. She couldn't. She couldn't bear to see his face.

"Brendan," she said, "we have a visitor."

She stared at the woman on the settee, who reached out one delicate hand to her husband.

"Hello, Bren."

Chapter Twenty-Nine

Callie held a sprig of pine, but she offered no smile of greeting.

And then he heard the voice—low, theatrical, unmistakable. And even before he turned, he knew his snug little world had just exploded.

As his arms dropped, he vaguely heard the sound of wood splitting and spindles snapping. No one moved.

"Iris?" He had to say the name. To make this nightmare real.

"Oh, goodness. I've not changed so much, have I? Come, Bren, surely you cannot have forgotten me. Not after all we've shared…" She laughed, a familiar, practiced laugh. So different from Callie's wonderful snort of genuine mirth.

Iris extended her arms to encompass the room. "Christmas, indeed! To finally be reunited with my child after so long!"

No one spoke. Silence hung as heavy and poignant as the waiting storm outside.

"La! Only Bren Cavanaugh would think to have Christmas in the dead of summer! Although perhaps Easter might be more apropos," she said, fixing him with a speaking look. "For apparently I have risen from the dead."

"What are you doing here?" he croaked.

"Goodness, I expected a bit more of a welcome after

coming all this way! And in the midst of a storm, too. I swear I thought I'd taken my life in my hands, the way that young man was driving."

Why had she come? And what did she want? He was pretty dang sure it wasn't her daughter. No, unless Iris had changed her spots, she must be after money.

He circled her, sizing up her weakest flank like a hunter stalking his prey. "How did you find us?"

"Brendan!" Callie exclaimed. "You are being extremely rude. Not only is she our guest, she is Rose's mother."

Callie. Dear God, what must Callie be thinking? And his Rosie?

His wife stood, holding a sprig of greenery over her belly as if it might shield her child from this sordid scene.

And Rose—she just looked down at her hands, completely unable—or unwilling?—to meet his gaze.

"No, Lady Clifford, he has a right to ask, and a right to hear—however deceptive he may be—but *I* am not one to judge. Mine is a very sad tale. But one hardly fit for my dear flower's ears."

She absently touched something pinned to her bodice. It quivered, as if in sympathy with her tale of woe. A jeweled butterfly.

"Let us just say that since you left me, my life has not been an easy one," Iris said.

Bren watched his daughter. He was good at interpreting the signs of a spooked animal. The girl seemed shocked, but not as if she were seeing a ghost. Had she suspected her mother might still be alive?

"Rose, would you please go ask Mrs. Billings to bring tea and some refreshments?" Callie gave her a tight smile.

Callie was doing right by sending Rosie on an errand so that they could deal with Iris Darvan without any kid gloves.

"Oh, yes, my blossom, would you? I am truly parched." She touched her throat. "The dust from the road…"

"Oh, of course, Ma—" The girl bit her lip, eyes flicking restlessly between Iris and Callie.

"Thank you, Rose." Callie stepped toward the girl and then stopped, staring down at the pine branch in her hand as if she hadn't the least idea where it had come from. She shoved it into the pocket of her apron, almost as if it were an embarrassment. "And please ask Harriet to make up the Jade Room and to lay a fire. This is truly a day to celebrate, the reunion of a mother and a child."

This could not be happening. He wanted to scream *she is not what you think!* But how could he pit himself against a daughter who had just found her mother? A mother she might love?

"Oh, you are so dear, Lady Clifford."

Rose crossed the room but hesitated in front of the bundles laying at his feet. One of the bright red ribbons had fallen free from the mess. She bent to pick it up, but stopped herself.

He wanted to reach out to her, to assure her that their family would not be broken by this intrusion. But he couldn't. No more lies.

Rose's departure—that snick of the lock catching—changed the tension in the room, from walking-on-eggshells to a tougher, more gloves-off, air.

He stepped around the gifts he had spent hours upon hours crafting. They would not be opened this evening.

He would pay her off. Again. And he would keep

paying her, as long as she left them in peace.

But what if Rose wanted to have her mother in her life? Didn't he owe it to his daughter to see if Iris had miraculously changed?

"I suppose you know about Lily..." he muttered.

"Yes." Iris bowed her head, like some painted Madonna. "At least she is at peace now."

"One way to put it." Guilt stabbed at his heart.

"What is that supposed to mean?"

"Never mind. What do you want from us, Iris? Why are you really here?"

"Isn't it obvious? I want to be reunited with my daughter!"

"Do you? Seems right convenient you show up just after I get a title attached to my name."

"Brendan!" Callie looked at him as if he were a stranger.

"Callie, I'm sorry. I never expected to see her again. I don't know what to do."

Callie smoothed her hands over the swell of her belly and stood straight as a raw recruit. "Well, I do. We must allow Mrs. Darvan the chance to know her child. Mistakes were made and so much valuable time lost, but we must be grateful for the opportunity we've been given to right a terrible wrong.

"I wonder if Rosie would think so?"

"How can you say such a thing? Mrs. Darvan is her mother!" Callie cried.

"My dear Lady Clifford, what he is implying is that my child will not wish to know me. No doubt, he has poisoned her against me," she said, pinning him with her startlingly blue gaze.

"You left them!" Bren yelled. "You were gone for

months! Years!"

Iris jumped up from the settee, pointing an accusing finger at him. "And who left me first? When I was carrying his children?"

"Brendan, is this true?" Callie whispered. "Did you leave her?"

"By God, it's already happening." Helplessly he took a step toward Callie. "I didn't mean to," he whispered. "I was young. Foolish. I thought she was finished with me. God help me, I didn't know." He shook his head trying to find a way to make her see.

Iris bowed her head, a faint smile on her lips.

"You see that pin she's wearing?" He pointed to the glittering bauble on Iris's breast.

Callie nodded.

"How 'bout you tell my wife about that little gem, Iris?"

Iris covered the brooch as if to protect it.

"No? Well, let me enlighten my wife, then. Iris Darvan was known as, The Butterfly."

The woman's smile froze for half a heartbeat then she straightened her shoulders.

"Why, you ask? Because she would flit from one poor slob to another, always in search of a sweeter reward. A gent with more to offer and, poof! She'd be gone in a flash." He shoved his hand through his hair. "Hell, if Rosie didn't look just like a Cavanaugh, I'd wonder if she was mine."

"Oh, how cruel you are, Bren!" Iris spat at him. "I gave you everything! My love, my fidelity, my devotion! I bore your children even though you'd left, left me alone and friendless. I wrote to you so many times, begging you to come back, to be a family. And, like a fool, I believed you when you promised you'd come, promised we'd marry and be a family. Promised you loved me! But those were all lies. And so yes, once more I had to become The Butterfly. I had to survive. I had to provide for my girls as best I could."

Iris flung herself onto the settee in one elegantly practiced move.

"That's a damn lie. I never wrote to you. Good God, I didn't even know I was a father until after my Pa died, and I found your letters locked away in his desk. As soon as I read them, I deserted and came to England to find you and my girls. But everyone I questioned told me you must be dead!"

"Stop! There can be no more lies," Callie said shaking her head.

He needed to cut to the chase. He needed her out of his house. "How much do you want, Iris?"

"What?"

"How much money will it take for you to leave us alone."

Callie gasped.

"You think you can buy a mother's love with a few quid?" Iris said, her tone as dramatic as the famous Sarah Bernhardt's. "That may have worked before, when I believed she was lost to me forever. But now I have found her—no thanks to you—*I* will not abandon her again!"

"Five hundred? Six? I warn you, don't be too greedy, Madam Butterfly or you'll get nothing."

"Brendan, stop it! Mrs. Darvan has just been reunited with her daughter!" Callie hissed.

"Callie, you don't know her. She didn't want Rosie then, and she doesn't want her now. Not really. She'll only use her as a pawn to get what she wants. Is that what you want for Rose? Because I surely don't. So, how much, Mrs. Darvan?"

"You see," Iris said rising from the sofa and stepping to Callie's side. "That's what men think, that money will solve everything. But we, we mothers know different."

Callie flinched as Iris set a hand on her arm.

Rage welled inside him that she would dare touch his wife. But Callie might never forgive him if he threw Rose's newfound mother out of the house.

"Callie, I'm asking you to trust me on this," he begged. "Don't let yourself be taken in by her. She's as different from your ma as chalk and cheese."

Callie flinched at his reference to her mother. But why would a gal as smart as his Callie be taken in by a snake like Iris, unless she were comparing Rose's situation to her own?

"Did you ask her why she abandoned her daughters? What excuse could she give?"

His wife looked so small next to that huge tree. Small, sad, and defeated.

He took her cold hands in his, made sure she was looking at him. "Callie-gal. You have to believe I didn't know she was with child."

She looked down at their hands as if they might hold the answer she so desperately needed. Then she looked up at him, resignation stamped on her face. "No, perhaps not. Still, I will not, I cannot, separate a child from its mother."

"Even when I tell you she can't be trusted?"

"Even so."

"Then you don't trust me."

She said nothing.

"You don't trust me," he said again. "You take her word over mine."

Callie took a deep breath and closed her eyes. "I only ask for the truth. Just confess the truth, and I can forgive you." She opened her eyes, her gaze full of pain.

"Truth?" He spat the word out. "Truth is only worth something if someone believes you, otherwise it don't mean a hill a beans."

"Truth always matters. It must."

"Why? What good is knowing something in your heart when the world thinks different?"

"Because it means you can live with yourself." She looked at him as if doing so physically hurt her. "Did you know Rose's mother was still alive? And did you keep the knowledge of it from Rose?"

He couldn't lie, not any longer. "I did what I thought was best for us all. Especially Rosie."

"Who are you to be the judge of what is best?"

"I'm her father!" he near yelled, making his wife flinch. He pulled her back, softened his voice. "Lord knows I'm not always the best judge, Callie. But Farren agrees with me about her. So, I'm asking you to trust us. Trust *me*. Believe me when I say letting this woman get her claws into Rosie would be the worst thing I can imagine. Because I know she'll only leave her again."

"You left her." Callie said in a near whisper.

"What?"

"Rose. Even after you found her again, *you* left her. Once to search for Iris, then back to the United States to clear your name, and then to wander the wilds of Scotland. We'd never have met otherwise."

He staggered back, as if she had slapped him.

"And you cannot deny you intended to leave her at Ryeland," she said with some real force. "You would have chosen to leave her with Farren and Nora. Again."

Her words rained down on him, washing away the thin veneer of confidence he'd managed to build up these last few weeks in Scotland. Leaving him shivering, his faults exposed to all the world.

Silence.

Except the hammering of his heart.

"You asked me to trust you. How can I trust you when you do not trust me?" Callie asked.

"I trust you with my life!"

"Really?" Callie shook her head. "Maybe with your life but not with the secrets of your heart. You are brave when it comes to risking your life, but what of your heart? I was foolish to think that I might penetrate your defenses, but you are as secretive as ever."

God, how he ached to rewrite his history. His failures, his callous mistakes.

But he couldn't. Callie was right. Leave it to her to cut right to the bone. He had left Iris Darvan. He had failed his daughters. First Lily, who had been forced to scrape out a living on the streets, her short life full of misery. And now Rosie. He abandoned her almost as soon as he could. A few damned swimming lessons would not heal such a breach. He was a fool to think he could escape his past. Hell, it was standing right in front of him in the form of Iris Darvan, a smirk of victory stamped on her porcelain face.

Thunder cracked overhead. He wanted to howl with laughter or rage, he didn't even know anymore.

He looked toward Callie, his wife, his heart, imploring her to believe him, to take his part in this, but she stood frozen, her mouth compressed into a stern line of disapproval.

The door clicked behind him followed by the familiar rattle of a tea trolley being rolled in. Seeing Mrs. Billings with those tiny china cups and little sandwiches piled in perfect pyramids made his stomach heave.

He spun, a kaleidoscope of twinkling lights and fluttering paper snowflakes blurred with his tear-washed eyes.

To think he'd believed he could recreate Sara's beloved Christmas in July. No, he couldn't rewrite the past, any more than he could bring back Lily, or Sara. He was a fool to think he could escape.

"Ladies," he bowed. "Seems you both got the short end of the horn. I'll leave you to get better acquainted."

He whirled past the gape-mouthed housekeeper and pushed out of the room, heading out into the storm.

Chapter Thirty

Callie concentrated on lifting her skirts and putting one foot in front of the other as she and Iris Darvan navigated the staircase. Certainly, she could have given Mrs. Billings the task of showing Mrs. Darvan to her room. The housekeeper would have been all too happy to do so, having asked Callie several times if "Madam didn't want to lie down for a while?"

"Thank you for being so kind to my Rose. I can see she loves you." Iris Darvan's lilting voice floated up, pressing in on Callie's temples.

My Rose.

"It is mutual, Mrs. Darvan," she pushed herself to make the response. Then, with more force, "I cannot imagine our lives without her." But as she said the words, she knew her dream of this snug little family was over. From now on, this woman must be a part of their lives.

They continued down the hallway in blessed silence. Callie passed Rose's room, not stopping to see if the girl were within. At the Jade Room, she turned the huge knob and pushed the heavy door open. Why had it been called such? She could not see even a hint of the color jade in the rather austere room. The only nod to the name, an elaborately carved eight-paneled screen of some far-eastern origin.

"Oh, what a lovely room," the woman said, her tone belying her words.

Callie crossed to the window, her fingers finding the curtain edge. *Where was he? Was he out in this storm?* Rain lashed against the glass. A flash of lightning knifed through the sky, illuminating the black clouds for an instant, before blackness once again claimed the land.

"You must not blame Bren for his suspicions. He knows nothing of the difficult life I have led since he left me. Nor how I have longed to be reunited with my girls—with my—"

"I saw you at Ryeland Park." Callie turned away from the storm. She had not meant to be so abrupt, but this thorn had been under her skin for so very long, she longed to have it out, one way or another.

Iris Darvan's hand fisted for the briefest moment in the silk fabric of her skirt before letting it go. "You saw me?"

"Yes. I should have confronted Brendan immediately about why he was meeting with a mysterious veiled woman the evening before our marriage. But I did not. I was wrong not to do so."

Callie did not think the woman was going to reply.

"You saw—Bren and me?" she asked, her tone deliberate.

"I was in the conservatory and spied you through the window."

"Ahh…"

"I only saw your veiled face and the glint of your pin."

"You couldn't have heard our conversation."

"No."

Iris Darvan fingered the pin on her breast. "I suppose my love of butterflies will be my undoing one of these days. Unkind of me to come on that very day, but I was desperate to find my sweet Rose. You see, I saw the announcement in the papers of your marriage to Viscount Clifford. At first, I did not understand. My Brendan, a peer of the British realm? Who could imagine such a thing!"

She crossed to the fireplace, her long, elegant fingers touching the stone mantel. Bathed in the ambient light, Callie could not see her face, just a lush figure gilded with a halo of golden blonde hair. "He sent me away, of course. Told me of the child you are carrying."

A razor thin blade of pain sliced through her, shocking with its sting. "He told you of our child?" That revelation, more hurtful than his lying to her. He had agreed to keep her pregnancy a secret. Only her father and Helena had known.

Only this morning, they'd decided to tell Rose, a surprise for their Christmas festivities.

"Oh, my dear, I see you are shocked that he shared such an intimate secret with me. But you see, I know what it is to be increasing and not have the support of the father. I could not in good conscience force him to repeat his transgression, even though he— But no. I will not come between you and your husband. I am not a monster."

Callie, who had not been sick for weeks, suddenly felt as if her child was squeezing her insides.

"You must not blame him for sending me away," Iris Darvan continued as if Callie's world were not falling to pieces. "What would people say, seeing his paramour at his wedding to another? I would have left, of course, even had he not pressed me to take his money."

The woman shook her head. "But, why did he not

tell me the truth, that Rose still lived? Cruel of him, so utterly cruel! He must have feared I wouldn't have gone quietly if I knew. What mother could?"

"He told you Rose was dead?" Could Brendan truly have been so heartless? To hide a child from her true mother? To have her experience the heartache of yet another death? And simply pay her off to be rid of her? Callie shook her head. The Bren she knew—thought she knew—would never do such a thing.

But perhaps she did not know him at all...

"Believe me, I never wished to hurt you, Miss Ainsw—forgive me, Lady Clifford—dear Callista—if I might be so bold as to address you thus—but I loathe deception. What is it they always say? Ah, yes, the truth will out.

"I was hoping Bren would change and act accordingly, but he—well, he being Brendan—honor, sadly, is not part of his makeup. But, to give him credit, he vowed he must go forward and try to be a good husband and a father to this new family. He could not go back, no matter how much he might wish..." Iris finished wistfully.

Go back.

To be a real father to both Rose and to Lily? Or to rekindle his first love? Is that what she meant? Iris hadn't said as much, but it was clear from her demeanor that she felt she and Brendan had missed their chance at happiness all those years ago.

Callie remembered that rainy night at Ryeland Park, the two of their heads bent together by the carriage. She had asked him later if he had loved the mother of his children. He had not answered immediately. She supposed he had not wanted to hurt her by admitting how deeply he had.

But what of his behavior today? Had it all been a sham for Callie's benefit? Was he just covering his tracks, so to speak?

Had he loved Iris so much that her spurning him and then keeping their children's birth from him, had made him bitter and vindictive?

No, it did not ring true.

"I am used to fending for myself," Iris declared with a sad smile. "And being disappointed in love. But to have the chance to hold my child again—well, that I could not compromise. I somehow knew you would understand."

Of course, Callie understood. Not just because of her own impending motherhood, but because of the pain her own mother had suffered, being separated from the child she loved. Alone in the world save for the bond of her child, the flesh of her flesh. Callie touched her slightly swollen belly. What would it be like to be separated from a part of herself? Her mother's anguished cries still haunted Callie's nightmares.

Callie squeezed her eyes shut, as if the action would banish such painful memories. But truth was truth. She must support this woman, must right a wrong.

"He is angry at me, and rightly so. You see I panicked when I became with child—well, children—I had no idea I was carrying twins—. He had no money, and I was so very frightened. I needed to feel secure. I spurned him." She shook her head, a sad smile on her face. "I do not blame Bren for taking his anger out on me all these years later. I hurt him badly. He left me in anger." She crossed to Callie. "But now he has you. And the chance to be a good and devoted father to his new child. Please, I am begging you to let me be a mother to my only surviving one."

Damn him!

And damn herself. She had not demanded truth, and he had not trusted her with his secrets. Not the ones that truly mattered. The ones within his heart.

How could he keep a mother from her child?

Callie felt as if she were going to throw up. "Mrs. Darvan—"

"Iris, please."

"If you will forgive me, I am feeling rather—tired. I think—I must lie down for a moment."

"Oh, of course! I remember all too well how wrung out I used to get carrying my girls. Such a surprise to find I carried two lives within me! Such a miracle!"

"Yes, I feel the same—a miracle." Callie nodded, her hand drifting to touch the swell of her belly. She started out of the room before remembering. "This room connects with Rose's through an antechamber. I thought the arrangement might help you get reacquainted."

"How kind you are! I had never hoped to be so embraced by Brendan's new wife. I am so very touched."

Callie only nodded.

"Oh, might it be possible to have a bath drawn? I am so travel-worn from the train then the cart ride up to Kinduggan." Iris Darvan arched her back thrusting her magnificent bosom forward.

"I'm afraid the keep has no piped water. Brendan has been working on a system—" She stopped herself. "I will have our potboy bring water and a slipper tub up immediately."

The woman crossed the room and took Callie's hands within hers. "Thank you, dear, Calista. You cannot know what a balm you are to my poor, weary soul."

The touch of this woman's hands, so much softer, and whiter than her own seemed to be some sort of period to this entire hideous day.

Callie pulled her hand from Iris's. "I beg you will excuse me. Do not hesitate to ring should you require anything."

After closing the door, she leaned back against it, spreading her arms wide, as if her action might keep Iris Darvan from damaging their family anymore. But of course, it was futile. The damage was already done. Had been done long, long ago.

She should go and lie down. But as she made her way toward her bedchamber, she could not face the bed she had shared only a few short hours ago with her husband.

Oh, why had he invaded her snug life, this brash American with his too-wide smile? His flashing dimple, his shock of guinea-gold hair, easy, loping gait and his thirst for life. Making her believe she could have happiness, could have love, could *be* loved.

Oh, why could it not have been Helena who had arrived instead of Iris Darvan? How joyous they all would be now instead of so broken and confused.

Callie picked up her sister's letter, the one relating her plans to come to Scotland, and brought it to her lips. Her father's still unopened letter lay in the drawer where she had stashed it days ago.

Should she read it now? So easy to put it away for another day. But, perhaps like Bren reading unwanted letters, she must read hers as well? Yes, it was best to face issues sooner than later.

She cracked the seal to reveal Gerald Ainsworth's neat, precise penmanship, such a contrast to Helena's scrawl and doodles.

Callista,

I have kept this letter (and many others like it) to myself all these years. However, you are a married lady now and, soon to be a mother. I believe you are ready to know the truth, which is neither black nor white, but somewhere in between-

Your father,

Gerald Ainsworth

Another letter was folded within his missive. The paper yellowed, but otherwise pristine.

Callie unfolded it and then sat up, her breath catching as her gaze caught the signature at its bottom.

Antonia.

A letter from her mother.

Chapter Thirty-One

Bren tore the stopper from the whisky and thrust the tower window wide. Seeking to be one with this raging storm. It's fury echoing his own inner turmoil. The rain lashed against him, blinding him, and the bottle slipped in his hand. He lunged, barely catching himself and the bottle before both fell to smash on the rocks below.

Christmas!

He lifted his head and the bottle, toasting his escape from death. Rain mixing with his tears, he watched the scotch run down the keep's stone walls into the muddy earth and rock far below.

What a fool he'd been, trying to revive the past. As if by recreating Sara's favorite celebration, he could erase his sister's death, erase the part he had played in it.

Erase his guilty heart.

He thought he'd finally found someone besides Farren whom he could trust, who trusted him. His brother always seemed to know what was in his heart without Bren having to say a word. But for Callie to know him, he'd had to reveal many of his scars, both outward and even some that lived deep inside.

Speaking those shames aloud might've scattered them—dandelion fluff, blown clean off the stem, like he and Sara used to do, watching the bits drift off wherever the wind took them. He'd figured a confession like that would just plant more trouble. But telling Callie hadn't left him bare. It had taken root, pushing back against all the old choking weeds. Maybe the Catholics had the right of it. Confession did a man good.

He took another swig.

Why hadn't he told Callie, then, that Iris was still alive? Had he thought his marriage so fragile it could be broken by the likes of Iris Darvan?

Still mired in his past. Too afraid of scorn and rejection.

Instead, *he'd* broken it, broken it with his fear, with his lies. Callie, who only wanted truth, only asked for truth. And he could not give her even that. He deserved to be left.

Turns out all this power, all this consequence and rank, was nothing. When push came to shove, a lying ghost from his past could fell him like the spindliest sapling. Take away everything he had built and raze it to rubble.

Their little family—

"Damn you, Iris!" he shouted, echoing the thunder. "Damn you for making me feel useless and good-for-nothing. Exposing me as a liar and a cheat!"

He looked around the room, the place he took himself when the world pressed too close. His haven.

Or perhaps it was his prison? Estate papers still littered the desk. He'd managed to read some of them, had even started to understand crop rotation and drainage. They lay next to his plans for piping water into the keep. And under those, notes and drawings for a new bridge, one that wouldn't be washed away each season.

He'd thought he'd made a beginning.

Whisky burned the back of his throat. He swallowed it down looking at the bottle in his hand.

"Kinduggan, Fine Whisky, est. eighteen-hundred and sixty-eight," he read out loud. "Yes, damn fine whisky!"

Belcher had mocked up a proposed label and pasted it on a bottle as a surprise for Bren at their last meeting.

Time was he would have drowned his sorrows in this bottle and then looked for yet another.

But whisky was no longer something to numb him into oblivion. This brew was born of his passion for creating something of excellence. Something he was proud of. And his time spent with Tam. The old man had believed in Bren until he actually began to believe in himself.

What had Tam said? Wood has its flaws and knots, and the grain is not always smooth. But that gives the wood character. Makes it special and one-of-a-kind. Perfection is over-rated. To be a man, one must accept the whole, scars and all.

By God, this time Iris would not win. He set the bottle down with some reverence. He was stronger now. He knew himself and what he had to offer. Lord knows, he was not perfect, but he deserved happiness. He deserved this woman, his wife. His Callie girl. And he deserved to raise both his children. The one he had yet to meet, and the one who he had begun to forge a relationship with. His Rosie. His beautiful near-grown daughter. He had been given a second chance with her. He would never again abdicate that honor—the honor of being her father.

Where was she?

Somehow, he felt she was the key to all of this. She would be able to tell him if he had Iris all wrong. But the fact that Rose had not returned to the drawing room, no, not even when the tea had arrived, said more than mere words.

He swiped his eyes and pulled the window shut, locking it tight against the pelting rain.

He struck a light. The huge burl he had found deep in the woods lay on the worktable like a wizened ogre's head.

He ran his thumb over the mottled wood and then both his hands, seeking to draw strength from its strength. Hidden within this beauty lay a beautiful bowl. He was going to find it, dig it out of hiding, then present it to Tam for actual Christmas. He could already see it formed in his mind's eye. And he could see Tam's face, delighted, yet all-knowing. Expecting nothing less from Bren, a man in whom he had so much faith.

Would Callie ever have that kind of faith in him? Could he trust her with his terrible secret? Would she forgive him? Would he forgive himself?

She didn't know him all that well yet. And that had been his fault—keeping some secrets from her—from everyone. Even Farren. But he was ready to gain her full trust. He was ready to take on this family.

He was not perfect, but she had never asked for perfection, had she? No, Callie had only asked for the truth, for a chance to grow together in honor and abiding love. She deserved that.

And by God, he deserved that chance as well.

Chapter Thirty-Two

Callie carefully refolded her mother's letter, slipping it back into her father's note and then tucking both inside her desk drawer. Her fingers drifted to the locket at her throat. *Only True Love.*

Then, with a calm that surprised her, she unclasped the locket, carefully laid it atop the letter, then closed the drawer shut.

She should find Rose.

She slipped Helena's letter into the pocket of her apron, wanting to feel close to her beloved sister. Her fingers found the sprig of evergreen she had tucked there when Iris Darvan had arrived. What a difference an hour could make…

Hurrying down the hall, she heard the sound of water filling the slipper tub from the Jade room.

"At least this last one is hotter," she heard Iris Darvan say, followed by a murmured response of Phillip.

Callie hurried by.

She knocked softly on Rose's bedchamber door, but there was no answer. Turning the knob, she pushed the door open.

Where was the girl?

She combed the keep's upper chambers, and even the tower, where she had hoped to find Bren. But all stood empty. Had Bren gone out in this storm?

Had Rose?

"Nae, I've not seen Miss Rose since she came to ask for the tea," Mrs. Green said when Callie hurried down to the kitchen to inquire after the girl.

Angus, having been told under no circumstances should he attempt to go back down the mountain in this weather, sat by the fire. He had been pressed into service to help bring water up to fill Mrs. Darvan's bath.

"I would not be surprised if that old bridge were out with this much water coming down," Angus offered.

"I don't like to say it, but it was wrong of Mrs. Darvan to insist you drive up with a storm coming," Mrs. Green said, wiping flour from her hands.

"Your ladyship?" Mrs. Billings came into the kitchen. "She's not in the library, or the morning room, or any of the other first floor rooms."

"Thank you, Mrs. Billings. Please let me know if any of you see her. She is—well, storms unsettle her."

Mrs. Green gave her sister a look.

"Your Ladyship?" the housekeeper asked, turning to Callie. "We were wondering, with all that's going on, if you'll be wantin' to still have your celebration?"

Oh! Callie had forgotten the great feast the staff had been preparing.

Now, the smells of their combined efforts—the rich aroma of roasting game birds, the cinnamon and nutmeg of Tipsy Laird, the yeasty scent of fresh-baked bread— hit her nose. "Oh, I am sorry, you all have worked so hard. I honestly don't know."

What would Bren wish to do?

"I don't suppose you have seen Lord Clifford?" she asked.

"Nae, madam. I would have said to check the tower, but you've already been there."

Callie nodded. "I think we shall have to postpone our Christmas in July. Perhaps August?"

The staff murmured, "of course", and "certainly", and the like.

"Sure, and a week or two won't matter. Heavens knows his lordship will likely kill twenty more pheasants in the meantime," Mrs. Green said, moving to the ovens.

"And our puppet show will be all the more brilliant with a few more days' preparation!" declared Harriet. Martha nodded in vigorous agreement.

"Thank you all, again. We are truly blessed to have such an accommodating staff." Callie smiled and then left them to their tasks.

On her way to see if Rose had returned to her room, Callie passed by the Jade room door which stood partially open. Had Phillip neglected to close it?

"Oh, my goodness, you gave me a fright!" Iris's voice with the sloshing of water. "How long have you been standing there?"

Callie was about to reveal herself when she heard Rose speak.

"I don't know. A while. I just wanted to watch you for a few moments."

Callie froze. Peering through the slit in the door, she could see Rose's shadow on the wall. She must be standing in the doorway to the connecting dressing room.

"What an odd child you are. Why didn't you return when the tea arrived, my poppet?"

"I—I don't know."

"Well, I must say it looked rather strange, disappearing right in the midst of our reunion. What must these people think?"

"I am sorry, Mama."

"No matter, my sweet flower, all is forgiven. I have found you now and we shall be such a merry family!"

A flame of jealousy leapt in Callie's breast. She tamped it down. There would be time enough for sorting her feelings after they figured out how Iris Darvan was to fit into their family.

She should leave.

"But where have you been, Mama? Where have you been all these years?"

Callie froze in her tracks at Roses's raised voice.

"Oh, everyone and their infernal questions! Will no one leave me in peace? No one cares a jot about the difficult life I have led!"

Callie heard what sounded like a hand slapping water. "If you must know, I met a man. A bad man, who took me away from you. And now let us speak no more of it. Those years are not happy memories for me. Now, be a dear and hand me that scented oil."

Rose was silent.

Callie found herself back at the cracked door.

"But where? *Where* did he take you?" Rose's voice, insistent.

"It's not important." Iris Darvan's voice sharpened. "The *oil,* my pet."

"But, Mama, did you ever try to find us? Did you even send us a letter? We waited for you, Lily and me. Mother Lockhart said you would come back for us. But you didn't. And then that terrible man came. Lord Milton. He pretended to be a good man—pretended to be my Poppa—but he turned out to be a very bad man. Lily was so strong and brave. She got away. But not me. I was too slow and too scared. I got caught."

"Goodness, Eunice Lockhart assured me—"

"Eunice Lockhart? You spoke to Mother Lockhart?"

"Oh, lord, you are getting me all confused with these upsetting questions. I misspoke. I *heard* about that despicable man, Lord Milton, much later. Yes, in fact I think I read about it in the papers. I'm sure I saw it in the papers."

"No, that could not be. There was no mention of it in the papers. My Uncle Farren made sure that my name was kept out of it. He told me that I need not worry. That no one would know. He assured me."

Callie was surprised at Rose's tenacity in the face of her mother's growing impatience. The Rose she knew had always been so obliging. Callie could not help but admire this young woman who was standing up for herself.

"Oh, don't be so naïve. I forget you are such an innocent despite your years. Why, when I was your age, I—well, never mind. It is best not to trust these men with their promises, my sweet flower. This Lord Milton, your Uncle Farren, even your beloved Da, will all fail you some day. Indeed, I expect today was a hard lesson for you, seeing your Da is not perfect. No, Brendan Cavanaugh has much to answer for. And I'll warrant your step-mamma has a new-found perspective on her marriage. A lesson *all* women must learn, as soon as may be. It's only right that you should learn it from your *true* mother. Now please, let us not speak of this any longer."

All Callie heard next was the splashing of water over Rose's reply. And then the lower tones of Iris's answer.

"You may think what you will, but never say I didn't warn you." Iris said. "Now don't dawdle, my pet, hand me that oil. I am shriveling!"

Callie turned to flee. Iris was right. Oh, why had

Brendan not just told her the truth? Why had he thought to spare her from conflict?

Callie found herself back down in the great hall. The Christmas decorations seemed ridiculous as the summer storm raged outside. The stockings all hung from the mantle, waiting to be filled. The smallest, for their unborn child, lay under the tree, for Rose to discover and hang.

A flash of a red bow caught her gaze. Like a sleepwalker, she approached the bundles. Bren's gifts to her and Rose.

She knelt and then pushed the wrapping aside.

"Oh," the word released in a hushed breath. Within the muslin folds lay the most beautiful cradle she'd ever beheld.

Three of the exquisitely scrolled spindles lay broken.

Thunder snapped and rain lashed at the windows as tears ran down her cheeks.

The words of her mother's letter came unbidden, lancing into her heart. *I beg you, do not importune me again. I cannot, will not come back. I do not expect you to understand, but I love her. I always have. She is my heart. Divorce me, so that you may marry another and have the heir you so desperately desire. It is of no matter to me; I will never wed again. I thought I could at least give you that before I left, but it was not to be, and I could not stay.*

Please take good care of Callista. My only regret is that you force me to leave her behind. As you say, her reputation would be irreparably damaged if she were to be allowed to come to me, even for a short visit. Still, my heart breaks knowing I will never see her again.

She will do well enough with you, but I cannot live without my love! My heart!

Antonia

She'd never known her beloved locket had been a token of love from her mother's true love. The blonde hair—a woman's—entwined with the red. Now it made sense.

Her mother had loved deeply, but her love had been unacceptable to the world. Antonia Ainsworth had hoped to have a son and leave her husband with an heir, but she had born a girl, and the thought of continuing in her sham of a marriage was too much for her mother to bear.

Callie's thoughts went back to that terrible day when she assumed her mother had come home because she longed to be with her beloved child, but in fact, it was her father who had found her and forced her to return with him.

But Callie had not been enough.

She squeezed her eyes closed against the flood of tears coursing down her cheeks.

Her father had told his young daughter that her mother was dead to spare her from that terrible truth. What had he written? The truth was never black and white but somewhere in between.

Hard facts—implacable and rigid—were also truth. Winter always came; the hawk took what it pleased. But perhaps some truths were more malleable—more forgiving.

Her father, in his own way, had tried to protect her from pain, even as he damaged their own relationship by keeping such a secret from her. And her mother had tried to protect her daughter's reputation, even as she broke her heart by leaving her behind.

A sudden memory, long buried, raced across her mind. Her mother and father standing in the doorway of his study, young Callie crying from the stairway, desperate for her mother, and her mother's tear-stained face looking up at her daughter, so full of pain, then turning away, disappearing back through the door.

Her mother, choosing to leave her.

Callie's hand drifted to Helena's letter still in her pocket. Her dear little sister.

She drew the folded paper out along with the pine-scented sprig. Smiling, she traced the little doodle of angel's wings Helena had drawn in the margin. Sweet, fanciful, Helena, confiding in her angel from the park. The angel who had given her a handkerchief—

A tear dropped down onto the drawing, making the ink run.

Callie blinked as the image began to transform.

Not an angel—

A butterfly!

****

Callie yanked open the door. "Mrs. Darvan? Or is it Mrs. Gillingham?"

Iris Darvan froze midway putting her arm into the sleeve of her robe. "Excuse me?"

"Or should I simply call you, The Butterfly?"

The beauty's mouth pulled tight, and her eyes narrowed.

"It was you who met my sister, Helena, in the park and gave her your handkerchief, wasn't it?" Callie stepped into the room. "She thought the embroidery angel's wings, but they are really a butterfly's, aren't they?"

Iris finished donning the robe and clinched it around

her waist. A robe brocaded with butterflies.

"Well, yes. But a mother will do anything to find her daughter. Sometimes one must stretch the truth to get what one wants. Something both Bren and I know quite well."

Callie ignored the woman's false assertion. "It was Helena who revealed that I am with child, wasn't it? Not Brendan, as you claimed. No, do not bother to deny it." Callie said as Iris's lips curved to shape what would surely have been a protest. "I know Bren would never have shared such an intimate secret. He might have bribed you to go away, but he would never have betrayed our unborn child."

A terrible thought occurred to her, one that she might not have considered but for the fact that her own mother had chosen to leave her.

"Did you know Rose was alive when you first came to Ryeland Park? Did you accept money in lieu of your daughter?"

Callie could see the woman calculating in her mind.

"Again, no need to answer. I know in my heart you knew."

"It's no more than Bren would have done, especially if he'd needed the money as much as I did. That man has no heart!"

"Bren has no heart? Would a man with no heart leave in the middle of a war to scour another country for children he never knew he had? Would he never give up even when imprisoned by a madman?"

Iris sniffed. "If he'd shown as much devotion to me as he did to them, they would have never been lost in the first place."

"You dare to blame their loss on him? When you

were the one who abandoned them? Lily and Rose, time and time again?

"I wouldn't believe everything Bren tells you, my dear. He'll lie through his teeth if he thinks it will protect him."

"Bren doesn't lie!" The words tumbled from Callie's mouth without hesitation. No, he didn't lie, did he? He might embroider or exaggerate to entertain, or keep some things hidden to protect his tender, bruised self. But he'd never outright lied to her, had he?

"Bren doesn't lie," she repeated, her voice stronger, surer. "You are the liar, Mrs. Darvan. Or Mrs. Gillingham. Or whatever your real name might be."

"You are a fool if you believe a knave like Brendan Cavanaugh."

"I have been a fool. Not for having faith in Brendan, but for needing to believe you actually cared a jot for Rose. I have let my history cloud my judgment. I needed to give you the benefit of the doubt. I needed to give Rose a chance to have you as a mother. I couldn't see the truth because I wanted you to love Rose as I love her. I needed you to be a caring and loving mother."

I beg you, do not importune me again. I will not come.

Her own mother's intractable answer when her father begged her to come home, to be a mother to Callie. Callie closed her eyes, absorbing this terrible new history. This truth.

"I spurned my husband because I needed to believe you would never leave your child—your children. I refused to take his part against you when he assured me he was doing what was best for our family, that he only wanted to protect Rose from you. And his instinct was to protect me as well. He didn't need to protect me, but he has yet to learn that. And I in turn did not trust him with my own truth—that I'd seen the two of you together at Ryeland Park."

Iris looked up from under her lashes, a self-satisfied smirk on her face. "Oh, yes, our little tête-à-tête, Bren and me."

"Of course I did not know it was you. I only saw a veiled woman with a butterfly pin. But if I'd only probed, I would have found out the truth. He was trying to protect me. I only hope he will forgive me. You are right in one thing, Brendan and I have much to learn of each other, but I look forward to every moment."

"You think you have it all worked out, do you?"

"I imagine you didn't want the inconvenience of a nearly grown daughter, who is a beauty in her own right, you wanted money. And when the money dried up, you thought to try and play the "mother" card again."

"You know nothing about my life, my trials."

"That is true, I do not know your history. The lot of our sex is often difficult. We have so few options. For my own part, I tried to exercise my autonomy from what my family and the world had prescribed for me. I imagine you've had far worse trials than having to marry a man simply because he is suitable. But my concern is not with you, my concern is with Rose and with my husband with whom I share a life and a child. I have been given a chance at love. A chance at a ready-made family. I know this is a rarity and I do not plan to squander my happiness. I will not let you take that away from me. Or from Brendan. He's not perfect by any means, but he has suffered enough in his life, and I mean to support him and his children. And as far as Rose goes, I will certainly not let you take away her chance to finally have a real family. So be warned. And now I am going to find my daughter."

"Yes, find her, by all means," Iris said cryptically.

The smirk on Iris Darvan's face made Callie want to shake her. But Callie knew she would only get more lies should she question the woman. Best to use the time to find Rose.

Please, dear God, let her be safe!

She left the room, firmly closing the door on the beautiful, pitiful sight of Iris Darvan.

Chapter Thirty-Three

Rose was the key to all this mess. He needed to see her, find out her feelings about her mother's return. But where was she?

Rose's bedchamber door stood open. Bren pushed the door wider.

"Rosie?" he called out softly, but he knew with a hunter's certainty that she was not within.

He heard the smack of something hitting water and then his nose registered the smell—oh, he knew that scent.

He stepped through the connecting dressing room to find Iris standing beside a slipper bath basin.

Her hair, which had been haphazardly pinned up, had loosened and fell in tendrils around her flushed cheeks and neck, teasing her breasts.

"Oh, Brendan! What a start you gave me!" Iris wrapped her arms around her body, pushing her breasts high. Her robe—a pink, frilly thing figured with—of course—butterflies, gaped. "Does no one in this house knock? But what a lovely surprise!" Her tone turned sultry and her stance coquettish. "Do come in."

He strode toward her and she held open her arms. As if he'd ever allow her treacherous hands on his body again.

"Tarnation, woman." He snagged a shawl off the floor and tossed it to her. "Cover yourself."

Her mouth a moue, the sulky pout he remembered all too clearly. She took her time draping the shawl around her shoulders, settling it over her breasts.

He did not turn away. How could he have ever been taken in by this woman? He'd been so young, so stupid, succumbing to such obvious coquetry. How different she was from his eager, honest, what-you-see-is-what-you-get Callie.

"Where is Rose?"

Iris shook her head. "Ah, our dear, sweet, hapless, Rose. All that beauty. Such a waste."

"Jealous, are you? Or just mad *my* Rosie didn't fall for your dog and pony show? Unlike Callie, Rose knows you too well to be fooled by your poor Madonna act."

"Ungrateful girl. I would never have spoiled her so, as your *lady* seems wont to do."

Bren resisted the urge to defend his wife. Callie might be taken in by Iris for the moment, but he doubted she'd be fooled for long. Callie had a way of seeing a person for what he—or she— truly was. "How long have you known Rose was alive?"

"What are you talking about? I came as soon as I discovered her whereabouts."

"I didn't ask you how you knew where she was. I asked when did you discover Rose was still alive? Did you know when you came begging for money at Ryeland?" Bren pressed.

"Of course not." But her sly eyes would not meet his.

"By God, you did. Farren said he wasn't sure. How long had you known before that? How long did you know and not come to get them? To save them?"

Iris actually looked contrite. "Lily was long dead by

the time I got back to London. And Rose was certainly being well-cared for."

"Well-cared for?" Blind anger lanced through him, making him jerk forward. He made himself take a breath. "You *knew* Rodger Milton had her?"

Iris turned away, but quickly spun back, facing him head on. "Yes, I knew."

He sputtered in outrage, but she only shrugged, then crossed the room to sit in front of a vanity mirror. "I dare say Milton coddled her. His hot-house flower. Far better than being thrust into the real world and experiencing just how cruel it can be." She gazed critically at her face and then smiled as if testing it out for its effect.

Rather than wring her neck, he made himself stay on the other side of the room, watching her reflection. "No experience of cruelty, you say?"

Iris waved her hand dismissively. "Rose had every comfort. I'm sure he treated her with the utmost care, despite his…oddities." She raised her chin, exposing a long column of neck, and then brushed her fingers down the expanse of white to her bosom, as if critically assessing her physical assets.

He found himself right next to her, his hands fisted by his sides. "Oddities? He sterilized children! He experimented on them!"

"Oh, get off your high horse!" She stood, forcing him to step back as she sailed by him, gesticulating wildly. Once, he'd been fascinated by such mercurial displays. "Good lord, the chit was living in the lap of luxury! Her closet held no less than thirty or more frocks of every color of the rainbow."

"Her closet?" Sick realization hit his gut. "By God! You were there? You were in that house and stood in her bedchamber?"

She whirled around to face him. "He gave her everything! While I had nothing!"

"He was a monster!"

"Yes!" she fired back. "Never gave me a cent for allowing him to keep Rose, the miser. Sent me packing with all kinds of threats. I had to resort to Gillingham, but he was soon drained dry. Poor Gilly. He'd always been in love with me. Hated you for taking me from him. If he'd had a feather to fly with, I might have stuck with him. But he could never stay flush."

"Yes, just like always, it comes down to money. Who has it, and how you can get him to give it to you."

"It's just me now, Iris, No need for a show. Besides money, what do you really want?"

Thunder snapped, and she jumped like a startled pea hen.

"Oh, this bloody wilderness!" She gave a dramatic shudder. "I can't understand how anyone can abide it!"

Wilderness? Kinduggan and these Highlands were his haven. His home. His and Callie's. And he wanted Iris gone from it as soon as humanly possible.

Again, he was struck by the difference in the two women who were, and would be, the mother of his children. The Iris he had known always grasping at life, clawing her way up through the demi-monde, and him right alongside her, enjoying the ride. He shook his head. What empty and meaningless days. The only good to come out of them was his beautiful Rosie-gal—

"I repeat, what do you want?"

"I thought I made that clear. I want my daughter back." She fingered the tie of her robe. "But now that I see you again, I wouldn't mind having you as well."

He ignored her sultry smile.

"The real question is, why did you never try to find me once you knew Rose was alive? I am her mother, after all," she huffed. "I am easily cast aside when no longer needed. But, you should know by now, I will not be dismissed. Lily is lost to me forever, but Rose is still mine."

"Is that how you think of her? As something to own? As a bargaining chip to get what you want?"

"And if she were? What kind of bargain might we strike?" She looked up at him from under her lashes, a clear invitation in her glittering eyes.

Bren jerked away from the sickening sight. But Iris didn't seem to recognize his revulsion, stepping close to his side. "You got a proper lady with child, and were forced into marrying her, if the rumors swirling about town are correct. It can't have been easy for you, marrying a virtual stranger. You never liked being trapped, did you?"

She sidled up to him and whispered in his ear. "I know how much you like to keep your options open. We are alike in that way, you and me. I understand you in ways she never will. Oh, she may have your title, and your child, but the poor thing will never have your heart. No woman will. I can accept that, even if she won't."

"You don't know a dang thing about me. All you've ever been concerned with is yourself."

She laid a warm hand on his arm. "I know you leave when things get sticky. Always looking out for the easiest way out. I understand. Because I'm the same way."

Was it true? Was he truly like Iris? Did he deserve to live without his Callie girl? His love? His heart? Was she better off without him?

"Wake up, my darling. You know as well as I that she'll come to despise you in the end. Your Callie wants a saint, not a real man. The proof is in the pudding. She doubts you at the first bump in the road. Too high-falutin' and mealy-mouthed to accept a real man. But I know who you really are. I want you for who you really are. An opportunist, just like me."

Bren stood frozen in the room between the door and Iris. Was she right? Was Callie better off without him? Was Rose? He used to think so. But what about now? What about the life they had begun to forge together? Could it be broken so easily?

"Bren, don't you remember how good we were together? Here, let me refresh your memory…"

Lush, soft curves pressed against his body.

Disgusted, he shoved her off. "Where is my daughter?"

Iris narrowed her eyes into glittering blue slits. "Oh, Rose. She got herself in a state, silly chit. So unnatural, turning on her real mother."

"What the devil are you talking about?"

She shrugged, maddeningly serene.

"Where is she, damn you?"

"Rose is easily led. Still a child, despite being a nearly grown woman. Why, when I was her age, I knew exactly which way was up. Had my first gent wrapped around my finger by the age of fourteen. Lily was more like me, though she lacked my ambition. But Rose? Beautiful, yes, but worthless. You all have been too soft on her. Well, that will change as soon as I have the charge of her."

"Leave her with you? Never."

"How tragic that she thinks you already have."

He stopped at the doorway and turned back. "What do you mean? What did you say to her?"

Iris smiled. "I might have mentioned the babe soon to arrive. The one who'll replace her."

"What?"

"Oh yes, Bren. Your precious secret's out."

"How the hell do you know about the child?"

"Your dear Callista told me. As you might expect, with all the lies you've spun—white and black—petit and grand— poor dear needed a friend to confide in.

"You? A friend?"

"You never did understand women. She was afraid you'd leave her—just as you left me. Sadly, I could not, in good conscience, give her the assurance she so craved."

"God help me, you're evil."

"Tut, tut. I only speak the truth. If that's evil, perhaps it's because you've fled from truth your whole life. Saint Callista will have her heir to comfort her. But Rose? She's nothing but a bastard. Even in her foolish little mind, she sees it: once you've a legitimate child, she's cast aside—just as you've done before. And her darling step-mama? Far too busy cooing over her own to care about a by-blow. I merely suggested she leave first. With me. She ran off—but she'll return."

"Where's Callie?"

"Saint Callista?" She gave a lazy smile. "Forget her. I'm here. Your Iris. The flower of your youth. The mother of your... well, one child, anyway."

He headed for the door.

"Don't bother, I expect she's gone."

He spun back. "Gone? What are you saying?"

"Now that she knows our full history, she saw how the land lay. So, she surrendered—left the field to the victor. Tore out like the devil was snapping at her heels."

"You're lying. She'd never go out in this storm. Not with the babe."

"Seems leaving you meant more to her than the babe's safety. Come now. Forget her. You were never able to resist me. Resist these." She let her robe fall open, baring her breasts.

Bren turned away. Could it be true? Could Callie hate him that much?

"She's a coward, Bren. Doesn't deserve you. Come to bed. Let me show you what real love feels like."

"When did she go?"

She flopped onto the bed. "You know I never keep track of time."

"Pack your things. The moment this toad-strangler lets up, you're gone."

He strode for the door. God above, how had he ever believed himself like her?

"Haven't you figured it out yet, Brendan Cavanaugh, Viscount Clifford? You ruin families. Ruined your own. Ruined Rose's. And now you've ruined this one. You'll never keep her. Not your saintly Callie. She'll never abide a coward like you!"

He ran for Callie's room, Iris's words echoing in the hollows of his soul.

Gulliver met him at the door, winding round his boots with a plaintive meow.

"Callie?" Bren's voice echoed in the quiet.

The cat trotted ahead as Bren passed through the connecting room—

Also empty.

"Meow!"

With a swish of his tail, Gully darted into the corridor.

Bren followed, taking the stairs three at a time. The doors to the Great Hall stood open. He peered inside.

Their tree—tall, proud, gloriously adorned. A monument to all they'd hoped for. A testament to the joy they meant to kindle.

There, on the floor, Rose's keepsake box.

When finally opened would his Shy Bird marvel at the inlay—native woods carved to reveal a rose entwined with a lily? Tam had clapped him on the back when he'd finished it, saying, *Couldnae ha' done better m'self, lad.*

Beside it lay the cradle, its rockers still swathed in a puddle of its muslin wrapping. Three spindles, broken, laying on the stone floor.

Had Callie seen it? Run her hands over the simple lines? Imagined their child tucked safe within its frame, wrapped in warmth and love?

It could be mended.

The cradle.

The trust.

His family.

There was celebrating yet to be done, and love to build upon.

By God, they would have Sara's Christmas in July.

No going back—but forward? Aye, that they could do.

Tam's words echoed in his mind, rough and real as ever:

Life's never perfect, laddie, and if ye think it is, ye're in for a world o' hurt. Take it a day at a time. Do yer best. Then forgive… or ask tae be forgiven.

He would do both.

He would ask Callie to forgive him for hiding the truth about Iris. And he would forgive her, too—for not believing him.

She would learn to trust him. He had to believe that. They'd already come so far. Shared so much. Surely Iris and her venomous tales could not undo what they'd built?

"Now I just have to find her," he said to Gulliver, who blinked at him as if in solemn agreement.

"And tell her I love her."

Chapter Thirty-Four

Gully meowed and streaked across the room toward the door and then headed for the back of the house. He turned once to make sure Bren was following. The cat stopped at the door that led from the still house out into a covered portico, which then led to a track toward the barn.

Bren pushed open the massive door. The rain had stopped, but streaky, black clouds still raced across the sky.

Angus was running back from the barn toward the keep, his shouts lost to the howling wind.

Bren met him halfway. "What's wrong?"

"Valentine, my cart-pony—she's gone."

Bren raced toward the barn, Angus following.

A ruffled petticoat lay on the hay-strewn floor. With her fear of horses, Rose would never have tried to mount even Angus's mild-mannered pony. The underpinning had to be Callie's.

"I was just coming out to check on Val—she can be skittish in storms—when I found this. I just can't imagine anyone—that is—beg pardon, your lordship, I—"

"Never mind, lad. Have you seen Miss Rose?"

"No, your lordship. And, beggin' your pardon, I wouldn't expect Miss Rose to venture out into this storm, sir."

"No, I wouldn't think so, either." But who knew what the girl would do given the events of this day. Certainly, her fragile world had been rocked.

"You didn't see anything amiss besides the pony gone?"

"No, your lordship. Just this—undergarment. I knew it had to belong to one of the ladies. I was just coming to get you when you found me."

The only animal left was ol' Verlan. Bren had brought the gelding up from the village just recently. He was near blind now, and Bren wanted his last days to be coddled ones.

"I'll have to take Verlan."

The horse swung his huge head up over the stall's half door and then snorted as if he could sense the task in front of him.

As Bren urged the animal out of his stall, Angus got out the saddle and bridle. The horse stood at the ready while Angus threw on the saddle and then reached under him to cinch the girth. Verlan lowered his head for Bren to slip the bit into his mouth. Bren hesitated. The horse's eyes were milky, nearly opaque, as if a fog had settled over them. The old boy blinked and butted his head against Bren's chest, as if to say, 'let's get on with it.'

A moment later Bren heaved himself on to Verlan's wide back and gathered the reins.

"Your lordship—I—I am so sorry," Angus said, shaking his head.

"No one's fault, lad." *Only my own.* "I expect my wife went in search of Miss Rose, but just in case, look out for her, will you? And have plenty of hot water and blankets for when I bring the ladies home."

"Aye, sir. That I will!" Angus pulled his forelock

and stepped away from the horse and rider.

"Come on, boy. Let's go get our family." He set his heels into the stirrups and shot forward into the tearing wind. The late afternoon light snuffed to a mere smudge in the bruised sky.

"Verlan, I can't lose them. I lost Lily. I lost Sara. I won't lose my Rosie. Or my Callie—my heart.

****

Bren scanned the gorse-choked verges flanking what had once been a rutted cart road. Now it was a torrent—small streams surging through a mire of sucking mud. If *this* path looked like a river, the real stream would be roaring.

Please, God—let me find them before the bridge.

He wasn't above fear, or loss, or ruin. Title be damned—he was just a man. A man with everything to lose, and no power at all if he failed to keep his family safe.

I'm scared.

He'd only experienced this kind of terror once before in his life. Not when the Sioux were at his heels, not when he was carrying secret missives through enemy lines, not even when he was being held by that maniac Milton. Only when—

He shook the memory from his mind. *Focus on the here and now.* This family, this woman, his unborn child. Want made you vulnerable. Want made you scared to lose. And he had so very much to lose.

He bent low over Verlan's neck, crooning encouragement to himself as much as to the poor beast.

He spied a bright patch to the side of the path ahead—something snagged in a thicket of gorse. A shawl. Rosie's? He couldn't be sure.

He sent up a prayer to whatever god might heed the sinner he was that she was somewhere ahead and unharmed.

Beyond a turn in the road, he saw a pool of white—another petticoat. It must be Rosies.

Good girl. Even sopping wet, in this wind, she'd like to have taken off like a dang kite had she kept the infernal underpinning on.

One more turn until the bridge. Dear Lord, what might the storm have done to that ancient pile of stone? The plans for a new one still lay unfinished on his desk.

Then he saw her. Callie.

She had dismounted and was trying to get hold of a skittish Valentine.

Without her stiff petticoat the wind plastered her skirts against the slight swell of her belly.

Another prayer sent upwards to please keep their babe safe.

"Callie!"

No response. The wind tore his call away as soon as it left his lips.

Nearly to her now.

"Callie!"

She saw him. Hand up to her eyes, her other still tangled in the reins.

"Let the beast go!" God Almighty, he could just imagine the dang horse bolting and dragging Callie with her.

"Drop the reins!" he shouted.

But she had turned from him toward the bridge as if she needed to get away. That she could not even look upon him.

He pressed his heels into Verlan's sides. "Come on,

you old soldier. I need you now!"

The horse seemed to hear him. He snorted and lowered his head, pushing against the tearing wind.

"Callie!"

But if she heard him, she paid no mind, intent on something beyond the bridge. Something on the other shore?

He leapt off Verlan, his feet stinging as they hit the ground.

"Callie, I—"

Her gaze remained fixed on the shore beyond the bridge.

He tried to take the reins from her, but she seemed to need them as an anchor.

"Callie-girl, won't you at least look at me?"

Valentine threw her head, unused to Verlan who now loomed over her. Callie's arms jerked along with the pony.

In one instant he had his knife out and slashed the twisted reins. Valentine snorted and then wheeled toward the keep and the safety of the barn.

Bren took Callie's cold, wet hands in his. Her gaze met his for only a moment before she turned away. In that instant, he had seen fear and desperation, but he thought he'd also seen love. A tiny flame of love.

She pointed at the bridge.

"What is it?"

"Rose!"

The wind howled, whipping sheets of muddy water across the stone bridge in a frenzied dance. His heart thudded in his chest, blood pounding at his temples.

"Where?"

He strained his eyes, searching for any sign of her.

Had she crossed already? Had the storm swept her away before they could reach her? His hand gripped the reins of his horse, his other arm around his wife, trying to keep her steady in the turbulent weather.

They stood at the edge of the swollen river, his gaze fixed on the far side where the low bridge crossed. The only path between him and his daughter? The water surged beneath the stone structure, dark and roiling, carrying debris—twisted branches and clumps of earth—swirling in the fast-moving current.

Danger!

Take care of your sister!

Don't let me lose my other half!

The memories pelting his brain.

"Rose!" Their combined voices cut through the wind, but barely rose above the roar of the river.

"Rosie, can you hear me?"

Beside him Callie echoed his plea.

Callie's hand tightened in his, she pointed to the stand of trees just beyond the bridge.

Sure enough, he could make out the shape of a girl. A girl in a sodden green dress, her head down against the wind.

"Rosie!" He dropped Callie's hand, waving his arms overhead to catch his daughter's attention.

She looked up then. "*Da!*" She stepped onto the bridge, eager to cross to them. My God, didn't she realize the thing could crumble at any moment? Part of the stone wall had long fallen away, replaced with a temporary wooden fence.

"Rose!" He shouted, his voice hoarse, pushing through the fear. "Don't move! Stay where you are! I'll come to you!"

But the wind threw his words back at him.

Rose took another step, her hands clutching the low stone wall.

"No—*no!*" He didn't know whether the scream was his, or Callie's. "Rose, wait!"

He held out his hands, trying to tell her with his body what his words could not. But she still kept coming.

Dear God, her smile, it was wreathed in relief…

But suddenly she looked down—her smiled turning into an O of surprise as the water swirled over her calves— and then she stumbled.

He leaped forward ready to charge over to her, but she pulled herself up, clutching the stone wall with both arms. "Go back!" he called.

Rose finally seemed to understand. She nodded and began retracing her steps, going arm over arm along the wall.

Bren breathed a sigh of relief. She would be safe.

Verlan threw his head and snorted just as Callie screamed.

Bren took his eyes from Rose to see what had driven his wife into danger.

Callie pointed a shaking finger at—a huge log, barreling down the stream, like a beast freed from its chains.

Straight at the bridge.

"Rose!" His voice cracked, raw with fear.

I cannot lose my other half!

In the blink of an eye, the log came for her—carried on the roaring surge. With a mighty crash, the wooden rail shattered, washing pieces across the span as the log then smashed into the opposite wall, tearing out a huge chunk of the bridge.

Torn away from her security, she lunged for the remaining wall, but the force of the surge swept her feet from under her and she fell. As the river's grip tightened around her, her scream was swallowed.

Callie's scream took up the cry as she gripped his arm.

Churning, muddy water swirled about her, pulling, pulling, until the inevitable, she plunged over the edge and into the river itself.

He thrust the reins into Callie's hands and then stepped to the edge of the mud-slick bank. Callie's cry for him to be careful was drowned out by the roar of the river and the pounding in his chest.

The cold shock of the water slammed into him like a fist. His feet found no purchase on the slippery rocks below, but his arms drove forward, pulling him with the current, his legs kicking, fighting the force wanting to drag him under. Debris spun around him, threatening to knock him off course.

He could just make her out ahead of him—her form, struggling against the current, arms flailing.

"Rosie!" he called to her, wanting her to know he was coming for her. But, if she heard, she made no sign.

The banks narrowed dramatically, like a bull in a shoot, the water now forced into even tighter confines. Further down, when the river opened up, he'd have a better chance.

But would he be able to reach her in time before the water hit the rocky stretch just before the waterfall?

He was a lot heavier than she, but Rose was also hampered by her skirts. Even without her cumbersome petticoat, they would be heavy.

Just as the thought came to him, she disappeared

under the water again.

Damn it! He was still too far away.

He forced his body to move faster as the water tried to swallow him whole.

"Rose!" Callie screamed from the shoreline.

She would need to come up for air! She was down too long! Panic hit him hard and he slipped beneath the water.

When he fought his way back up to the surface, he saw only a pale pool of green floating on top of the water where his daughter should be.

Nooo! His heart screamed!

Then, like a fountain, she burst out of the water, her mouth open, her hair whipping as she shook water from her eyes.

"Rose!" Callie shouted again.

With renewed strength, he pressed forward toward her. *Please God, let me reach her.*

But then he saw a miracle. She was swimming! Flailing mightily, but swimming!

And, by Jingo, she'd managed to hold her breath long enough to shuck off her skirts! Even now the mass of fabric was sinking slowly beneath the water. He wanted to howl with laughter and pride.

Now, close enough to the shore, she was able to gain her feet, and stand. Callie was scrambling down the bank to help her. But Rosie pulled herself up and on to the shore on her own—sure enough, only in her bloomers!

She immediately turned back to the river, to him. His nearly drowned and thoroughly muddy daughter, as skittish as they come, and her face told it all. A smile the size of the newly formed state of Texas bloomed on her lips.

His heart sang. *Safe! Safe! Safe!*

But before he could answer her smile, a great shadow blotted out her beautiful face. A sickening crack. Then only blinding pain.

The world spun violently, the force of the blow sending him reeling through the water. His vision blurred.

Pain lanced through his head, making his teeth clash. Blood filled his eyes. A weak shaft of sunlight broke through the clouds just before the water closed over his head.

****

Neither she nor Rose saw the log until it was too late.

A sickening crack. A bloom of blood. Callie nearly retched. The log spun away as Bren sank beneath the churning waters.

Rose nearly dove after him, but Callie seized her arm. "No! He wouldn't want you in danger again. Come on!"

Callie, Rose, and Verlan scrambled along the bank, tracking the trail of blood, and the occasional flash of Bren's clothing. Every time he surfaced, they shouted.

He never answered.

****

Safe.

His Rosie…She hadn't needed him after all. She was strong enough on her own. And Callie was safe on the shore next to her. The women he loved would be fine. The realization allowed him to relax and not fight the current anymore. The water's current, the current of his memories …

…Take care of your sister …

Danger!

Please, God, don't let me lose my other half ...

The words ran through his mind, pulling him back in time to a summer's day nearly twenty-five years ago...

He couldn't sleep.

Pa was gone, as he often was. Sometimes for days. Sometimes weeks. They never knew when he'd take off or return home. He'd just reappear, as if no time had lapsed, with no explanation, demanding his dinner.

Seemed like his departure this time had signaled the gods to rain havoc. Nearly a week of toad-strangling storms had turned the garden to mud, the roads to bogs, and the roof into a sieve. They'd gone to sleep with the steady drip, drip pinging against nearly every pot and vessel they could find.

But today the sky was clear, and the fish would be biting!

Sunday. Church, and a few chores, but then most of the day and evening to fish.

Whistling, he took the stairs three at a time, making his way to the kitchen.

Ma was nowhere in sight. She was usually up early, relishing her quiet time before everyone came scurrying down demanding things of her.

There was a note on the table next to a rising loaf of bread. Addressed to Farren. Of course.

Her spidery hand was too fancy for him to make much sense of. Ma had been called away? Miz. Chapman's time...

"Yee Hahh!"

"What's all the caterwaulin'? And where's Ma?"
Farren shoved his hand through his hair making him look even more like a surprised porcupine than he

usually did.

"We hit the jackpot today, brother. No church. So, fishing all day!"

Farren looked skeptical. "Where's the note?"

His brother never liked to defy their ma's orders. Farren had the cockeyed notion that he could still somehow worm his way into her heart.

He skirted the question. "Miz Chapman's time."

"Another one?" Farren croaked. "Isn't she near fifty?"

Bren shrugged. Made no never mind to him. The only thing he cared about was the new fly wrapped carefully in a square of paper tucked in his vest pocket. He touched it now, just to make sure it was still there. It was a beauty. A Hare's Ear, made from carefully selected two-toned hair, its hot spot a red silken thread, its finish a tiny golden bead, the last two bits both snitched from the very bottom corner of his mother's sewing basket.

"Come on, let's get some grub together and set out for the stream."

"Shall we gather at the river?" Sara's thin soprano preceded her. "Where bright angel feet have trod. With its crystal tide forever. Flowing by the throne of God."

Sprout came into the kitchen halfway done up in her Sunday best, fists rubbing her sleepy eyes.

Ready to launch into the second verse, she stopped and frowned. "Where's mama?"

Doggone it. He'd forgot about Sprout. The note said, be sure to take care of your sister.

"Miz Chapman's about to hatch. Sprout, you're on your own today, Farren and I are going fishin'."

"I want to fish!"

"No you don't. You don't like fishing. You like talking. And singing. Which is as close as you're gonna get to a river today." He smirked at his little joke about her choice of hymn.

"I wanna go!"

Bren could see Farren waver.

"Next time, Sprout," Bren told her. "Remember I got you that book you wanted. Jane Eyre? You've been hounding me about it for months."

"But you promised to take me this time!" This last directed solely at him. That little gal could make a stone weep.

Heck. He dropped his head and heaved a sigh.

"We can't leave her, Bren," Farren said, holding up the note Bren had stuck under a pot.

Ah, hells bells.

"Change out of that rig." He was halfway out the back door. "And bring that dang book!"

What seemed like an eternity later, they were finally ready to go. Sara still hadn't changed. What she'd done instead, he'd no clue, but he wasn't waiting another second.

"You get so much as a speck on that fancy frock, my hide'll be tanned."

"I'll be careful. Sides, I got some britches for when I fish." And then she slid her warm little hand in his.

Goll dang, he loved that little gal. But sure as milk turned sour there would be hell to pay over the ruination of her Sunday best.

He wouldn't think of that now. Sides, the whippin' would be worth it.

He was a ways ahead of Farr and Sara. Sprout had to point out every gol darn bug and leaf along the way.

Bren got to their spot and couldn't believe his luck.

An old ash tree had come down just by the side of the stream. Huge rocks and old stumps had been caught behind it, making a temporary dam. Perfect for fishing.

Someone had posted a sign on the twin tree that still stood next to its fallen fellow. Danger! *Or at least that's what Bren thought it said. He didn't bother trying to make out the tiny words below it.*

Dang it! If Farren caught sight of that sign, he'd put the kibosh on this haven for sure. But, dang it all, this was the place. He could feel it. The trout would be in paradise in this new pool, ready to gobble down anything that came over the edge.

Bren picked up a flat rock and used it to pry the sign off the tree. He tossed it into the woods just before Farr and Sprout crashed through the trees.

"Lookee here! Mother Nature has made us a perfect spot!" Bren crowed, gesturing to the newly formed pond.

Farren eyed the damn. "Looks precarious."

"Naw, it's perfect, Farr. I ain't movin'" He threw down the old quilt under a nearby tree and the tin of biscuits and bacon. "Settle yourself right here, Sprout, and don't move. Last thing I need is for you to come home with that dress all muddy."

"But you promised I could fish!"

"In a bit. Let me just see where the fish are bitin' first and then we'll get you set up."

But he was already setting his lure, wading into the icy waters.

Time slid by as it always did when he was fishing. He'd moved downstream, trying to find a bit of peace. Sara and Farren kept up a steady flow of banter, just as he knew they would with his little sister in tow.

"Look at meeeee!" the trill of his sister's cry made his line jerk.

"Dang it all, Sprout! I will tan your hide!"

Then he heard a terrible crash, blood-freezing screams. Farren yelling, "Sara!"

The once-placid water suddenly churned. He struggled to keep his footing as it raced by him, pulling him farther downstream. He knew before looking, the dam must have broke.

He fought to get to the bank, throwing his rod away as it tangled on a nearby branch.

Scrambling up the muddy slope, he pulled away ferns and roots. Branches tore at his face and arms as he pushed through the brambles and deadfall.

He saw the yellow of her dress first. Looked like a dang flower, with her skirts all ballooned up around her. Only a matter of time till they pulled her under.

He dove in, heedless of what might be beneath the churning water. When his head broke the surface, she was only a few feet away. He'd get to her.

He smiled now, reaching for her, but she didn't return it. Her lips moved, trying to tell him something, but her face kept being swamped with water.

He grabbed for her, for the yellow fabric surrounding such a tiny, fragile body.

"Farr!" She gulped.

Bren turned back to the river. But he couldn't see his brother.

He kicked, pushing Sara toward a clump of tree roots half submerged in the roiling water.

"He dove in but didn't come up!" she gasped as she clutched for a root. "Go! Help him!"

The water raced around her. He turned back to the

stream. Still no sign of Farren.

"Hold on, and don't let go!" he told her.

She nodded. He let loose of her.

Battling upstream, he looked for a dark head, a blue shirt, any sign of blood. But the burst dam had churned up the water into a murky mess. He dove in.

How long had it been? Time seemed endless. Again, down into the water. But, dang it, he couldn't stay down long enough, had to keep coming up for air. Near panic, he dove again. There! A leg! Bren yanked with all his might and pulled Farren toward him, toward life.

Their heads broke the water, Bren gasping, Farren white and not breathing. Bren's muscles strained and burned as he laid Farr on his chest and backstroked toward the shore. Jagged rocks tore at his back and his feet slipped in the mud, yet he held onto his brother, his other half.

Now up on the bank, Bren pumped on Farren's chest, praying to God not to lose his beloved brother. His face so white, his lips a purplish-blue. He bent over him to give him his breath. To give him his life, if it would save him.

Please, anything, just don't let me lose my other half!

Farren gasped and Bren turned him to his side. Water gushed from between his blue lips and he coughed and sputtered. Blood ran freely from a gash on his head, but Bren remembered that head wounds bled a lot. He ripped the tail of his shirt and pressed the wet cloth over his brother's temple.

Farren's eyes finally opened.

Bren grinned through his tears. "Sprout, I guess we're going to be stuck with him. He's alive!"

It took him a moment to register that there was no reply. Only the rush of the water and a crow cawing overhead.

"Sprout? Sara?"

Bren heaved himself up and clambered down river to the tree with the extending roots.

Nothing.

"Sara!" He ran further down the bank, sure he would see her safe on the shore, ready to give him hell.

"Sara!"

Panic hit him head on, his heart pounding as if it would burst through its cage of bone.

Nearly fifty feet down river, at the bend they used to call the horn, he saw a spot of yellow.

"Sara!"

When he finally got to her, she looked like she was sleeping, all curled up, her head pillowed on a mossy rock. Her sweet bow mouth open.

He pulled her towards him, gently, so gently. But he knew—knew even before he saw how her head flopped at an odd angle, he knew. The awful truth. She was gone.

Please God, anything, just don't let me lose my other half…

God had answered his prayer.

****

"Can you see him?" Callie shouted to Rose over the roar of the water.

"No, not for a while now. But he is strong," the girl said, with conviction.

She'd been watching a log in the river, marking its progress down the stream. Was it as heavy as Bren? Branches slapped her face, and her feet slipped on mud-slicked stones and moss as she scrambled with Rose along the stream bank.

Thank goodness the terrain on this side was clear of larger undergrowth, Verlan followed, likely listening to her and now Rose's calls. She could not spare him a glance as he stumbled and snorted behind them.

Needing reassurance, Callie reached back for Rose's hand. The girl grasped it firmly. This was her daughter. Come what may, she would fight tooth and nail for this young woman.

And for this man, who she loved so very much.

"Here! Help me up!" Callie shouted to Rose, gesturing toward Verlan and the jutting branch downstream. "We'll never make it in time this way!"

Rose interlaced her fingers and boosted her. Callie swung into the saddle, clutching the reins as the great beast surged forward beneath her.

"Come on, old boy," she murmured. "Bring him to me, one more time."

Verlan lunged forward. At the sharp bend in the river, Callie pulled hard. "Whoa!"

She grabbed a hank of mane as she nearly lunged over the horse's head.

She flung herself down and landed hard. One slipper lost to the sucking mud. Freezing water stole her breath; sharp stones sliced her feet.

She waded in, eyes fixed on the branch—their last hope.

It was heavier than expected—slick with moss, pulled by the current. She clenched her chattering teeth and pushed it farther into the racing stream.

"Please, God—please, just let me tell him I love him. Just once."

A splash behind her. Rose, panting.

Together, they fed the branch into the rushing water, cold biting their hands, the current trying to tear it away.

Then Verlan whinnied.

A blond head appeared in the water.

My God, not too late—

"Bren!"

"Da!"

****

Please, God, anything, but don't let me lose my other half!

He had lived with God's ironically cruel gift all these years. The heavy weight of his bargain always pressing down on him. Hell, maybe it hadn't been God, but the Devil who'd answered his plea? Made sense that the Lord of Darkness would've stepped in to aid him instead of the Almighty. As much sense as his meeting his end in a watery grave.

So easy to give in. Just open his mouth. Let the water have its way and be done.

Out of the blackness a light appeared, glowing and shifting ever so slightly. Then it transformed.

Sara!

His sister's sweet face bobbed in front of him, a soft smile on her lips. Bren felt the touch of light hands against his arms. He tried to smile back at her, but his head swam, and his lungs burned. The hands seemed to shift to cover his pounding heart. Again, he tried to smile, to let her know he was ready to come to her.

She shook her head, her hands pressing on his heart and lungs. The face floated toward him, her lips coming to brush his. It was impossible, but she seemed to give him air. To give him life.

Brenny, it was not your fault...

Had he heard her speak? Forgive him?

The knowledge of it bloomed in his heart, replacing the heaviness with buoyancy and light. Yes, she forgave him. He knew it deep in his heart.

He'd tried. By God, he tried his best. It had been a terrible accident. He was not to blame. My God, he was not to blame.

Brenny, it was not your fault...

And he smiled.

Her face dissolved into light, and then into darkness. Part of him wanted the light to come back, to take him, too. But Sara had shaken her head. It was not his time. Too much left to do, so much left to live for.

He tasted blood in his mouth. Iron. He opened his eyes. Water surrounded him. Water cloudy with blood. His lungs burned, squeezed so tight. Must be a record. Hell, he'd not been counting, but this must be his longest yet.

Something deep within him fought to come to the surface of his flagging brain. Something he had yet to do, something he'd yet to say.

What was it? Blackness and pain in his lungs crowded his mind, but there was something else, a need. Such a need.

He would ask Sara. But then he remembered, his little sister was gone.

I cannot lose my other half...

Callie!

Callie did not know. He had to tell her to have the final peace he craved. Sara's forgiveness was not enough.

He needed to tell Callie he loved her. No, much more than simple words, he needed to show her—try to be a father to Rose and to his unborn child. To live to be a better man. Not a perfect man, but one who would rise above his mistakes, not be drowned by them.

Hell, Callie might be done with him, just as Iris had said. She might have decided he was not worth the effort.

Well, if she had, he'd just have to persuade her otherwise. He wouldn't let Iris win. The burden of guilt no longer a weight to drown him.

He thrust up with all his might. His head broke the surface, and he sucked in air.

"Bren! Brendan! Hear me!"

"Da! Da, please!"

He shook his head and swiped blood and hair from his eyes.

A huge horse stood on the bank—Verlan?

A long branch waved crazily above the water. Two figures holding it—

Callie and Rosie!

"Grab it! Grab it, my love!"

My love—

Not too late! Not too late—for happiness, for dreams, for family. Even to be a danged viscount.

If only he could keep the blackness from coming. If only he could stay conscious long enough to do as they asked.

Just reach out. You can do this. You deserve life. You deserve happiness.

"Now! Do it, now!"

He reached out his arms toward them, to hold them close once more.

"Yes! Yes!! Hold on. You must hold on!"

He wrapped his arms around something, not soft, not his warm Callie. But it didn't matter. Callie was telling him to hold on, and so he would, because he loved her so.

The terrible pull on his body lessened. His legs tangled in reeds. He tried to blink the blood from his eyes.

"Let go, Da. You can let go now. You're safe. We have you. Mama and I have you."

Something brushed over his eyes. Hands bracketed his head. "Open your eyes, my love. Please open your eyes and stay with us."

"Callie." Did she hear him? His eyelids so heavy, blackness creeping in. Had she called him her love?

"Please, my dearest, please open your eyes! Don't you dare leave me now. Do you hear me!"

She needed him. Wanted him. Even knowing he was a scoundrel.

Her beautiful face loomed over him, earnest and so very dear.

I love you.

Could she hear him?

I love you, Callie-gal.

But before he could make her understand, the world went black.

Chapter Thirty-Five

Callie called out to Verlan, but the horse was already plunging into the water, steady and sure—as if he understood their need.

Together she and Rose managed to pull Brendan onto the horse's broad back. Callie climbed up behind him, wrapping her arms around his icy body while Rose led them forward.

At the road, Callie nearly wept with relief. Angus and the cart were just turning toward the bridge.

"When Valentine returned, I got worried," Angus said, as he packed heated bricks around Brendan. "I hitched her up at once, and Phillip brought blankets. Mr. Billings wanted to come, but his missus wouldn't hear of it." He gave Verlan a fond pat and tied him to the back of the cart.

She held Bren against her, crooning nonsense to him, willing him to wake. Rose did likewise.

He would wake. He must.

She sent up a prayer of thanks to the shifting clouds.

Miraculously mercurial this Scottish weather. Torrents of rain and wind, and then—sudden sunshine filtering through wisps of western cloud, gilding the mountainside with a heavenly opalescent light.

The wind fell to quiet squalls, ruffling puddles left along the road. The rush of the river still murmured through the trees, but now birds joined it—high notes in nature's halting symphony.

Please let this change in weather foretell a similar healing in Brendan's body.

Everyone was waiting on the portico when they arrived. Mrs. Billings immediately took charge, directing hands and hearts alike. All seemed grateful to be useful, and soon Brendan was upstairs, dry, bandaged, and settled in their bed.

"Wake up, my love. Please, wake up." Callie clutched his cold hand against her heart, willing her strength into him, as if its beat might summon him back.

Rose hovered near the bedpost, rocking slightly, whispering to herself.

"Bren, we need you. We haven't yet had Sara's Christmas. We can't do it without you."

Purple bruises looked nearly black against his ghostly white face, his skin—cold as stone.

"Is he breathing?" Rose edged forward, her voice brittle.

"Yes, shallow but—yes." Callie reached back to take Rose's hand. The girl's fingers were nearly as cold as Bren's. "He will wake. He must."

Hours passed. People tiptoed in and out, bearing food that went untouched, tea that mostly grew cold.

Gully sat sphinxlike, one paw draped across Bren's arm, his green gaze unwavering.

Rose had finally been coaxed to bed, with the promise she'd be called the moment anything changed.

Callie slipped beneath the covers and nestled beside him, trying to give him what warmth she could.

Oh, why had she doubted him? Why had she taken Iris's part so easily?

Because of her mother.

Because of Antonia.

Antonia Ainsworth was no saint. Just a woman. One who had risked everything for a chance to love honestly. Even when it meant losing her only child.

That was the truth. The hard, bruising truth.

Her mother had loved deeply—too deeply to pretend otherwise—and by shirking her duty, she'd broken the rules of a world that offered no place for her. And so, broke her family's heart.

But she hadn't stopped loving Callie. The paradox tangled painfully in her chest.

Rose had known the truth from years of living with Iris—had felt the neglect deep in her heart. Her mother didn't want her.

Not enough. Not in the way a child longs to be wanted.

Iris was selfish. Impulsive. Easily swayed.

But Antonia?

She'd left, yes—but not to run.

To live, maybe.

To survive.

The longcase clock in the hall tolled the hours. Three. Then four. Would he wake on the fifth?

No.

Six.

Seven. Then eight. Still nothing.

Callie flung open the curtains, as if light itself might rouse him. She wanted brightness. She wanted a miracle.

The doctor had been summoned. Angus and Phillip had patched the broken bridge, just enough to carry Iris Darvan down the mountain. From there, Angus rode for the doctor, but help would take hours—perhaps days.

Rose now sat beside her Da, his hand in hers, her

voice a soft song Callie couldn't quite make out. Whatever she said, it seemed to soothe her.

The day slipped away. Their child stirred in her belly as if anxious for the father it had yet to meet.

Her mind thick with fear and exhaustion, she fell into a light sleep, but her dreams, filled with nothing but water—the river, swirling and dangerous, always pushing Bren further away.

Rose had been persuaded to go have a proper tea in the kitchen with the staff.

Callie crossed to close the curtains on another day.

She gripped the heavy velvet, leaning out the embrasure to catch the last glimpse of the sun as it inevitably slipped downward. She had the fanciful notion that he must wake before it disappeared—or he might nev—

She shook her head and rubbed her eyes. Too little sleep. Too much worry.

The last wink of light vanished, snuffed into reflected pinks and golds. Gone now.

"Callie-girl?"

She could have sworn her heart stopped, then leapt as if it must burst from her.

"Bren?" she whispered.

"Eeeewooo!" Gully stood looking at Callie and then butted his head against Bren's neck.

"Bren?" she repeated as she rushed to his side.

"My Callie-girl," he rasped.

Oh, those beautiful green eyes.

"Da?" Rose stood in the open doorway. "Oh, Da! You are awake!" She went to her father, taking his hand, her body sinking down to her knees as she lay her cheek against their entwined hands.

Callie sat on the bed next to him, stroking his hair. "Rosie…"

"Oh, Da, I was so afraid. I was so frightened you would never wake up!"

"Shh, Shy Bird. I'm tough as they come."

Still Rose seemed so forlorn as she buried her face in the bedclothes.

Bren reached over to stroke his daughter's head. "Where's my brave girl who held her breath for so long? Who swam?"

Rose looked up at her Da. And Bren smiled.

"That was quite a trick—holding your breath like that. Been practicing, haven't you?"

Rose offered a tentative nod. But then shook her head and burst into a flood of tears.

"Oh, Da, I'm so sorry. It's my fault—I should've told—I should've said—" she ducked her head again.

"Hush now, what's all this nonsense?" He glanced over at Callie, but she was as in the dark as Bren.

With tear-stained cheeks she met her father's gaze "I lied—well, not really, but I kept a terrible secret." She closed her eyes and more tears came. "I knew Mama was alive. I didn't tell because—well, because—I just… I thought if I told, she'd come and take me. And I didn't want to leave you. Not then. Not ever. I know it was wicked."

"Shh, now, darlin'. I happen to know wicked, and that just isn't you. Not one hair on your head or bone in your body is wicked."

Bren stroked her hair as she wept, her small frame trembling under his hand. Soon she recovered, wiping her tears with her sleeve.

"Rose-love… how did you know?" Callie asked,

gently.

The girl sniffed and took a breath. "I saw Uncle Farren meeting Mama the night before the wedding. When you found me on the stairs, Da—I'd just seen them through the upper window."

"Farren?" Callie's hand froze. "It wasn't you, Bren? But you were gone—and your hair, it was damp... Farren said he needed to comfort one of the children..." She looked into his eyes. "Oh, heavens, it was Farren all along?"

"It was. I did escape the party, but only long enough to get a breath of air. I went to the garden, to visit—to visit Lily's spot. I picked some flowers to give to you—"

"But you met me first and gave them to me instead!" Rose turned to Callie. "Da never even spoke to her. Only Uncle Farren."

"Oh—I thought it was you, saying goodbye to some... old friend. Someone you couldn't let go of." Callie shook her head. "I should have asked. I should have trusted you."

"Now, don't get all twisted up," Brendan said gently. "I'm no saint myself. I didn't know Iris was alive—not then. But a few days ago, in the letter I got from Farren—he wrote he'd met with her, paid her off. I should have told you both right then, but I was—" He let out a deep sigh. "Scared. I was trying to buy us a little bit of peace. A little start, before the storm."

"She's gone, Da. We sent her away." Rose said firmly.

Bren looked to Callie who only nodded.

"We gave her money," Rose continued. "And she left."

Bren took a deep breath. "I'm so sorry, Rosie." He opened his mouth to say more, but really what else could be said? Callie knew he hated that she and Rose had dispatched Iris, but actually, Rose had been the one to initiate her mother leaving.

Callie would tell him all about his fiercely brave and just daughter. How she'd handled her selfish mother. He would be so very proud of his Rosie.

Callie smiled. "Seems we all had secrets. But we were trying to protect the same thing—each other."

"In the future I promise to always tell you both everything!" Rose said with the innocent fervor of a girl on the precipice of womanhood.

Callie and Bren exchanged a knowing look. Callie certainly hoped Rose would have at least one or two lovely secrets to cherish.

"Oh!" Rose scrambled up. "But now, I must go and tell the others! I promised to let them know as soon as you awakened! And I cannot break a promise." She took her Da's hand. "I am so very lucky to have you as my Da. I love you so very much!"

Rose swiped away her tears and gave her father a brilliant genuine smile.

At the door she turned back. "And I love you too, Mama."

Mama... Rose had first called her that at the river. But now, in the quiet calm, the word resonated deep in Callie's heart.

"I love you too, my sweet daughter."

Rose offered one last smile before slipping out of the room.

"Mama?" Bren said.

Callie nodded. Her throat too tight to speak, she let

her eyes tell him everything.

"Seems like my Shy Bird is finding her wings." He squeezed his eyes shut against the gathering tears. But they still spilled over his cheeks, rolled into his ears.

"Bren—"

"Callie—" he said cutting her off.

He swiped the tears from his eyes and held up a staying hand. "I know a gentleman ought to let a lady go first, but this can't wait another breath. I love you. I love you so much. It took me a while to cipher it out, I reckon—I had to square myself first, before I could see clear. Before I could love you the way you ought to be loved."

"Oh, Bren, I—"

"Just let me get this out, it's been building in my heart for so long that I am like to burst with it. "

Her hand moved to cover his thumping heart.

"I lost myself when Sara died. Farren—he was strong enough to heal up, make a fine life for himself. But me?" He shook his head. "I realize now I've been holding my breath ever since she died. Oh, I made a trick of it, staying underwater like that, but I realized even out of water, I was still holding my breath. Waiting to fail. So rather than face the pain, I just left."

She longed to rush in, to assure him, but she waited.

"I'm done holding my breath. You are my heart now, my Woodland Witch… and I can finally breathe free."

She kissed him then. Fiercely, as if she might prove her enormous love for him.

"Oh, I love you so much. I have been wanting to tell you as well." She cradled his face between her hands. "You are brave, and kind, and so very smart. You are my hero, Brendan Cavanaugh, flaws and all. I am so very blessed that you stumbled into my life."

He answered her, his mouth devouring, his tongue searching, pressing, filling her. "I want you, Callie-girl. I need to be inside you."

"What about your head?"

He gave her that boyish grin, the sly one, like he had a wonderful secret, and guided her hand down between his legs. "Seems right fine to me."

She shook her head as she cradled his face between her hands. "Oh, you utterly vexing man."

He pulled back, looking into her eyes.

"Vexing? Did you call me vexing, Callie Cavanaugh?"

"Yes, Lord Clifford, I surely did," she answered, making her tone grave.

"I'll show you vexing, my viscountess!" He reached for her.

She snorted and then climbed right on top of him.

Later, much later, they lay spent in each other's arms, her head tucked beneath his chin, his breath, deep and even as he slept.

The fire's embers glowed as another log crumbled to ash, casting the room into darker shadows.

She too had been shaped by a deep wound—the loss of her mother. And like Bren, she'd built her whole history around that hurt.

But history could be rewritten, couldn't it? Not without pain. But the promise of new chapters to come.

Perhaps that was the truth of love—not always getting it right the first time, but choosing, again and again, to stay. To forgive. To build something lasting out of what was once broken.

She laid her hand over his heart.

"Rest now, love," she whispered. "We are stronger than we know."

Their child stirred within her—as if answering. A quiet promise of the next page, waiting to be written.

Callie smiled and closed her eyes.

Epilogue

The applause was thunderous—well perhaps enthusiastic might be more apt, as every one of the small gathering of family and friends rose to their feet clapping and cheering. Brian Belcher let out a shrill whistle, the sound piercing the air thick with the smells of pine and gingerbread.

Harriet and Martha bounded out from behind the puppet theatre, paper crowns perched on their heads, glittering with bits of foil. Rose slipped between them, flushed with excitement and pride. Her puppet—a dun-colored horse draped in a tartan shawl—bobbed jauntily by her side.

"Ach, Tam, did ye see that?" Brian Belcher wiped a tear from his eye. "The cheek of the braw puss! How dare it try ta snatch that pur wee mouse as he tried to save the princess!"

Tam grunted, nodding. "Aye. Clever beastie, he wasna one ta set idly by. He wanted a part. Or fancied the lass for himself."

Callie smiled. Gully, wanting a role, had leapt onto the stage and nearly toppled the whole theatre while battling the puppets' strings.

Callie reached for Bren's hand, but discovered he'd not risen with the rest of the company. He sat quietly dabbing at his eyes.

Well-wishers soon enveloped the girls, showering

them with praise and questions.

Rose slipped free from the crowd and made her way to Callie and Bren. "Da, do you think Sara would have approved?" she asked.

Bren sniffed and nodded. Then stood. "Oh, I know she would, Rosie-gal. She would have been right proud of you ladies."

He took her hands. "Now that fish—the one who helped the prince dive for the pearl—that's a creature your Aunt Sara would've especially loved."

Rose smiled at her father. "*You* were my inspiration for that character, Da."

Bren's only reply was to enfold his remarkable daughter in a fierce bear hug.

"I liked the part where 'ol Verlan read that magical message delivered by the fairies with only his nose," Phillip offered shyly as he joined the girls.

Tam grunted in agreement as he took a pull from his pipe. "Aye. Just because a body is auld, dosna mean he's useless. It near brought a tear to the eye."

Bren laughed. "Sprout loved a good moral, but she had the knack of revealing it so you didn't even know you were getting taught."

"Tam Cree," Mrs. Green teased, "did ye hear that??"

"Aye, wisdom falls to those who are thirsty, Mrs. Green" he said, and lifted his pipe with theatrical dignity.

"Well, I hope it comes to those who are hungry as well. We have enough food here for a week of Christmases!"

"Oh, quick, Rose—" Callie grasped her daughter's hand and set it against her belly.

"Oh! Oh, Mama—Da! I felt it kick!"

"Yes, it's a lively one. I suspect it takes after your

Da already.

Rose smiled. "You think it's a boy? I'd like a little brother…"

Callie exchanged a glance with Bren, the memory rising—how carefully they'd chosen their words when they sat Rose down, wanting to mend the bond Iris had tried to break.

They'd told her gently, just after Bren had regained his strength, assuring her again and again that nothing—nothing—could ever make her less theirs.

"Well, boy or girl, you will be its big sister right around Christmas proper," Callie said with a smile.

"Aye. We'll get an even bigger tree then, won't we, Billings?" Bren called out to the butler.

"Aye, my lord. T'will be grand," the old man gamely answered.

"I am so glad we are staying here at Kinduggan—home." Rose smiled.

"Yes, home," Bren agreed. "That sounds right nice."

"Did you write to Farren about our plan?" Callie asked.

"I did. Rosie helped me with all the spelling. I reckon once Farr rants a bit, he'll come to see that his managing Ryeland is the best solution for us all. Besides, he's nearly as fond of Belcher's Brew as I am. Would be a sin to the world not to carry on. Besides, I want our wee bairn to be raised to learn the woods and lochs of our beautiful Ben Crannoch."

Callie nodded. "How is the new batch coming along?"

"Brian thinks it'll be the best yet. We'll start up the distillery in full force next spring."

The door banged open.

"Am I late?"

"Helena!" Callie cried.

Her little sister swept into the room like a summer storm, her arms piled with gifts, her hair a wild tangle around her ears.

"Happy Christmas!" she cried, dropping a bulging sack before catching Rose and Callie in a flurry of hugs.

"We knocked and knocked—didn't we, Angus?" She tossed a grin toward Angus and Sharon, who had followed her into the great hall.

"Angus finally took us to the still house door. Honestly, we could have just followed all the noise!"

Sharon offered a neat curtsey, and Angus gave another deep bow, his gaze lingering on Rose with something like wonder.

"Oh, what a lovely surprise! Welcome to you all! You've missed the puppet show, but we have yet to exchange gifts and have our feast." Callie said squeezing her sister's hands.

"We, too, come bearing gifts—and news!"

Callie glanced sharply at Bren. Helena had called Iris Darvan her angel—could she have fallen under her spell again?

"What sort of news?" Bren asked, stepping closer.

"Well—seems fitting you're celebrating birth and Christmas—because Nora's had her baby!"

"Oh!" Rose grabbed Helena's sleeve. "We hadn't heard—we nearly packed up to come south!"

"Entirely my fault," Helena admitted cheerfully. "Well, not entirely. Nora was late delivering, and then I was late departing. I begged them to let me be the one to tell you. A special gift for your Christmas."

"Then please don't keep us in suspense! Boy or

girl?" Rose cried.

"Is Nora well? The baby?" Callie asked overlapping her daughter.

Helena laughed and shook her head. "I meant to stage a dramatic reveal, but I simply can't hold it in— still, you must guess!"

"A girl," Rose said at once. "Mum's too beautiful not to have a daughter that looks just like her."

"A boy," Bren shouted. "Another Cavanaugh lad to bedevil Farren."

All chimed in, shouting their guesses. Even Mr. Billings arted in.

Helena turned to Callie who had remained quiet. "Well? What say you, Cal?"

Callie tilted her head, a grin teasing her lips. "You are both wrong and both right. I say a boy and a girl! Twins!"

Laughter rang off the rafters.

With a theatrical flourish, Helena presented a small parcel to Rose. "Open it."

With trembling hands Rose carefully unwrapped the paper, then paused, eyes going wide. "Oh…"

The girl covered her mouth. Callie stepped forward to go to her, but Bren put a hand on her arm.

She drew out a delicate ornament, embroidered with a heart of lily-of-the-valley, the name "Lily Jayne" looped in pale green thread.

"It is a little girl," Rose whispered, blinking fast. "And she is named after Lily. My sister."

And after Sara, too. *Jayne* was Bren and Farren's sister's middle name.

Callie felt Bren's hand tighten around hers.

Helena nodded solemnly. "Nora declared it was the

only name that felt perfect."

Tam and Brian murmured something about needing more whisky, and the rest of the company gathered in little clusters apart from the family, their voices hushed.

Bren drew Rose to his side, enfolding her, the ornament clutched to her breast.

Her little family. Callie swallowed, her throat suddenly thick.

She turned to Helena. "And how are Father and Hermione?" she asked, mostly to give father and daughter a bit of privacy.

"Oh, the same, I suppose. Mother is very keen for my next season, and Father—well, he is Father."

Callie smiled. Yes, her father was—well, her father. Yet, she had a new appreciation for him. He had tried, albeit, in his autocratic way, to keep their family together. Who knows if he had ever loved his young wife? Callie suspected he had. But his love had been doomed from the outset, for her mother had already loved another. That was her mother's truth. And her father's? Well, he was a cold man, disappointed by love and family, without doubt. But still, he had tried to manage love as best as he was able, and that was worth something.

"Oh, and I have another piece of news—about Opal."

"Opal?" Bren, his arm still around Rose, turned to Helena. "The girl with the missing ear? The one who once took a fortune off me in cards?"

"The very girl! She disappeared after Charlotte Sealing's ball—Nora was beside herself—but now she's been found. She's in Scotland, too!"

"Scotland! Where?" Callie remembered hearing

about Opal from Mari.

Helena lowered her voice ominously, "Some crumbling castle said to be older than even Kinduggan. And they say it's owned by an eccentric scientist who chops up bodies to study them!"

"Helena, honestly."

"Cal, I only repeat what I hear. Oooh, perhaps *he's* the one who cut off Opal's ear."

Callie snorted. Rose shuddered, and Bren laughed outright.

"Now I must get all these gifts under the tree!" Helena picked up her bag and turned to join Sharon, Harriett, and Martha. The other puppeteers were soon unloading gifts and exclaiming over various ornaments.

But Rose hung back. "Da?" she asked, her voice a mere whisper.

"Yes, Shy bird?"

"Do you think Lily Jayne will be brave, like Lily was?"

Bren did not answer right away. "Well, I don't rightly know for sure. But one thing I do know, she'll be surrounded by love, Rosie. And that's the beginning of all the best kinds of courage. Besides, she'll have you as an example." He placed a kiss on her forehead.

In that room full of warmth and laughter, Callie knew she had found everything she had once believed she would never have: family, and truth, and love that was real and enduring.

Her mother's locket now lay wrapped up under the tree in the beautiful keepsake box Bren had made for Rose. It no longer held the emotional meaning she had once given it. She hoped Rose would treasure it in her very own way—a new beginning.

"Ready for a toast?" Bren asked, holding out a bottle of Kinduggan whisky.

Glasses and mugs were filled with various libations, and then raised.

"To Lily Jayne," Bren offered.

"To auld friends and new whisky," said Brian.

"Lang ma eyer lums reek!" Tam crowed.

"He means, Long May Your Chimney's Smoke!" Mrs. Green scoffed fondly.

"To family," said Rose, lifting her cocoa with both hands.

Callie blinked fast as Bren wrapped his arm around her.

A cheer rang out and they all drank.

Callie closed her eyes, wanting to seal this Christmas—the first of many to come.

To family and to home.

Sneak Peek at
Crazy for the Countess

Prologue

January 1864
Mayfair, London

Nora St. James, Countess of Havermere, should not have attended the burial.

Gently bred women did not go to such events. They were deemed too frail, their emotions too uncertain to withstand the ritual of consigning a body to the earth.

An equally held belief was that women, being sisters of Eve, were sinful by nature, therefore not worthy to tread upon consecrated ground. The *ton*, no doubt, would ascribe the latter to Nora.

And last, but certainly not least, the good folk of London believed she had murdered the deceased.

She went anyway.

Men in black armbands slanted looks at her beneath their stovepipe hats. Some disapproving, but most slyly coveting. Their eyes slid over her veiled face and red hair to settle on her breasts, waist, and hips.

No matter. She was used to it.

Removing her glove with two quick tugs, she bent and dug her fingers into the dark earth. Musk and pungent decay filled her nostrils. She wanted the black beneath her perfectly manicured nails. She wanted it to seep into her body and somehow make this death real.

With a fistful she rose, squeezed, and then let it fall in a clump. It burst open, scattering over the pristinely polished ebony and rosewood casket.

Bile burned her throat at the memory of his white face turning yellow, the blood pooling in his lifeless body and the tang of urine as he finally released his brutal grip on life.

Nine years married. Just a raw, naïve girl when he'd claimed her.

Now he was gone.

Praise God.

An incredible lightness enveloped her as if she were suddenly within one of those hot-air balloons soaring over the top of the churchyard. She rose to her toes and lifted her chin higher. But she remained solidly on the frozen ground, imprisoned by mourners all huddled around the gaping hole and the black iron fence that surrounded St. Martin-in-the-Fields.

With the final benediction pronounced, she offered her own silent prayer—quite different from the Reverend Harmon's hope of eternal joy in heaven for the fifth Earl of Havermere—and then turned her back on death.

Penny press reporters, who had hung about like carrion on the edges of the churchyard, now swooped in to surround her. Their mouths formed questions, a barrage of words fired like so many shots, making her hot ears ring, their pencils poised to capture her answers, so eager to twist them into lies.

"Did you do it, Countess? Did you poison your husband, Lord Havermere?"

"No chance of the old earl sending you off to Ballencrieff Asylum now that he's conveniently dead is there, Countess?" another shouted.

"You must be relieved to have the inquest behind you. What will you do now? Perhaps find another rich husband?"

Havermere's plan to send her to Ballencrieff Hall, a madhouse in the Scottish Highlands, had been quashed by his apoplexy. No longer able to speak or write, he had lingered, lying in bed for nearly three months while servants wiped spittle and food from his twisted lips, faithfully turning his wasting body.

Once a day Nora had made herself enter his room to endure his accusatory glare. It could not touch her. *He* could no longer touch her. Hurt her. She'd breathed in the sour smell of death and stared back, her truth deflecting his vitriol.

That last day, she'd watched as he gummed down his favorite cake, delivered each morning from Downs Bakery. He smacked his papery lips, impatiently gesturing to his nurse for more.

Disgusted, Nora had turned away. Only a moment later, a panicked gasp had her whipping around. The old man lurched, and the cake flew, the plate clattering to the floor. Nearly knocking the nurse aside in his haste to haul his lordship into a sitting position, a footman thumped on the old man's back. White froth bubbled between his blue lips.

Heedless of his peril, he seemed to use all his remaining strength to raise his arm and point an accusing finger at Nora.

Try as she might, she could not move. That boney finger and glassy gaze pinned her to the wall as if she were already imprisoned in iron shackles.

In the ensuing pandemonium, the cake had been thrown away. No evidence.

However, poison had been found in his body. Nora would not have put it past the old reprobate to do the deed himself if only to drag her down with him. But the brief inquisition ended with the ruling, "Death by persons unknown." Still, gossip had run rampant.

And now, with the old earl's funeral, it seemed the newly widowed Countess of Havermere was still a tasty morsel for a few voracious curs, yapping to tear over the last shred of scandal.

Nora ignored them, moving steadily toward the refuge of her waiting carriage. Her heavy black lace veil lent a curtain of protection, and her coachman's hand and gaze were sure and steady as he helped her inside.

She welcomed the dark interior and sat back into the squabs, pressing her fingertips against her dry eyes. "Drive on, Thomas."

Her voice surprised her. It sounded as if it belonged to someone else.

Someone with hope.

A word about the author...

When I was a child, words often seemed to tumble on the page, refusing to line up no matter how hard I tried. I would lose my place, skip lines, or struggle to make sense of what everyone else seemed to find so easy. Much later, I learned this had a name—dyslexia—but in 1868, when my hero Brendan lives, such a word didn't exist. A boy like him would simply have been called slow, careless, or worse. I gave Brendan this challenge because I know how deeply it shapes not only the way one reads, but the way we see ourselves. And yet, it doesn't define him—it pushes him to see the world differently, to notice what others overlook, to listen more keenly, to understand people in a way that goes beyond words. For me, books were both a struggle and a refuge. Writing this story was a reminder that love—whether romantic, familial, or the love we finally learn to give ourselves—can be the force that steadies us when letters and life alike threaten to slip out of order.

If you've ever struggled to feel "enough" in a world that seems built for other people, I hope Brendan's journey brings you comfort and courage. Because sometimes the very thing that makes us feel broken is what makes our story worth telling.

And if you enjoyed Brendan and Callie's story, I hope you'll leave a review. Stay tuned for my next: Daft for the Duke!

jessrussellromance@gmail.com

Thank you for purchasing
this publication of The Wild Rose Press, Inc.

For questions or more information
contact us at
info@thewildrosepress.com.

The Wild Rose Press, Inc.
www.thewildrosepress.com